Helen Rolfe writes contemporary women's fiction and enjoys weaving stories about family, friendship, secrets, and community. Characters often face challenges and must fight to overcome them, but above all, Helen's stories always have a happy ending.

You can visit Helen at:
www.helenjrolfe.com
@helenjrolfewriter
@HjRolfe
helen_j_rolfe

Christmas at the Village Sewing Shop

Helen Rolfe

ORION

An Orion paperback

First published in Great Britain in 2022 by Orion Fiction,
an imprint of The Orion Publishing Group Ltd
Carmelite House, 50 Victoria Embankment,
London EC4Y 0DZ

An Hachette UK company

1 3 5 7 9 10 8 6 4 2

A CIP catalogue record for this book is
available from the British Library.

ISBN (Mass Market Paperback) 978 1 3987 0618 7
ISBN (eBook) 978 1 3987 0619 4

Typeset by Input Data Services Ltd, Somerset

Printed and bound in Great Britain by Clays Ltd, Elcograf S.p.A.

www.orionbooks.co.uk

This book is dedicated to The Write Romantics – a group of ten writers, including myself, who met online in 2013 and have been together every step of the way during our individual writing journeys. The support from each and every one of you is nothing short of amazing. Cheers to a lifelong friendship and many more books between us! xxx

Chapter One

Loretta

'Ouch!' Loretta gasped.

Daisy snatched a tissue from the box on the counter in the Butterbury Sewing Box, the sewing shop that had been in the family for over seventy years. 'You'd think in all the decades you've been sewing you could manage to hem some curtains without causing an injury.' She covered her mother's finger, soaking up the blood. 'Is everything all right?'

'I'm the parent. Shouldn't it be me asking you those sorts of questions?' Loretta at least had an excuse to frown now she'd hurt herself. With everything she had on her mind it was difficult to keep up the pretence, keep smiling and act nonchalant.

Daisy rolled her eyes, something the youngest daughter of the Chamberlain family had well and truly perfected. 'I'm thirty-one, Mum. It's time to let me be a grown up.'

'Mothers never stop worrying.'

Daisy shook her head and got on with opening the cardboard box that had come in this morning's delivery. The shop had had a happy life here in the village of Butterbury, so had Loretta, but with what she'd discovered a couple of months ago the fabric of their very existence might well be about to fall apart, and she wasn't sure that even with the strongest of thread and the best skill in the world she'd be able to stitch it back together this time.

Loretta got a plaster from the first-aid kit they kept out the back of the shop and wrapped it around her finger. She caught sight of herself in the oval mirror against one wall and hoped that by looking into it she'd get herself together enough to convince Daisy or anyone who came into the shop that she had nothing to worry about, her life was easy, an absolute dream. Isn't that what everyone was trying to do these days? Sharing only the nice parts on social media, the parts that made it look as though life was a breeze.

Loretta scrutinised her appearance. Her hair had gone grey but it had held onto its volume and enough bounce that she could get away with wearing it just below her collarbones. Cut in choppy long layers and parted to one side, it hid some of the lines that had begun to appear, and a pair of thick-rimmed dark glasses hid the frown that seemed to have deepened between her eyebrows. But if it got much deeper she might need some of those clever filters Daisy talked about – the ones you could use in photographs to make a person look as though they had flawless skin, brighter eyes. Loretta's mum, Rebecca, had always been about growing old gracefully, told Loretta that any lines and wrinkles that appeared on the face and body were signs of a life well lived and they should be grateful and proud of every single one. Loretta knew where she was coming from but, at sixty-five, she wasn't quite ready to let age and gravity get the upper hand.

She went back to the front of the shop and, with her guard up and hopefully the worry erased from her expression, finished hemming the curtains and did her best to drag her mind from fretting about Daisy or either of her other two daughters. She knew that what she had to share with Fern, Ginny and Daisy was going to come as a shock, but she also knew she wouldn't be sharing the news quite yet. She wasn't ready and wasn't sure she ever would be. This was one Christmas revelation that wrapping paper and bows couldn't make any better.

Curtains finished, Daisy managed the inside of the shop while Loretta took a stepladder out to the front and got on with the task of cleaning the mullioned windows. In the summer months they barely needed much attention, come autumn it would be a weekly job at least, but now, in the winter, it seemed the wind and the rain had it in for them and every morning she liked to give the frontage a once over to keep it looking as inviting as always. A family business was different to working for someone else, it instilled an extra sense of pride.

She felt the bite of cold and worked quickly using the hot water from a bucket and the sponge to do the glass and the wooden frames before climbing up the steps to wipe the iron-bracketed oval sign depicting the name of the shop with '*Est. 1948*' written in italic beneath, which was a regular bird perch and thus saw the birds leaving behind the odd treat. The moment she was finished, she hurried back inside with the bucket of water and the cloth and then the stepladder. 'It's freezing out there. Arctic!' It didn't help that she'd nipped outside without buttoning up her coat or putting on a scarf. She'd thought she'd be fine in a chunky woollen sweater and a pair of fingerless gloves.

'Why do you think I didn't volunteer?' Daisy grinned

3

as Loretta pushed the door with glass panels that matched the windows closed. Daisy slotted the last few reels of cotton onto the plastic display to refill what they'd sold and hung up a couple of packets of needles, filling the row on a hook on the far wall alongside other haberdashery accessories.

'Don't forget the front step still needs sweeping.' Loretta took the notepad her daughter had used to jot down what else needed replenishing and disappeared past the tea and coffee area out at the back and went upstairs to find more supplies. It was best to make a few trips rather than try to carry everything back down at once.

The space above the shop had originally been a flat and it was where Loretta and her late husband, Harry, had lived when they first married, before they started a family. But now the upstairs to the Butterbury Sewing Box was a series of storerooms as well as a dedicated venue to host sewing groups, knitting lessons and quilting workshops. The old bedroom and dining room had walled shelving units, the kitchen was used for catering for the groups and for Daisy and Loretta's lunches. It had evolved exactly as they'd needed.

Back in the shop Loretta found Daisy peering at something on her phone. Daisy was a good worker most of the time but that was another thing about a family business, working with parents, siblings, children, it wasn't always easy to ensure employees were doing exactly what they should be. Loretta knew that in any job your mind might wander – in an office there'd be conversations by the water cooler, perhaps a conversation about something non work-related at a desk – people rarely spent the entire day focused solely on work. Personal life crept in, she knew that, but lately Daisy's focus had drifted. She dealt with practicalities well – stocking shelves, sorting through invoices – and was always polite to customers, but there was something bothering her and Loretta couldn't get any information out of her youngest daughter. Loretta had a horrible feeling that whatever was troubling Daisy was deep-rooted and something Loretta has missed along the way – and as a mother that was the worst feeling of all.

'Did you sweep the front step for me?' Loretta asked Daisy when her daughter finally put her phone back into the rear pocket of her jeans.

'I'll do it now.'

On the one hand, maybe she shouldn't assume that because she was hiding something, everyone else was too. But on the other, she wished Daisy would tell her what was on her mind.

Daisy reiterated the 'Arctic!' comment the minute she came back inside. 'It's a thankless task, you know.' She put the dustpan and brush away beneath the counter. 'The step will be covered in leaves and debris before lunchtime, I bet you. You're making more work for us. I say leave it until the spring.'

Loretta laughed. 'The village will have to burrow their way in to the shop if we do that. And remember, your grandad is stopping by today – you know I like him to see the shop at its best.'

Ivor, Loretta's eighty-eight-year-old father, had once worked in this shop with Loretta's mother, Rebecca, after they took on the family business from his mother, Eve, when the time was right. It had been their pride and joy and now it was still something that made Ivor happy whenever he was here. Ivor had, however, refused to come and live with Loretta in her house or contemplate having the flat at the shop converted back to accommodation especially for him. Instead he'd taken one look around Butterbury Lodge – the care home at the top of the hill the other side of Lantern Square, which sat in the heart of Butterbury, in the dip between the road that led in the direction of the lodge and the road that stretched out of the village and led on up to the local farms – and opted to grab a highly coveted place there. The lodge was, in his words, 'Close but not too close.'

'He does love the shop,' smiled Daisy. 'What time will he be here?' She'd softened and picked up a feather duster to tackle the uppermost shelves, not something she usually did unless it was requested. It was testament to how much she and her sisters adored their grandad – he was the way to their hearts when all else failed.

'Soon,' was all Loretta said before she grabbed the broom to sweep the internal floors that needed doing a few times a day. 'Do you need to rush out?' Loretta always liked to remain flexible, let Daisy have her life, and it worked both ways. Between them they managed the workload and customers but allowed for errands and each of them to do their own thing when they needed to. And given Daisy was thirty-one, Loretta didn't always ask too many details about what her daughter was up to.

'Not until later so I'll get to see Grandad.' She dusted the lower shelves near the counter and held the door open for a group of women chattering as they bustled inside.

The trouble with a shop that had stood the test of time was that the windows, the floors and the structure were all a part of the history and not always geared up for a December day that made them feel as though they were into February and not still the better side of Christmas. And so Loretta turned the heating up in the shop. But the drafts and everything else inside the Butterbury Sewing Box were all a part of the memories, and besides, when it was cold, it gave Loretta and Daisy a chance to show off their knitted garments by wearing jumpers with big roll necks as they worked. Today Loretta wore a camel-coloured jumper in cable knit and Daisy had gone for a wine-coloured jumper that suited her rich chestnut hair, the same shade Harry's had been when he and Loretta first met.

The women had gone slowly up and down each of the three small aisles in the shop, picking up items and dis-cussing their needs, and after Loretta rang up the orders for the customers who were visitors to Butterbury – a pack of assorted needles for a sewing machine, a packet of premium quilt batting, and a dozen balls of mulberry wool – she wished them a merry Christmas and turned to find Daisy had made her a cup of tea.

'I picked up some cookies from the Lantern Bakery too.' Daisy indicated the space beneath the counter where she'd left the paper bag.

'Now we're talking.' Loretta took out a cookie and bit into the soft, gooey centre. Daisy did the same and for a moment, silence descended now that the customers had left.

Loretta took the opportunity to walk around the shop and enjoy her tea, straightening the odd out-of-place packet, a ball of wool that may have been returned to the wrong section, a packet of buttons that had fallen to the floor.

The Butterbury Sewing Box, started by Loretta's

Grandma Eve, had been fuelled by a pure love of fabric, colour and Loretta's gran's ability to create. It was nestled at the edge of a village street with not much else around apart from a small corner shop selling newspapers, bread, milk and the odd thing you might well need before you next made it to the supermarket, and a shop that fixed lawnmowers. Out past the grounds of the old manor surrounded by a Cotswold stone wall, and before you reached the rambling green fields and countryside footpaths that bisected the land, the road where the shop sat wasn't a thoroughfare, they weren't subject to the ebb and flow of footfall dependent on the seasons, but a steady custom had kept them and still kept them here. Butterbury was a village that had held onto its charm with a range of independent shops, and the jewel was Lantern Square at its heart, with well-tended flowerbeds, weaving pathways, and compact lawn areas surrounded by iron railings. Lantern Square was often a drawcard with a handful of annual events and this side of Christmas meant the village tree at one end, food and mulled wine carts, and the merriment that came from living in a village large enough that you could maintain a personal life, yet small enough that people still raised a hand to wave in greeting.

The interior of the Butterbury Sewing Box still had the same dark wood shelves it had always had, give or take a few sympathetic replacements, the panelling on the walls remained, as did the glass shelves that had some of the family creations made over the years, which would forever be a part of the shop: a pearl-grey miniature yarn basket knitted by Rebecca with knitting needles poking from out between its brown leather handles; a rhubarb-and-custard coloured bobble hat Ginny made was shaped around a polystyrene mould; Loretta's knitted doll with a smile and rosy cheeks in a patchwork dress with long legs dangling and knitted Mary Janes on her feet. Ivor's love of knitting and crochet was here for all to see too, because for each of his granddaughters he'd knitted their favourite nursery rhyme – Fern had Humpty Dumpty sitting on a knitted wall, for Daisy he'd knitted the clock from 'Hickory Dickory Dock' and added the white mouse, and for Ginny, she's always loved 'Jack and Jill' and so the two knitted figurines, Jack holding the pail and wearing his crown, stood side by side on the shelves with everything else. It was personal touches like this that piqued customers' interest and made the Butterbury Sewing Box what it was today.

Loretta set her cup down on the walnut counter that had stood in the same position for decades, at the back with a view of the front door. At one end sat an old-fashioned till that, according to Loretta's eldest daughter Fern, seriously needed an upgrade. Fern had mentioned it more than once, telling her mother it needed bringing up to date and modernising. Daisy always said it added character to the place, but of course, she would, anything to argue back her point with her eldest sister. Ginny, the middle daughter, hadn't got involved in the argument, she did her best to avoid that or any other confrontation having been the peacemaker for so many years.

As Daisy did the honours and served a gentleman who came in to buy a pair of gloves, Loretta perused the photographs on the wall that sat at a right angle to the counter, the wall they passed every time they came and went from the back of the shop to the front. The wooden panelling held some of the most treasured memories grabbed over the years starting from the black and white print of Loretta's grandparents, arms around one another, smiles beaming, in front of the shop when it first opened. Customers loved seeing this one, knowing how the Butterbury Sewing Box came to be. Among the memories on the wall was another of her Grandma Eve sitting on a stool holding a quilting hoop on her lap as she worked on a quilt that covered her legs, her face knitted in concentration. Every time Loretta saw this picture it reminded her of how her gran had been the one to teach her quilting for the very first time, a skill she'd worked on over the years with Ivor and Rebecca's help as time went on, and then passed on to her own daughters. Quilting had been just a tiny part of Grandma Eve's portfolio of talent – she made clothes, from trousers and skirts to play dresses and outfits for best. Her passion had started in war times and it was the inspiration behind the Butterbury Sewing Box. Grandma Eve had even embroidered the prettiest handkerchief for Loretta's sixteenth birthday, intricate pink and white roses on the frilly border that curved and dipped with a ridge of deeper pink. The handkerchief was tucked away in Loretta's drawer in her bedroom, a treasured piece that had once been in her grandma's hands and was now in hers. She smiled, remembering how her grandma had told her that young ladies should always carry a handkerchief with them, it was simply what you did.

On the same wall as the photographs was a square pinboard and on that, fixed beneath colourful headed pins, were all Ginny's postcards from her trips far and wide. Every time another one landed on the mat, Loretta would devour it and pin it up on display with the rest, glad her daughter was having such adventures. The card showed a colourful depiction of the tulip farms in Holland, a stunning image of the Belvedere Palace in Vienna, the vibrant Christmas markets in Basel and sparkling winter snow in Copenhagen. And no matter whether Ginny had been somewhere before, she'd always send another card.

The photograph at the end was one of Loretta's three girls, sitting in age order, Fern on the left, then Ginny, then Daisy, all of them focusing on the special quilt spread across their laps as though they were discussing it, its intricacies and meaning. The quilt had been lost some time ago, sadly, but here it was, captured in black and white with the three girls gazing at it in awe. Harry had taken the picture without any of them realising and what Loretta treasured most was that the photograph depicted the closeness the three siblings had once shared, the sisterhood that had somehow evaporated along the way.

Loretta thought about that quilt and many others, the way the girls had worked together and bonded over them every Sunday. Back then the shop had only opened during the week and on a Saturday, Sundays had been a true day of rest, and Loretta had always spent it with her family. The next picture along on the wall was again taken by Harry and this time Loretta was with her daughters, all four of them on their hands and knees as they positioned squares, all of which had to be pieced together to make the quilt that lay across Loretta's double bed to this day. The material had gradually dulled over time, its slight imperfections – the crooked stitching between an emerald green square and another with sunflowers, the jagged way the piece of lace had been sewn onto a countryside scene in another square – were what made it unique and special, and the sentiment as well as the closeness of that activity had never faded for Loretta. She would forever adore the quilt with its blue base and backing, squares of bright turquoise, midnight blue embroidered with silky pale crescent moons, pale blue checks taken from Fern's old school dress, the puffy white clouds against an exquisite sky blue that Ginny had painstakingly cut out by hand before sewing on. The quilt had a couple of denim squares too, material Daisy sourced from a cut-up pair of jeans that hadn't actually been in line for recycling. Loretta could see those denim squares in the photograph now and smiled at the memory as she always did, remembering Daisy's expression when she was scolded for hacking to pieces the perfectly good pair of jeans Harry had bought her rather than an old pair that no longer fit. The scolding hadn't lasted long though, it never did with Daisy. Over the years Loretta had made the odd repair to the quilt, replaced some of the batting as it lost its oomph, and it had never stopped being a reminder of her family and closer times.

Loretta wished it was as easy to get her three girls together now as it had been then. Looking at the carefree trio in the picture she wondered when they'd moved from being close-knit to having their sibling relationships hanging on by a thread, swinging in the wind, likely to break with the smallest tug.

When Fern was born forty-one years ago, Loretta had wondered whether it would be she who would take over the shop eventually, but then Ginny arrived a little over four years later, and finally Daisy six years on from that, and then Loretta had been in a cloud of parenting and hadn't given a second thought as to who would want the shop she was so busy raising the girls and keeping the business going. She'd indulged, however, on more than one occasion, imagining all three girls wanting to take on the business, perhaps even together. But that had never happened. Fern had lost interest in sewing, quilting, or anything creative at all, so much so that Loretta found it hard to believe they shared the same DNA. Once Fern got to her teens Loretta would've been hard pushed to get her eldest daughter near a sewing machine even if she'd bribed her with a stack of gold coins. Ginny had been a lot more interested, but for some reason even she had stepped back along the way.

Loretta watched Daisy ring up the man's order on the till and she smiled over at him when he put the pair of burgundy knitted gloves on straight away.

'I'm ready to tackle a Butterbury winter now!' he declared with a flourish before he left.

Daisy put the other gloves he'd tried on back on display and Loretta watched her. She'd been such a troubled teen, the only one of the three who really ever had, and Loretta had never known why. She's assumed it was what it was and had simply tried to be there for her daughter. What she never would've predicted was Daisy's decision to stay here with her in the Butterbury Sewing Box rather than further her studies in a totally different direction. But when she was old enough, that was what she had done. Her sisters had begun to follow their own paths, their dad was gone, and Loretta just assumed her youngest daughter was doing what made her the happiest. And with so much upset over the years, Loretta hadn't thought it her place to question it.

With Daisy quiet once again at the other end of the shop, replenishing shelves, Loretta assumed, Loretta stocked up the baskets of mixed wool near the front door. She pushed in leftovers from bigger batches that would sell cheaper because the shades wouldn't quite match what they had in stock now, but they'd be perfect to pull together a brightly coloured blanket, a tea cosy – unbelievably some people still used those – or a crazy knit jumper for the more adventurous. She put the last of the chocolate-brown wool onto the shelf stack near the window and straightened the pole that had rainbow-decorated fabric draped over it. The poles of material were horizontal rather than vertical, allowing customers to flip through the selection easily. But customers didn't always leave the fabric straight and a good tidy up was always on the agenda. Loretta was third generation Rawlins – she became a Chamberlain once she married – to take the helm at the Butterbury Sewing Box and Daisy might laugh at her high standards and fastidiousness when it came to keeping the shop clean and well-presented, but in the not-too-distant future Daisy would be the one in charge, she'd be the boss for the fourth generation in a row and Loretta felt a spark of joy that her Grandma Eve's legacy would continue. All she needed now was to make sure Daisy's head was really still in the game because these days she worried that it was anything but.

Loretta found Daisy at the end of the shop, but she wasn't filling the shelves as Loretta had assumed. She was engrossed in something on her phone yet again.

'Don't worry,' Daisy quickly leaped in, 'the stock is already replenished, I'm not shirking my responsibilities.'

'I never said you were.' But she was up to something.

'You're so suspicious, Mum.' The eye roll that came with it told Loretta she'd get nothing else out of her daughter as she shoved her phone back into the pocket of her jeans. But Loretta didn't miss a mischievous smile. Either she was up to no good or there was a man on the other end of that text message or whatever contact she'd just got. And that, Loretta supposed, would be a good thing. Daisy hadn't seemed interested in having much of a love life lately and it made Loretta sad to think her daughter was missing her younger years when she should be out and having fun, and might even be lonely. Daisy had never said as much but she was forever going off alone camping, something she and Harry had often done together, or to photograph things – the countryside, local events, scenery at a new camping ground. And it was one thing for Loretta to be on her own when she was in her sixties, but it was quite another for Daisy to be doing the same thing at her age.

Daisy was alerted to movement outside the shop. 'They're early.'

Loretta spotted the minibus from Butterbury Lodge that had just pulled up. 'Don't panic, it'll take them a good five minutes to disembark.'

'I'll run and put the heater on upstairs, get the room nice and toasty.'

Loretta greeted the seven arrivals at the door and, as predicted, it took them a while to get out of the minibus and file inside.

'We're here!' It was Flo, one of the residents at the lodge, and for a woman who had once kept herself to herself, she seemed to be in charge of everyone else. She was first inside the shop and as Loretta embraced her father, announced, 'We've got a name, you know. For our group.'

Loretta finished ushering everyone inside out of the cold.

'Don't you want to know what it is?' Flo went on as Daisy reappeared, bypassed everyone to give her grandad an enormous hug, and then resumed professionalism by offering to take coats. She was soon weighed down with an armful, laughing from behind the material and insisting she run those upstairs before anyone handed her anything else.

'Tell me, Flo,' said Loretta as she gathered the remaining coats and scarves. She gave her dad another hug, noticing he was wearing the chocolate brown jumper he'd knitted himself.

Flo's eyes danced. 'We're calling ourselves Oldies in Stitches.'

Loretta laughed as she handed Daisy everything in her arms and her daughter took the rest of the garments upstairs. 'Good for you and very appropriate.'

Maggie, the staff member who'd driven the minibus, came back inside armed with a box. 'The knitting projects they've been working on are all inside.' She leaned in and whispered to Loretta, 'Make sure their chairs are far enough apart, knitting needles tend to get waved around in all the excitement and I don't want any injuries.' Maggie seemed to deal with residents with a tireless efficiency and missed nothing with sharp eyes behind rounded spectacles. She'd been in charge at the lodge for years and seemed well-versed at keeping things in order but with an injection of fun that many of these elderly residents so desperately needed, especially those who didn't have a family network visiting regularly.

'They'll be fine with us.' Loretta smiled, although it was Daisy taking charge leading the way upstairs with Ivor at the rear, jostling everyone into place. He'd volunteered to help with the basic knitting skills workshop and had already got everyone off to a flying start up at the lodge apparently.

Left alone once again in the shop Loretta felt a sense of peace descend and for the next hour until the Oldies in Stitches were collected and ferried home again, she finished off the tidying, served a handful of customers and exchanged brief snippets about their days, she discussed a pattern for a baby blanket on the phone with a customer who requested she post out some items, and even had a chance to flip through the catalogue that had come in the post that morning and choose some exquisite fat quarters of material to add to her own personal collection.

An hour or so later and six of the residents had been collected by Maggie, but Ivor stayed behind. He often did this and it meant he and Loretta got to stroll through Butterbury, take in the countryside surrounds, make their way down to Lantern Square before heading on up the hill and back to the lodge. Bundled up in their coats, scarves and gloves, Ivor with a hat Daisy had made him last Christmas in a cherry red he said was just his colour, they nipped home first and collected Busker, the golden retriever Daisy had adopted when a friend of hers left for university and her parents, who worked in London full-time, realised they wouldn't be home enough to look after it. Loretta linked her dad's arm all the way, a steady stroll, time together that was always precious.

It was still cold but the wind had died down a bit and its direction was in their favour as Busker, despite his advancing age, insisted on darting into any bushes they passed, sniffing his way around. Ivor adjusted his hat, pulling it further over his ears to cover the back of his grey hair completely, careful not to dislodge his wire-framed glasses. 'Daisy had the group very well organised today. She's efficient, and they all adore her.'

'I love that she spends so much time up at the lodge with you.' Hearing that Daisy really was up there and not off doing something secretive was quite a relief to Loretta. 'I just wish—'

'She'd hang out with people her own age?'

'I don't know, Dad. Sometimes I wonder how she's ever going to meet anyone stuck in a sewing shop with her mother and spending the rest of her time hanging out with the Oldies in Stitches.'

'You worry a lot about her.'

'I worry about all my girls.'

'Have you phoned Fern and Ginny yet?' When she shook her head he said, 'You're putting it off.'

'Wouldn't you?'

His long sigh said that he wouldn't. He'd never been one to back away from a challenge, no matter how hard it was. 'You've always valued honesty above all else, Loretta. And I admire that.'

'I wonder where I learned it from.'

They took a detour into one of the fields to give Busker a bit of a run and when they emerged into the open space Ivor tried to bend down for the stick Busker dropped at his feet. But he only got halfway. 'Do the honours?'

Loretta put a reassuring hand on her dad's arm and bent down, picked up the stick and threw it for Busker. Ivor was slowing down, it was life, but it didn't mean to say she wanted to think about him ever leaving this world and her behind.

Busker retrieved the stick and seemed happy enough

to trot along the dirt track carrying it between his jaws as if to say, 'I've got the prize, I'm the winner'. They came to an uneven part of the path and Ivor gripped tighter onto Loretta's arm until they were back on even ground. Butterbury was beautiful in any season and a frost still lingered on the uppermost branches of the nearby oak tree and fell as though it was snowing when they passed beneath.

'Did you see the photograph Daisy took of this field?' Loretta asked her dad. 'She captured the frost just right.'

'She's a talented young lady.' He paused. 'You need to call Fern and Ginny. They won't thank you for keeping this from them, not in the long run. Do what you have to do, tell a lie just to get them here if you have to, but don't leave it until it's too late.'

'I don't know what to say to them. Would you?'

He shook his head.

But his understanding didn't make it any easier. Loretta knew what she had to do. If she wanted her family to get through this then she needed to get her girls together and see if they could be those three sisters who'd once shared everything, who'd once joked that they were sewn together as well as their gran's best quilts. It had never mattered back then that there was ten years difference between Fern and Daisy, there'd been something for each of them to learn, to embrace, to enjoy. They'd pull together scraps of material from wherever they liked, each girl would rummage in the plastic tubs Loretta had filled with offcuts. There was no end of colour to choose from, a vast array of designs, they could be as eccentric or conservative as they liked. The girls had loved getting crazy with spots, stripes, clashing colours. *Anything goes!* had been Harry's way of describing it as he'd watch them all working away before he and the girls would sit down to watch a movie. He always chose family movies that would be appropriate for all three, Fern and Ginny watching films they'd already seen but that they loved and Daisy seeing them for the first time.

Quilting had brought Fern, Ginny and Daisy together as kids, it had brought her joy too. And Loretta wondered, could it be that in order to bring her girls together and make them strong enough for what was about to come their way, they would have to go back to where it all began?

Chapter Two

Fern

'You're the most efficient member of my team,' her boss, Nick, remarked with a double tap on Fern's desk. 'We need to clone you.' She'd just handed him her report chock full of recommendations she'd drawn after analysing departments in the company that were under-performing, those that were doing better than expected and pulling those results together with external information including industry research, consumer trends and competitor analysis.

'Thanks, Nick.' It was always nice to hear that she was valued.

Fern pushed her chair beneath her desk at the end of another working day, and despite the tiredness creeping up on her she kept her expression bright, her voice lively. 'I'll see you tomorrow. And I've put all the information you need for your morning meeting on your desk already.'

Fern was eager to get home now with an evening of organising ahead of her. Christmas was fast approaching and every year in mid December she held the neighbourhood Christmas party. Tonight she needed to finalise the invites – she'd chosen a high quality, elegant style with gold swirly writing and a lit-up tree design, each one headed with the words 'Hosted By Mr & Mrs Tayman' – and once they arrived, she'd hand deliver each of them to people on both sides of their street. She felt a flip of excitement at once again putting on the party of the year.

'Go home and relax,' her boss encouraged as though he could see her mind whirring with plans. 'You've earned it.' He waved the report once in the air to signify his commendation and headed towards the glass walls of his office. Fern worked long days, but he'd still be here for hours yet following an afternoon of back-to-back meetings.

When Fern's mobile rang she took the call as she stowed a collection of papers into her bag to take home and work on after the party planning. It was Everett, probably letting her know he'd be late, his usual reason behind a phone call these days. She was proud of his dedication and ambition, but for a married couple they had very little time for just the two of them, and Fern wondered whether she was the only one who'd noticed the cracks beginning to show.

The moment Everett mentioned their youngest son Jacob's parents' evening that would take place in January she ran a hand around the inside of her collar and closed her eyes as she realised what she'd done. 'I totally forgot the booking system opened late last night.' And unfortunately getting an appointment wasn't easy – they disappeared, fast, to the lucky parents who were quick enough. Usually Fern was ready and waiting and had her choice of timeslots. But not this time.

She sighed, sure that when she was at school parents evening had been a lot more straightforward. She didn't remember her mum and dad having to battle to see a teacher as if it was a grand prize rather than an important update on your child's progress.

'I would've done it, Fern, but you told me you had it under control.'

'I'll email the teachers individually,' she said quickly, 'I'll line up appointments for the new year.' Parents' evening was a while away yet so she could still save the day.

'I'll do it now. I'm still at the office so I might as well. I just wanted to check with you in case the confirmation email had gone to my spam folder. Honestly, it's fine. See you at home later.'

It didn't sound fine. She ended the call, said goodbye to Maxwell, the only other colleague remaining, head buried in papers, gold strip desk lamp lighting up the words just enough for him, and made her way out of the department and towards the lifts.

As the lift whooshed from the seventh floor down to the basement car park, she tugged the bottom of her suit jacket to ensure it was in place and turned her head from one side to the other to make sure no errant wisps of hair had escaped the high ponytail she wore when she was at work. It was sleek, courtesy of her hair straighteners, and in tip-top condition, thanks to regular salon appointments every six weeks like clockwork to keep the very dark brown and not yet grey tresses the way she liked them.

The lift opened out into the underground car park. Newcomers to the company looked on in awe at anyone who got to park at the offices and drove in and out of the barrier closed off to outsiders. But Fern had earned her space there after eight years of waiting. Ever since she graduated she'd been working in London as a financial analyst at the major publishing company who produced a plethora of magazine titles annually. She hadn't paused in her career apart from when she took maternity leave for each of her sons and her job was something she treasured. She was proud of what she'd achieved. She felt valued, she excelled, and she felt like she was doing something well.

What she wasn't doing quite so brilliantly with was marriage and parenthood. It seemed the harder she tried, the more she failed. Fern felt as though she was making mistakes and letting people down more and more lately. And it wasn't just with parents' evening. Last week she'd missed Cooper's hockey game, she'd forgotten to pay for Jacob's school trip to the Science Museum, which meant he very nearly didn't get to go, and on Cooper's birthday having booked and paid for the wrong movie at the cinema for him and six of his mates, she and Everett between them had had to ferry them all somewhere else more than forty miles away after having cleared it with each parent that that arrangement was fine. Last week she forgot to pick up Everett's dry cleaning even though she'd insisted she do it when he had so much on at work, and yesterday she'd knocked Everett's late mother's Mandarin hand-painted lidded jar off the shelf in the study and it had smashed to pieces. Everett lost his mum a little over a year ago and coped by throwing himself into his work more and more. For a while Fern had just let him get on with it, he was in pain, but somewhere along the line without realising he'd kept up the habit and she felt as though she'd taken a backseat in his life.

When had they moved from being Everett and Fern to being Jacob and Cooper's parents and nothing else? Or was this what happened to all parents, they lost a bit of themselves in order to become a family?

Fern put the windscreen wipers on as she emerged from

the depths of the car park into the open air. The fog from this morning had lifted but in its place was drizzle. Not the rain that hammered down and pelted the windscreen and made you feel alive, the sort of pathetic equivalent of trying its best but not quite making it as precipitation. The darkness of winter had already lowered her mood. Gone were the long sunny evenings of summer where she'd drive home, windows open, music playing and relaxing her with every mile between there and the new-build house she and her family had called home for almost six years. This evening even thoughts of organising anything for the Christmas party weren't enough of a distraction to lift her spirits.

When she arrived home, she could hear Cooper's music pounding from his room. At fifteen years old Cooper seemed to have ventured into the tunes that for some reason had to be played at full volume and on top of that, they were more often than not accompanied by lyrics Fern deemed a little unacceptable. Fern was only glad they lived in a detached property so at least she wasn't upsetting the neighbours, and even more glad she'd invested in a pair of noise-cancelling headphones that allowed her to get some work done at weekends if he was around. She was never sure what reception she'd get from Cooper either. Sometimes a request to lessen the volume was met with a murmur of agreement and the music dulled to a bearable level, but other times he'd snap at her to stop moaning at him, she'd end up telling him off for being rude and the whole house would be filled with unpleasantness. It certainly didn't fit in with the dreamy parenting idyll she'd imagined. Of course that was a view she'd had before she became a parent. When you didn't have kids it was all too easy to judge a naughty child or a parenting technique, but put yourself in that family's shoes and it was quite often a different story.

Fern and Everett had desperately wanted a family and both of them had made adjustments. It all seemed to work like clockwork in the early years – juggling day care, different start and finish times with their jobs, meetings scheduled out of the blue, jumping in to help each other out when they could. But it had become harder as the boys got older. They weren't as much work physically, there were no exhausting visits to the park to run around and play tag or kick a football with them, but it became more tiring emotionally as they got older. Fern knew she had to keep reminding herself that they were great boys and that attitude and backchat were things to take in her stride. But some days, like today, when she was tired and weary of it all, it was difficult to make herself see sense. Between Cooper and his music thumping away and Jacob playing on his PlayStation as though his life depended on it – like he was doing now in the room at the end of the hallway as she shut the front door behind her – she didn't get much of a look in with either of her sons unless they needed something or were sick. She wasn't sure what she'd envisaged as they grew up and she supposed even the tightest of circles were bound to squash into a different shape as personalities developed and time marched on. It was what had happened to her and her sisters, Ginny and Daisy, their once close bonds stretched further and further apart as they simply got on with their own lives.

Fern got changed and focused on pulling the dinner together quickly and efficiently. The chicken breasts had been marinating since she put them in the fridge this morning with freshly chopped chillies, lemon juice and garlic, it didn't take long to peel potatoes and cut up a selection of vegetables. The next hour was a mix of *Hello, Mum. How long till dinner? Where is my school tie?* Followed by *Mum, tell him not to go in my room without asking!* And *There's no toilet roll up here . . . I need it, now!*

By the time Everett came through the door Fern had everything in hand, glad she'd had some time to calm down. The last thing she wanted was for Everett to see her angry, unable to cope. In her workplace she swore there was another divorce announced every few months and she didn't want to become another statistic. Fern knew some of the women at work moaned that they had to do everything at home but the set-up in this house wasn't like that. Everett pulled his weight. He had high demands at work, they both did, and Fern just wanted to hold on to the carefree Everett, the gentle-hearted man she'd fallen in love with from the start. Which meant they really did need to spend some alone time together and talk. Perhaps she'd suggest it tonight.

She smiled at her husband and hoped the weary look on his brow wouldn't last long. 'How was work?'

'Good.' With a sigh he ran a hand around the back of his neck.

'Did you get in touch with Jacob's teachers?' Better to start with casual conversation than admit she thought they had problems. She multi-tasked by washing up the sharp knife lying on the chopping board so it didn't mistakenly get put in the dishwasher.

'I haven't heard back from all of them, but we've already got three appointments lined up in the new year a couple of days after the official parents' evening.'

'Thanks for sorting it,' she said, still not able to gauge his mood.

'We're both parents, remember.'

She finished drying the knife and pushed it into the block on the kitchen worktop. 'I know.'

'Sometimes I wonder if you do, Fern.'

She felt an unexpected lurch in her tummy at the frustration still lacing his brow, the tone of voice that suggested this was about so much more than her forgetting parents' evening. She should've told him she was worried about their marriage months ago. But then again, perhaps he should've been the one to address it, it couldn't all be her fault.

In a calm voice she explained, 'I intended to do it, I forgot, and I'm sorry.'

'I'm capable of doing everything you are, yet you insist on doing it all yourself.'

Before she had a chance to wonder whether he was being argumentative because he'd had a long day or was frustrated at her lack of trust in others doing things the way she would, she said, 'Is this about me always needing to be in charge?' There was a time he'd admired her for her strength, her ability to take control, when those sorts of comments would've been teasing to show he didn't mind the state of play one bit. When had her admirable qualities become more of a frustrating trait than anything else?

He held her gaze for a moment and then as though he was exhausted by it all he added nothing extra and stepped closer to pull her into a gentle hug. 'I'm not suggesting that, Fern. I'm just saying . . .'

'Dinner is cooking,' she murmured after a while, when

she felt him relax the way she managed to do too, the hug a reminder of the closeness that still lurked deep down rather than the distance that seemed to be increasing between them these days. 'Would you like a glass of wine?' A peace offering might be a better idea than attempting to talk about anything else.

'Can't. I've got a squash game in an hour.' He pulled away and ran a hand across his smoothly shaven jaw that would show stubble in the morning, hints of the same grey that had begun to fleck his dark hair.

She turned back to the sink to wash the wooden chopping board that wouldn't go in the dishwasher either, picked up the steel wool and gave it a vicious scrub.

'I did tell you this morning.' His voice came out soft, wary, not missing the change in her mood.

'It's fine,' she rallied, feeling put out that she desperately needed some alone time with her husband yet this wasn't the first time he'd announced other plans. 'You go to your game, I'll keep your dinner warm and the wine can wait.' Squash games, online meetings in the evenings, even playing on the PlayStation with his son, pushing her further and further down his list of priorities. They had little time for one another these days, unless it was between the sheets. They never seemed to have had a problem with that.

He pulled her back against him perhaps with a change of heart. 'I could always cancel.'

She was tempted to ask him to but he always came home a little bit calmer after a game. 'You go, I need to order the invitations for the Christmas party anyway.' And she wanted them here well in advance, even though save the date cards had already been distributed. Fern had never liked to do anything last minute, never mind forget tasks altogether.

He pulled her in for another hug and when his mouth moved down against her neck, kissing the little space above her collarbone that always drove her crazy, she sighed. Despite any bickering, intimacy had kept them going lately and she never wanted to lose that part of their relationship. 'How about we have that glass of wine when I get home?'

'Sounds good to me.'

When Jacob called out again about being hungry, anxious not to let go of the moment, Fern kissed Everett on the mouth and whispered, 'I'll wear the lingerie you love and have the wine waiting.'

He made a low guttural groan as though the interruption was painful before he turned to greet his youngest son with a ruffle of his hair. Cooper came downstairs next and asked about dinner, even though it hadn't been long since he'd eaten some toast.

'No, you won't keel over and die if you don't eat soon,' Everett assured them both, his mood better already. 'And you're both old enough to find your own pieces of school uniform,' he added when Cooper asked about his school socks and Jacob said he couldn't find his spare sports top for PE. 'And, please, stop bickering. Turn the music off, the PlayStation too. It's almost dinner time.' He loosened his tie, winked in Fern's direction and headed upstairs to get changed.

And just like that she was transported to the Fern and Everett they'd been when they first met.

Fern had fallen for Everett the day he picked up her railcard in the London Underground and chased her up the escalator. She'd dropped it at the bottom and not being one to stand on the right and wait behind everyone else, she'd quickly ascended the escalator on the left and was already at the next one by the time an out-of-breath Everett caught up with her. He'd handed her the ticket and she thought she'd never see him again, the well-built man who filled out a suit nicely and who'd looked at her with his ocean blue eyes as though he already knew her. She'd thought about him for the rest of that day, finding it hard to concentrate at work, hearing his velvety voice even though he was nowhere near, wishing they'd had more than a snatched conversation. She looked out for him every day at the train station and on the Tube but she didn't see him again until almost a month later when he walked past her in Covent Garden. He'd taken her for coffee that day, then lunch the next, then drinks at the end of the week. And they'd barely had time apart since.

Everett, three years older than Fern, was still working with the same company in London except now he was the chief finance officer. He took the train to and from work each day, five days a week. Sometimes he bemoaned the journey but Fern knew he didn't hate it that much. He always read the morning news with a large coffee taken in his Thermos, and she sensed it was his down time before a hectic day at the office. She rarely took time for herself, but not because she couldn't if she wanted to, more that she had no idea what to do with herself if she wasn't busy. Funny, she knew a lot about numbers, but not a whole lot about relaxing. She always wore a watch that counted her steps, made sure she got the requisite ten thousand a day, marching on the spot at home if she didn't until the little buzz on her wrist told her she'd attained her target.

When Fern was much younger she'd been a keen runner. She'd been on the school's cross country team, she'd run every morning when she and Everett got together, but slowly the demands on her time had taken over and the habit had fallen away. She'd tried going to yoga a couple of years ago thinking it might perhaps be the answer to help de-stress, but on the contrary, she found her mind racing and an inability to switch off and so she gave that up. She moved on to trying Zumba to work out some frustration, but then the class she went to was moved to a lunchtime, which was impossible for her, and so that fell away too. Fern didn't have many female friendships either, what with the demands of her job and her family. And anyway, sisters were supposed to do that job, weren't they? Unfortunately it hadn't worked out that way with the Chamberlain girls.

Fern called Jacob and Cooper for dinner and covered Everett's plate so he could reheat it when he was home after his game. The boys wolfed their food down and went right on to bananas and ice-cream for dessert before they reluctantly headed off to do their homework after Cooper stacked the dishwasher, his chore on the calendar today, and Jacob put the rubbish into the wheelie bin by the back gate.

Fern put some music on while she wiped down the table and washed up. When her phone rang and her boss's name popped up on the screen she put it on speaker. As he spoke, she froze, tap still running, frying pan in one hand, cloth in the other. 'What do you mean I haven't given you what you need? I left it all on your desk, Nick.'

'You didn't include the balance sheets or the cash-flow statements, and the executive summary is for Carters.'

Carters weren't even a client anymore. How had she managed to print off the wrong executive summary and not even notice? She usually triple checked everything, she didn't make mistakes. 'I don't know what to say, Nick. I'm sorry. I'll do it first thing in the morning.'

'I need it for the breakfast meeting.'

A tightening pain across the top of her head made itself known as she realised that actually, she couldn't remember writing up the finalised executive summary, which meant trawling through information and pulling it all together. 'It's not a problem, Nick. I have all the information I need, just a matter of collating it all together and I'll email it through tonight.' She made it sound so simple when it wasn't. And it wasn't quick either. She closed her eyes and took a deep breath even though she wanted to lob the phone across the kitchen and swear.

Her boss ended the call relieved, Fern on the other hand felt her stress levels rise. She got back to rinsing the pan and when it fell from her grasp and the water splashed up the front of her sweatshirt she screamed, 'Fuck it!' at the top of her voice.

She didn't swear often but lately it was as though the words were out before she had a chance to think about it. The last thing she wanted was to teach the boys bad habits. She stood, hands bracing against the sink and closed her eyes but sensed she wasn't alone.

Jacob was hovering in the doorway. 'Malcolm in my class said that the other day and got suspended.'

Deep breath in. 'Well Malcolm shouldn't say it. And I shouldn't either, I apologise.' The best thing to do was not focus on it, move on. She was sure she'd read that in a parenting manual over the years. 'Did you do your French homework?'

'I hate French.'

'That wasn't what I asked.'

'Yes, I finished.'

'That was quick.'

He shrugged. 'Only had to learn twenty words.'

'I'll be upstairs to test you in half an hour.' That did it. He didn't linger. The thing with Jacob was he did do his homework, but he'd do the bare minimum to get by unless he had an extra push. Fern remembered helping Daisy when she was around the same age and stuck with her maths homework. Daisy hadn't been at all interested in the subject, which made it all the more difficult, but Fern liked to think she'd helped enough. Sometimes she forgot those moments, the tiny memories that made up the tapestry of childhood and family and could easily be lost.

Despite the missing report and the work she had to do nagging at the back of her mind Fern managed to help Jacob learn the rest of the vocabulary before she heard Everett come in downstairs.

'Delivery for you,' he indicated when she joined him in the kitchen. He'd put a package onto the table. 'Must've come when you were upstairs. They left it at the front door.'

She tutted. 'I wish delivery drivers wouldn't do that. I was here all the time, I would've heard if they'd bothered to knock.'

He glugged back a glass of water. 'What is it anyway?' He gave her a peck on the cheek as she used scissors to open the top of the box.

'Outdoor festoon lights for the garden.'

'Whatever for?'

'For the Christmas party.'

'We're doing that again this year?' He refilled his glass.

'I told you I'd sent out the save the date cards. And we do it every year.'

'Exactly. *We* do it every year. We invite the neighbours, we supply a lot of the food and drink, *we* clean up after they've all gone home for a rest.'

She shook her head and couldn't hold back a sigh. 'It's Christmas, it's neighbourly.'

'So let someone else do it.'

'OK, Grinch.' Her attempt at humour fell flat.

'I'm going for a shower.'

'Fine,' she said as though she was thirty years younger and having an argument with her sisters over who had to do the drying up or set the table for dinner.

Fern's stress levels had already risen after the phone call with her boss and now her husband hadn't helped. But instead of dwelling on it Fern went online and ordered the invites – just enough plus a few spares because she'd hate to forget anyone. What was wrong with putting on a party for the neighbours, anyway? It was a nice thing to do, wasn't it? And Everett always had a good time.

When Everett finally came back downstairs she'd just taken another couple of deliveries and left them in the hallway.

She heard him cry out and swear from where she was sitting in the dining room. 'You OK?'

He just looked at her. He'd stubbed his toe on one of the boxes – the case of wine for the Christmas party. 'I'll live. What are these?'

Did she have to explain everything? 'A case of wine and the other is a box of wine glasses.'

'Perhaps we should've asked the neighbours to bring their own if we don't have enough,' he moaned.

Her mouth fell open. 'Who has a party and says bring your own glass?' He'd lost all sense. 'And it's not that we don't have enough, it's that a lot of the ones we do have are a bit worn or don't match. I want everything to look perfect when people arrive. I'll have the beautiful gold tablecloth, everything arranged, food on the matching white serving dishes.' She went to her husband's side and put a hand on his arm. 'You'll enjoy yourself and have a wonderful time, I know you will.'

'I don't know why you have to spend so much money. You do this every year.'

'So it's about the cost?'

'No, actually it's not.' He looked defeated. 'But last year you bought new patio furniture and a fire pit, the year before it was a garland for the back door as well as the front so guests could appreciate it if they went out to the back. Every year you spend hours, days, weeks even getting ready for one night that always falls on us.'

She swallowed hard. This felt like a personal attack and it had taken her by surprise. 'Everett, where is all this coming from?'

His glare faded away and as though he was exhausted from it all he told her, 'It's as though you've lost sight of what Christmas is all about.'

'It's about people, I know that. Hence the neighbourhood party.'

He set the microwave to the correct time to warm his dinner. 'It's about family and friends. It isn't about perfection. It isn't about formal invitations, extra luxuries to make guests more comfortable, the right glasses, the right wine, the right accessories dotted around. What's wrong with a casual invite, everyone bringing a plate of food and some drinks, popping in when they like?'

She wasn't even going to answer that. 'I'd love to hear about how terrible I am for organising a party, Everett, but I have work to do.' She poured herself a glass of wine. With any luck she'd be done this side of midnight if she actually made a start.

'Why are you working tonight?'

'It's hardly uncommon, Everett,' she snapped.

He reached for her hand and she let him take it, his touch calming her enough for her to explain, 'I screwed up, dropped the ball.'

'That's not like you.'

And before she could think that understanding and communicating were a start, she snapped, 'Well, after parents' evening we both know that's not true, don't we?' And she took her hand away.

The microwave pinged, he took out some cutlery and sat himself down. 'Regardless of that, Fern, it's not like you to make a mistake at work, that's all I'm saying.' He looked as fed up with their sniping at one another as she was. The way his hair, still damp from his shower, had left a crescent-shaped water mark seeping onto his marl grey T-shirt, made her want to reach out to this man who was her world.

'You don't seem to like me very much lately.' Her frustration with the tension between them meant her accusation was out before she had a chance to think about whether she really wanted to say it or not.

He looked at her as though she might be crazy. 'How exactly do you work that out?'

'Your criticisms of me, the fact you would rather play squash than have an evening in with your wife.'

'You're putting words in my mouth. And you told me to go even though I offered not to. Don't analyse me like you would one of your clients.'

Before either of them said anything else, she stalked out of the kitchen, narrowly avoiding slopping the wine from her glass in her haste.

'I'll make sure the boys don't disturb you,' Everett muttered after her without looking up from his dinner.

In the dining room she switched on the laptop and wished it was so easy to ignite her energy levels, which felt as though they'd depleted ten-fold since she got home. It wasn't long before she heard the faint murmur from the television Everett must have turned on in the lounge and imagined him putting his feet up for the rest of the evening. Lucky him.

Fern was forty-one and as she'd edged into her fifth decade she'd occasionally wondered whether Everett would lose interest and trade her in for a newer, sexier model. Sometimes she wouldn't blame him. Not that she didn't trust him, it was just that despite living in the same house they seemed so far apart from one another. And Everett was too good at keeping his thoughts to himself rather than blurting them out like she'd just done – perhaps that was part of the problem, that he didn't feel the need to talk the way she did, and so as time went on they shared less and less about how they were feeling and nothing ever changed.

She made up her mind there and then that no matter

how tired she was or what hour she finished her work, she intended to put on her sexy lingerie and make love to her husband. It would be an unspoken way of making peace. And although it wouldn't get to the bottom of their problems, she needed the connection, to remind herself there was plenty to fight for when it would be all too easy to give up. And it was one thing to drop the ball at work but it was quite another to do it in her marriage.

Fern worked for hours. Only when she'd checked everything in triplicate and emailed the documents to her boss, did she switch off the laptop for the night. When her phone rang at a little after ten o'clock and she saw it was her mother her thoughts instantly went to panic mode. Was she all right? Was Grandad? They usually spoke once a week. Fern regimentally called her mum every Sunday night at around seven o'clock, never this late. It was a pattern they'd got into when the boys were little and Fern had had to manage bedtimes and her work and it had stuck.

Panic simmered down to relief when she answered and Loretta assured her that everyone was alive and still breathing.

'I'm calling to check arrangements for Christmas,' Loretta told her.

It seemed odd she'd chosen to do it so late at night, but Fern reiterated the plan they'd already agreed upon. 'We'll come to you on Christmas Eve and stay two nights, if that's still OK?' It was always a squeeze and tensions ran high over the festive season squashed into the house with at least one of her sisters, but Fern and Everett did it every other year like clockwork. Next year it would be their turn to see Everett's dad.

'I've been thinking,' Loretta went on. 'Two days isn't really enough, is it?'

Fern, Ginny and Daisy had seen one another on and off over the years, but it was usually fleeting. In the summer they'd all been in Butterbury together for their mother's birthday, but other than that, they hadn't all slept in their childhood beds under the same roof at the same time for years. Two days would be plenty. None of them would ever admit it but it was as though they did their best to avoid being in the same place, together, for too long. The Christmas before last when it was Fern and Everett's turn to be in Butterbury, Daisy had gone off to New York with a friend who had a cousin with an apartment that was a steal apparently, an opportunity not to miss, and Ginny had been in Europe finally making it to Butterbury on Boxing Day in time to wave goodbye to Fern. Two years prior to that Ginny had been in Vienna from Christmas until new year, and with Daisy tucked up in bed with the flu, Fern hadn't had much to do with her youngest sister at all.

Loretta carried on. 'Your grandad is getting older—'

'He's not sick, is he?' Fern's mouth went dry. Whenever Fern returned to Butterbury she always saw her grandad and sometimes she spent more time with him than she did at her mother's house.

'You know what he's like, he'd never complain. He's settled at the lodge but he's slowing down a lot. You just never know do you . . .' She was right, of course. Their dad had died suddenly, there'd been no warning, they hadn't known what was coming their way. Fern would've given anything to have one more day with him, one more conversation, one more hug.

'Never know what?' Her mum did this sometimes. She didn't come right out with what she wanted to say but instead dropped little hints until you either pieced it together yourself or finally managed to get her to actually tell you what she was getting at.

'You never know how much time you have. I want to make this Christmas really special for him. I'd love for you three to be around to see him as much as you can, show him you're still the sewing sisters.'

Fern began to laugh. 'Nobody has called us that in a very long time, Mum.'

Their grandad had adopted the name for them ever since he saw all three girls making clothes for Daisy's dolls. Daisy had been very young at the time but Ginny had had the patience to involve her and guide her with a needle and thread to stitch together a tiny top for her Sindy doll, and a pair of trousers for Barbie. Ginny had taken to any needlework or sewing project with gusto. Fern had never completely understood the attraction although it was part of her family, had been for generations. Grandad was a dab hand at both knitting and crochet and so Fern had wanted to be a part of it all too and had got involved as much as she could. And anyway, it was fun helping Daisy with her doll's clothes. Ginny had been the one to help Fern with her needlework project for school too despite being much younger than her. In fact most of Fern's grade in that subject could be attributed to her sister's efforts – Grandad used to say that while Ginny had given Fern needlework know-how, Fern had imparted enough maths knowledge for Ginny to scrape a pass in her own exam.

The sewing sisters had been a team through and through. But not anymore. And Fern hadn't even picked up a needle and thread in years, it was Everett who mended the boys' uniforms or sewed on a missing button.

'So will you come to Butterbury for longer?' Loretta pressed on. 'I'm not suggesting Everett and the boys come too, they're all busy with school and work, but would you come and have a longer visit with your sisters and your grandad? I know it would mean the world to him to have you all together again.'

Ah, the guilt trip. Fern might have known it was on its way. Come to think of it, Grandad had said almost the same thing last time they'd spoken. *I would love to see you three girls together again. I want to see you giggle and chat and conspire about something or other.* She remembered him watching on during those times and the twinkle in his eye. Fern guessed it was the pleasure of being a grandparent.

Fern thought about her work, the home, the boys and Everett. And she thought about her dad. Her mum was right, you never knew what was around the corner. And she supposed she was owed some time off work; she rarely took much at all. 'I'll see what I can do,' she said.

'Oh thank you, Fern. Thank you.'

But then her heart sank. What about the Christmas party?

'I mean I know you're busy with your important job,' her mum rambled on. 'I know you have your own life. It's just that—'

'I promise I'll try. What have the others said?' After all, if they refused to do it, maybe she'd be off the hook. Or she could go to Butterbury and come home just for the party itself before returning to be with her grandad again.

She rubbed at her temple, everything getting more complicated by the second as her mum told her that Daisy would definitely be around all over Christmas because she was needed in the shop and didn't have any trips planned, but Fern got the impression her mother was yet to call Ginny. She wondered what her middle sister would make of the request. Ginny was totally different to Fern – she had a job but she flitted from place to place on a temporary basis and she travelled *all* the time, something that had never appealed to Fern in quite the same way. Fern went on holidays, but she'd never been tempted to swan off whenever the fancy took her. A strong family life with foundations and permanency was far more for her.

Fern hung up the call and looked at the picture in the frame positioned next to the lamp. In a silver square was a photograph captured of the family before everything changed – Fern and her sisters, their parents. Taken one summer, all of them were smiling as though they couldn't stop and it warmed Fern every time she looked at it. She could still remember the day they'd been punting on the Cam after Loretta took a rare day off from work, closing the shop and throwing caution to the wind for the sake of making family memories. A bystander had offered to take their picture and after Dad sat down once he'd passed the man the camera, he'd almost fallen into the water.

Fern kissed the tips of her fingers and touched them to her dad's cheek on the photograph. 'I miss you, Dad.'

She turned off the lamp and headed up to bed.

Everett was nearly asleep but she quickly brushed her teeth and after slipping on her favourite lingerie she'd taken into the bathroom with her, she tiptoed back into the bedroom and climbed into bed. Sex would make everything better. They were compatible in that department and it usually worked to placate him if they'd had an argument, they usually forgot what they'd even been rowing about. But when she snuggled up next to him and looped an arm around him, kissing his shoulder, expecting him to turn to her, she got no response and realised he'd already fallen asleep.

She turned onto her back, her mind buzzing too much to shut her eyes. What happened to her orderly life? The clean and happy-go-lucky kids, the happy husband, the laughs they'd had and time spent together?

What happened to the romance with Everett, the staying up late just so they could talk to each other? She'd asked Everett that in all seriousness once and he'd looked at the boys before saying, *They happened*. She wouldn't change it for the world, but she missed her husband. It was crazy when they lived together, day after day. But it wasn't the physical closeness she missed, it was the emotional connection. And both of them seemed to have lost focus on that along the way.

Fern had intended to ask her boss tomorrow morning for time off but as she lay there staring at the ceiling in the half light from the moon beyond the window, she realised she needed to demand the break. Because as well as wanting to spend time with her grandad, Fern suddenly felt the urgent need to have some time to regroup, to pull herself together and stop making these mistakes, forgetting things, snapping at her husband and her kids. If she didn't she wasn't sure she and Everett would ever take a step back enough to talk properly and move forwards.

She looked across at Everett, willing him to wake up.

But he didn't. She thought about what he'd said to her earlier, that she'd lost sight of the true meaning of Christmas. She thought about the brand new glasses, the fire pit and patio furniture, the recipe books sitting waiting for her perusal to cook the best and flashiest dishes to impress her guests at the annual party. A tear trickled out of the corner of her eye. She was only trying to make it the best for everybody, and that meant doing it right.

Failure wasn't a concept she ever wanted to entertain. Not when it came to the party, not with motherhood, not with marriage or at work.

She sniffed quietly. Because tonight she realised that not only was she risking failing at all those things, somehow she was failing herself. When had she last felt completely together? When had she last felt totally happy, as though she was in control?

She knew the answer to that.

Not for a very long time.

Chapter Three

Ginny

Ginny had ditched the suitcase after her first ever trip to Europe and swapped it for a bright blue backpack, easily visible on train carriages, and once hauled onto her back and fixed in place with the straps across her chest and others sitting comfortably on her hips, way more portable as she moved from place to place.

She leaned against the wall, taking in the night view from the top-floor apartment on the Parisienne street in the 8th arrondissement, the twinkling lights of the skyline in this magical city. This was her last evening in Paris before she left tomorrow morning and she was meeting her best friend, Melanie, who'd married her Belgian fiancé, Jonas, in a lavish ceremony in Bruges a couple of weeks ago. They'd returned to Paris this morning and Melanie had insisted she see Ginny before her friend headed back to the UK.

Ginny and Melanie had met at university when they were both studying midwifery. Since then Melanie had worked her way up the bands to become a midwifery sister in the UK before relocating here to Paris. Ginny on the other hand had given up the permanent position she'd held with an NHS hospital for four years and instead signed up to an agency who contracted her to work whenever a vacancy came up, wherever that might be, both in the public sector and private, meeting women from all walks of life. She loved the variety in her work – one day she might be advising a woman on her birth plan, the next she might be attending a straightforward delivery followed by a session counselling a woman through a particularly difficult labour. She gave advice on breastfeeding, she took new recruits under her wing, and she loved interacting with mothers-to-be, anxious fathers, relatives who turned up to meet the newest addition to their family. The flexibility of the private sector and often increased rates of pay meant Ginny could travel wherever and whenever she liked – she'd been to Thailand, Australia, Japan and Toronto, she'd been through Europe more times than she could count – and the arrangement suited her just fine. Or at least it had for a long while. But recently she'd had niggling doubts that this was how she wanted to be long-term.

A glance at the clock took Ginny away from admiring the view of Paris out of the window and reminded her it was time to go. She checked her hair in the mirror, teasing the strands until they fell just so around her face. All three of the Chamberlain sisters had had really dark hair when they were born but over the years they'd all evolved in their own way. Fern's hair was still a deep glossy brown – it wouldn't dare veer off course either – and Daisy's was a rich chestnut. Ginny's hair fell between the two shades into a caramel hue that lightened every summer. Their mum had had the same colour when she was young, in her wedding photographs and right up until she was in her late fifties when gradually tiny slivers of grey had crept in until finally her whole head was a shade of grey that really suited her. And when Loretta put on her thick-framed black glasses to see her needle and thread, somehow it looked just right.

Ginny sighed. Seeing the world was one thing but it wasn't only the backpack on her back that sometimes made her tired, lately it was more than that. Somehow her whole way of life had begun to lose its allure. Perhaps some time at home might help to get some clarity. Although if she didn't travel and wasn't a midwife, what on earth was she going to do with the rest of her life?

At the restaurant, Ginny wasted no time ordering a bottle of red wine even though Melanie hadn't arrived yet. This was something else she'd got used to, eating alone, not needing to have someone else there. She'd probably got a little too used to it, sadly.

She hooked her bag over the rickety wooden chair at their table and let the low lighting and the murmur of foreign accents wash over her. Another holiday almost over, but it had been an eventful one. Ginny had been a bridesmaid at Melanie's wedding in Bruges. The wedding had been a dream and Ginny had followed it up by extending her stay to absorb the delights of Bruges, the Belgian city that was every bit as captivating as everyone said it was. Ginny, or rather Melanie, had timed it rather well too with the start of the Winter Glow Festival in Bruges, which brought thousands of lights to hundreds of trees and bustling street markets. As she'd walked along enchanting cobbled streets, lit-up shop fronts had beckoned her into their cosy interiors. Reflections on the canals had depicted the magic of a fast-approaching Christmas, the scent of chocolate that filled the air year-round had been all the more intoxicating with the promise of the winter wonderland that would soon be upon this European city. She'd sent a postcard home to Butterbury, of course, the way she always did even if she were somewhere she'd already been and she always chose classy pictures on the front, knowing that Daisy would see it every day at work too. With her sister's natural talent for photography, Ginny wondered more often than not why Daisy was still stuck in the shop, but it was the way it was, she couldn't change it.

Melanie arrived at the restaurant all smiles and kissed her friend on both cheeks, the Parisienne way, and the waiter reappeared from nowhere to take her coat.

'Where's Jonas?' It seemed as though Melanie had come on her own.

Melanie nodded when the waiter swiftly returned to offer her a glass of red wine. 'He said he'd leave it to us girls. Think he's had enough of me.'

'Two weeks of marriage and he's already looking for a way out?' Ginny winced. 'I'd run now if I were you. Where's the commitment?' But she grinned above her menu. Those two were rock solid. Unlike any of Ginny's relationships. The only one that had approached serious had been with Lucas Abney. They'd started dating in high school. Lucas with the soft caramel eyes, the dark blond hair and muscles that showed he had never and would never be suited to working behind a desk. Plenty of couples had split up when they ventured off to university but Lucas and Ginny hadn't. They'd had staying power, for a time, despite Ginny studying at university in the north of England and Lucas being at the opposite end of the country to study marine biology, a path his parents had insisted on him pursuing rather than assuming he'd follow in their footsteps at Hawthorn Lane Farm, the Abney family's fruit and vegetable business. Not long after Lucas graduated he was offered the opportunity of a lifetime to go to work in Florida.

Ginny couldn't deny that things between her and Lucas hadn't been the same since her dad died. Lucas had been there for her, of course, but she'd struggled to make sense of it all and somehow they'd lost the easy relationship they'd always had. Lucas had ended it when the Florida opportunity came up and she'd been devastated at the time. Melanie had been the one to help Ginny pick up the pieces, to listen to her in lengthy telephone calls, and the only thing to make it easier had been knowing that Lucas had left Butterbury, that if she went home she wouldn't have to worry about bumping into him.

But then he'd come back and he'd been living in Butterbury for some time. Ginny still wondered how he'd reached the decision to return, to take on a major role in the family business, the business he appeared to be happy to leave behind. But she'd never asked him because whenever she went home she made sure to avoid the road leading up to the farm, she kept her head down when she was out and about. And so far it had worked, largely because of her determination rather than good luck or perfect timing. What were you supposed to say to the man who left and took a piece of your heart with him? Maybe if she'd got serious with someone else it might be different, she'd be able to flash a ring at him, tell him she was starting a family, that she had everything she'd ever wanted, but she couldn't claim any of those things.

'I wish you weren't leaving in the morning.' Melanie poured the last of the red wine into Ginny's glass after she finished her mouthful of steak. 'It's been great having you around again. Like old times. It's a shame we have to grow up, isn't it?'

'Don't let Jonas hear you say that.' Ginny smiled.

'I just mean that it's nice having a good friend here.'

'But you're settling in, aren't you?'

'Of course.'

'And when you have a baby there'll be mother's groups so you'll make friends there.' She sneaked a glance at her shellshocked friend. 'That's what you're planning, right?'

'Am I that transparent?'

'I'd say you're not pregnant yet because you had a good dose of wine, but you plan to be soon, hence not suggesting any cocktails like the last time you and I were together for your hen night.'

'Correct on both counts. Not pregnant yet, but planning to do it soon.' Her apple cheeks were already glowing as if pre-empting the change and with her ash blonde hair wound up into a chignon, Melanie couldn't disguise the feeling of joy on her face at the thought of becoming a mother. The both of them had often talked about motherhood the way you did when it was such an enormous part of your job to watch families form in new ways, but since Ginny had forged a different path, she'd tried not to think about how she might like her own life to take shape one day.

'I think it's wonderful,' Ginny complimented. 'Now, come on, how about you show me a bit more of Paris one last time, a final farewell.'

They left enough cash on the silver tray to cover the

bill plus a generous tip and Ginny handed it to the waiter before they pulled on their scarves and coats ready to face the cold.

'How about you?' Melanie asked as they left the restaurant and moved with the crowds as though it were still the middle of the day.

'How about me what?' Ginny linked an arm through Melanie's as they headed towards the Avenue des Champs-Élysées where wider pavements would cater for the seasonal crowd.

'Are you ever going to settle down?'

She could play this one of two ways: pretend this nomadic lifestyle was still everything she'd ever dreamed of, or admit the truth. She went with the latter. 'I've loved seeing a bit of the world. I never understood why Fern didn't want to, why Daisy never did. All those photographs she could've taken, you know how much she loved taking pictures.'

'Hey, this isn't about your sisters.'

It had always felt as though it were about her sisters. Growing up she'd felt suspended somewhere in the middle. Daisy was younger and their mum was busy making sure she didn't get dragged up but got as much attention as the others. Fern had already got to a point where rather than being babied she loved to be the grown up. And Fern had had their dad, Harry, both of them shared a love of maths, something neither Daisy nor Ginny had either inherited or ever wished to get involved in. Fern and Harry had been in their own little world half the time, Daisy had clung to Loretta like a limpet, and Ginny? Well, she'd fallen somewhere in between and had learned to be independent very early on.

'Lately I've been wondering what I really want.' She moved around, made friends easily, kept things interesting. But she was thirty-seven and well aware that most of those friends had evolved and begun to settle down, whether as a couple or in a place they wanted to be or with a career they had no intention of altering. And lately Ginny had no idea what came next. She felt like a hot air balloon that had had its ropes severed and here she was drifting high above the landscape, taking in the beauty of the world around her but with no idea how to get herself back down to earth and move forwards with a sense of permanency.

She explained to Melanie how she'd been feeling for the last few months. 'I love so much about agency work – it's flexible, I work with different teams, I don't have to worry about bureaucracy when I'm not in the same workplace, there's less stress involved, and better pay.'

'I agree, all those plus points are selling it. So what's the problem? Are you saying you don't want to be a midwife anymore?'

'Sometimes I wonder whether I need a total change.'

'If you're going to suggest a job behind a desk then I'll tell you now, you won't last.'

'Probably not,' Ginny agreed. 'But I've reached a crossroads and I really don't know which way.'

'I felt a bit the same way when the hospital made so many changes, I didn't know whether I was coming or going. There was a time I wanted out.'

'But you didn't leave. You would still be there if you hadn't moved here to be with Jonas.'

'True. And I soon realised that I'm one of those people who will never change career. I want to have a family, but once I do and the kids are at school I'll be getting out there, putting my career back on track. I love it too much not to.'

They walked on for long enough that Melanie insisted they stopped for hot chocolates, prolonging their time together. And when eventually it came time to part ways Ginny felt a sadness wash over her that she couldn't identify. How was it that with three sisters to talk to she only ever shared her deepest feelings with friends these days? The three sisters had once been close despite the age gaps, but since their dad died, something between them had broken and they'd never been able to mend it.

On the final leg of her journey from Paris to Derby, Ginny's phone rang only minutes after the train shunted out of the station and the name *Mum* popped up on the display. Excellent timing. Her mum loved a good chat but it would've been better to do it when she wasn't on-board. She didn't want to disturb the other passengers, but she took the call if only to explain she was in transit and that she'd call back later. She did her best to be considerate and keep her voice low as she told her mum where she was and when she estimated she'd be home.

But Loretta didn't want to talk later and got to the crux of the conversation.

'All three of us, home for a few weeks for Christmas?' Ginny repeated her mother's words in disbelief.

Ginny went to Butterbury a handful of times during the year but she usually didn't spend much concentrated time with her sisters, and she couldn't even recall when all three of them had spent more than one evening together, let alone an extended period. This didn't make sense to

Ginny. Usually her mother didn't fight the fact that they all had their own plans, when Daisy decided to flit off with friends somewhere as was her right, when Fern had commitments with Everett's family. So why now? Why the insistence they all come back to Butterbury and stay for not only Christmas but the lead-up too?

'It's your grandad,' Loretta carried on, as though reading her mind.

Ginny's insides clambered in anticipation of the answer and then went into free fall. 'Is he sick?' Her voice shook, she closed her eyes remembering the life-changing phone call about her dad all those years ago.

'He's getting older, we all are. I just want to make this Christmas special for him, Ginny. You know how much he adores all three of you and I'd love to have Christmas dinner around our table with him at the helm.'

Ginny opened her eyes and watched the countryside whizz by outside the window. 'I have work for a few days, I've already agreed to it.'

'You can come after that. I can cover your train fare if needs be.'

Mum really was desperate for this to work. 'No need, I'm all set.' If this was about Grandad, she couldn't not be there. She had no intention of letting history repeat itself. 'I'll book my ticket and let you know the timings.'

She didn't miss the relief in her mother's voice and with that settled Loretta had obviously forgotten Ginny was on the train and wanted to know all about Paris, Bruges and the wedding before she reluctantly hung up to go and attend to customers in the shop. For some mothers discussing Melanie's wedding would've been the perfect precursor to launch into questions about when Ginny was

55

going to meet someone and settle down, but thankfully Loretta wasn't that way inclined and Ginny appreciated it. Being asked those sorts of questions was annoying if you'd made a choice to stay single and focus on other things. But it was even more annoying when you hadn't because then you needed to do your level best to pretend the very fact hadn't begun to get to you. Her mum hadn't mentioned Lucas much since he'd got back to Butterbury either. She'd informed Ginny and left it at that. She knew her daughter had been heartbroken when he ended things, but what she didn't know was that once Ginny got over the initial shock, she'd felt an inexplicable sense of freedom she was thankful for. And it was that freedom, the chance to do what was right for her, which had stopped her from being too resentful towards the man she'd once thought she'd be with forever.

The rain started teeming down ten minutes before the train drew into the platform at Derby railway station and so it was a brisk walk from the station to home, the only detour a stop at the corner shop for a bottle of milk and a loaf of bread.

She dumped her bag in the hallway of her flat as though it were a lead weight and although her mum's phone call had made her begin to worry about Grandad, it made her feel something else too.

It made her realise she really needed to go home to Butterbury. There was a pull she hadn't realised was there until now and she knew that the time and space in her home village might just be the way to give her some thinking time and work out where she went to next.

Chapter Four

Daisy

Despite being a big lover of the great outdoors Daisy wasn't sorry to be inside the shop at long last. It might only be the beginning of December but the early morning temperatures left you in no doubt that it was time to hunker down for a long winter. And today the wind was howling, the window panes in the shop rattled and a draft didn't mind pushing its way beneath the door.

In the summer months Daisy savoured the walk and the fresh air before work far more when she could enjoy the sunshine. This morning even Busker had seemed to be dragging his feet as though the damp and the cold were too much for him. But still Daisy loved being outside and she'd got some great photographs. Her dad had always told her there was no such thing as the wrong weather, only the wrong clothes. She was the only one of the three sisters who liked to go camping, always had and still did. Even now she'd happily take herself away for a couple of nights' break, pitching up her little sky blue and navy tent that had been her companion for years seeing her through sun, rain, snow and high winds. By day she'd take her camera and explore capturing breathtaking scenery, landscapes she could've stared at for hours, wildlife including deer, squirrels and even spiders, their impressive webs glinting in the sunshine or sparkling in the frost to show off their intricacies. She'd finish her days cooking on her mini stove beside a small campfire, weather permitting, and then she'd cocoon herself in her sleeping bag and sit at the entrance to her tent looking up at the stars, nothing between her and them, just freedom.

Daisy finished the mug of tea her mum had left her. Loretta as usual had opened the shop first thing while Daisy walked Busker, then as Daisy arrived Loretta made the tea either for both of them or if she had something to get on with – errands to run – she'd leave Daisy a mug and get on. It had been the same arrangement for years. Daisy picked up her camera and scrolled through the photographs that she'd taken this morning. She paused, remembering the last time she and her dad had gone camping, Loretta and her sisters gladly staying behind with none of them fans of the outdoor pastime. For three wonderful days Daisy and her dad had camped in the Brecon Beacons, they'd hiked, they'd cooked in the tiny tin pans over the little hotplate, and she'd carried her camera everywhere. It was the last time Daisy remembered being truly happy around her father, until she found out he wasn't the man she thought he was and no matter how much she tried to get past it, she never had such close times with him again. She went away with friends instead after that. He said he understood, but she could see the hurt in his face. And back then, she'd almost been glad he didn't get to have everything perfect in his life either.

Daisy's eyes had filled with tears as they often did when she thought of her dad but she batted them away when

Mrs Ledbetter, local woman to Butterbury, emerged from where she'd been perusing the fabric selection.

'What have you got there?' Mrs Ledbetter was looking over Daisy's shoulder at the shots on the camera she was holding.

'I was out with Busker this morning.'

'Poor Busker, it's freezing.' She took in the picture of the family dog, eyes half-closed against the wind, his fur blowing.

'Any day is a beautiful day for photography.' Daisy smiled, glad she wasn't looking at anything incriminating. Mrs Ledbetter was friendly enough but was well-known to enjoy a bit of local gossip. And Daisy didn't much want her business broadcast around Butterbury. Not that there was anything to tell. She did the same thing day in, day out. Mrs Ledbetter probably led a wilder existence than she did.

Mrs Ledbetter tried to look closer at the photographs. Daisy had captured the rugged beauty of the deserted landscape that morning, at first shrouded in a low-lying mist, then the dark, unpredictable clouds brooding up above before they'd moved on too.

'My eyesight isn't good enough,' Mrs Ledbetter concluded. 'That or the screen is too tiny. If you ever get them printed then I'll take another look. Now, can we talk curtains?'

'I would love nothing more.'

Mrs Ledbetter at least had a sense of humour and raised an amused eyebrow at Daisy's sarcasm.

'Are you making these curtains yourself?' Daisy asked.

'Loretta is helping me and we're doing tie-backs. Your mother is wonderful, you know, so generous with her time and her efforts. And you've inherited her talents and her nature.'

Daisy wasn't so sure about that. She got by, she knew the business, she could manage the shop alone if she had to, because she'd made it her mission to know all the ins and outs, to keep the promise she'd made to herself that her mother would never have to worry, that for once her life would stay on track and she'd get exactly what she wanted. And what Loretta had always wanted was for the Butterbury Sewing Box to stay in the family.

Mrs Ledbetter pulled out a piece of paper with the measurements of her window and her curtain rail and handed it to Daisy. Daisy calculated the amount of material she'd need, scribbling down the details, and checked she'd worked it out right before she took the large roll of fabric over to the counter. Mrs Ledbetter admired the design as it was unrolled along the beautifully polished, smooth, dark-wooden surface from one end almost to where the till sat. A tape measure was fixed to the longest edge of the counter to make the job easier and when Daisy was sure of her accuracy, she picked up the scissors and carefully cut the fabric. She recommended the best colours of cotton to use alongside the material, found the most appropriate, and rung them up with the order.

'I'm looking forward to getting started.' Mrs Ledbetter beamed. 'Thank you, Daisy. Between Miriam's haberdashery at the opposite end of Butterbury and this place, you have everyone's needs covered. And with Miriam away dealing with a family emergency, thank goodness you're still open or I would've had to wait to get started.'

'Glad to be of service.'

Daisy couldn't remember the last time her mother had

shut the shop like Miriam had done – although, to be fair, Miriam's absence was more to do with her extended family needing her than simply taking a break. Daisy took short holidays whenever she could but Loretta seemed resistant to leave the place. Daisy wished her mum would realise that she could cope without her for a few days. Or perhaps it was Grandad that kept her mum so unwilling to leave the village. Loretta was close to her dad and now he was in the lodge she was up there daily, they both were. And as they both knew, life could change in a heartbeat, days with one another were to be cherished before something stole them away.

'You know I always thought Fern would take over this business,' Mrs Ledbetter observed, missing the way Daisy bristled at the mention of her eldest sister, the assumption that being the eldest meant you were the one who had the best ability. 'Then I thought, perhaps Ginny, because she always loved to sew. I'd see her in here, cutting up material, making her own clothes.'

Daisy plucked a brown paper bag from beneath the counter and put Mrs Ledbetter's reels of cotton inside. She folded up the fabric carefully, inserting tissue paper between the folds, and put it into another bag. She didn't really want to talk about life, sisters and this place, given she so obviously hadn't been on Mrs Ledbetter's radar to be able to manage the shop, and so she changed the subject. 'How's the cleaning going up at Butterbury Lodge? Grandad says you're still working hard.'

Mrs Ledbetter did up her coat again ready to brave the cold. 'It takes a lot of work, especially in the winter, all the mud that gets trodden in and the leaves and debris.' She rolled her eyes dramatically.

'Then it's a good job they've got you.' Daisy smiled.

When Mrs Ledbetter went on her way Daisy slotted the roll of material back into its allotted space and ensured the other rolls were tidy, and with no other customers in the shop she thought she'd better get on with unboxing the latest delivery. She brought the box from out at the back into the front of the shop and opened it up to find a whole range of fat quarters for quilting. There was a bundle themed in red with polka dots, humbug stripes and poppies, and another cream fabric with traditionally wrapped sweets, which made Daisy smile. While she didn't have a huge passion for the family business in its entirety in quite the way her mother did, quilting was something else. Quilts had always been special in their family, the associated meaning and togetherness conjuring up memories easily swept aside. She still had her childhood quilt at the end of her bed and come the winter months, she'd pull it over herself, feel safe, loved, like nothing had ever changed.

The post arrived and Daisy shuffled through it. Dull, brown envelopes mostly, a flyer about the GP surgery and how they were now offering online appointments too for convenience – a smart move in Daisy's opinion. And then a postcard from Ginny. Most people would flip it straight over and read the words but Daisy was instantly drawn to the picture instead, the way the photograph on the front captured the higgledy-piggledy buildings of Bruges bordering dreamy canals, which were like something out of a fairy tale.

Loretta arrived back at the shop and almost immediately after she came through the door she spotted what Daisy was holding in her hands. 'From Ginny?'

'Of course from Ginny. Who else sends postcards to the shop?'

'Well what does it say?'

Daisy passed it to her mother. 'Read it for yourself, I'll sweep up.' Leaves had blown in after the postman and even more after Loretta so Daisy grabbed the dustpan and brush from beneath the counter.

Loretta still had her coat on and as she read the card she loosened the neck button. 'I'm glad she had a nice time, we should get the Paris postcard soon enough as she's already home now. She said Paris was magical, she and Melanie had a wonderful time at dinner, just the two of them, on the last night.'

'You spoke to Ginny?' Loretta was hanging her coat on the hook past the wall of photographs and the pinboard with the postcards. 'You never said.' Loretta was usually so vocal about being in touch with Ginny or Fern, as though Daisy might forget she had sisters if their names weren't mentioned often enough.

'I thought I did,' she dismissed.

When her mum didn't expand, Daisy recapped what jobs she'd managed to get done in the shop, what she hadn't quite got to yet. They were well-versed in this type of handover. She left her mum unpacking another box of fat quarters, shrugged on her coat, looped her scarf around her neck, tugged on her gloves and picked up the bags she'd tucked away out of sight earlier.

'Did you read the card?' Loretta's question stopped her before she could escape. The card was already pinned up with the others.

'Of course,' Daisy lied.

'What have you got there?'

She didn't miss much. 'Just some old clothes for the second-hand shop.'

'You should've said you were going to drop some off, I have a few things I want to get rid of.'

Daisy quickly pre-empted any suggestion her mum might run to their house at the end of the street to get them. 'Sorry, I can't hang around. I promised Grandad I'd be up there by one o'clock.' And she had no intention of going to the second-hand shop either.

Loretta looked again at the pinboard of postcards. 'You know, you could take yourself off for a long weekend in Europe if you liked, I really wouldn't mind.'

'I know you wouldn't. But I'm not all that fussed.' Nobody else had ever understood Daisy's fixation with the great outdoors, as though Europe and a hotel or apartment were the preferred experience. Loretta, Fern and Ginny had no desire to embrace nights beneath canvas, waking to the rugged outdoors that Daisy and her dad had both had a passion for. Daisy loved how the weather made it different every time and no matter how inclement she always embraced it and the wonder of the skies, the clouds, the way mother nature was the boss on each and every day of the year.

Daisy had almost made it to the door of the shop, by-passing an elderly man and pointing him in the direction of the turquoise wool, when Loretta's voice stopped her in her tracks. 'I've asked your sisters to come home for Christmas.'

Perhaps blurting it out when Daisy was in a rush and they had a customer had been on purpose. 'For a couple of days, you mean? And both of them?' They hadn't all shared Christmas for years and Daisy was sure she wasn't the only sister to be glad of that.

'I've asked them both to come for a few weeks, some concentrated family time.'

Daisy almost burst out laughing. *Concentrated family time?* It wasn't something that the Chamberlains did well at all. 'It'll be lovely to see them,' she said, putting on a front, because she could tell her mum was serious.

It wasn't that Daisy didn't love Ginny and Fern, and it wasn't that she didn't like them either, it was that none of them seemed to understand one another at all. Fern was a high-flying career woman who somehow juggled family and a husband to huge success, Ginny lived a life without bounds flitting wherever the mood took her, and Daisy was here in the shop taking responsibility and making sure their mother got the happiness she deserved.

'I want you all to be on your best behaviour,' Loretta went on.

'We're not children.' Daisy felt eleven years old rather than the grown woman that she was.

'You're *my* children.'

'Why this year, why all of a sudden?' A feeling of panic flooded her bones. 'Mum, are you sick?' *Please don't let that be it, please don't let this be a prelude to something sinister.* She'd almost forgotten there was a customer at the other end of the shop he was so quiet until he put the wool he'd selected onto the counter by the till and told Loretta he was going to select some buttons.

Loretta came to Daisy's side and spoke quietly, reassuring her youngest daughter. 'I'm not sick, no. Do I look sick? Is it this lipstick, is it the wrong colour?'

Daisy began to laugh. 'Don't joke, you got me worried.'

'It's your grandad.' Before Daisy could ask whether he was sick, she added, 'He's fine, enjoying his new life at Butterbury Lodge, as you know, but when I talk to him there's a sadness. He misses you three girls. And I don't mean individually, you all see him, you most days and your sisters whenever they're home. But I'd like to give him one more Christmas with us all as a family. It's been years since we all sat around the table together and I know how special it would be.'

Daisy's eyes filled with tears at any reference to her grandad getting older. Daft, it was a fact of life, but she couldn't bear the thought of being without him.

Joshua Abney chose that moment to come into the shop, almost knocking into Daisy with the door. 'Sorry,' he grimaced. He was carrying a rather plentiful wooden box of winter fruits and vegetables. A stalk of Brussels sprouts poked out of one side as he leaned around it and added, 'Didn't see you there. Are you OK?'

'Of course.' She shook away the tears and the look of melancholy that clearly gave her feelings away. Along with the zing from the lemons and the sharp aromatic scent from the grapefruits balanced on top of something else came a subtle undertone of a woody aftershave that Daisy realised had begun to be a familiar association with Joshua as much as his deep brown eyes which were almost a match for his hair.

The Abneys, much like the Chamberlains did with their business, had been running the Hawthorn Lane Farm for generations and Joshua, who was only a few years older than Daisy, worked on the land at his family's fruit and vegetable farm along with his brother, Lucas, and their parents. When Ginny had dated Lucas, Daisy had had the biggest crush on Joshua. He'd been dating someone at the time and Daisy had become well versed at hiding her feelings, resisting his good looks, the hair with a little peak in the fringe that suited him, sexy thick dark eyebrows and full lips her gaze was drawn to every time he spoke.

Loretta beckoned Joshua into the shop. She, and Mrs Ledbetter, knew full well that Joshua liked Daisy. Daisy just hoped neither of them had cottoned on to her own feelings because although tempting at times, she really had no desire to get lost in romantic notions of falling in love and living happily ever after when people could hurt one another so badly.

Luckily, local gardener Rhys arrived at that moment with a beautiful and fragrant Fraser fir for the shop and Daisy saw her escape, leaving the men to carry the tree over to the awaiting stand at one end of the Butterbury Sewing Box.

Daisy made her way from the shop towards Lantern Square. The big switch on of the Christmas lights at the end of November had been as special as it was every year, with the huge tree in the corner of the square, an iron-railing surrounding space with flowerbeds, pathways and grassed areas. There were illuminated wooden creatures dotted around, including a hedgehog in the flowerbed she could spot now from the other side of the railings and a lit-up reindeer closer to one of the gates to access the square. Butterbury always did Christmas well and Daisy, despite any reservations about the daily grind, loved living in the village and couldn't imagine being anywhere else. It wasn't too busy, it wasn't a big town or city, and being nestled in the Cotswolds meant they were close to rolling hills, picturesque villages and some of the best walking trails the country had to offer.

Daisy made her way past Lantern Square and up the hill on the opposite side that led out to acres of beautiful countryside. She reached Butterbury Lodge at the top of the hill and unlatched the little gate at the front of the path, closed it behind her, and paused to look at the view that even in winter was impressive with the village spread out and the square situated in the dip before a hill led out in the opposite direction towards farmland. The Abney farm made up part of the land and past their business was another fruit and vegetable farm, owned by another local family, slightly smaller, but equally as popular. Living in Butterbury you were never short of fresh produce supplies and Daisy hoped it would always be that way.

Daisy said good morning to Hannah in passing. Not too dissimilar to Daisy in age, Hannah was engaged to the local doctor and ran Tied Up with String, a care package business that had become increasingly popular. Hannah hadn't lived in the village all that long but she'd settled in quickly enough and volunteered up here at the lodge. She'd grown close to Mr G, one of the elderly residents and one of the chattiest men Daisy had ever met, and Daisy smiled as she went in through the front entrance, knowing Mr G had met his match with Ivor. The two of them would keep the staff here on their toes, that was for sure.

Once she'd signed in at reception she found Ivor in the expansive lounge at the rear of the property. The residents all had their own rooms and differing needs, yet help was on hand, company too, if that's what you were after, in communal areas like this. Out of the window past the

Christmas tree that brought a waft of pine and the season into the room were pretty gardens, a pond and a fountain that, on quieter days, you could listen to as it trickled water in a soothing fashion. The lodge was so much more than a care home. The residents had access to a book club, cookery classes, and Charles Bray, a local man who'd lived in the square until moving here, had requested someone come in to provide dance lessons, which were starting at the end of the year. Now, thanks to Ivor's influence, many of the residents were beginning to embrace their creative side. Daisy had started coming here to the lodge at the beginning of the year as a favour to him, to spread the love of sewing, knitting and quilting. She'd thought the initial session would be it, but so many people flocked to her after her spiel, asking about learning some new skills, that she volunteered to make it a more regular thing and give some basic lessons. She might not be passionate about it all like her mother was but she still enjoyed coming here or giving the lessons in the workshop above the shop. Some residents she found were grumpier than others, a few didn't converse much, but on the whole they were good company.

'What have you brought for us today?' Ivor sat in the chair beside the window and adjusted the cushion behind him. He moved well for a man of eighty-eight and although he hadn't needed to come here, he had made the move before Loretta could worry herself into making him live with them. He'd confided in Daisy that such an arrangement would've totally cramped his style.

Daisy pushed her gloves into her coat pocket on the back of another chair and then opened up each of the carrier bags she'd brought with her to reveal a rainbow of coloured balls of wool. 'I've been sneaking these now and then over the last few weeks, as usual, but Mum spotted me with the bags today.' She'd been taking one or two balls here and there, adding the money to the till as though a customer had made the purchases, and built up a decent collection every time she did it. She was usually more careful and zipped home to grab the bags rather than stashing them at the shop, but today she'd been too pushed for time and hadn't thought her mum would take that much interest in what she had in a couple of nondescript bags.

'Don't blow our cover,' Ivor urged.

'I won't,' she giggled. They'd been working on something rather special since Easter when her grandad first formed a sewing group – that Daisy now knew was called Oldies in Stitches – up at the lodge. Everyone was in on it, the secretiveness was all part of the fun and Daisy loved spending so much time with her grandad. With her dad, it had been camping and the great outdoors, but with Ivor it was this.

Ivor took out the four balls of pillar-box red wool, the end of a batch she'd got cheap, and enough for what they still needed to do. He, Mr G and Ernest who'd come to join them waded through the bags admiring the rest of the colours.

Daisy thought about what her mum had said to her about Grandad and she was right. Ivor did deserve to have his entire family together for Christmas, all three of his granddaughters in the one place at the one time on an occasion that usually brought people together. Except Daisy knew that while it was nice in theory, unfortunately Christmas was also a time of year that had the ability to drive people apart. She wasn't sure what did it – the pressure of perfection the season called for, the meal itself, the build-up to the one day that was Christmas? Whatever it was, she knew that this year she didn't want her mum to have any added stress, and she made up her mind that not only could she be responsible enough to step up and be the one to take on the family business, she could also hold it together with her sisters when they came home for an extended stay. Time together had been in manageable chunks for as long as Daisy could remember, but looking at Ivor now as he passed some of the snowy white wool across to Ernest, distributed more to others who'd come to see the latest haul, Daisy was determined not to mess this up for anyone, least of all Grandad.

Chapter Five

Loretta

Joshua had insisted he help Loretta get the Christmas tree into its stand while Rhys went back to his truck parked outside and got on with delivering trees to the rest of the residents in the village just like he did every year. He was still in the shop now, helping her get the tree properly straight.

'I'd better not decorate it until Daisy's with me, I'll be in trouble.' Loretta grinned. They finally had the tree in position and while Joshua held it, Loretta bent down to fix it into place with the screws against the base of the trunk.

Over the last few months Loretta had noticed a definite spark between Joshua and Daisy, but for whatever reason, Daisy kept insisting she wasn't interested. Loretta had no idea why she wouldn't be – he was local, gorgeous, trustworthy . . . in fact the Abney brothers were exactly the type of men you wanted to join the family. Then again, didn't daughters always resist the men their mother thought were perfect for them?

Joshua's older brother, Lucas, had dated Ginny for seven years until he ended things and took a job in Florida. Ginny had been so upset, but deep down Loretta had been glad Ginny didn't announce that she was moving to America with him, because what if they'd stayed over there? What if Ginny had started a whole new life overseas and never returned? It wasn't that she, as her mother, wanted her to forever be clinging onto the apron strings, it was more that Ginny might never have rekindled the relationship she'd once had with her sisters. And to Loretta that would've been heartbreaking.

Ginny had visited Butterbury on and off since she moved away, but she'd never once bumped into Lucas who had been back in the village for a few years. Lucas had come into the shop when he first returned to Butterbury, faced Loretta as though she was about to haul him up in front of a judge and a jury for dumping her daughter, but she'd embraced him in a hug because once upon a time he'd been like a son to her. And Ginny had used her heartbreak to her advantage. She'd channelled her energies into something new and got her life on track with work, with travel, and found her happy place right there.

Loretta stood back to admire the tree, already planning in her mind how it would look with ornaments and lights. But she'd have to resist doing anything to it, because she'd meant it when she said Daisy would not be happy if she decorated it without her.

Somehow all three of her daughters were strong-minded and although proud of that fact, Loretta still felt guilt creep up on her now and then at how she'd been when Harry died. The girls had shouldered their grief and when Loretta should've been the tower of strength for all of them, some days she'd found it difficult to even drag herself out of bed. And more than that, she was ashamed that in the weeks and months following their loss she'd never sat down and talked about it at length with any of them. Loretta wondered, had she managed her grief better, would the sisters still be close? The best of friends? She'd missed something along the way, the root cause of their problems, and now years later unearthing it felt impossible.

'How are Fern and Ginny?' Joshua asked as he circled the tree once more to check it was definitely positioned properly. He reached up and adjusted the uppermost branches on one side where they'd tangled around one another.

'They're well.' Joshua was also polite, another tick on Loretta's approval list. 'And they're both coming home for Christmas.'

He didn't hide his surprise. 'All three of them, here together?' It seemed the Chamberlain girls had got into such a habit of not coinciding visits for any length of time that others in the village had noticed. Neither Fern nor Ginny ever stayed long and they spent part of their time visiting their grandad, which meant they didn't have to hang around Butterbury very much at all. Fern and Ginny seemed to have put a distance between the village and their new lives, and all three girls, more disturbingly, had put a distance between themselves.

'Well hopefully I'll see them both around,' said Joshua.

'You might well do. They're staying for a few weeks.'

He whistled through his teeth. 'I never thought we'd see the day your three were back together.'

Loretta hadn't either, and she wished it was as simple as his words suggested. She'd love to see all three of them sharing stories with one another, discussing their woes, giving each other advice.

Joshua buttoned up his heavyweight khaki jacket and pulled on his gloves ready to brave the outside. 'Perhaps I'll see you at the tree farm soon. I'm doing a stint in the grotto.' He lowered his voice when a local father came in with two toddlers in tow. 'I'm the Father Christmas up there this year, a few times a week, swapping evening shifts with another volunteer. I'm Father Christmas at the bookshop too.' He put a finger across his lips.

'Your secret is safe with me,' she whispered in return before waving him on his way.

If only Daisy could see what Loretta saw in this man with a heart of gold, a man who knew what was important in life.

Loretta also had a chance to make a start on the Christmas window in between serving customers. She positioned the wire tree at the very edge of the bay window, waving to Jeffrey the postman who walked past with his very pregnant wife heading towards Lantern Square. She opened up a cardboard box to an array of colour and, one by one, took out the pompoms that acted as baubles, remembering how one winter when Ginny was fifteen she'd had the flu and even after a week in bed was still too weak to return to school. For something to do, Loretta had had Ginny sitting out at the back of the shop making these coloured pompoms of varying sizes, in the brightest of colours as well as traditional Christmassy reds, golds, silvers and ice blue. They'd threaded each one with matching cotton and that year Loretta had made this wire Christmas tree upon which to hang them, and it had gone up every year since. She hung the baubles, only pausing to source cotton for the few pompoms that seemed to have lost theirs, or serving customers as they came into the shop.

By the time Daisy returned, Loretta was positioning the wooden bedhead that just about fitted in the raised platform of the window and on top of two cardboard boxes next to one another. Across the boxes she draped a Christmas quilt that showed off some of her favourite festive quilting fabric with a snowy playground scene and a house with a chimney and Father Christmas on the roof, his sleigh and the reindeer waiting. Every year people would be enticed into the shop by the festive window and Loretta would point them in the direction of ready-made quilts she had in stock or the materials to make their own.

Daisy was by the stunning Fraser fir, safely in position. 'I'll never grow tired of the smell.' She pulled off her gloves and put a hand to the tips of the branches, her fingers inspecting the needles. She inhaled deeply and smiled. 'Actually, I'd better have a word with Rhys about a tree for the house.'

'Perhaps I should've thought and ordered them both at the same time,' said Loretta. She'd picked up a stocking decoration for the window display and hung it on one end of the bedhead. 'I remember you girls choosing a tree every year when you were younger.'

Daisy took off her coat. 'Who are you trying to kid? It was me and Dad who chose the tree, us who carried it home. We didn't have a Rhys back then, we carried it be-tween us. Ginny and Fern would've turned their noses up at putting on wellies and traipsing up and down to find the perfect tree. And Fern especially would've complained about the mud. You know what she's like, she's always dressed immaculately, her hair is always styled.'

'You are indeed very different girls, nothing wrong with that. And your sisters always loved the tree when it was inside the house.'

She conceded. 'They did.'

Was she agreeing because that's what she thought Loretta needed to hear? Sometimes Loretta found it harder to read her youngest daughter than she would've liked. Although she was pretty sure Daisy hadn't been going to the second-hand shop earlier. She was up to something and it made Loretta uneasy. 'Maybe we could head up to the tree farm together after closing. I know they're open late. I could choose some new ornaments, you could check out the trees, you always had a good eye for them.'

'Let's do it,' Daisy agreed. 'We could take Busker up there too.'

'I'm not sure that's a good idea. We might lose him among the trees and it's too cold to be looking for a dog in the dark. You know how much he loves to explore.'

'I gave him a long walk this morning, I suppose,' said Daisy.

'Why don't I nip home now, take him out for a brief walk, and he can curl up in his basket here for a while so he has the company. Then after closing I'll drop him home and you and I can go up to the farm.' Busker would just have to be understanding tonight.

Loretta put the empty box that held the pom-poms be-tween seasons out at the back ready to take upstairs. She caught sight of the photograph of Busker on the wall, the shot Daisy had captured as he snuggled into his basket on top of a multi-coloured blanket Ivor had made especially for him when he became a part of the family. Her eyes fell onto the photograph next to that one, the picture of all three of her girls snuggled beneath a beautiful handmade quilt and their dad at the very end squeezed onto the sofa that had been plenty big enough when they were tiny but only fitted them then because Daisy was beneath Harry's arm and leaning against him. Daisy must've been around eight years old, Ginny fourteen, Fern eighteen.

Loretta reached out to touch the glass as if she could somehow feel the softness of the quilt, the joins where the squares had been sewn together, some expertly, others clumsily. Quilting had never been Harry's thing but he'd insisted he help make this one because he'd been the one to suggest they have a special quilt just for movie night, Harry and his girls. Daisy was only three at the time, but she'd chosen some of the material as the project got under-way and she'd always been there with them all, she even helped to arrange the pieces when it was time, although they'd had to watch her when sharp cutters, scissors and pins did the rounds. Ginny had been much more able to participate by then and so had Fern, both girls laughing at Harry's cluelessness when it came to sewing. But it hadn't been an activity in which participation was equal or man-datory, but rather a bonding experience that would stay with them. Daisy didn't remember making the quilt at all, of course, she'd been too young, but this picture on the wall was forever a reminder along with those nights all together in front of the television. The quilt had been such a source of joy, until it became one of heartbreak.

'What time is the tree farm open until?' Daisy's voice reminded Loretta she needed to get a move on.

'It's open for hours yet, we're fine.' She left Daisy at the helm, went home and collected Busker who was pleased to see her as always and even more so when she picked up his lead.

Out for their walk, Busker pulled in the direction of the fields but Loretta didn't want to go that far and so he accepted a brief outing into the centre of Butterbury instead and all the way to the end of the high street.

Loretta noticed a man lurking near the haberdashery run by local woman Miriam who quite often sent customers Loretta's way, and vice versa. 'The shop's closed, I'm afraid,' she called out. 'They're away visiting family for a couple more weeks.' When he sighed she asked him, 'Are you looking for anything in particular?' She didn't like to tout for business when he'd obviously come to see the competition, but if he was desperate, it was only fair. Perhaps he had a wife at home who was waiting anxiously for supplies to carry on with a project and finish in time for Christmas, you never knew.

'I needed to see the owner rather than anything she sells.' The man smiled, a kind gesture that reached eyes behind thinly framed glasses. Perhaps he was used to dealing with Miriam and only she would do. Loretta understood, she had customers who said the same of her, particularly when they reached this man's age, around a decade older than she was if she were to hazard a guess.

'Try again in a couple of weeks,' Loretta suggested. 'They're open Monday through Saturday.'

He tipped his cap. 'Will do.' And he climbed slowly back into the car he'd parked right outside, moving with a bit more ease than her elderly father but not much more. He had a sadness about him and it made Loretta think, there was only so much you could pick up from appearances and snatched remarks. She wondered what his story was.

When they finally closed the shop for the day and Busker was safely ensconced at home, Loretta and Daisy made their way up to the tree farm on foot. The scent of mulled wine made straight for them from the cart next to the small gate they'd let themselves in beside the main one that allowed farm vehicles and cars to pass back and forth. In wellington boots the mud didn't matter, they squelched on their way over to the big barn where there were pre-cut trees, customers milling about, some loading trees onto roofracks, kids darting about glad to be outside after dark.

'The smell is intoxicating.' Daisy stood for a moment and closed her eyes, breathing in the fresh, wintry aroma of the land and the trees.

'There's really nothing quite like it.' But Loretta's attention was already on Joshua as he spotted them and came over. She tried not to make it too obvious that she was watching her daughter too, the way her eyes twinkled at the sight of him even though she was doing her best to appear nonchalant.

'What are you doing here?' Daisy asked when he came to her side.

'Delighted to see you too.' He greeted Loretta. 'I'm actually working here tonight.'

'With trees?' Daisy was curious. 'I thought you were a fruit and vegetable guy.'

'I have a lot of talent in another area.' He tapped the side of his nose and winked at Loretta before he left them to it.

'What's he up to?' Daisy didn't seem happy not to have got a straight answer.

'Perhaps if you were nicer to him, he'd tell you.' She wasn't going to let on that she knew why he was here. It was a frustration of hers that her daughter's love life should've blossomed in her twenties and thirties but instead she seemed determined to push everyone away. Occasionally Loretta would talk to her about it, but not often. It came under the title of *none of your business* and usually induced a reaction that couldn't be classed as good.

'Let's head to the fields,' said Daisy with only one glance in the direction Joshua had disappeared. 'We'll choose our tree and then tag it.'

'Sounds good to me.' Loretta gave the nod but had to add, quickly, 'Slow down.' She'd never been a fast walker in wellies, especially with so much mud involved, and Daisy was already striding ahead. 'They've got hundreds of trees,' she called after her daughter as she zipped up along another row. 'They're not about to run out!'

But Daisy ignored her in the excitement. Loretta had thought Busker would be a problem in the great outdoors with all this freedom, but perhaps she should've been more worried about her youngest daughter.

The farm was lit up well with ample lighting along the rows far enough that they could see the trees and it wasn't long before they found one they both deemed perfect. They tagged it and Daisy marched back to grab a helper to come cut it down and take it to the shed for them to make their payment and arrange delivery.

The lady at the till wearing a pair of fingerless gloves she'd bought from the Butterbury Sewing Box rang up the order while her assistant netted the tree. They were about to let her know a time for delivery when a deep voice said, 'I'll take it to them.'

Daisy turned and laughed at the sight of Father Christmas, his bright red suit and big bulky belt with the gold buckle and a bushy beard down to his chest. 'I don't think that'll be necessary, Father Christmas. You stick to delivering presents, I think we've got it from here.' She turned back to the lady with the notepad awaiting further instruction.

And when Loretta let out a laugh Daisy turned around again, wrapped in a cloud of confusion until Father Christmas tugged down his beard and revealed a smile with a cheekiness that matched the twinkle in his deep brown eyes.

'So what's it to be?' Joshua asked, his eyes fixed on Daisy. 'Pay extra for delivery or have Father Christmas bring the tree to you later on, free of charge?' He leaned closer to Daisy and Loretta didn't miss the way her daughter looked down shyly when he whispered, 'I promise not to try to squeeze it down the chimney.'

When it appeared Daisy was lost for words Joshua told them, 'I drove here in my truck anyway, it's no big deal. I'm happy to do it.' A smile played on his lips as Loretta informed the lady on the till that delivery wasn't necessary, and then he picked up the netted tree to presumably fix it to the roof of his truck ready to go as soon as he finished his shift. Beard back in place he fell into his role of Father Christmas and let out a booming 'Ho, ho, ho' as he walked away.

'Come on,' suggested Loretta to Daisy, 'I'll buy you a mulled wine for the walk home.'

Polystyrene cups filled at the cart to catch customers at the gate before they left, they strolled home, arms linked, at a much more leisurely pace than they'd adopted around the tree farm.

'He looked good in a Father Christmas costume,' Loretta braved saying as they walked. When Daisy said nothing she added, 'I don't understand what's wrong with him? He's hot—'

'Mum!'

'Well he is! And he's so kind, the right age, clearly interested . . .'

'You've said all this before. And he might be interested, but I'm not.'

Loretta sipped her wine, the warmth a pleasant addition to the chilly night air. 'Your sisters will be back in Butterbury before we know it, perhaps you could all decorate the tree together.' She couldn't gauge Daisy's reaction, what with the darkness as they navigated the quieter part of the road without a footpath and Loretta had to fall in behind her daughter.

'Whatever you like, I really don't mind, Mum.'

Out of her three daughters Fern seemed the most settled in life, but then again she was always a bit too serious so that concerned Loretta. Ginny seemed to have found a balance with travel and work but had very little time for personal relationships. And then there was Daisy, who was in Loretta's life on a daily basis and although at times Loretta wasn't sure she was completely happy with the choices she'd made along the way, at least she was a lot more together than she'd been in her teenage years. She was the one who'd worried her parents the most of all when at fifteen years old she'd gone completely off the rails. Loretta had to wonder sometimes whether Daisy had ever truly got back on course.

Parenting appeared to be a delicate dance between backing off, stepping in when needed, giving advice and knowing when not to. And it seemed this Christmas would be no different.

Chapter Six

Fern

Fern handed Everett the shirt she'd brought back up to the bedroom. He'd ironed it this morning but left it downstairs when she was on the phone and he darted upstairs to avert a crisis. Their sons were fighting because according to Cooper, Jacob had used his toothbrush and according to Jacob the only thing he'd be using his brother's toothbrush for was to clean the dirty marks out of the toilet bowl.

Everett leaned in to kiss Fern and picked up on her tension. 'They're siblings, they fight, nothing to stress about.'

'They didn't used to fight this badly.' She put in one of her earrings and took the other from her palm. 'They once got along well.'

Everett did up the buttons of his shirt and turned up the collar to loop over his tie. 'They still do, but bickering is a fact of life.'

'What's that supposed to mean?' She'd been applying her lipstick in the mirror but turned to face her husband now.

'Nothing.' He took position in front of the mirror, secured the knot in his tie and shifted it up to the buttons.

'But we have been bickering more lately, haven't we? I suppose it happens in every marriage.'

'Not in our marriage.' Or at least it hadn't been happening until recently.

'I've got to go, Fern. I'm late as it is.' He looked at his watch as though to prove a point. 'We'll talk more later.'

'You're miffed I'm going to Butterbury.' She didn't want them to stop talking, not yet.

He sighed. 'I'm not *miffed*. A little surprised, that's all.'

'I've said I'll come back for the Christmas party the day before, get everything sorted and then return to Butterbury.' It wasn't ideal but it was the only practical solution. 'And besides, perhaps some time apart might do us good.'

Her remark had scared him more than she'd intended. 'You want time away from our marriage?'

'That wasn't what I said, it's a few weeks, that's all.'

'I get the feeling there's something you're not telling me. Is there?'

'Of course not. I'm worried about my grandad, I told you.'

What she hadn't told him was that she was worried about so much more. In the middle of the night she'd woken up with a desperate need to pinpoint exactly when she'd last felt herself in control but not in an over-the-top kind of way. And she'd realised it had been years ago. Before her dad died, before her life was smashed to pieces and her family was tugged this way and that. Ever since, she'd gradually become more and more focused on doing every little thing right. Because staying on top of things, giving her life structure, meant she was ready for anything bad to come her way and it wouldn't knock her sideways if it did.

When the doorbell went, Fern dashed downstairs and took in a delivery.

Everett followed her down soon after. 'What did you order this time?' He eyed the box while she poured the fresh coffee she'd had brewing into a Thermos and handed it to him.

She was grinning. 'You're going to love them – I ordered some festive booze balls, kind of a bonbonniére for the guests at the party – adult guests. I'll fill each one with red wine.'

He thanked her for the coffee and set it onto the side table while he put on his shoes. 'We've plenty of the Shiraz from the last wine order, use that for the bonbon things,' he said, tying the second lace as he sat on the bottom stair.

'I was thinking the merlot.'

He shook his head and looked as though he was biting down on his lip when he stood up.

'Everett, if you've got something you need to say just say it.'

'I wouldn't dare.'

Did he have to make it worse by using such a condescending tone of voice? With the frustration still looming from last night, his attitude this morning, Fern felt the pressure inside her head rise.

The next thing she knew she was hissing at him in a low voice so the boys couldn't hear. 'You know what, sod the party this year! You clearly don't want it, it's obviously an issue. So I am done.'

'Fern, calm down.' He put on his coat and picked up his coffee. Clearly her losing her temper wasn't enough to stop him getting to work on time.

'I mean it, the party is off, I've had enough.'

'Fern—'

But she wasn't hanging around to see if Everett had anything else to add. She could already hear another fight escalating between the boys in the kitchen and went to deal with that instead.

She found them arguing over who got to have the last Weetabix in the box and who had to make do with All-Bran. 'I'm shopping later today, it's one morning, for goodness' sake. What's wrong with you both?' There was mess all over the floor where one of them must've snatched one of the Weetabix from the other's bowl and Fern's fuse, already shortened, burned right down and she yelled at both of them. 'Upstairs, this minute! And when you can have a sensible conversation, you can have breakfast!'

How did one remark from your husband and an inconsequential kids' argument have the power to set the tone for your mood and potentially shape the rest of your day? She'd woken up feeling organised, somewhat in control, but now? Now she wished she could climb back into bed and wake up the same Fern who'd been full of energy with her young boys, who'd made love to her husband even after the longest day. She longed to be the Fern who was truly happy, the Fern who turned up on time, the Fern who was never late for a meeting or missed an appointment. She wanted to wind back the clock to when her life had run smoothly, when it didn't feel as though things were beyond her control. But it had been so long since it had been that way that she wondered whether it ever could be again.

She cleared the floor, grateful she'd at least managed to sort things out at work. She'd also advised her boss that a family necessity meant she needed to be with her mother in Butterbury for a few weeks. He'd been happy to accommodate her last-minute request and she'd calmly scheduled her holiday with human resources and methodically worked through what was on her desk, organising others to cover where needed and be a point of contact in her absence. When she'd got home she'd told Everett and the boys she was going to Butterbury before they would this year. She'd cited the excuse that this was all for her grandad, that he was getting older and really wanted to spend time with Fern, Ginny and Daisy together. The boys' questions came firing out one after the other – *Who's going to take me to Saturday morning hockey? What about the open evening at school? Can I still go to Scotty's birthday party because you were going to take me?* Everett had leaped straight in and clarified that he had been a parent before and knew how to drive a car, how to socialise with other people in the case of the school event, and was perfectly capable of sourcing a birthday present for the friend whose party it was. *So why don't you do it more often?* Cooper had asked and his dad had told him it was because Mum was so good at it.

Fern wished Everett hadn't left this morning without them talking properly. She wished she'd been able to tell him her real reasons for going to Butterbury all of a sudden, that it wasn't just because Loretta had requested it or that Grandad needed it, but that she needed to get away from the norm here and try to get her head straight. She wasn't sure how to accomplish it – it couldn't be measured like the financials and the performance at work – but she knew action was required and her home village seemed like the best place to start.

After Fern dropped the boys at school, she headed

straight to the supermarket. With a couple of days to get the house and family organised before she left, she intended to spend the afternoon batch cooking so Everett and the boys would have plenty of meals and wouldn't exist on frozen pizzas or takeaways.

She headed up and down the aisles plucking fresh and nutrition-packed ingredients. She found pantry staples – brown rice, pasta, couscous – and as she shopped she realised she was beginning to feel excited about her solo trip to Butterbury. The only misgiving she had was that it would be concentrated time with her sisters and she wasn't sure how that would go. Still, it could be worse. A colleague who Fern lunched with on occasion was going home for Christmas too and apparently her parents had downsized the second she and her three brothers had left home and so now it was a race to see who got the spare bedroom, and it wasn't always ladies first. At least Fern didn't have that problem, the girls all had their own rooms. Fern sometimes wondered why Loretta had kept such a big house when it was just her and Daisy, why she'd insisted their bedrooms remained the way they'd always been. It was as though she was clinging onto a past that no longer existed. And perhaps that was what she was trying to do now, expecting the sisters to come together under one roof and get on like they once had.

Fern hoped for all their sakes that it worked out that way.

After a walk Fern spent the afternoon in the kitchen and found that compared to how she usually felt by the end of the day, she felt more clarity than she had in ages. She'd never wanted to get away on her own before. It had seemed like a needless luxury, but as she'd chopped ingredients and cooked, the thought of being Fern – not Mum, not a wife, just Fern, in her childhood room with her beautifully handmade quilt at the foot of the bed – filtered her body with a calm she couldn't explain to anyone else.

'You're home early,' she observed when Everett walked through the door a good hour before he usually would.

'I decided I needed to be,' he said warily. And the simple act of what he'd done wasn't lost on Fern. He recognised they were in trouble too. He hadn't said as much, but coming home to her told her all she needed to know.

She paused after she dropped peelings into the compost bin. 'I'm sorry I lost my temper earlier.'

'Are you really cancelling the party?' he asked softly.

She looked at him briefly before getting back to what she was doing. As she'd cooked she'd realised coming back for it would be silly, a lot of pressure to have everything just right, and take away from the time out she so desperately needed. 'I'm really cancelling the party.'

'Do the neighbours know?'

'Nope.'

'I can let them know.'

She nodded. 'That would be great, thank you.'

'Who knows, maybe one of them will realise what an effort you go to every year and put on a party themselves.' Everett wrapped her in a hug from behind. 'I'll miss you when you're away.'

She smiled, glad to be in his arms again, but their time alone was short-lived when the boys, who'd both been upstairs doing homework, came downstairs and Jacob headed for the fridge while Cooper raided the pantry.

Fern made sure they both had something half decent.

'I'm old enough to eat what I want to eat,' Cooper snapped.

'Call it life experience,' she told him. 'You'll thank me for not giving you a heap of sugar and processed foods when you're older,' she called after him as he schlepped back upstairs with the peanuts she'd given him and the banana from the fruit bowl. 'It's not like I never give them treats,' she said to Everett. But her attention was snatched away to Jacob who'd gone to start up his PlayStation. Fern wiped her hands on her apron and followed her youngest son. 'Twenty minutes,' she told him. 'Then finish your homework.' He hadn't been upstairs long enough to do it, he was trying his luck, and his nod of agreement proved he knew she was onto him.

It was hard to get the balance between time out and school work, but she knew if she got her boys into good habits, it would help them in the long run. 'Don't let him be on that thing too much when I'm away,' she told Everett, back in the kitchen where she put away the tomatoes she hadn't used, adding in a comment that they could be sliced and used in sandwiches as well as an instruction not to let them go off or be wasted.

When Everett didn't reply she asked, 'Did you hear me?'

He loosened his tie, undid his top button and then reached for the carton of orange juice in the fridge. 'Heard you, loud and clear.'

'Everett . . .' She was momentarily struck by the animosity in his tone. Here they were, back to petty remarks and snapping. How was it possible to miss someone you were standing this close to? 'Are you annoyed because we got interrupted?' Perhaps that was it. They'd been alone before the boys put a stop to it.

'I'm not a teenager with hormones all over the place, Fern.'

'I didn't say you were.'

But he left her in the kitchen and whatever contentedness she'd felt while she was cooking and preparing meals for her family was replaced by a tension that saw her splashing water when she dumped utensils into the sink, and invited no humming of whatever tune had been in her head earlier.

Everett came into the kitchen as she was taking the mince out of the fridge for tonight's dinner, ready to make a chilli con carne. He took the packet of mince from her hands. 'I'll cook tonight.'

It was a welcome peace offering. She was about to insist that she could manage, but she'd made so much this afternoon even she wasn't sure she could face any more cooking.

As Everett chopped the onion, minced the garlic and found the kidney beans from the back of the pantry they talked. They discussed his work, they went over hers, they talked about his boss who was new and had slotted in well. 'Your boss was understanding,' he said of Fern's. The muscles in his forearm tensed as he used the tin opener to take the lid off the tin of kidney beans. 'To give you the time off with such little notice shows he values you and can see that you need the break.'

'I don't need the break, but I am entitled to it.'

He turned around briefly to look at his wife. And with that one look she knew. Everett could read her better than the newspaper he held on his lap on the train each day, work out her clues more easily than he could solve those of the crossword puzzle. And with that one look her way Fern felt a rush of love but also a rush of shame. She'd failed, she had weakness, weakness she didn't want anyone to see let alone Everett. Being strong and dependable was part of who she was. It always had been.

'I'll be taking my laptop,' she told him. 'That way I can be contacted if they need me.'

'Did Nick insist on you doing that?' His knife paused in mid-air from cutting up the courgette he'd dice really small to sneak it into the chilli without the boys having any idea.

Fern didn't answer the question because of course he hadn't insisted, he hadn't even hinted at it. Everett was right, Nick was a good boss and Fern got the impression he sensed her need to take time off and so hadn't questioned it. But it was one thing for Fern to admit she needed time to regroup to her boss, not that she'd had to come out with it in so many words, but quite another to let her family know the same.

'What are you looking for?' she quizzed as Everett shifted through things on the pantry shelves.

'Tomato sauce,' came the voice.

'There should be a couple of jars still left, right at the very back.' Fern made her own tomato sauce and each time, it was enough to last for months, the exquisite flavours captured in the jar tasting better than anything that was store bought.

When Everett still didn't have any luck Fern took over the search and got down on her hands and knees to check the very bottom of the pantry. 'I meant to make more. I should've thought of it earlier.'

'Don't stress.' He put his hands onto her upper arms and guided her back to her seat. 'You drink your wine, I'll sort this.' He called his eldest son and instructed him to go and grab four tins of diced tomatoes from the corner shop. And Fern didn't miss his mutter to grab himself a can of drink if he liked.

'He shouldn't drink fizzy all the time,' Fern said when Everett came back in to carry on with dinner preparation.

'He doesn't. Everything in moderation.'

'Sorry about the tomato sauce.'

'You must be the only person who makes your own.'

'I like to do the best for my family.'

He didn't turn around this time as though he'd got tired of the same fight. 'So do I, Fern. So do I.'

Dinner was going to be a while and Fern took a glass of wine upstairs and ran a bath. As she lay there soaking Fern made a list in her mind of what she needed to pack for her trip to Butterbury – plenty of winter outfits, a few choices of footwear. Her sisters would shake their heads when they saw her laptop, her mother would pretend to understand, but Fern couldn't be without it yet. If things got too difficult it would be an excuse to escape, something to hide behind if she needed time away from the others. She wasn't about to show them that she'd taken time off to get her head straight, she wasn't going to show her weaknesses or let her façade slip. That only ever happened behind closed doors.

Going back to Butterbury had never been easy since her dad died, and it got a little bit worse every time with the tension between Fern, Ginny and Daisy. But at least she'd be getting away from here, she'd give her marriage a bit of breathing space and try to pull herself together.

She'd soon be back to the wife and mother who juggled everything and kept it all together.

And once Butterbury and Christmas were out of the way, she could start fixing things between her and Everett. That was what she wanted the most of all.

Chapter Seven

Ginny

The train finally trundled into the station in Butterbury and Ginny was greeted with the cloudy skies her app had predicted. She stood up, pushed her arms through the loops of her backpack, lifted it onto her back and secured the straps before the train had even come to a stop.

The last time she'd been home, Daisy had met her from the train in one of the worst storms to hit Butterbury. She'd picked her up in the Caribbean aqua Mini Cooper she'd had since she gave up on the idea of getting her degree and instead fell into the family business, earning money straight away. All Ginny could remember was being grateful Daisy had used her money on a car and not frittered it away. She was the youngest, had once been irresponsible and all over the place, and the car had been like the mark of a new start, a grown-up life that would make everyone else's lives a lot calmer. The wild streak had, it seemed, become less of a problem as her sister grew up.

Ginny emerged onto the platform and filed out of the station with everyone else. Already she could sense a change in the mood as she made her way from the station towards the village, the shift from a city or town-like at-mosphere. A cold breeze blew against her, making it a little harder to walk with the backpack. No need for a gym, no need to squeeze in a run or a weight's session when you did all this walking and had a job that kept you on your feet. She thought how Fern had been a runner over the years, going every single morning without fail as though she had a timetable that must be adhered to. Although the last time Ginny had talked to her sister and deigned to ask whether she still went running, Fern had bitten her head off with retorts claiming how family life as well as a demanding job didn't allow for much else. Ginny had left it there, she hadn't wanted to add any more fuel to that particular fire. Her sister had talked to her as though she resented what Ginny had when Ginny envied Fern and her well laid-out life, the direction she never wavered from. And what Fern failed to see was that perhaps Ginny's freedom had come at a price and perhaps it wasn't all happy and rosy every day of the year.

As Ginny walked she remembered fondly the times she'd walked this route with her dad. Sometimes she'd go and meet him from the station when he finished work. He and Fern were always talking maths problems at home in the evenings, Daisy loved to cuddle up on his lap and watch television when she was very little and then they'd had their camping trips, and so Ginny had carved out some of her own time with him by going to meet him off the train. Her mum had been too busy in the shop to tell her off for going out when she had homework, and Ginny had even done it when it was dark, insisting to her dad that Butterbury was perfectly safe. They'd walked home talking about their days, general chit-chat not of interest to anyone else, but it was enough for her. They'd pause and look at the birds hopping to the feeder in the front garden of the house beside the church, they'd turn the corner near the bus stop in winter where the man who owned the house always put up a nativity display in what looked like an old rabbit hutch. Those were her favourite days, when the walk became more of a stroll, and when they'd stop at the Lantern Bakery and buy peppermint fudge to enjoy before they got found out by Loretta who would tell them off for spoiling their appetite before dinner.

Ginny smiled when she saw the nativity display exactly where it was every year. A mother had brought her kids along to see it tonight and she passed them and made her way towards Lantern Square. She smiled all the more when the square came into sight, marked out by the beacon of the enormous Christmas tree in situ.

As she drew closer to the heart of the village and crossed over to walk beside the square and peek at the illuminated creatures in the flowerbeds, embrace the Christmas lights strung from one side of the street to the other, she watched a robin redbreast hop from the iron railings to the branch of the nearest tree, behind the foliage and out of sight. She was never quick enough to take a photograph. Daisy would've been, the robin would've likely posed for her.

She was so deep in her own thoughts as she walked on that she almost collided with a Christmas tree coming right for her.

'Sorry, didn't see you there . . .' Local gardener Rhys peeked out from behind the tree and when he saw who it was a smile spread across his face. 'Why if it isn't Ginny Chamberlain.'

She beamed. 'Rhys!' Rugged and handsome local boy with his heart in the right place, he looked after the flowerbeds and lawns in the square as well as the grounds up at Butterbury Lodge.

'I'd pick you up and hug you right now if I wasn't holding this tree.'

'I'm hugging you anyway,' she grinned, stepping closer and hugging him the best she could without getting a face full of pine needles.

'It's been too long, Ginny.'

'I know, but great to see you now.'

His eyes darted to the left and then back to her. He had a mischievous look on his face when he leaned a bit closer and whispered, 'I see someone else who wouldn't mind a hug from you.' He gently tilted his head to one side in the direction of the pavement across the road and when Ginny glanced over she saw Lucas popping something into the red postbox.

Her heart in her mouth having not seen him in years she barely heard Rhys when he added, 'We'll catch up in the pub soon, yeah? I'd better get this to my customer.'

She mumbled an agreement as, unable to take her eyes away from Lucas, her stomach betrayed her by flipping like the pancake she'd tossed last Shrove Tuesday. Except this time it didn't settle back into the frying pan the way it should. It hovered, unsure what to do.

And it seemed he had no idea either. Because he'd just spotted her.

It was Lucas who finally made the move to come across when it seemed her legs weren't about to oblige. 'That looks heavy.' He eyed her backpack. 'You didn't think of getting a taxi from the station?'

She felt awkward beneath his gaze and banter as though they'd only seen one another weeks rather than years ago, as though they didn't have a deep history, even his smell was a reminder of their familiarity – the woody scent, a combination of the earthy outdoors and the cold with a special warmth that came from close proximity to someone who'd once been so much a part of your life. His caramel eyes were like the stickiest of toffee, impossible to come away from. 'I walk everywhere,' she stammered, discombobulated by seeing him all of a sudden. 'It keeps me fit,' she added, desperate not to sound like a total imbecile.

He paused as if he didn't know how to respond to that. 'How long are you staying?'

'A few weeks.' She wondered whether he could see the rise and fall of her chest. She could feel every movement as she tried to rid herself of the nerves that refused to stop fluttering. 'I'd heard you were back in the village for good.'

'Sure am. Have been for a while.'

She wanted to ask him what happened, why he'd decided not to pursue the different career he'd studied for. But perhaps that privileged conversation belonged to someone else now. Men like Lucas didn't stay single for long. She'd shared a bed with this man, they'd once assumed they'd be together forever. How had they gone from that to these staccato sentences, barely able to relax around each other?

'I guess I'll see you around.' He looked at her the way he always had, as though she was the only woman in the world. Or perhaps she was imagining it, wishing for it in some way.

'I'm sure you will.' She said her goodbyes, waved across at the local doctor, Joe, and his fiancé, Hannah, as they headed towards the post office armed with parcels, and left Lucas to chat with them while she escaped in the direction of the Butterbury Sewing Box. She'd go there first rather than home because otherwise she'd get Busker all excited at her arrival and she'd have to leave him.

Ginny finally reached the shop and pushing open the door felt as much like coming home as it would do going to the house. The familiarity washed over her, the colours of the fabric, the sense of warmth as Loretta rushed over to envelop her in a big hug.

When her mother eventually let her go Ginny shrugged off her backpack. She left it out at the back while Loretta made the tea and Ginny went into the shop. She smiled at the sight of the window display, the baubles that she'd made once when she was off school for what felt like the longest bout of flu in history. The wool had held its colour and Ginny ran her fingers across a couple of the pieces, remembering those days like they were yesterday.

Daisy was off seeing their grandad today so it was just Ginny and her mum. Ginny moved over to look at the tree and then the different stock they'd got in the shop since the last time she'd been here.

She admired the roll of material still on the counter. 'Mum, this fabric is gorgeous.' A blend of creams and greens on a caramel background, it was festive, depicting ice skaters, figures wrapped up in winter attire, scarf tails flying in the breeze as they pushed sledges about the ice.

Loretta handed her a mug of tea. 'It's a brand new design this year. Beautiful, isn't it? It would make a lovely quilting fabric. You could make something with it if you like.' She peered over the top of the glasses that had slipped down her nose a little.

'You know I don't have time for needlework these days.' Ginny dismissed the idea and instead wandered around to see what else was new.

As Loretta served a customer, Ginny finished the remains of her tea and was about to take her cup out to the back when she noticed a girl peering in through the front door. She was pretty, looked around fifteen or sixteen years of age, if Ginny were to guess, with blonde hair in the sort of waves in its length that reminded Ginny of beach waves. Effortlessly natural.

Ginny opened up the door. 'We're open, come inside out of the cold.'

But Loretta stepped forwards and took over. 'Ginny, would you mind fetching the tapestry bag from upstairs. It should be on the table in the room at the front. This young lady left it here a few days ago.'

The girl looked awkward, perhaps too shy to explain the situation to anyone other than Loretta, and Ginny headed upstairs to fetch the bag.

By the time she got downstairs there were another three customers milling about near the fat quarters and from what Ginny could overhear they had no idea about where to start with quilting. 'Want me to handle it?' she asked her mum who handed the young girl the bag as she and Loretta stood beside the Christmas tree.

'Thanks, Ginny.'

Ginny didn't mind. She could still remember the basics and when she spoke to the customers they were clearly total beginners. She showed them a couple of books they had on display in the shop that would teach them how to get started, so they bought some of the fabric on special offer, some thread, and left excited that they were going to give it a go.

'We'll be back for lessons in the new year,' one lady wearing a pink woollen coat called over her shoulder to Ginny before the door clunked shut behind them. The girl Loretta had been talking to had left, so it was just the two of them again.

Ginny nodded to the till. 'You're still resisting any suggestion of a new one?' It was a bronzed relic that had been through a major restoration a few years ago. You had to punch the buttons hard as they often got stuck, as did the drawer, which needed a tug and then a shove to complete any transaction. 'I wondered whether Fern might have finally persuaded you to upgrade, get everything up-to-date so you could monitor sales and inventory.'

'Not a chance, my customers love it.' Loretta smiled.

'Well I'm glad you're keeping the till. It's part of the shop, part of its charm, always has been.'

'I have a little machine for card payments now too, so the system works just fine.'

'What time is Daisy coming in today?'

'Knowing her and your grandad she'll be hours. I honestly don't know what they find to talk about. She runs workshops up at the lodge, but not today.' Loretta looked as though she was now questioning Daisy's real whereabouts too. 'And her camera was at home earlier so she can't be flitting about taking pictures of whatever she can find.'

Ginny looked around the shop. She'd always thought her little sister would go on to be a photographer, a famous one even. She always had the drive and the skill, forever snapping pictures of them, sometimes when they least expected. She had an ability to capture emotion on faces that most people would miss as though the camera shot had seen into that person's very soul.

Unfortunately Ginny could also remember a time when Daisy's photography hadn't been welcome.

Daisy had taken a picture of Ginny weeks after their father's funeral, curled up on the sofa when she thought she was on her own. When Ginny found the photograph days later she'd yelled at her sister, accused her of having warped emotions, no sensitivity. And then she'd torn the picture into little pieces and thrown it at Daisy's feet, anger not only fuelled by the picture itself but by losing their father, and by Daisy's selfishness that had led to all three girls losing something so precious to them all.

Something that could never be replaced.

Chapter Eight

Daisy

Daisy emptied out the bags of wool she'd brought to Butterbury Lodge with her today. The residents were well aware of the secret project but nobody else in Butterbury would be for some time yet. Being here also had the added bonus of allowing Daisy to psyche herself up some more before she had to face Ginny who was arriving today.

'Grandad, this is wonderful.' Daisy kissed Ivor's cheek as she admired the midnight blue rectangle he'd set to one side, which had a white snowman knitted on the front complete with a black yarn hat and a red scarf. 'Who knew you had this sort of talent. I thought you said this would take you quite a while.'

'I've been busy. You know me, I don't like to fall into bed too early. And I'll admit Flo may have helped me once or twice over the past week,' he added as Flo herself came over. 'I didn't show you our progress until now as I wanted it to be a surprise.'

'Well it's a lovely surprise.' She smiled at Flo and passed on her compliments.

Flo explained, 'Once we decided he didn't need to knit the snowman pattern into the garment it became a team effort. Ivor knitted the rectangle while I used a pattern I've had ever since I knitted a toddler's scarf for one of my neighbours many years ago. It was of a snowman, the same snowman you see there.'

On top of the midnight blue the snowman had curved edges and Flo or Ivor's stitching to fix it in place was flawless. It would make a wonderful addition to their project.

'I made sure we used acrylic wool,' Flo went on, 'like you said.'

Last time she'd been here one of the residents had offered some wool she had left over from knitting projects over the years but Daisy had explained they needed to be wise with what they used. Acrylic wool was key to this project. Not only was it cheap and lightweight, it also came in an array of colours, and more importantly wouldn't react so tragically in the rain. Other types of wool got too heavy and sagged and nobody wanted that to happen to their beautiful creations that were slowly being collected and stored in the cupboard Maggie had allocated them specially.

Back beside her grandad Daisy asked, 'Who's that over there with Victor?' A pretty blonde teenage girl was crouched down chatting with the always-polite yet very timid man who hadn't wanted to join in with the project. Somehow this girl had managed to get him making what looked like a pom-pom. 'I didn't think Victor had any family to visit him.'

'He doesn't. That's Carrie and she's with the choir and she also volunteers from time to time to keep old codgers like me company.'

Daisy laughed. 'You're not an old codger, Grandad.'

'What am I then?'

'You are unashamedly you, Ivor Rawlins.' She gave him a nudge and looked over to Victor who was chuckling quietly at the tangle of wool he'd somehow managed to hook around his knees. 'She's got him helping out for the project, well I never.'

'I'm impressed,' agreed Ernest as he came over to see what they were looking at. 'Maybe we could rope her in to helping out with delivery of the project too.' He tapped the side of his nose. Residents were loving all the secrecy surrounding what they were doing, the mischief was part of the fun.

'Do you think she'll keep it a secret?' Daisy wondered.

Her grandad suggested Daisy go over and remind her, make sure she knew this wasn't to be talked about in the village.

Daisy headed over and introduced herself to Carrie as Victor continued to beaver away at a white woolly pom-pom.

The girls stepped back from him and Daisy asked Carrie, 'How ever did you manage it?'

'You mean getting him to make something?' The girl smiled, her blonde hair falling in waves around her shoulders. 'We've got to know each other recently. I told him I couldn't knit but that I really want to learn a new craft and then I admitted I could do basic pom-poms, which would be very useful for the project everyone is talking about.' She shrugged. 'He asked me to show him.'

'Well the more people on board the better. But just remember, it's hush-hush.'

'I know, Ivor told me. Don't worry. I won't tell a soul.'

Daisy got the feeling she could trust this girl.

'Ivor is good company,' Carrie went on.

'Yeah, he is.'

Carrie hesitated before she confided, 'He was a bit upset yesterday.'

'Upset?'

'His favourite Christmas quilt got ruined in the wash.' She pulled a face. 'He didn't want to make a fuss about it, but someone here put it in at too high a temperature apparently, but I can tell he's devastated.'

'That's terrible.' He'd be so upset. His quilts were always one of a kind and Daisy knew what it was like to lose something so special.

'It would make a good idea for a Christmas present,' Carrie suggested.

Daisy nodded across at Ivor who'd been watching them and then turned her back so there was no chance of him overhearing. 'You're right, but unfortunately those quilts take a long time to make from scratch.' And it wasn't long until Christmas.

'You have some gorgeous ones in the shop already.'

Surprised, Daisy asked, 'You know the shop?'

'I've been in once or twice.' She stumbled over her words. 'Trying to learn . . . crocheting . . . knitting . . . quilting. Anything really. I can't do any of it apart from pom-poms, which to be fair any six year old could master.'

'Don't put yourself down.' Daisy thought harder. 'The quilts in the shop *are* beautiful. But no way, Grandad would need his own.'

'And there really isn't enough time before Christmas?'

'Not doing it on my own there isn't,' she mumbled almost to herself.

'I thought you had two sisters,' she added bewilderedly before Daisy could get back to her grandad. 'And Ivor told me they're coming home to have Christmas together for the first time in a long while.'

Those two really had talked. Although come to think of it, Grandad loved to talk to anyone and getting to know new people was something he especially enjoyed.

When Maggie called out that the mince pies were warm and hollered over to Carrie and Daisy to ask whether they'd mind handing them round, they both headed to the kitchen.

Carrie took one plate, Daisy took another and as they emerged to serve them to the residents Daisy confided, 'My sisters and I used to quilt, but I can't see us quilting together again somehow.'

'Maybe just ask them and see?' Carrie glanced away shyly. 'My mum used to tell me that if I never asked, I'd never get.'

'Very true,' Daisy laughed. 'Your mum is a wise woman.'

'She was,' Carrie said, voice soft.

'Oh, I'm sorry.' And so young as well. She knew exactly what it was like to lose a parent when you were a teenager. It had to be painful at any age, no matter how old you got, but she would've given anything to have her dad in her life for a bit longer to give her more time to find her way before everything changed forever.

'Thank you.' Carrie smiled. 'But you should . . . you should ask them.'

Daisy took a deep breath. 'You know what, you're right. I need to just come out with it. They can only say no, can't they?'

They barely had to pass the plates of mince pies around because residents flocked towards them and Daisy left her conversation with Carrie there as Carrie went back to helping Victor who was beaming as he held another pom-pom aloft and added it to the couple he'd already made.

Daisy enjoyed a mince pie standing by the tree that filled the space well and stretched right up to the ceiling. Their tree at home was still bare, of course, because Loretta had insisted all three girls be home to decorate it. But it still smelt glorious and it had greeted Daisy this morning with its scent wafting into every part of the house it could find.

A warm feeling cascaded through her when she thought about Joshua taking it back to the house for them and hanging around to help her put it up. Her mum had left the room with the excuse of making tea and cutting slices of ginger cake.

'Shift it a bit to the right,' Daisy had told Joshua when he called out from behind the branches to ask whether the tree was straight. 'No wait, back to the left a bit.'

He poked his head around the tree. 'How about we swap places?'

'Fine.' She was happy to be the one manoeuvring the tree.

'I was only kidding.'

But she'd already gone over and put a hand through the branches to grab a hold of the trunk.

He was standing close, not moving an inch. 'Daisy, you've got hold of my hand.'

'Oh, sorry.' She hadn't realised her grip was around him as well as the tree, so she took her hand away and moved it further up. 'You stand over where I was.' She quickly reached another hand through the branches for a better hold.

Over where she'd originally been standing, he declared, 'Definitely more to the left.'

'Are you sure?'

'Isn't that the point of me being here?'

Daisy moved it as suggested. She hadn't realised how heavy the tree was when you had to hold it for someone to walk around and inspect from different angles like Joshua was doing now. He was being pretty pedantic about it too. And pulling faces, running a hand across his chin, thinking hard. 'What? Come on, this thing isn't getting any lighter,' she groaned.

He smiled and crouched down to turn the screws in the base of the stand. Daisy, arm aching from holding the tree, now not only had the stunning tree to admire, but Joshua's physique in black cargo trousers when he moved round and bent over.

He stood up and when he turned his chest was almost against hers. 'Daisy, you can let go.'

She shook herself. 'Oh . . . right . . .' And she stepped away from him to admire the tree. 'It's perfect. Thank you for helping.'

'My pleasure,' he said.

She felt a crackle of electricity as his arm brushed hers but when Loretta brought through tea and cake the moment was over and it wasn't much longer before Joshua headed for home himself. Daisy had gone to bed wondering whether she was a fool to have made up her mind a long while ago that relationships just weren't worth it. They were messy, even the people you loved and trusted the most could hurt you somewhere along the way, and she wasn't sure she ever wanted to open herself up to that pain.

Ernest brought over the knitted green that he'd fixed around a piece of sponge so it resembled a gift and stopped Daisy staring at the Butterbury Lodge Christmas tree and thinking of Joshua, strong arms bringing in the tree at home and carrying it along the length of the corridor to the sitting room . . .

'I can't claim credit for the knitting,' Ernest explained. 'That was a friend.'

Daisy touched him on the shoulder. 'It's wonderful. Could you do another two between you and your friend in different colours for me?' She waved over at Carrie when she noticed her leaving and then Betty called out for some help with her crocheting. Grabbing some yarn and an extra crochet hook, Daisy suggested they do it together, both going through the same motions, side-by-side. After three rows, Betty had a bit of confidence and Daisy left her working away. With residents dotted around working on various crochet, knitting and sewing projects Daisy didn't miss an opportunity. She took out her camera from her bag she'd left at the side of the room.

Surreptitiously moving around the space Daisy captured the smiles of delight, the furrowed brows of concentration, laughter when mistakes were made, serious chatter about what they were doing. When Daisy and her grandad had thought of this idea it had been met with a great deal of enthusiasm from complete beginners to the advanced. Even the naysayers who'd insisted they wouldn't be around by Christmas had jumped on board and got involved. And so since Easter when she'd introduced the concept, Daisy had been planning this with military precision. She'd timetabled it all and estimated how long it would take to make the items they needed, then she'd doubled her estimate. She always checked the work too – discreetly, of course – before she put it away in the cupboard. Sometimes she'd add a bit more stitching for extra security. And they were well on track to be finished in time for Christmas.

Daisy made sure she got plenty of photographs. She planned to display them on the big pinboard in reception once they went public with the project so everyone could see what a mammoth task this had been.

Betty's son had been hovering on the periphery drinking a cup of tea. Daisy sensed he'd seen his mum but she'd shooed him away for a few minutes so she didn't lose concentration. He'd been talking with Maggie but came over to Daisy's side and thanked her for helping Betty.

'It's my pleasure, she's getting the hang of it finally, I think.' They looked her way. 'She's one of the keenest, I'll give her that.'

'Did you get any good photographs today?'

'Loads,' she confessed and proceeded to show him some of the shots.

He admired them all, especially the one where Betty's cheeks were flushed and she had an air of delight and accomplishment on her face as she pushed a chunky needle through two pieces of wool to fix them together.

'I've been worried about her settling in,' he confided in Daisy. 'But after talking with Maggie and seeing her here immersing herself in what's going on, I feel much more reassured.' He hesitated and then told her, 'If you don't mind me saying, your talents are rather wasted.'

'Excuse me?'

'Those photographs really are quite something. In fact, I wouldn't mind buying the photograph of my mother from you. It captures her happiness well and it's the way I like to think of her between visits.'

Daisy was touched her photograph had conveyed so much meaning for him. 'I'll have a copy waiting for you the next time you come. But I don't need payment.' She had something far better than money in her hand. She had approval, an accolade from a stranger, and it meant more to her than the man would probably ever realise.

Chapter Nine

Daisy

'Sorry I took so long,' Daisy called out as she pushed through the door to the Butterbury Sewing Box and held it open for a woman clutching one of the embroidered knitting bags they sold as though she'd found treasure with her purchase.

Her mum pushed the till closed and smiled at her youngest daughter. 'How's Dad?'

'Grand, as always.' She hung up her scarf and had just shoved her coat onto the hook after it refused to hold on at first, when her sister emerged from the back. Ever since that day Ginny had freaked out when she had snatched the photograph that Daisy had taken of her and torn it into little pieces, Daisy had been wary of the sister who up until then had always been the calm one, the one you least expected to go off.

'Hello, Daisy.' Ginny came towards her and wrapped her in a hug Daisy wished would last a bit longer than it ever did.

'Welcome home. What needs doing, Mum?' Conscious she'd been at the lodge for a long time she flipped straight into work mode.

'You and your sister chat, I'm fine out here.'

'I've been gone for hours,' Daisy insisted.

'I noticed.'

Daisy was trying to think of an excuse not to be thrust into her sister's company just yet, but she didn't need one because the shop suddenly got busy and before she knew it all three of them were helping customers, taking orders, keeping the shop shipshape right up until closing time.

It suited Daisy just fine. And, she suspected, Ginny might be relieved too.

Back at the house Ginny fixed the dinner – a beef and red wine casserole – as they all talked. And slowly Daisy began to feel more comfortable around her sister. One down, one to go. And if it was this easy the whole time they wouldn't have a problem at all.

Ginny told them she'd seen the nativity display on her way here from the station, she complemented the tree in the lounge awaiting its decorations, and she told them about her travels and the wedding.

'Rhys told me you'd seen Lucas already,' said Loretta, shifting the atmosphere slightly. 'I'm allowed to mention his name, aren't I?' She grimaced.

'You can't get away with much around here,' Daisy observed, watching her sister squirm.

'We said hello in the street, that's it,' said Ginny. 'And yes, you can mention his name.'

'He's still single,' Daisy teased, wondering a little too late whether she really should've said that at all.

Ginny met her gaze. 'So is Joshua.' But she didn't say it with malice, there was an impish twinkle in her eye at least.

Daisy got up to strain the potatoes ready for mashing while Ginny took the casserole out of the oven, set the lid onto the worktop and stirred the thickening mixture. 'Mum, you really shouldn't try to interfere in our love lives.'

'I was doing no such thing.' Loretta wiped her glasses after they steamed up when she leaned in to smell the casserole.

'You were a bit,' said Ginny. 'You wouldn't like it if any of us did that with your love life, Mum.' She put the lid back on the casserole while Daisy added butter to the potatoes once they were out of the water and back in the pan.

'I apologise if that's what you think I was doing. But it's only because I care.' Loretta filled three glasses with water and set them on the table. 'And no need to interfere with mine, I've had my one true love, I don't need another.'

Daisy opened her mouth to say something but changed her mind, shut it again and carried on mashing the potatoes. 'What time is Fern getting here? She's going to miss dinner at this rate.'

'There was a mix up with the car,' Loretta explained. 'Hers went in for a service and it wasn't finished until the afternoon rather than the morning. That's what she said, I'm sure. She'll be here later on.' Loretta swished a hand through the air as though the reasons for their sister's absence didn't matter. She was on her way, that was the main thing.

After dinner, with the evening stretching out in front of them and with Loretta watching both Daisy and Ginny as though expecting one or the other of them to say something controversial, Daisy surprised herself by suggesting to Ginny that they escape to the pub. At least that way they weren't under their mum's watchful gaze and, who knew, perhaps it would even help them to relax a bit in one another's company. As long as they didn't dredge up the past, they'd be fine.

'Is it me or is Mum really tense?' Ginny asked, fastening the last of her coat buttons as they began the walk from the house down towards Lantern Square.

'It's not you. She is tense.' Daisy pulled her maroon woolly hat down a little further as the wind picked up and it hurt her ears. The weather forecast was cold, some rain on the way, and she hoped that by Christmas and beyond, at least until new year, they'd be blessed with the bright blue skies and cold days that made winter pretty and pleasant.

'So what's the real reason she's summoned me and Fern home and demanded we all spend Christmas – a prolonged Christmas – under one roof?'

Daisy looked across at her sister. 'You were hardly summoned. Heavily persuaded might be more Mum's MO.'

Ginny's laughter came out white on the cold air that whipped up and down the Butterbury streets. 'That sounds like an apt description.'

'How did she persuade you, by the way?'

'She made out Grandad was on his last legs.'

'Really? To me he seems to have shed ten years since being up at the lodge.' They rounded the corner and took in the sight of Lantern Square resplendent with the Christmas lights dotted everywhere, strung across the street, the enormous tree tall and proud at one end. 'Then again,' Daisy added, reality kicking in, 'if there's something wrong, he'd be the last one to complain.'

'That's what I'm worried about.' Ginny shivered. 'I hope we get to enjoy Grandad for a lot longer yet.'

'I guess you never know when the time's up,' Daisy muttered dolefully as they walked past the railings that surrounded the square where people milled about and the scent of doughnuts and churros tried to entice them over.

The pub came into view and when they opened the door to the Butterbury Arms, Christmas music flooded out.

They'd bustled all the way to the bar and, once they were in position, removed hats and scarves. Ginny took out her purse. 'What's it to be?'

'Ginny!' It was Colette the landlady and she flew around to their side of the bar to hug the new arrival. 'Welcome home! I haven't seen you in forever, you never come in when you're here.'

'I'm usually busy with Grandad,' Ginny confessed, although Daisy knew it was more that she didn't want to bump into Lucas. Daisy suspected had she not seen him already, she might not have agreed to come to the pub. Ginny usually avoided such places when she was home and although she'd never told Daisy, Daisy had to wonder how strong her sister's feelings for Lucas still were. Their break up had broken Ginny's heart at the time and all it had done for Daisy was cement her belief that no matter how strong a relationship, something could still come along and break it.

'What can I get you?' Colette listened to the girls recite their orders, Daisy requesting a bottle of Becks.

'No gin for you?' Ginny quizzed as they went to find a space to stand towards the end of the bar.

'I no longer drink gin, or any other spirits, for that matter.'

'Glad to hear it.' And she added a smile, probably in case it started an argument, because Daisy didn't have the best track record when it came to alcoholic beverages, and she'd never been allowed to forget the mistakes she'd made because of it.

Daisy shouldn't have worried about what to talk to Ginny about because so many people at the pub came over to say hello that they were rarely alone. Daisy even began to relax and have a good time, the pressure off, at least for now.

The girls had been in the pub a few hours when they decided to say their goodbyes, only for Ginny to bump into Lucas again. Daisy surreptitiously watched them as they stood far closer to one another than they needed to, he said something and she laughed, and Daisy wondered whether she was the only one in here who could practically see the sparks flying off each of them. No doubt her sister still had feelings for the man who'd once broken her heart.

She decided to give them some time alone to catch up and headed for the door to go outside and wait in the fresh air. But she didn't make it very far because Joshua was next to come in to the pub and as the crowd swelled as though last orders were about to be called rather than being a long way away yet, they were thrust together, Daisy's chest pressed against his.

'Stop apologising,' he insisted, and with his hand gently on her elbow guided her away to the side of the pub and a bit of space. 'It's crazy in here tonight.' He looked over people's heads.

'Lucas is here already.' She assumed that's who he was looking for. 'Talking to my sister.'

Eyebrow quirked he asked, 'Really? It's been a while for both of them. So you're giving them space?'

'I thought I should. I don't think they've talked since they split up. There was no real closure for either of them.'

'Do you think that's what they want?'

She watched his lips move as he spoke. 'Honestly? No.'

'Me neither,' he said returning her grin and holding her gaze for longer than he needed to. He offered to buy her a drink and she took another beer even though she'd probably had enough. She suspected Ginny wouldn't be in a rush to go now. She was still talking to Lucas as though he wasn't due to meet his brother and she hadn't arrived with someone else. It was as though time had stood still for both of them and Daisy felt a stab of envy that Ginny might well be prepared to take a chance on love when putting her heart on the line like that had always filled Daisy with dread.

'Talking of relationships,' Joshua said, handing her a beer and clinking his bottle against hers as he came back to the side of the pub where they had some breathing room. 'How's it going between you and Ginny?'

'Fine.' Her lips twisted awkwardly. 'OK, so not *totally* fine. It's civil, it's polite, and actually a lot better coming here. It's less under Mum's watchful eye, which I think helps as well as having other people to talk to.'

'Fern not shown up yet?'

'No. And I'm not sure how it's going to be when she does. How dysfunctional is that?' she sighed. 'Three sisters who can't have a decent conversation these days.' The alcohol had definitely loosened her tongue already, but he was easy to talk to.

He leaned one arm on the wooden ledge jutting out from the wall in a space that wasn't filled with empty glasses. 'It's not like it's been years since you've seen one another.'

'I know, and like I said, we talk, but . . . I don't know.'

'You lost your dad.'

Her gaze snapped upwards locking with his. His words were like a thump into her chest. Not just because of the reminder, she hardly needed that, but because without having to tell him he seemed to have deduced that that was when things had really changed between Fern, Ginny and Daisy.

'Shit happens.' She shrugged.

He put an arm against her shoulder before she could turn away to look for Ginny and hurry her along. 'Don't say that, don't dismiss it. I'm lucky, I have both parents and a brother I get on with.'

'Did you and Lucas always get on?'

'We've had our moments.' She watched him tip back his head to get another swig of beer, the stubble which crept further under his chin than she'd realised, but averted her eyes when his gaze lowered again. 'When Lucas said he was going away I was happy for him. I started to get my head around taking on the business solo. Then he said he was coming back, and I'll admit it took some adjustment. I think what made it harder was that he wasn't quite sure of himself when he first came home. He'd had a great time doing this career that was completely different, but here he was telling us all that he wanted to work back at the farm long-term.'

'How did he prove he was serious?'

'We sat down and had a really long talk after he'd been back in Butterbury a few months. By then his own doubts seemed to have lifted and I could tell he wanted to be here. And honestly? It felt good that I'd be taking over the business with my brother. We made proper plans, divided responsibilities, discussed our commitment and saw that both of us really were in this. It sounds simple, but it gave me sleepless nights for a while.'

'I can imagine.'

'Look, I can't pretend to understand what it was like for you three when your dad passed away, especially for you being the youngest.'

She was about to tell him that it was shit, terrible, the worst pain imaginable and the only thing equivalent would be losing someone else she loved. And the only thing worse than that, losing someone else without her sisters by her side.

'I know you were going through a pretty bad time back then already,' he said.

The whole village had likely been well aware of the mess Daisy had been in. She'd come home drunk enough times that it wouldn't have gone unnoticed. Joshua had walked her home one evening after she'd been drinking in the square with her so called friends. She'd always looked up to him, perhaps because she'd always liked him, and somehow she'd always got the feeling he understood her. That night he told her she needed to sort herself out and she'd laughed *Yes, sir!* as he held her up and made her put one foot in front of the other. It was those instances that had really driven a wedge between Daisy and her sisters, who nagged her to pull her act together. The drinking had started well before losing her dad. After Harry died it hadn't continued, she'd almost felt numb, she'd gone around the village as though she were a bit of a zombie, barely talking to anyone.

'Losing Dad hit us like a thunderbolt.' Just like all those years ago she found herself able to turn to Joshua. 'He wasn't sick, we had no time to prepare.'

'I don't think you ever can.'

Tears pooling in her eyes she looked up at him. 'Up until the morning he died, I'd been horrible to him.'

'What? I'm sure that's not true. You should see me and my old man, I can be rude, so can he.'

Daisy shook her head and dug her thumbnail into the side of her finger as she made her admission. 'This was different. I found something out about him. Something that I never told anybody else. I'd known for ages before that day.'

He must have put two and two together. 'Is that why you were in such a mess?'

She nodded.

'Daisy . . .'

Her name, said so softly on his lips had her closing her eyes to find the strength to explain to him, 'That's when I started slacking off a bit at school, hanging out with people who couldn't care less about much other than drinking and acting up. I was mean to Dad. But that morning, the day he died, was the first time we'd laughed together in a long while.' She giggled remembering. 'Ginny's postcard from a ski trip landed on the doormat and her PS had the suggestion we do a family ski trip one day. Dad told me he didn't see the fun in strapping your feet to two planks of wood and throwing yourself down a mountain.'

Joshua laughed. 'I must say the appeal isn't there for me much either, I agree with Harry.'

She wished her dad were here now, almost as if he'd be able to urge her to give love a chance, let this man into her life more than she was managing to do. But something always held her back. 'I tutted at his comment about the two planks of wood,' she said. 'I told him that skis were hardly planks of wood. He'd looked down at his everyday loafers, looked across at me and I can still remember his face when he said, *Whatever, I'm not doing it.* He'd had his briefcase in one hand, suit jacket slung over his arm and added *Just remember how my foray into roller skating went when you were seven.*' She told Joshua how Harry had once hired a pair of skates so he could accompany her around the rink with the bigger kids. 'He'd ended up falling on his arse half a dozen times, he was covered in bruises. *Never again!* he said on the way home.'

Joshua gave her hand a squeeze. 'See, that's a lovely memory to have of your dad – you laughing with him that day I mean, not the bruises on his arse.'

Daisy smiled. He was right. But the reality was, before that day she'd kept her dad at a distance for what he'd done. She'd thrown herself into inappropriate friendships, gone out until all hours, avoided being at home or near him so she didn't have to play a part in any of the deceit. And in doing so she'd forgotten how much she loved his company.

Her voice wobbled when she admitted to Joshua, 'I never gave him the opportunity to prove that he was more than his mistakes, still the dad I adored, still the dad I always thought he was. Because less than eight hours after he'd left her that day, he was dead.' A gasp escaped and shocked her, she hadn't expected all this to come out tonight, to Joshua, and somewhere so public.

He pulled her to him and she buried her face in his jumper as he held her long enough to comfort her, not so long they would draw any attention from people around them.

'I almost took off when he died,' she told him. 'I wanted to go far, far away and never look back. I've thought about it more than once.' She looked at him, registered the uneasiness he had now. 'God, I'm sorry.' She sniffed, blew out her cheeks, recovered. 'Right, enough of this misery, can we *please* talk about something else.'

He smiled and obliged by asking her about her last camping trip to Northumberland and when she suggested he go some time he said, 'I will if I get the chance. But life on the farm is full time, my life is here in Butterbury.'

'Well go if you get the chance, it's a beautiful part of the country. Waking up to those hills – there was nothing like it. It was a freedom that's hard to explain.' A thought zipped into her mind of Joshua camping, with her, tucking them both beneath a blanket and looking up at the wide expanse of a starry night sky.

'Did you get many pictures?'

She tilted her head to one side.

'OK, silly question.'

'Most are on my camera and my laptop at home, but –' she took out her phone '– I do have some I emailed to myself – I'm paranoid the backups of my backups won't work,' she said, smiling.

She showed him the pictures she'd taken of the sunrise, when she'd had the privilege of watching the breathtaking skies bursting with colours that were different every time. The rise of the sun had brought with it a crisp, clear day, as burned orange faded to blue and shadows of the surrounding trees on the ground were cast long and thin around her.

'You have a real sense of adventure, Daisy.'

'I'm not sure about that.'

Rhys came over to them. 'Look up, guys,' he said.

They both obliged. And dangling right above them was a sprig of mistletoe. Green stems forked in different directions, clusters of pearlescent berries clutched at their hidden meaning as Rhys told both Joshua and Daisy that they had to kiss, it was a rule.

'So that's why nobody was standing over here,' she said wryly.

'And we walked right into it,' said Joshua, although he hadn't looked away from Daisy.

And they were still standing beneath the mistletoe.

'Come on, you two, where's your Christmas spirit?' Rhys clearly had plenty and Daisy suspected they weren't going to walk away from this.

And now Joshua wasn't looking at her. In fact he looked embarrassed, awkward as though if he were to oblige, he'd be taking advantage. It was an emotion she'd never read in him before. He'd always seemed so confident when he'd asked her out, so sure of himself.

And in a quick decisive moment, Daisy, with enough beer inside of her to give her the confidence to talk to the man she'd opened her heart to moments ago, put Joshua – and Rhys – out of their misery.

With her fingers against Joshua's cheek she turned him to face her. She put her hands against his chest, the muscles defined beneath the thick winter jumper. And then she stood on tiptoes and planted a smacker on his lips. But rather than pull away now the deed was done they both melted into the kiss, his surprise at the gesture doing nothing to diminish the skill of his tongue.

Daisy only pulled away when she realised they were being watched and more than one wolf whistle echoed around the pub as she heard someone yell *Go, Daisy!* And someone else call out *It's about time, you two!*

Breathless and aware Ginny was watching too, she pulled on the woolly hat she'd stuffed into her pocket and left the pub without saying another word.

Ginny had followed her and outside her sister didn't have much to say apart from, 'That was unexpected.'

Daisy didn't have a chance to explain what happened to herself let alone anyone else and before she could say anything the sound of heels accompanied by a familiar voice grabbed their attention.

'Mum said you'd be here, I came to meet you both.' Fern attempted a smile. 'I thought you were here for a quiet drink but it seems wild in there, or at least it was from what I saw through the window.'

Daisy, confused, realised not only had they been beneath the mistletoe but the mistletoe was hanging so that anyone outside the pub could see exactly what was going on. 'You saw me kiss Joshua,' she concluded. Great, she couldn't have timed it any better if she tried.

Ginny was first to hug their older sister. 'I'm glad you're finally here.' She stood back and smiled. 'And it really was a few quiet drinks but, you know what it's like, you get talking to people in there. It's hard to remain incognito.' She turned to face her youngest sister again. 'The kiss, however, is another thing entirely. Quite unexpected,' she said, sharing a look with Fern.

And there it was. Two sisters against the youngest, the one who didn't know what she was doing, who supposedly didn't have a clue. They'd both been in the village for less than a day and already Daisy was feeling as though she was about to be squished back into the mould she'd fought so hard to escape. No matter how hard Daisy had tried over the years she felt sure her sisters had never shaken off their opinion that Daisy's middle name was Irresponsible.

Daisy ignored the jibe and hugged Fern hello. 'Good to have you home.' And it was, if only for Grandad and the family Christmas he'd treasure.

As they began to walk in the direction of home Daisy looked across at Fern, the tallest of the three siblings. Fern might well be on holiday but she looked far from relaxed. Her hair was in that same severe ponytail it always was, the dark brown tresses tamed by straighteners, never covered by a hat and likely too scared to fly about in the wind tonight. Her dark brown, expressive eyes their dad had always likened to a colour of fine whisky seemed mistrusting, and most of that was directed at Daisy right now as she asked her again what might be going on with Joshua.

'Joshua has been keen on Daisy for ages,' Ginny put in as they walked. 'And I'd say the feeling is mutual.'

Daisy didn't say a word, just kept on walking. She wasn't going to rise to any teasing.

'He's gorgeous, I'll give him that,' Fern concluded. 'And you looked pretty interested from where I was standing, Daisy.'

'Well I'm not.'

Fern's forehead lifted in surprise. 'Then you must be a very good actor to kiss someone like that when you don't feel a thing for them.'

'Why don't you go on a date with him, Daisy,' Ginny suggested, 'if he asks again.'

'I don't need approval from either of you.' Daisy snapped more than she'd intended to.

'Perhaps we should just go home,' said Ginny, Fern on one side of her, Daisy now on the other, taking up the width of the pavement.

'Maybe it was the gin that made her kiss him,' Fern laughed in what Daisy assumed was supposed to be a whisper to Ginny. And when Daisy shot her a look she added, 'What? Alcohol loosens us all up.'

Daisy almost said perhaps she should have a couple of drinks then and lose the serious aura that accompanied her everywhere she went but instead she said, 'That wasn't what you meant though, was it?'

'Daisy—'

'No, Fern, I'm fed up of it. You two will never let me forget those days. I was fifteen, for crying out loud.'

'Fifteen and reckless,' said Fern, who never liked to lose an argument.

Daisy faced them both, arms out wide as she announced, 'I *was* fifteen and reckless. But the key word in all of this, is *was*. I was young, you're supposed to have fun when you're young. Just because you wouldn't know fun if it jumped up and bit you on the arse, Fern.' And with that she turned and stomped past the square towards home, not caring whether the other two were with her or not. She'd wait at the front gate, represent a united front to their mother or whatever they needed to do to just get through these few weeks and Christmas until they could all resume their normal lives.

The sisters held it together in front of Loretta who made them cocoa as though they were five, eleven and fifteen rather than thirty-one, thirty-seven and forty-one years of age. But it worked, at least for Daisy, who felt calm by the time she went up to bed.

In her bedroom she set a glass of water on the coaster on her bedside table and opened the drawer. She took out a silver bell from the very back and held it in her palm, remembering her dad and the Christmas he'd left it for her to find outside. She closed her eyes, wishing they could have their time again, especially those days when she'd believed in the magic of Christmas and he'd kept her imagination floating along on a cloud. Back then she'd thought he could do no wrong, he would never do anything to hurt her or any of his family. She'd never thought she and her sisters would drift apart either. They were a strong trio, it didn't matter about the gaps between their ages, if anything she'd always felt it pulled them closer. When the sisters were growing up, their parents had always told them it was their differences that made them unique, what made them interesting, it was all a part of being a sibling. But Daisy wasn't sure they could ever be those three happy-go-lucky girls who'd once been nothing but smiles.

She put the bell away and turned to open out the quilt that lay folded at the foot of her bed. She needed it at night when the temperature fell and the duvet wasn't quite enough.

There was a knock at the door and Daisy had no idea which member of her family it would be and therefore had no idea whether to feign sleep or say a friendly *Come in.* She chose the latter.

It was Fern. Great.

Fern closed the door behind her and sat down on the bed, on top of the quilt. She was wearing silk pyjamas that looked like something out of a posh catalogue and Daisy wondered whether they even kept the chill out at night. Although usually she had a husband to do that. Perhaps she didn't need the brushed cotton Daisy always wore, the red-checked ones she had on now – nothing out of the ordinary. And she had plenty more varieties in the same thickness to keep her going all through winter.

Fern ran her hand across the quilt squares, her fingers stopping at the silky-soft binding that ran around the edge and finished the whole thing off. Her hand moved over to the square in faded denim blue with intricately embroidered daisies linked in a chain. 'I remember Ginny helping you with this piece.'

Daisy instantly softened rather than letting her anger and expectation of an apology rule the atmosphere. 'I couldn't work with anything so small,' she remembered. 'I got frustrated and annoyed at myself. Ginny didn't just help me, she basically did it *for* me. I didn't really mind though, I wanted it to look good.'

Fern smiled. 'She always did love her sewing, her quilting and knitting.' They were both looking at the sister square, the same square each of them had in their own individual quilts. Loretta had made three near-identical squares, as identical as they could be without templates, each with three matchstick female figures standing in a row at varying heights. Beside each figure was something individual to each of them – a camera for Daisy, embroidered with precision, black with a little yellow viewfinder. For Fern there was a sum to show her passion for anything mathematical, for Ginny a stitched-on sewing machine.

'I always thought Ginny would be the one who stayed in the shop with Mum,' Fern confessed.

Daisy could've been angry that Fern might be having a dig, saying Daisy wasn't good enough, but the air of vulnerability that came with her older sister's make-up free face, the hair that had been released from its ponytail to allow the dark brown locks fall over her bare shoulders, was enough to make Daisy believe there didn't necessarily have to be a hidden meaning beneath her remark.

'I thought that too,' said Daisy. She'd assumed it would be Ginny, then she'd thought it would be Fern. But they both made their own way and the second Loretta admitted she needed help in the shop Daisy had leaped in. It had been her chance to prove to everyone that she wasn't the irresponsible, recalcitrant Daisy they all assumed she was. And it gave her the chance to be there for her mum who had already had to put up with so much, more than either of her sisters would ever know. Because Daisy knew something, something she'd become well-versed at bottling up inside so if she never told anyone, she could pretend it had never been true.

Fern's hand settled on a pattern of daisies Ginny had embroidered in the corner of a plain white quilted square with a lacy frill running across diagonally. Daisy wondered whether Fern was thinking of when they'd all made these quilts at Loretta's suggestion, their mum wanting to teach them, pass on skills that descended from generations. Was Fern thinking about her own quilt in the bedroom she hadn't slept in alone in a long while? Or was her sister's mind on the quilt they no longer had but the one that meant so much?

'I'm sorry, Daisy,' Fern said finally. 'I'm sorry about earlier. I was a total bitch.'

Her harsh words to describe herself made Daisy thaw. 'It's all right. I wasn't very nice either.'

'We sure bring out the best in each other,' her older sister sighed.

'What I said was mean. I should never have been that nasty to you.'

Fern paused and then, not meeting Daisy's eye, said, 'I did have fun, you know.'

Did? That implied she no longer had any fun these days. But perhaps now wasn't the time to deal with semantics.

'Actually there was something I wanted to run by you and Ginny.'

'Go for it.'

Daisy explained what Carrie had told them about Grandad's quilt.

'He'll be so upset,' said Fern, a hand against her chest, 'and too polite to complain. I feel like going up there to say something, but I won't, it would upset him if I stuck my oar in.'

'I think we need to give him another one for Christmas.'

'We can do that. What's in the shop? There are always a few gorgeous ones.'

'I think we have to make him his own, make it special, select material that means something.'

'Well that sounds ideal, but it's not that long until the big day, you don't have time for that and I doubt Mum has either.'

Daisy bit down on her bottom lip. 'Would you help?'

Fern began to laugh until she realised Daisy was serious. 'Oh, Daisy, I haven't picked up a needle and thread in years, I wouldn't know where to start. And neither has Ginny as far as I know. You're the only one who kept it going all this time.'

Daisy was gutted. But at least she'd asked, that was all she could do. 'Don't worry, just an idea, a crazy one this close to Christmas,' she dismissed. 'So are you going to see Grandad tomorrow?' Daisy asked instead of dwelling on what could never happen. Perhaps if they were closer it would be different, her sisters might leap at the chance to do this once more like they had in their younger years.

'Ginny said she'd go with me in the morning,' said Fern. 'Hey, if it's quiet in the shop, you should come too.'

'I'll see what I can do.' It felt good to be included, even better that her older sister had come in here tonight to make peace. There was a time when she might not have bothered. Perhaps being a mum had changed her in ways Daisy didn't always see.

Fern was looking at the photograph of Harry in the frame beside Daisy's bed. Taken of him sitting on a park bench in the snow, all three sisters had the same shot that captured his smile, the love for all of them in his eyes. 'Sometimes I expect him to be here, you know, at the house, and then when he's not . . .'

'I dream about him sometimes.'

'I don't think I have in years.'

'Waking up is like going through the grief all over again.' She blew out her cheeks. This was the second time tonight that she'd got all melancholy. First with Joshua, now with Fern. She'd make an effort to go with the others tomorrow. 'I'll try to come up to see Grandad with you and Ginny.'

'Great. But we'll understand if you can't, you have the shop after all.' Fern stood up to go. 'I'd better get to bed. I am sorry about earlier, Daisy.'

'Me too.' Daisy looked at her sister. 'I know I've made mistakes. But what you need to know is that I'll never forget them, please try not to keep reminding me.'

Fern nodded her affirmation. 'Just tell me one thing . . .' Daisy hoped this wasn't yet another reminder and she braced herself for it. 'At least tell me whether Joshua is a good kisser.'

Daisy gasped and picked up her pillow, whacking her sister with it. Fern responded by picking up the spare pillow and doing the same in defence before Ginny came in to see what all the commotion was about.

Fern filled Ginny in on the question Daisy refused to answer.

'You like him though, don't you?' Ginny asked softly, perching on the end of the bed.

'I'm not looking for a boyfriend,' Daisy told them. 'I'm not,' she said more firmly and then, despite how tired she was, asked, 'When will we do the Christmas tree?' It was looking very sorry for itself and neglected downstairs in the lounge where she and Joshua had set it up.

'Now?' Fern suggested.

'It's a bit late,' Ginny moaned.

'We'll never do it otherwise.'

She was right and so between them they took the boxes of decorations from where they'd been waiting patiently, piled up at the far end of the landing, and traipsed downstairs shushing one another because Loretta had already gone to bed. They coaxed Busker into the sitting room with them so he wouldn't feel he was missing out and for the next couple of hours they strung lights, hung baubles, laughed at some of the childhood ornaments Loretta insisted would never be omitted from the Christmas rituals. And perhaps it worked out better that they were all tired. There was no bickering, not much chatter to be construed as having hidden meaning, it was simply the mark of the start of their time here all together.

Daisy was exhausted by the time she finally climbed into bed but she was content, not only because she wasn't at war with her sisters when it could so easily have gone that way given the visit to the pub earlier, but also because talking to Joshua had really helped. She felt lighter than she had in a long time and even though the weight was still there on her shoulders, some of it had at least begun to lift.

She snuggled beneath her quilt and thought about the kiss. The kiss that likely had the whole village talking, the kiss that would've gone on and on had the hecklers not dragged her attention away.

And Daisy felt sure she'd fall asleep with a big smile on her face.

Chapter Ten

Loretta

It was early and still dark when Loretta's alarm went off. She'd gone to bed last night happy all three of her girls were home, together. They'd come in the door from the pub and although you didn't have to be a genius to see there was tension, it was a start. And somehow, without her forcing them in that direction, between them they'd decorated the Christmas tree in the sitting room. Loretta had doubted bringing them together under one roof for an extended period, but her confidence was growing that this could work.

Loretta made four mugs of tea and took them to her daughters' bedrooms. Fern sat up and smiled, thanking her – Loretta suspected she was an earlier riser and lie-ins weren't going to be a part of her visit no matter how cold it was outside. Ginny was a bit harder to wake and groaned more than once but managed a thank you. And Daisy's first question was *What time is it?* before she turned over to go back to sleep at Loretta's answer. Loretta told her not to let her tea go cold and reiterated the same as she had to the others, that breakfast was in thirty minutes.

Loretta stood in the kitchen, glad of Busker's company to settle her. Seeing her girls moments ago, each of them tucked beneath their own unique quilts to escape the overnight chill, had melted her heart. They might all be grown-up but a tiny piece of their childhood still existed when they were under her roof and with each of those quilts came memories Loretta would treasure forever, memories of sitting down with her daughters at the week-end to spend time with one another, to pass on the skills that had been handed down to her.

'This won't do, will it, Busker?' she said with a ruffle of the dog's head as she pulled herself together to continue with breakfast.

She'd been to the Lantern Bakery yesterday afternoon to grab a farmhouse loaf – Ginny and Daisy both loved chunky toast, doorstep-style, the bigger the better, she remembered. Daisy loved her eggs whatever way they came and Fern ate healthily so Loretta decided she'd be catering for all three with scrambled eggs, wilted spinach and grilled tomatoes, on top of thick-cut slices of toast.

Fern was first to emerge before Loretta had even fin-ished washing the tomatoes, and Loretta shuddered. 'You're making me feel cold.' She took in the silk dress-ing gown covering equally inappropriate pyjamas for winter.

'I'm fine, you don't need to worry.' She rinsed her empty mug and stashed it in the dishwasher. 'Now, how may I help?'

'No, this is down to me, you have another cup of tea or read the newspaper – I think it's on the mat, I'm sure I heard the letterbox go.'

'Maybe I'll shower quickly, free up the bathroom,' Fern suggested instead. Loretta had to wonder whether she was cold and wanted to warm up but didn't want to admit it.

As Fern was showering Ginny emerged, not saying much, just heading for the sofa against the far wall of the kitchen beyond the table. She flopped down, her head resting on the cushion at the end. 'Want some help?' she asked without opening her eyes.

Her daughters were nothing if not polite and she liked to think they were good house guests wherever they went, a value Loretta had taught them from a young age. Whenever they'd gone to sleepovers at their friends Loretta had always reminded them to thank the parent for having them, to do as was asked, and to respect the different house rules.

'I can handle breakfast for four,' Loretta answered. 'You do realise I cooked you three meals a day for years, and ran a house, and had a job—'

'Oh no, not *back in my day*,' Daisy said rolling her eyes as she joined them in the kitchen rubbing her forearms as though she was freezing despite her cosy brushed cotton pyjamas.

'Less of the cheek, you, or I'll cut your toast thin,' Loretta warned, picking up the breadknife as she took out the loaf from the wooden bread bin.

Daisy froze. 'Please, anything but thin bread, I don't think I'd survive.' When her mother assured her she would make the slices thick if she behaved, Daisy collapsed onto the opposite end of the sofa to Ginny and muttered a good morning to her sister.

Fern came downstairs minutes later, dressed in a sophisticated burgundy cashmere jumper with a white shirt beneath and a pair of jeans. Her feet were without socks and Loretta could see her toenails were painted siren red, it made her look more relaxed walking around with bare feet, although the high ponytail was back again. It had been good to see her first thing this morning, her hair splayed out on the pillow. It was a Fern less guarded, more open, and a woman who didn't have the weight of the world on her shoulders. Because as much as Loretta had wanted to bring her daughters home and together, she had also sensed for a while that there might be something bothering Fern. Something wasn't quite right, but she hadn't pushed it. Fern would, as she always had if absolutely necessary, come to her if she needed to. Or she'd sort whatever was bothering her out before she even had to involve anyone else. Not the way Loretta preferred it, but her daughter was very much her own woman and she respected that.

'Is the heating even on?' Daisy moaned.

'Of course it's on,' Loretta replied. 'Grab a blanket or the quilt from your bed if you're cold.' You'd think after all these years living in the same house Daisy would be used to its quirks and the drafts that were inevitable in an older property.

Unlike her sisters, Daisy hadn't been as eager to fly the nest and Loretta had asked her more than once whether it was because she didn't want to leave her on her own. Daisy had dismissed the suggestion citing the shop's proximity to home, the cheap monthly board she paid, being family, how she loved Butterbury but wasn't in a position to afford anywhere her own, and she'd posed the question *Who would get custody of Busker?* Which was of course a good point. Daisy had brought him into the family but they all loved him and neither Daisy nor Loretta would ever want to give him up. Along the way Loretta had stopped pushing her youngest daughter for answers and instead decided Daisy would up and leave when the time was right. Although Loretta sometimes wondered whether she should give Daisy a bit of a shove. She had a whole young life to lead and Loretta knew she wasn't really doing that. Where were the nights out with friends? Where were the boyfriends? Where was Daisy's sense of adventure and passion, because as time rolled on, Loretta was pretty sure it wasn't at the Butterbury Sewing Box.

Loretta sighed. You didn't know worry until you became a parent. She gazed at the three pictures she had in white chunky frames on the kitchen wall, one of each daughter. Daisy had taken the photo of Ginny working away on the pink sewing machine she'd once adored and used every day. Loretta had taken the picture of Daisy, capturing her lifting up her camera towards her face, the wind whipping her hair across her cheek. And Loretta had captured the beautiful shot of Fern too, taken the year she packed up and went away to university. She was lounging on the sofa, pencil in hand and a book of puzzles resting on her knees, her hair loose around her shoulders with a sense of freedom she didn't seem to have anymore.

Loretta stirred the eggs as they began to scramble, the smell enough to make her tummy groan in anticipation. The kitchen was well-suited to having lots of family around, particularly the five-ring gas hob and extra wide oven that allowed her to cater for the masses. The upstairs of their home may not have changed much at all apart from a new bathroom suite, and it might take a while to warm up in the mornings, but they'd done a bit of work to improve it over the years. Their home, a terraced house, was old on the outside with its Cotswold stone walls that had stood for decades, the low wall at the front of a compact lawn bordered with beds that changed colour with the season, and a peacock-green door. But inside, the layout no longer comprised the traditionally separated reception rooms downstairs. The main sitting room had kept its beautiful fireplace and a view of the back garden, the hallway flooring had been replaced from carpet to sleek yet naturally distressed oak wooden floorboards and the walls were painted a soft white and lined with shelves at intervals upon which were pot plants, framed photographs of the family, and trinkets collected over the years. The dining room and kitchen had been knocked into one, making cooking and eating sociable affairs. The kitchen was sleek and modern with touch-to-open cabinets and space enough for a sofa as well as an armchair beyond the table, the armchair Harry had bought her shortly after they were married. It was one of those comfy designs, rounded, with an ability to almost swallow you up whole. Harry had cooked a lot, particularly when Daisy was very small, and Loretta had dozed in the very same armchair and cuddled her youngest, letting the other two girls watch the television in the sitting room.

As Loretta began to dish up the breakfast, the sisters set the table, found glasses and a jug for the orange juice. They helped ferry the food from the kitchen worktop over to the table and Ginny grabbed the butter, which Loretta had kept at room temperature for spreading. Talk fell to work and Daisy recapped how the shop was going, the popularity they had year round and especially at Christmas.

'Butterbury residents have always loved to sew.' Fern smiled. 'Some villages would never sustain two sewing shops – I assume Miriam's haberdashery is doing OK still?'

'It's doing well, I think, she does slightly different products and services to us with only a small overlap,' Loretta explained. 'Although I think I'm getting some of her customers while she's away.' She thought again of the elderly man in the cap asking after Miriam and disappointed to find the haberdashery closed for a while. 'I do hope it's going smoothly with her family.'

Daisy slathered more butter onto her toast as Loretta prompted Ginny to tell them about her work as a midwife.

'Still with the agency?' Fern helped herself to more of the wilted spinach from the bowl in the middle of the table.

Ginny nodded. 'It stops me getting stale, bored of the same environment.'

'You could never be stale,' said Loretta, 'you're always off seeing new places. Such an adventure. Sometimes I think I should take myself off and see a bit of the world.'

'You should,' Ginny urged. 'I don't think I can remember the last time you took a holiday.'

Loretta thought hard. 'July, seven years ago.'

Daisy laughed. 'You remember the specific month and year and you haven't been since?'

'I went to a sewing exhibition in Edinburgh.'

'So work-related,' Fern concluded. 'Not a holiday.'

'It was for me. I loved every minute of it.' She sipped the cool orange juice. 'Perhaps I should think about a holiday.'

Fern tipped her fork in her mother's direction. 'Don't think about it, do it.'

'Talking of taking a break,' Loretta said to her eldest daughter, 'I saw you brought your laptop with you.'

'I'm hoping I don't have to do much,' Fern replied. 'But it's there just in case. I'm due a lot of time off so it worked out well that you wanted us home.' She looked at both of her sisters and then Loretta.

Daisy finished her juice. 'Mum, did you hear what happened to Grandad's Christmas quilt?'

Loretta stopped on her way over to the stove. She had heard, but she wanted to see where Daisy was going with this. 'What happened to it?'

'It's ruined.' She reiterated the story to her sisters, how Carrie, who helped out at the lodge, had told of Ivor's upset, how he hadn't wanted to make a fuss. 'Carrie suggested we give him a new one for Christmas.'

'We've got some beautiful quilts in the shop,' said Loretta.

'I did mention to Fern that perhaps we should make one.' Daisy looked at her sister. 'I know we agreed it was insane to try to do it so close to Christmas what with the shop and neither you or Ginny having done anything sewing related in a long while, but I woke up this morning wondering whether we could make it happen. I'd really like to.'

It seemed Daisy had been rehearsing her spiel and she took a deep breath. 'What do you think?' she asked, looking at her sisters.

Judging by their faces each of her daughters was remembering the time and effort it had taken to make those quilts at the ends of their bed and every other quilt that had ever been in the family.

Fern for once looked unsure of herself. 'I told you I don't sew anymore, I wouldn't have a clue where to start.'

'I suppose we could,' Ginny began. 'It'll be a lot of work, but it'll mean everything to Grandad.'

'Are you three really going to do this?' Loretta looked at each of them, this big commitment looming.

'If we all do it together we can have it finished for Christmas, can't we?' Daisy asked before looking at Loretta. 'I'll obviously work in the shop, but I can bring my quilting in and do it between customers or on my breaks.'

'I'm in,' said Fern all of a sudden. That was the Fern they were all used to – decisive, an action-taker. 'But I'll warn you, I'm rusty.'

'Where do we start?' Ginny asked.

Fern frowned. 'I don't remember it being a problem when we were younger.'

'That's because you all just leaped right into it,' Loretta said. 'None of you held back. And I didn't care whether things matched or colours complemented one another, I was a great believer in letting you make your own choices.'

'Leave those,' said Ginny when Loretta began to clear plates. 'You go to the shop. Fern and I can clear up while Daisy walks Busker.'

Loretta left them to it. No broken china at breakfast this morning seemed a good start.

And to see them planning a quilting project, together, was more than Loretta could've wished for this Christmas.

'Fern's making a leek and chicken pie for dinner,' Loretta told Daisy later on that day when they were in the shop. Daisy was by the shelves of material that, lined up, resembled a bookshelf with a set of colourful book spines. Loretta was dusting the counter, which she always kept spotless and ready for opening out beautiful fabrics.

'She's probably missing cooking for the men in her household,' Daisy replied as she found what she was looking for and pulled out the yellow material with even paler yellow checks.

'I don't think so.'

'What makes you say that?' Daisy brought the material over to the counter where she opened it up and lined it up with the metal measurer fixed on the edge.

'Just a feeling I have. She didn't say anything to you last night about what might be bothering her?'

'I barely saw her last night, Mum. And since when has Fern ever confided in me about her marriage and her sons?'

'She didn't hesitate to come home here earlier than Everett and the boys.'

'I hate to point out the obvious, but you asked her to.' Daisy took out the sharp fabric scissors and carefully cut the material to the size required, folded it with tissue paper between layers and popped it in a bag ready for the customer who'd called earlier and would be stopping by to pick up the fabric order.

'Yes, but usually she would've put up a fight, told me she was incredibly busy, her company and her clients needed her.' She bit her cheek in thought. 'Will you let me know if she's stressing about anything?'

Daisy had wound the material back around its pole ready to return to the shelf. 'I'm not spying for you.'

'I'm not asking you to.'

But the way her daughter looked at her told Loretta she wasn't going to get any gossip from her. No matter whether the sisters were best friends or not these days, there appeared to be an impenetrable code of sisterhood.

She supposed she should be proud they were still loyal to one another; it was a value she'd tried to instil in them as they grew up despite any rift that may have surfaced.

The door opened and in came Hannah. 'I bumped into Jeffrey at the post office,' she gleefully announced, and with arms in the air added, 'It's a girl!' It wasn't so long ago that Hannah had fallen in love with Joe and Loretta wouldn't mind betting those two would be starting a family of their own one day.

'That's wonderful!' Loretta loved baby news, it brought back such special memories.

'Six pounds seven ounces and called Rosie,' Hannah went on. 'I thought, seeing as Jeffrey is our loyal postman and we all love him dearly, it would be nice to put together a care package for him, his wife and the baby.'

Loretta leaped at the chance to be involved. 'Come this way.' She took Hannah to the section where she had knitted mittens and booties on display as well as a couple of little cardigans. 'I'll throw these in, my part in the gift, how does that sound?'

Hannah beamed. 'It's going to be an enormous care package. I've got books from the bookshop, some beautiful toys, a teddy bear, muslin cloths, nappies. All I can say is thank goodness I'll hand deliver and won't have to post it.'

Hannah went on her way with several knitted baby items and while Daisy saw to a customer who'd come in looking for some satin blanket binding, Loretta tidied up the shelf of fat quarters, rearranging those that had been put in the wrong place, turning some face up so the designs were more obvious. They had some beautiful fabrics and Loretta loved to be surrounded with so much colour every day – she moved the snow white with ruby red cherries next to the solid red fabric, the plain lilac next to a lavender with white daisies, a cream with brightly coloured cars next to a deep green with farmyard animals, which would make the perfect baby quilt.

When the door opened again it brought in a rush of cold and Carrie. 'Good afternoon,' Loretta smiled. But by now Daisy had finished with what she was doing and rushed over to greet Carrie.

'My sisters are going to help with the quilt,' Daisy told her in a rush.

Carrie looked unsure, glancing at Loretta, then back at Daisy but Loretta merely carried on tidying some of the older stock, which was closer to the front of the shop and priced down, selling well. She retied the string bows around the fabric with candy canes, and another with Father Christmases on a pine green backing.

'I'm glad they said yes,' Carrie said softly before passing a small brown paper bag to Daisy. 'I haven't known your grandad for long but I found this material in a charity shop this morning and thought it might be perfect for the quilt.'

Daisy took out a folded piece of white fabric with winter berries and several robin redbreasts on the print. 'It's gorgeous.'

'He's always pointing out the robins in the gardens at the lodge, I thought he might like it.'

'I think you're right. And thank you . . . not just for this but for convincing me to ask my sisters. I'm just relieved they actually agreed to help. It's a lot of work to do this close to Christmas.'

Carrie, hands in the pockets of her pristine cream coat, nodded. 'I'm a beginner so it takes me forever to sew the smallest of pieces. I think I'm a long way off being able to actually call myself a quilter.'

'Hey, we've all got to start somewhere.' Daisy smiled kindly. 'Actually, if you've got some time it would be great to have an extra pair of hands. You know Grandad, he talks highly of you, and it'll give you some practice at the same time. If you want to, that is.'

Carrie froze. 'Oh, I couldn't, it's a family thing for you and your sisters. And as I've said, I've not much experience.'

'We'd really welcome the help,' Daisy encouraged.

Mrs Addington bustled into the shop and announced she'd lost a glove in the square and needed another pair. Loretta led her over to the display of readymade gloves and left her to choose.

'Basic sewing skills are all that's needed,' Daisy assured Carrie. 'You don't have to be adept with a machine or anything, and there's always the cutting out to do, the pinning of fabric.'

'It sounds complicated.'

Daisy shrugged. 'It's more laborious than anything. Honestly, any help we can get so late in the game with Christmas around the corner is a blessing.' When another customer came in and lingered needing help Daisy added, 'Just think about it.'

'No . . . I mean, no, I don't need to think. I'll help.'

'Great!'

Carrie went on her way, as did Mrs Addington, who was thrilled with the chocolate-brown woolly gloves she'd selected.

'That was kind of you,' said Loretta, although now she was worried Carrie would feel like she had to help just because Daisy asked her.

Daisy shrugged. 'Carrie's nice, I like her. And Grandad said with school finished for the summer she's been at a bit of a loose end. She's interested in learning more about sewing, quilting, basically creating, so we'll be helping her as much as she's helping us. And Grandad will be chuffed to bits that she helped. If we ever get it done,' she added doubtfully.

'You will,' Loretta smiled. And with a hand on her heart she went out to the back to make them both a cup of tea. Daisy had bobbed along on her own for so long in the village that it was nice to see her opening up to the possibility of new people in her life.

Her three daughters were here in Butterbury and about to embark on a project together, and maybe it would help each of them to learn a bit more about themselves in the process.

Chapter Eleven

Fern

F ern had to admit she'd forgotten how much colder her
mother's house was than her own. In her own home
they had super-duper double glazing, the bumper insulation characteristic of a new-build, but here in Butterbury
it was different. And her silk nightwear wasn't doing the
job it needed to do. She grabbed her quilt from the end
of the bed and wrapped it around herself once she'd put
on the silk dressing gown, which may as well not be there.
The nightwear made her feel sexy and Everett had always
loved it, but right now she was going for warmth.

Unlike yesterday, their mother hadn't woken them all
for breakfast today and Fern had appreciated the lie-in.
She rarely did it and hadn't set her alarm because she'd assumed her body clock would do the job, except it hadn't,
and by the time she emerged from her bedroom and made
her way downstairs, the house was quiet apart from one
person in the shower, who had to be Ginny with the other
two having to work at the shop.

Fern was used to getting up early in the mornings. She
had things to do. Get herself ready for the office, get the
boys organised, make sure she got anything she needed
out of the freezer for dinner, make fresh coffee for her

and Everett, putting his into the Thermos he took on the train every day. She liked to leave the house with a sense of calm and organisation. She certainly wasn't used to this – sitting around in nightwear beyond nine o'clock – but that's exactly what she was doing when her sister joined her in the kitchen where she was snuggled up on the sofa.

'I'm ready before you?' Ginny couldn't have looked more surprised.

'Looks like it.' Fern grinned. 'But surely you're used to some crazy work hours with labouring mums. Everyone knows babies don't adhere to office hours.'

'They don't, but I've learned to rest up well on my days off.' She flipped the switch on the kettle and held a mug aloft with the offer of tea for her older sister.

Fern pulled a face. 'I don't suppose you could do me a coffee?'

'As long as you don't mind instant?'

'It'll do,' said Fern. The reason why she hadn't made one yet was because she was missing the freshly ground coffee from home.

Ginny opened and closed a couple of cupboards before she found the instant coffee, a miniscule jar Loretta likely had in just for Fern. Perhaps that was an idea for Christmas – a cafetière. She knew her mum loved a good coffee too. She made a mental note to look for one when she went shopping in the next few days.

'I'll bet you don't lie in when you're travelling.' Fern sat up a little bit more so she could see her sister at the kitchen worktop. She'd never asked Ginny many details about the places she'd been to, the experiences she'd had along the way.

'Of course not, otherwise my postcards home would be photographs of hotels.' She smiled wryly.

Ginny set Fern's mug on the side table nearest to her, and clutched her own between her palms as she settled down at the other end of the sofa facing her sister. She was bundled up in a beautiful berry-red high-necked jumper with ribbed cuffs and hem that finished on her thighs. In dark jeans and with her caramel brown hair hanging loose around her shoulders, her inquisitive hazel eyes never once giving any hint of worry, she seemed to Fern to be the most relaxed of the three sisters since they'd all been thrust together. Or perhaps that was just Ginny. She'd always been the more chilled of the trio, with a colour in her cheeks Fern envied now more than ever.

They talked about Fern's last holiday in Croatia – Ginny had spent some time there too and there were plenty of places they could both reminisce about, a shared interest that Fern realised made talking far easier. The last time Fern and Ginny had sat this long together, just the two of them, Fern could only remember her younger sister making some remark that it was all right for her, she knew what she wanted and she went and got it. It had been a remark that took Fern by surprise and Ginny hadn't said anything similar since. Fern had forgotten about it until now because Ginny was more often than not easy-going. What she had thought about was how wrong her sister had been – Fern might come across as organised, together and in control, but along the way she'd fought to be those things when she could've very easily fallen apart. When their dad died, the other two were younger, it was up to her to be there for them, to hold it together enough that it put no more pressure on their mother who was doing the best she could.

'Admit it,' said Ginny when Fern, still bundled in the quilt, coffee finished, said for the second time that she should really go and take a shower. 'You're bloody freezing.'

'I am not, I'm perfectly warm.' She tried to collect the mugs to take to the sink to wash but it wasn't easy with one hand trying to cling onto the quilt still wrapped around her body.

'You're huddled under a quilt.' Ginny took the mug out of her sister's hand and along with hers took them over to the sink for rinsing and stacking in the dishwasher. 'I'm all for dressing sexy, but a T-shirt and jogging pants is probably a better idea when you're wandering around this house.' She leaned her head around the doorway and checked the thermostat in the hallway. 'Mum never whacks the temperature up.'

'Never above twenty degrees,' Fern mimicked Loretta, wagging her finger at the same time and making her sister laugh.

'Never above twenty.' Ginny grinned back at Fern.

Their mum had fought them on the heating as they were growing up. The dial frequently got nudged up by one of the girls, nudged down by Loretta, up again when the girls discovered it had been adjusted, which inevitably led to a lecture of how much the heating bill would be. They'd been told to put on layers, make use of their quilts. And Fern couldn't deny the quilts were cosy in their warmth as well as their memories.

'Are we still planning to see Grandad at lunchtime?' Fern checked with Ginny before she headed for a turn in the bathroom.

'Yep. We'll swing by and grab Daisy around midday.

Mum says the shop should be quiet enough and if not she'll manage.'

Fern climbed the stairs. In a way it was odd to be back here, away from Everett and the boys, as though she was a kid again. Everett had called her earlier and been surprised to catch her asleep even though she'd done her best to pretend she wasn't. She hadn't been communicating with him as much as usual with texts and calls, which was likely his reason for contacting her and he did seem worried, but she'd assured him she'd just been busy seeing Grandad and spending time with the family. What she hadn't shared was that coming here felt like taking a huge step back from her normal life and already she could see how much she'd needed to do that. The lie-in never would've happened at home. The moment her eyes pinged open she would've been out of bed and on with the day, making sure everything was just the way it should be. Being here almost reminded her of those years in her late teens when she'd had no responsibilities and it was liberating. She wondered whether Everett felt that way too, whether this time would help them both see that they needed to reconnect and change the habits they'd fallen into. The habits that weren't making either of them as happy in their marriage as they deserved to be.

Fern made her bed and lay the quilt out on top of it ready to fold in thirds and place at the foot of her bed where it belonged. She ran her hand across the material, drinking in the memories, the cream sister square that was almost identical to Daisy's and Ginny's, the square that she'd insisted should go in the centre because the sisters were the centre of the universe. They'd once been so close, and as she folded up the quilt she wondered how their relationship had become so disjointed, how they'd gone from that closeness to lives that rarely crossed paths, and polite conversations rather than confiding in one another.

As she'd sat with Ginny she'd wondered what it might be like to tell her about Everett, about how she thought she was failing at marriage and at parenthood, that the confidence everyone assumed she had in spades wasn't really there at all. She thought back to sitting on Daisy's bed, when she'd apologised for being horrible to her after seeing her kiss Joshua at the pub, and imagined how it would be to share her troubles with Daisy too.

But for now, small talk was all they could manage.

And Fern supposed it was a start.

Fern and Ginny, umbrellas at the ready for the forecast downpour later, stopped at the shop to collect Daisy before they all set off for Butterbury Lodge.

Before they reached Lantern Square Ginny paused outside the newsagents and groaned when they saw advent calendars on display in the window. 'I meant to bring Mum one back from Bruges, with real Belgian chocolates.'

'We can stop off for one of these on the way back from the lodge,' Fern suggested as they walked on. 'Not quite the same, but nice anyway.'

When they reached the lodge Daisy dashed away before they'd even taken their coats off and signed in at the reception.

'What's the rush with Daisy?' Fern asked Ginny, un-looping her scarf and hanging it on the coat stand with her coat.

'You know Daisy . . .' Ginny pushed her gloves into the pockets of her coat and double-checked they weren't likely to fall out. 'She can be unpredictable, who knows what's going on with her.'

Fern felt guilty talking about their little sister like this when earlier this morning she'd been thinking they were all starting to respect one another that little bit more, to see each other for the individuals they'd become. 'Is something going on with her that we need to know about, do you think?'

'Not that I know of.' Ginny sighed. 'And I shouldn't have described her as unpredictable. She wouldn't like it if she'd heard me.'

Fern liked to think Ginny's remark wasn't only because she was the peacemaker but because she wanted all three of them to reconnect, the way Fern did, the way Loretta had to be wishing for and the way Daisy would surely welcome. 'Has she said anything else about the kiss with Joshua?'

Ginny shook her head and her expression suggested their younger sister was coming back to them.

'Sorry about that.' Behind Daisy was a girl, blonde, very pretty, but seemingly a very shy teenager as she seemed reluctant to meet anyone's gaze. Daisy introduced her. 'This is Carrie.'

Carrie managed a smile to Fern and Ginny while Daisy explained that Carrie, who was in the choir and volunteered up here, had agreed to help with the quilt.

Fern was a little put out. This was supposed to be a sister project, wasn't it?

But she quickly berated herself for being so mean-spirited. 'That sounds wonderful, all hands on deck!' And besides, she hadn't done anything creative in years, let alone worked alongside her sisters. They'd need all the help they could get.

'I hope you know what you're in for, Carrie,' said Ginny. 'It'll be hard work and we are well known for being a bit of a handful.' She looked at the others. 'Oh come on, it's true, I'm sure there'll be more than a bit of bickering along the way.'

Fern was about to deny it, especially when she noticed a look of horror wash over Carrie's face. 'We will behave, I promise.'

'Anything you want to suggest is great,' Ginny told Carrie. 'And Daisy will keep you up to date on our plans to make a proper start.'

'She seems lovely,' said Fern to Ginny when Carrie went off to talk with someone over on the far side of the room and the sisters went to find Ivor in the residents' lounge. She instantly felt even more terrible for thinking selfishly that this was their quilt for their grandad. When did helping out become something so awful?

After a hug for each of his granddaughters, Grandad made some brief introductions – or rather reminders because both Ginny and Fern had met plenty of these residents on previous visits. Or perhaps it was more for the residents' benefit than theirs. They met Flo, a quiet yet friendly woman who seemed to not mind Daisy but was wary of the other two. They said a hello to Ernest who had earphones in and was listening to an audiobook, and plenty of others' passed comment on how wonderful it was to see all three of Ivor's granddaughters here together.

'I appreciate you all coming to Butterbury for a few weeks rather than a rushed visit,' Ivor said, after Frankie who usually manned reception brought them over a plate of Rich Tea biscuits to enjoy along with a pot of tea.

'I had to juggle a few things to do it,' Daisy joked, 'but I got here.'

'Well thank you, all of you. I love Christmas and to have you all here in the lead-up is the best part for me, even better than the dinner on the day.'

Over tea and biscuits they spent over an hour with Grandad reminiscing about Christmases past, lots of them with their dad at the helm, finishing on the year before they'd lost him. That year it had snowed properly, blanketing the whole of Butterbury in white, quietening the streets, muffling the world for a brief moment. The only sound had been Harry and Ivor roaring with laughter about the couple who lived next door and who had hired a snow machine to cover their garden and feel more festive on the first year they had real snow anyway.

When they overheard one of the young boys visiting telling their grandma that this morning's treat in their advent calendar had been a chocolate snowman, Daisy reminded Ginny not to forget to stop off at the newsagents on the way home to grab a calendar for Loretta. 'Better late than never,' said Daisy, because they were already into December.

Ivor asked, 'Whatever happened to that advent calendar you girls had?'

All three girls thought for a moment until Ginny remembered. 'You mean the quilted advent calendar? I don't think I've seen that in well over a decade. I'd be surprised if Mum still has it.'

Ivor shook his head. 'She'll still have it, probably in the loft with all the other junk. Find it out, I'd love to see it again when Loretta next brings me over to the house.'

Fern wasn't sure they had much time to go hunting

for old things that might not even be there anymore, not when they had the Christmas quilt to make. But they assured Grandad they'd have a good look for the advent calendar.

When it was time to go they bundled up in their coats and three umbrellas pinged open one after the other as they stepped out of the lodge and into the downpour that had been promised.

Daisy shut the little gate at the front of the path and they set off down the hill, back towards Lantern Square. It wasn't yet dark but it was that time of the year when the sun set so early you felt as though you'd miss the day if you weren't careful.

'Do you think Mum's telling the truth about Grandad?' Fern asked the others. 'He's acting as though this is his last chance to recap on all the memories. Perhaps he really is—'

Daisy spun around. 'Don't say it.'

'Perhaps he really is dying,' Fern said anyway, disregarding Daisy's request but adding, 'It's a part of life, unfortunately.'

They walked on quietly until Ginny said brightly, 'Carrie seems nice. I'm glad she's going to help.'

'Me too,' admitted Fern, realising she actually meant it. And she welcomed the change of subject. 'Well done for getting her on board, Daisy.'

'No need to patronise me,' Daisy snapped back.

Fern sighed. She'd thought Daisy was moving past this, assuming her two older sisters were always ganging up on her when they really weren't. 'That wasn't what I was doing at all. I was simply saying thank you. No hidden meaning.' She waited a moment before saying, 'Sometimes I want to tell my boys not to argue, that they should appreciate one another as brothers.'

'Don't tell me, they ignore you?' grinned Ginny.

Fern laughed out loud. 'Pretty much.' She turned to Daisy. 'All I'm trying to say is that we are here now, together, and if Grandad really is sick then it's up to us to make this the most wonderful Christmas for him.'

'Agreed.' Daisy shook off her umbrella when they reached the shop so Ginny could buy an advent calendar. 'But please have a think about the way you two sometimes think of me as the useless little sister.'

'Nobody ever said—' But Ginny's words were cut off by Daisy's.

'I'm here, I'm working in the shop and holding things together for Mum just as I have for years. Me, I'm doing it, not you –' she pointed at Ginny '– and not you,' she directed at Fern, her extended index finger making her point.

'Daisy—' Fern wanted to stop her, she didn't want her sister to be upset, but she could see that she was. And umbrellas down, they filed into the shop one by one.

There was a time when Daisy never would've challenged them the way she was doing now. But what made Daisy think it was her who'd held things together for their mum? Hadn't it been Fern who'd done that when their dad died and during the years after? Being the eldest she'd comforted her sisters, held Daisy and rocked her when her world came crashing down, she'd answered the phone at any time of the night when Ginny needed someone to talk to, someone who understood.

When had anyone else done that for her?

Chapter Twelve

Ginny

'Don't be such a wimp.' Ginny peered down at Fern after she stepped off the top of the ladder and into the loft space at the family home in an attempt to find the quilted advent calendar Grandad had reminded them about and that Loretta said was likely up here.

'I'm not being a wimp,' Fern bit back. 'You know I hate spiders.' And then more gently she asked, 'Check for me, would you?'

Ginny rolled her eyes but did the honours anyway. As she performed her spider inspection she realised that as well as the stilted, polite conversations she and her sisters had had since they all congregated in Butterbury, they'd also begun to do a few things together. Granted Daisy flitted off to walk the dog or visit the lodge whenever she had a spare moment, and Fern disappeared into her room with her laptop when Ginny was pretty sure she didn't have to, but apart from that they'd been up to see Grandad together and now, they were doing something else as a trio. It felt, to Ginny, like a step in the right direction.

'Found anything?' came Fern's voice. Daisy came up the ladder, tutting at Fern for making a fuss.

'All clear,' Ginny called down to Fern.

'You wouldn't be much good camping,' said Daisy when Fern's head tentatively poked up from the loft hatch and she gingerly climbed off the top of the ladder. 'Creepy crawlies get everywhere, some even get into your sleeping bag.'

The look of horror on Fern's face had Ginny laughing but not as much as when Daisy crept her fingers over Fern's shoulder and tickled her neck.

Fern jumped a mile. 'Don't mess about, it's dangerous.'

'She's right.' Ginny stopped grinning, although it was nice to see the teasing between the two of them. It felt like they were really sisters again and Ginny swallowed a lump in her throat. She hadn't expected to feel so emotional, she'd expected this visit home would be something to endure rather than enjoy, but here they were actually managing to have a bit of a laugh. There'd been tension between all three of them for years, with Daisy putting so much strain on the family when it seemed she had no interest in getting her life on track. Fern came home to help out with funeral arrangements and anything else that needed organising – Ginny couldn't remember a lot of it, it was all a blur of grief – but she did remember Fern being there for Ginny to talk to, a shoulder to cry on, and for Daisy, although she hadn't always wanted her sister's help. Fern had a way of organising people that didn't always go down well. Ginny had spent many a day waiting for the rows to explode, on tenterhooks anticipating raised voices and arguments. And since then, things had got progressively worse. There hadn't been anything specific to trigger it, it was just that over time they all moved on with their lives and never really found that same bond they'd once had.

Ginny shone her torch into the storage areas in the search for the advent calendar. The boxes up here in the loft were stacked around the outer edges, some haphazardly, others neatly enough. Some were labelled, with others your only hope was opening them up and rifling through.

Daisy pulled a box into the centre of the loft which had enough space for them to undo and shuffle through a couple of boxes before they had to be returned to their side storage spaces so they could check more. They found packed-away board games, Fern's old school books she set to one side to go through and either take home with her or get rid of. Daisy's camping gear was neatly stacked to one side and Fern marvelled when she opened up a box to see what Daisy used to cook her food when she was away. Ginny knew Fern's kitchen was immaculate and organised, a pan or implement to suit every possible culinary need. To Fern, Daisy's ability to survive with this equipment and live that way as a chosen holiday was probably hard to fathom. They were such different girls. Fern was decisive, strong, never wavered off course. Daisy was adventurous, you never knew what she might want to do next, and Ginny often wondered whether she was happy living that way, whether she was content in the shop and being the one to stay here in the village.

Ginny found that she fell somewhere in the middle of the personality types, like she'd taken part of her character from her older sister and part from Daisy. She was independent like Fern, she didn't waver too much off course and had built a solid career that was nothing to do with the family business. On the flip side she threw caution to the wind, travelling and seeing the world, gaining new experiences, being unpredictable much like Daisy had been over the years. As far as her sisters knew she was calm, collected and didn't question much. Yet she felt out of all three of them she was the most lost. Finding out that Lucas had returned to Butterbury had shocked Ginny more than she would ever admit to anyone else. He'd been so sure of following a different path, she'd assumed he'd stay in America, settle down into a new life. But somewhere deep down his heart had always been here in Butterbury and knowing that about him, seeing how happy he was to be working in the family business with his life here for good, had made Ginny question whether her heart had really ever left the village either.

Fern undid another box and lifted out a faded pink sewing machine. 'I haven't seen this in years, Ginny.' It'd been a gift from her parents for Ginny's ninth birthday.

Ginny gave a tight smile before moving on to another box and when she opened it, slitting the Sellotape with scissors before pulling back the folds of cardboard, inside was a soft quilted material placed in a plastic vacuum storage bag. 'Bingo!' She pulled apart the plastic seals and took out the quilted advent calendar.

Daisy stood up, took one end of the material and between them they opened it out. 'Mum was pleased with the chocolate advent calendar, Ginny, but Grandad was right. There's no way any chocolate could ever match up to this.'

'It's a classic all right,' Ginny agreed as memories of this hanging in the hallway, of each of them taking out another material ornament and hanging it, wrapped around her.

'I'm so pleased Mum kept it.' Fern was looking at the quilt rather than her sisters, her fingers touching the material as they all felt the nostalgia of childhood fill the space at the top of the family home.

'Me too,' said Daisy.

Loretta had made the quilted advent calendar when chocolate advent calendars weren't really a thing. Even if they had been, Ginny suspected they would've still bucked the trend in favour of this unique way to count down to Christmas. The calendar had white snowflakes on a red rectangular background measuring around a metre in length. A rich green Christmas tree had been sewn on top of that with white snowflake buttons and below it, twenty-four pockets had been intricately sewn onto the surface. The pockets all had an embroidered number on the front and a hand-sewn ornament inside each with a loop of ribbon so they could be hung on the protruding buttons on the tree above. Ginny remembered they'd take turns with the calendar – with twenty-four days between them, Fern, age fourteen and already showing an aptitude and, moreover, a passion for anything maths related, had announced that it worked perfectly because it was divisible by three so there wouldn't be any squabbling over who got to hang the most ornaments. Ginny could remember lifting Daisy, who was only four at the time, up so that she could hang an ornament for herself when she struggled to reach.

'They're all there.' Fern had a tear in her eye as she observed that not a single one of the ornaments had gone missing from the pockets over the years.

'I'd be gutted if we lost any,' said Ginny. 'Memories like this should be looked after and treasured forever.'

'Too right,' agreed Fern. 'We were lucky our parents invested time in projects that meant so much.'

Ginny realised Daisy wasn't saying anything and a bad feeling glided through her when she saw Daisy's expression, like she was about to explode. 'Daisy, are you all right?'

'Fine,' she said curtly, suggesting she was anything but.

'You're clearly not,' said Fern.

'The hint wasn't very subtle, that's all,' Daisy complained.

'What hint?' Fern sounded exasperated, as though she'd had enough of treading carefully around their younger sister.

'The hint at how special those memories are, another subtle reference to the quilt that was special to all of us before it was lost. And of course that's my fault too because if I hadn't been in such a mess the quilt wouldn't have been out of the house, and if it wasn't out of the house—'

'Daisy, for goodness' sake,' Fern scolded. 'Don't take everything so personally, don't always assume the worst.'

Daisy dropped her end of the quilt. She at least left the torch when she took the ladder too quickly for Ginny's liking. She was glad to hear the thud of her footsteps once she reached the safety of the landing.

'She really needs to learn to chill,' Fern muttered as she and Ginny carefully folded the quilt and slotted it back in the bag to take downstairs.

'Were you hinting?'

'Not you too.'

Ginny put a hand on her sister's arm. 'No, not me too. I believe you.'

They locked eyes for a moment. 'Thank you.'

When they heard the front door slam shut as Daisy presumably returned to the shop, Ginny and Fern put the last of the boxes back until Fern went to pick up the one with Ginny's sewing machine. 'Where do you want this?'

'Back where it came from?'

'You don't want it?'

'Nope.' She closed the box herself and slid it across the floor to the edge. She moved another, lighter box to the farthest point and slid the box with the sewing machine into the space it vacated. 'Come on, I think I just saw a beetle run up the rafter.'

That did it. Fern needed no convincing and no longer wanted to examine the whys and wherefores of Ginny no longer using the machine.

After they'd taken the calendar down to the laundry and popped it in the washing machine, they went into the kitchen and Ginny flicked on the kettle.

Fern sighed. 'I really wasn't hinting at Daisy's mistakes when we were up there in the loft.' She fussed Busker, who seemed glad of the company, around the ears. 'She always takes things the wrong way. And we're all devastated that the quilt went missing, it was special to all three of us.'

Ginny poured boiling water onto coffee grounds. 'Daisy is likely fixated on the both of us really going off at her when we realised the quilt had gone. I mean, it wasn't even really her fault.' A look shared with Fern told her that her sister knew she was right. 'Things get lost over the years, it's a fact of life.'

Fern nodded. They'd both apologised to Daisy back then for their outbursts but the damage had been done. And now, it appeared, Daisy still couldn't let it go. It felt to Ginny a bit like the stubborn stain on her bedroom carpet from the night she and Lucas had drunk mulled wine in there the first Christmas they were home from university – he'd tickled her, sending the drink slopping over the edge. The stain had been scrubbed at plenty of times, it had faded, but deep down it was still among the fibres. It was only ignored because it was covered over by a sheepskin rug these days, although Ginny had run a hand over the stain last night. Down on her hands and knees she'd thought about Lucas, about seeing him again after all this time, about how she'd almost been transported back all those years to when they were together, when they thought they would be forever.

'Perhaps this Christmas we could try to make Daisy realise that it's not two against one.' Ginny put the suggestion out there for the first time in years.

And Fern looked at her and smiled. 'I think that's a really good idea.'

Ginny had always been the bridge between her youngest and her eldest sister but being back here in Butterbury all together was already making her realise how easy it would be for them all to fall back into their roles. Fern had always had a tendency to sound as though she thought she knew best, Daisy had a habit of being on the defensive, and Ginny had been the mediator.

This year maybe it was time they changed things a little. And having Fern agree that Daisy shouldn't be feeling as though it was her against her older sisters was a step in the right direction for all of them.

Chapter Thirteen

Daisy

'How's it looking?' Ginny asked the next morning when she saw Daisy inspecting the quilted advent calendar laid out on the airer in the laundry.

After her outburst up in the loft yesterday, Daisy was still embarrassed. Somehow whenever either of her sisters were around, she reverted to a much younger version of herself. And when there were two of them it was hard not to feel as though they might gang up on her like they had when teenage Daisy had been troubled, she'd not known which way to turn and she'd batted away any attempts at help from the members of her own family. It had been Fern and Ginny against her when they realised their special quilt was no longer anywhere to be found too, and that was what had made her lose her temper in the loft yesterday. But it was only moments after she'd stormed out of the house and slammed the front door behind her that Daisy had started to question whether the assumption her sisters were against her might be more in her head than in theirs. Maybe she'd got so used to thinking of Fern and Ginny regarding her as the troublesome one, the daughter who caused their parents the most grief, that she'd closed herself off from each of them. She'd never told her sisters the things she'd shared with Joshua in the pub that night, yet talking to him had come so easily with a trust that had been there in all the years she'd known him. And hearing that Joshua had his moments with Lucas, that even their relationship was challenging at times, had instilled a sense of acceptance Daisy felt she'd been battling for a long time. Perhaps it was time she opened herself up to trusting her sisters again rather than assuming the worst.

'It's all dry,' Daisy told Ginny and carried on unpegging the individual pieces from the bottom rungs of the airer and stacked them next to the laundry sink. She put the last of the ornaments onto the pile and Ginny lifted the quilted advent calendar from the airer. Daisy had expected Ginny to leave her to it but she lingered the way their mum did when she wanted to ask something and wasn't quite sure how to say it. Loretta had done it often when Daisy was a teenager, when Daisy had way too much going on in her head, more than any fifteen-year-old should.

In the hallway Daisy and Ginny hung up the calendar, slotting the ornaments into pockets at random. Each ornament was a square with a different picture on it – there was an elf embroidered onto a snow-white background, a Santa with a big brown sack slung across his shoulder embroidered onto midnight blue, a twinkle in his eye to match the stars up above him, a reindeer with a bulbous red nose embroidered in scarlet. There was a tiny gingerbread house on one ornament, its colourful sweets intricately detailed using the finest needle, an angel with golden wings and a halo that sparkled. And as each piece went into a pocket Daisy felt a little bit of their childhood trickle back, the memories of their mum and dad sitting at the bottom of the stairs close together, watching their daughters as one of them got to take that day's ornament and find a space on the tree above.

Daisy popped the angel into one of the pockets. 'I should take Busker out quickly and then get going to work.'

'How is the shop?'

'Busy,' she answered, looking for her keys and finding them beneath yesterday's newspaper on the kitchen worktop.

'I thought, given I'm not working and not travelling, perhaps I could come and give you a hand today.'

Daisy turned, unsure whether this was a criticism that she couldn't cope but after yesterday she knew she had to try harder not to jump to conclusions. She picked up Busker's lead, ready to take him for his walk.

'We could talk quilting,' Ginny went on, perhaps conscious of making an effort too. 'I'd have a chance to raid through the material box in the stockroom to find things for Grandad, and it means Mum gets some time out.'

'Mum and I have already set aside a few bits and pieces.' Daisy smiled.

'Great, I'll see what I can add. And hey, why don't I take Busker for a walk and you get to have some time to yourself before work?'

'He's all yours. Maybe I'll head out and take some photographs of the square.' She handed Ginny the lead and ran upstairs to grab her camera. She almost suggested she went with her sister but she wasn't ready for a heart-to-heart just yet and she had a feeling that was close to happening. The others had to be thinking about it too, surely? It was just getting over the final hurdle and actually doing it that seemed insurmountable right now, at least to Daisy. It had been one thing confiding in Joshua, but it was quite another to finally tell Fern and Ginny why she'd been such a mess as a teenager, why she'd been so angry, why she had closed herself off from her family and their offers to help. Joshua was an outsider, but the thought of another confrontation with her sisters, especially before Christmas when they were all supposed to be here for their grandad, filled Daisy with dread. It could be just what they needed or it could go the opposite way and they wouldn't want to hear her reasons at all, especially when they were so deeply personal and about their family.

When Daisy came back downstairs Ginny told her, 'I saw some more of your photographs in the shop, they're really wonderful. You're very talented.'

'Thank you.' She quickly added, 'Have fun, Busker.' And then she was off. Because she didn't want Ginny to bring up the photograph that had upset her so much, the one she'd torn into pieces. And she definitely didn't want Ginny to delve into why photography had never verged past a hobby for Daisy. She'd asked once before and Daisy had made a joke that she had it too good in the Butterbury Sewing Box to ever consider another way of earning a living, and now she couldn't deny that lately she'd been thinking exactly the same thing herself.

Daisy had a lovely hour walking around Lantern Square photographing the woodland creatures all lit up with white fairy lights and hidden in the flower beds or at the foot of the trees. It was a quiet time of the day, and with the sun shining she captured some of them in a beautiful golden glow from the right angle. Back in the days of cameras with a film Daisy had been more selective and less experimental with her photography, not wanting to waste a shot that was anything less than near-perfect. Her dad had told her it was an opportunity to learn and that she shouldn't worry about using film, it was what it was there for. He'd also told her to always follow her dreams, to never settle, and it was advice that had carried Daisy through until her world had fallen apart. She'd had her dreams mapped out. She'd planned to do a degree in photojournalism at a university on the south coast of England, she'd thought she had it all in hand. And then everything had changed. She'd discovered something she'd kept to herself, her dad went and died unexpectedly, and the only thing Daisy knew to do at the time was finally be the one to come to the rescue and be there for her mum in the shop no matter what. And the strength of proving herself to be responsible had spurred her on, until now. Now, Daisy was well aware she'd got into a rut and she didn't know how to edge out of it. If she'd been more decisive like Fern she would've said no to the whole idea in the first place, she never would've volunteered when her heart wasn't in it as much as she tried to convince everyone else that it was.

When Daisy headed to the Butterbury Sewing Box to start her shift Ginny was already upstairs and she was surprised to see Fern in the shop. But rather than reference the moment up in the loft, Fern merely showed her some material she'd found for Grandad's quilt. 'It was in the cheap lot by the door, you know the odd bits that don't necessarily go with much else.'

'He'll like this, it's beautiful.' It was pine green with snowflakes and candy cane designs.

Fern nodded, seemingly pleased to have done something

right, and Daisy saw what she didn't pick up on very often – a slightly unsure version of her sister, someone who had her doubts along the way too.

Fern lifted a notepad from the counter, pencil in hand, which was never a good thing, it meant she was about to get organised and, worse, bossy. 'I've been thinking,' she began. 'It's not long until Christmas and we want this to be the most perfect Christmas for Grandad.'

'It will be,' Loretta called out as she rearranged the frosted pine cones in the window display. Kids often picked them up, toyed with them and left them around the shop wherever they liked.

'We need to plan the food,' Fern went on.

'About that,' Loretta continued, bending down to retrieve another pine cone from beneath a shelf and brushing the dust from it. 'You don't have to take on the responsibility of all the cooking, Fern.'

'I'm happy to pitch in,' said Daisy. 'And I'm sure Ginny will.'

Fern nodded. 'So what'll we have?'

'The usual?' said Daisy. She went out to the back to hang up her coat and when she came back into the shop Fern looked over at her expectantly and so she elaborated. 'You know – turkey, roast potatoes, pigs in blankets, roasted carrots.' Fern was frantically scribbling as if she didn't know all this herself. 'Oh, and cranberry sauce.'

Fern sat up straighter, a finger poised in the air. 'I have a great recipe for home-made.'

Ginny came downstairs from where she'd been sorting the stock, which sometimes got in a mess all on its own. With a variety of balls of wool in her arms she dropped them all into the bargain basket. 'Recipe for what?'

'Cranberry sauce,' said Daisy.

'No need for that,' Loretta called over as she finished with the window display. 'The farm do a wonderful jar and it'll save us the hassle.'

'I love cranberry sauce,' said Ginny.

'Lucas makes it up at the farm.' Daisy raised her eyebrows in Fern's direction because her eldest sister's interest was piqued at the mention of Ginny's former boyfriend's name. 'Perhaps if you ask him nicely, Ginny, he might let you try before you buy.'

Ginny flushed a distinct shade of scarlet and busied herself hooking the beginner embroidery kits onto the hooks after a couple had fallen off, most likely disturbed by whoever had moved the pine cones.

'Stop teasing,' Loretta warned under her breath when she came past Daisy and went over to Fern to carry on with discussions about Christmas food.

'How about a nice trifle,' Loretta suggested. 'I can make that, I'd enjoy it.'

Fern wrote it down.

Daisy pulled a face. 'I hate trifle. Nobody likes soggy sponge. Has to be Christmas pudding,' she told her sister. '*And* it's Grandad's favourite.'

Fern wrote it down and decided, 'We'll have both.'

'Are you sure it won't be too much?' Ginny quizzed.

'It sounds as though you three have the cooking sorted this year,' Loretta smiled. 'Your grandad will be pleased.'

Ginny broached the subject on all their minds when she said, 'About Grandad . . . You are telling us *everything*, aren't you?'

'Of course.' But the second Loretta fiddled with the neck of her jumper, running her fingers under it as though it had suddenly begun to irritate her, the girls shared a look to say they knew she wasn't telling them everything, far from it. Because she always did the same thing, whether it was with the neck of a jumper, the cuff of a shirt or the collar of a blouse. She fiddled with the material and then protested denial, innocence or whatever she'd been challenged with.

Daisy felt something shift between her and her sisters, a silent understanding, a camaraderie, the way it had been when they were all so much younger.

'As I've told you all,' said Loretta, 'it would just be lovely for us to spend time together. And I appreciate you all being here. Your grandad does too.' She did that as well, Daisy noticed, put Grandad's name into the conversation like a full stop to put an end to any speculation. 'I thought I'd bring Dad back to the house for afternoon tea today so he can see the quilted advent calendar for himself.'

'That's a nice idea,' said Fern. 'But why don't you bring him for dinner instead. And we must remember not to mention the Christmas quilt to him.'

'Agreed,' said Daisy. 'Why don't you leave us in the shop this afternoon, Mum. Go see Grandad and then we'll all be home to see him for dinner. He can watch us hang the ornaments on the advent calendar. We're already well into December so we've got a few to catch up on.'

Loretta accepted the suggestion readily, blew kisses to each of them and went on her way.

'She's very cagey.' Fern watched their mother go. 'But let's not worry about Grandad until we have to.'

With the list made for Christmas lunch they turned their attentions to the Christmas quilt. They brought down a couple of boxes from upstairs and rifled through to find any scraps that might be of use and stashed them along with others they found in the shop into another box with everything they'd need to take home to make a start.

Fern headed into Butterbury to do some Christmas shopping while Ginny and Daisy were in the shop and bustled in a couple of hours later with several bags that she took out to the back. 'No peeking!' she hollered over her shoulder.

Daisy tutted because as well as unidentified gifts she'd also brought in a clump of leaves and a sprinkling of dust, right on the floor she'd only swept minutes ago. She cleared up the mess again and stowed the dustpan and brush beneath the counter as Fern hung up her coat and Ginny stood at the counter.

'Cup of tea?' Daisy asked Ginny who had so far turned down any offer of a break.

'Yes, please.' Ginny was dusting the counter and the relic till.

'I picked up some treats from the Lantern Bakery,' said Fern, minus the bags, coat off and cheeks still rosy from the wintry air. She opened up the paper bag to release the smell of freshly baked cookies.

'Tea all round then.' Daisy smiled. 'And I'll get some plates for the cookies.'

She popped the kettle on, ran upstairs for the plates and by the time she came back she realised they had customers because she could hear voices.

In the shop Daisy came face to face with Joshua and tried to quell her pleasure at seeing him in case her sisters noticed. All her thoughts were on that kiss, how his lips had felt against hers, and by the way he was looking at her now, his gaze dipping to her mouth and back up again, he was thinking about it too.

She managed to find her voice. 'Won't coming in here blow your cover?' She grinned, taking in his Father Christmas outfit.

'He ripped his trousers,' Ginny told her. 'I'll grab the red cotton.'

'You might need to take them off,' Fern suggested, the corners of her mouth tugging in amusement.

'What cotton do you think is best, Daisy?' Ginny called over from the rotating stand she was looking on. Daisy suspected she knew full well which would be best.

'What's the material?' Daisy asked him.

He risked pulling his beard down but only after checking for any kids in the vicinity. 'You expect me to know? It's costume material . . . thick, hot.'

Daisy put a hand to the sleeve of the jacket – she assumed the trousers were made of the same – and decided they'd need a heavier-duty thread than the cotton Ginny had her eye on if they wanted it to work best with the thicker fabric. 'That won't be strong enough,' she called over to her sister who had a few reels in her hand ready to colour match. Daisy swore she was being dim on purpose.

Daisy went over to the section with stronger thread and after holding up three different reels against the red of his suit, all the while avoiding the looks her sisters were casting her way, she stayed professional and found the best match.

'Where is the repair anyway?' She couldn't see it. But then she realised he'd had one hand behind him all this time.

The awkward grimace when she looked up at him told her it was in a place he didn't want to be seen, at least not in public. He turned around and when he lifted the red coat he revealed the big tear in the back of his trousers. She got a good view of the black, fitted jockey shorts beneath, the tight gluteal muscle and the dark hair where they met the back of his thigh as he told her, 'I caught them on a nail in the tree barn on my way out to talk to Lucas and I'm going to disappoint a lot of kids if I don't hurry up and get it fixed and get back.'

Daisy tried not to think too deeply about the body beneath his suit and the bare skin of his toned butt he likely wasn't aware she'd caught a glimpse of too when she told him, 'You've torn your jockey shorts as well.'

'Seriously?' He began to laugh. 'Let's just fix the trousers today. I can throw the underwear out later.'

Daisy looked around for Ginny in the hope she could leave her sister with the job while she did the tea but Ginny had already darted off to help the next customer through the door and Fern was watching Daisy and Joshua as though they were part of a Christmas window display, a little gleam in her eye as if this were a fairy tale in the making. But then Fern had always had a different way of thinking to Daisy. Marriage and family to Fern were something she never doubted. Perhaps if she'd known the truth, what happened to even the strongest of marriages, she might think a little differently. Then again, maybe part of the reason she'd come to Butterbury so readily meant that not everything was as perfect in Fern's world as Daisy assumed it was, something Loretta had hinted at but something Fern hadn't shared with anyone, least of all her little sister.

Daisy went over to the counter with the thread. 'It'll be a better repair and quicker if I can whizz the trousers through a sewing machine,' she told Joshua.

'Then I'd better get them off or that could be painful,' he agreed.

She called over to Ginny, 'I'll be upstairs for fifteen minutes or so.'

'Take your time!' Ginny hollered back.

'Take no notice of them,' she said as he followed her up the stairs out at the back and it was impossible to ignore the giggling between Ginny and Fern as they went. As irritating as it was, Daisy felt a tiny flicker of warmth at the teasing, fun and harmless, with no hidden meanings. 'Ignore them,' she said. 'My sisters love nothing more than to wind me up.'

'Hey, I get it.' His black-buckled boots clumped up the stairs to the very top. 'Lucas does it to me all the time, doesn't matter how old we get.'

She was nervous, she couldn't help it, especially when he trained his eyes on her again as they stopped on the landing. 'You can get changed in there.' She pointed to the first store room.

He pulled off his beard and quirked an eyebrow. 'I could, except I don't have anything to wear.'

Her lips twisted awkwardly. 'Hadn't thought of that.' She went into the store room and looked around for anything suitable. There wasn't much but when she spotted a folded-up towel in the corner she grabbed it and handed it to him.

'A hand towel?'

She squirmed. 'Fair enough. Forget the towel. And you'll be fine without it, it's warm up here, and I'll be quick.'

While Joshua took off the Father Christmas trousers and moved around making sure he didn't turn his back to her, protecting his dignity as much as possible, Daisy set up the sewing machine. 'This shouldn't take too long.'

He'd slumped into one of the chairs. 'To be honest, even though it's winter it gets way too hot in this kind of get-up. The beard is scratchy and you've no idea how nice it feels to get some air to my body at last.'

She'd positioned the fabric correctly and did her best not to let her mind think of how good he looked in the black underwear or the strong thighs she could see in her peripheral vision. 'You'll scare the kids if you take them off to get air again. Probably get arrested too.' And she pushed the foot pedal down so the needle did its job.

'You and your sisters seem to be getting along well enough,' he ventured.

Daisy looked up from what she was doing. 'It's getting better.'

'Glad to hear it.'

She paused. 'You helped me, you know.'

'Did I?'

'When we talked in the pub . . . it made me realise maybe we're more normal than I've always thought.'

'All normal and all very strong women.' He held up his hands. 'Not a criticism in the slightest. But I'm glad you're beginning to see the normality, that's a good thing.'

All being here in the shop never would've happened a few months ago, they all would've pushed against it, yet somehow it had happened naturally today and none of them had flown into panic mode that it could be the worst idea ever.

She rotated the material to fix the rest and ended up with a pretty good repair, and after inspecting her handiwork handed the trousers back to him. 'I'll be downstairs.' She was about to walk away but he reached for her hand and pulled her back. Deep brown eyes became impossible to look away from.

'Are we ever going to talk about that kiss?' he murmured.

She'd been comfortable talking about her sisters, not quite so at ease when it came to the kiss.

'You know I've liked you for a long while,' he began and before she could decide whether to blurt out that she liked him too, he said, 'I'm not sure you really know what you want.'

She wanted to kiss him again, that much she knew. It was everything else that came with it, the longer-term she had a problem with, the fact she'd need to learn to trust and accept the bumps along the way. She wasn't sure she'd ever be ready for that.

'I'm worried I'm not enough for you.' He pulled his trousers back on.

His claim came as a shock. 'Whatever makes you think that?'

'You need a change, I can see it. You say you're happy here at the shop, but you have other passions too – the great outdoors, photography. And I think it's those things that will truly make you happy.' Fingers beneath her chin, he tilted her face upwards. 'I'm just not sure whether you'll find what you're looking for here in Butterbury.' Was he about to kiss her?

He moved closer, they were inches apart, but he pulled back at the last minute. 'I'd better go.'

She barely managed a nod. His closeness made her dizzy, almost unsteady on her feet.

'I guess this makes us more than friends, you know that, right?' He smiled tenderly, not taking his eyes away from hers as though it went against all of his better judgement not to kiss her now the way he had beneath the mistletoe. 'You've seen my bare butt today. That *definitely* makes us more than friends.'

She laughed, she couldn't help it. 'I'll see you back downstairs.'

But despite the jokes on his part, Daisy had to wonder, was he as insecure about starting something up as she'd always been?

Chapter Fourteen

Loretta

Ivor lowered himself onto the third step of the staircase and Loretta squeezed in beside him.

'Wonder how long we'll have to sit here before they find us,' Ivor chuckled. He and Loretta were ready to turn back time and watch the girls hang ornaments on the quilted advent calendar, but all three of them were cooking in the kitchen. 'I know I'm old and I sometimes need a bit of a head start to get somewhere, but I don't want to sleep here.'

'Come on, girls,' Loretta called, exactly the way she had done when they were little, when the house had been chaotic, loud, a commotion but in a good way that was, quite simply, their family. Already her daughters were coming together in ways she'd hardly dared to imagine. They'd been sourcing material for Ivor's quilt, they'd been talking through ideas, and with each passing day it felt as though slowly the family was coming back together.

Fern was first, the other two girls filing after her. She was still wearing Loretta's beige apron with the yellow and white daisies imprinted on it as well as a big splash of what looked like red wine. 'The dinner is almost done,

I've set the timer for it to rest for ten more minutes,' she announced, glass of wine in hand.

'And I've mashed the potatoes,' Ginny added, 'the veggies are ready too.'

Ivor rubbed his hands together in anticipation. 'Butterbury Lodge does have a good menu but there's nothing like a home-cooked meal with your family.'

Loretta watched her daughters admiring the calendar and giggling between them as they debated who got to be the first to hang an ornament. She interrupted the banter. 'You do realise we're well into December. Each of you will get to hang a few, so does it really matter who goes first?'

Fern reminded them all of today's date. 'And ten divided by three is three, remainder one.'

'Always the mathematician,' Ivor smiled.

'Grandad, it's hardly Archimedes-level maths.'

Loretta watched her daughters and for once Fern seemed more relaxed, as though enveloped in a warmth and steadiness she hadn't had in a long while. But as nice as it was to witness, it had Loretta worrying that there might really be something wrong at home with Everett or with the boys, or even both, something she wasn't about to share with anyone. And she hoped whatever it was Fern wouldn't leave it too late to sort out.

'Who's Archimedes?' Daisy whispered into Ivor's ear, distracting Loretta from her worrying. 'What? Maths was never my thing,' she told her older sister who cast a bewildered look her way.

Fern explained who Archimedes was before Ginny said, 'Come on, let's get this show on the road.'

Daisy agreed and handed her glass of wine to Loretta. 'There's a glass waiting for you in the kitchen, Mum. And you can relax, I'll take Grandad back to the lodge later.'

'You sure?'

Daisy waved a hand as though it was no problem. 'Flo apparently needs a bit of help with one of her projects.'

'She's in a bit of a pickle,' added Ivor.

'Who's doing the first of December?' Ginny grinned at Daisy. 'You could do it. I'll lift you up to reach the tree if you like.'

'I don't think that'll be necessary.' Daisy let out a yelp when Ginny ignored her and tried to lift her off the floor anyway. She only managed to get her feet dangling an inch or two above the wooden floorboards before she admitted defeat.

After Daisy batted Ginny away she pulled out a material ornament from the square embroidered with a '1' on the front. It was in the shape of a dancing elf, its pointy ears and look of mischief a match for Loretta's youngest daughter. She hung it on the tree before Ginny took out an angel on a pale blue background from the second pocket, Fern a reindeer from the third, all of them excited as though this was far more than hanging material items onto a bigger piece of quilted fabric, which of course, it was. It was a part of their childhood, a memory to draw them together, and Loretta embraced the sound of their giggles as they regaled anecdotes one after another.

Ginny picked up her wine again. 'Do you do the snowy footprints for the boys?' she asked Fern, who was leaning against the bannisters next to where Loretta and Grandad sat. 'Like Dad did for us.'

Harry had always left Father Christmas footprints in the hallway for his girls. He would put on his wellington boots and Loretta would follow him with a sieve of flour dusting the top of each boot before he took the next step.

'Not anymore. It's a shame they're too old to believe.'

Ivor protested, 'I still believe.'

'Yeah, sure, Grandad.' Ginny grinned.

'Christmas was more magical when the boys were young,' said Fern. 'They'd be unbearable on Christmas Eve, bouncing around with excitement. Everett and I were exhausted every single year waiting for them to fall asleep before we could sneak in and leave stockings at the ends of their beds. Everett's excitement was almost on a par with theirs. He loves Christmas.' It was as though Fern's memories had transported her off to a place she badly wanted to get back to, as though she wasn't quite there anymore.

Loretta began to smile. 'You caught us doing the footprints one year, Fern. Do you remember?'

'That's terrible!' said Ginny.

Loretta shook her head. 'She knew the truth by then, don't worry. She was always up so much later than you or Daisy. She ended up joining in that year. Don't you remember the smaller footprints?'

'You always told me those were made by the elves!' said Daisy, registering the lie that had kept the magic alive.

'You've got to be quick to think as a parent, especially when it comes to the all-important Father Christmas conversations.'

The girls launched into a discussion about their other rituals – the carrots they'd leave for the reindeer, the mince pies they'd set on a plate for Father Christmas next to the glass of milk because the girls had decided it would be terrible to encourage the big man in red to drink and drive.

'Do you know my favourite thing Dad ever did at Christmas?' Daisy leaned her chin on her hands as they rested on the newel post. 'One year, on Christmas morning, I ran to the back door to see if it had been snowing and there was a big silver sleigh bell lying in the frost on the step, glistening back at me. Dad told me it must have fallen off the sleigh. I went outside to get it and I kept it in the pocket of my dress all day, I kept it with me until I went to sleep. And I still have it. It'll always be special.'

Loretta felt the skin on her arms beneath her jumper prickle in anticipation because she knew what was coming.

Fern looked at her youngest sister. 'That wasn't Dad, it was me.'

Daisy stood up straight, eyes glistening with emotion. 'It was you? You did it for me?'

Fern shrugged. 'I wanted to make the magic last for you. It's sad when it all stops.'

'I don't know what to say.'

The timer pinged in the kitchen and it was all systems go for dinner.

'I'll set the table,' Ginny announced as Daisy grabbed Busker by the collar before he could charge in front of the girls and trip one of them up.

Something between Fern and Daisy may well have shifted tonight. In that moment, acknowledging a gesture that had meant so much to Daisy and to Fern for different reasons, it was as though the memories of Christmas were bringing her daughters back together, slowly but surely.

Dinner was a delight. Ivor was in top form, chatting away with his granddaughters, making them laugh, pulling them together in conversations rather than dealing with them all separately – instead of talking about Fern's work, then Ginny's travels, and Daisy's life here in Butterbury, he talked about wider things. Complimenting the food led to his memories of when he was a boy. He'd been born during the Second World War, a teen when it finished, and he remembered rationing and the different way they'd approached mealtimes back then, how it was hard to eat too much when it all had to be shared around. All three girls were eager to know more, they always were when Ivor held court, they hung on his every word as much now as they had as kids.

They moved from the topic of food rationing to talk about fabric rationing and how fabric had been used in the war to make uniforms. Ivor told them all about the Make Do and Mend scheme, which was government backed and encouraged people to revive and repair their worn-out clothes.

'Talking of repairing,' said Ginny, a look of mischief in her eyes, 'Daisy did a repair in the shop today. A very special repair.'

Loretta wasn't sure what they were getting at. She finished another mouthful of mashed potato coated in the delicious sauce. 'She does repairs all the time.'

'Yes, but it's not every day she sees Joshua's butt,' Fern added, roaring with laughter.

'Tell me more!' Although Loretta didn't really care whether Joshua had come into the shop totally naked if it had this effect on her girls. They all looked so happy.

Ivor was thoroughly enjoying watching his granddaughters too and when they'd recovered from talking about Joshua's butt and explaining the tear in his trousers that had gone through to his jockey shorts, Ivor told them how he'd mended clothes as a boy scout. 'Never for a Father Christmas,' he winked in Daisy's direction, 'but I mended plenty. Not many men do that nowadays, more's the pity.'

'I know Everett isn't much good with a needle and thread,' Fern agreed.

'You send him to me, I'll teach him a thing or two.'

They moved on to talking about the Victorian era of crazy quilts with haphazardly shaped pieces, sometimes silk, the lavish embroidery used. 'They were never intended for everyday use,' said Ivor, 'they were much too decorative for that. Quilting has evolved a lot over the years and it's stood the test of time. I'm glad to still see it in the shop.'

'You'd have loved The National Quilt Museum in America, Grandad.' Ginny put her cutlery together as she finished her dinner and poured another glass of water from the jug in the centre of the table, letting a slice of lemon plop into her glass.

'You went?' Loretta was surprised. She hadn't heard Ginny talk much about her previous passion for sewing. Her pink sewing machine had been relegated to the loft and she'd got busy with her career and her life.

'I did. And it was quite something. There were quilts dating back all the way to the 1600s, from all over the world, reflecting different traditions and methods used. Sometimes the origins of the quilt weren't really known but other times you could read about the history of the person, what their life had been like, how quilting became a part of their life.' She stopped as though she'd gone off on a tangent she hadn't meant to follow. 'Anyway, I've got plenty of photographs, if you'd like me to show you.

They're in albums back at my flat, I'll bring them next time I visit.'

'I'd like that.' Ivor smiled. 'You know I've always loved a good quilt.'

Loretta didn't miss the look pass between the girls, the nudge from Ginny to Fern and vice versa.

After cups of tea, it wasn't long before Ivor declared they'd better get back up to the lodge so Daisy could help Flo before she turned in for the night.

With Daisy and Ivor gone, Loretta and Ginny left Fern alone to call Everett and they took Busker out for a quick evening walk, down to Lantern Square and back again.

'Fresh air after a big meal is always good.' Loretta waved over to Mrs Ledbetter who was hanging a garland on her front door. 'And I haven't had much of a chance to talk with you yet.'

'We've talked loads, Mum.'

'Not really. We've discussed the quilt for Grandad, you've told me all about your travels, your work and how much you like swapping over from one environment to another, but we haven't really talked about *you*.' And it was high time.

'Not this again. You always want to know long-term plans and goals.' But she said it with an air of amusement and Loretta couldn't deny it.

'What's wrong with putting a little bit of planning into your life?'

'I do plan. I travel, I work, that takes a lot of juggling, believe me.'

Loretta sighed. 'You know what I mean. Are you telling me you always want to be chopping and changing, you don't want to put down roots?' Usually whenever they talked Loretta asked questions, but Ginny didn't give much away about what she wanted long-term.

'I have roots, Mum.' She coaxed Busker away from sniffing the bushes in a front garden when he lingered that bit too long for a cold winter's night.

'So where to next?'

Ginny took a deep breath of the cold night air. 'I don't know.'

'But you always plan the next trip after you come home.'

'I usually do.' She waited before she added, 'But this time . . . I don't know.' She looked around them, at the lights on the big tree, the illuminated windows in the homes facing Lantern Square, people heading home from the pub, others out for a late night stroll.

Loretta came out with the question she'd been wanting to ask since Ginny came home and it wasn't hard to see that something was different this time. 'Would you ever consider moving back to Butterbury?' She fussed the top of Busker's head and around his ear until he decided that she could do that anytime and with this being the last walk of the day he really should be making the most of it and trotted ahead of them, nose to the ground to see what was what.

'I'm not sure.' It wasn't the response Loretta had expected at all. But it was said in a way that wasn't dismissive, in a way that said Ginny had a lot of thinking to do. And Loretta had to wonder how much of it had to do with her sisters, or perhaps Lucas being back in the village, or even the family business that Ginny had once had a real passion for.

Loretta put an arm around her daughter's shoulders

and gave her a squeeze. 'Well whatever you decide, it's really good to have you home.'

When they arrived back at the house Daisy and Fern were already in the sitting room and had upended the big box of material they'd been collecting ever since they decided to make their grandad another Christmas quilt. Out onto the floor tumbled an assortment of fabrics, a variety of designs and patterns, different textures, jaggedly cut scraps, neater quilting quarters.

Ginny had shrugged off her coat and when she joined her sisters she knelt down on the floor next to them. 'It's a bit late to start this tonight, isn't it?'

'We won't get it done otherwise,' said Fern.

'She's right,' Daisy put in, 'And I won't sleep tonight if we don't make a start. We've finally got all the material we're going to need, no time like the present.'

'This piece is perfect.' Loretta bent down and plucked the piece of fabric with a vintage town design, snow falling, a pale blue background. There was even a classic car driving along the street.

'I thought that piece looked like the car Grandad had years ago,' said Fern. 'I found it in a second-hand shop.' Fern sighed. 'Can we really pull this off and get it done by Christmas?'

'Of course we can,' Ginny rallied.

'But I'm so rusty,' Fern said, doubting herself. 'I've forgotten everything, I'm sure of it.'

'Don't forget that lovely girl up at the lodge has said she'll help with the pinning and some of the basic stitching. Having an extra pair of hands might be just what we need.' Usually the least decisive of the three, Ginny wasn't this evening, she was taking control, her face alive with enthusiasm.

'Would anyone like a cup of tea?' Fern suggested. She seemed nervous about how her part in all of this would play out, unsure of herself for one of the first times in her life. Or perhaps she did it more often than Loretta realised, she'd just got proficient at covering it up.

'Please.' Ginny was lifting up pieces of material and matching them to others, toying with ideas.

'I'll do it, you sit down,' said Daisy to Fern. 'Choose some fabric.'

Busker almost tripped Daisy over when she brought back the tray holding mugs of tea, Ginny got her hair caught on a pine cone hanging from one of the tree branches and Fern untangled it for her, and all three of them knelt on the floor for the next couple of hours going about the project, filling the house with the sounds of a normal family going about their lives, together.

When she'd found out Carrie would be helping with the quilt, it had filled Loretta with a mixture of dread and excitement. For her girls to be so welcoming was a gift, but what if it all fell to pieces?

Loretta had a tear in her eye, but her daughters were all so busy rifling through the material that they hadn't noticed. Seeing them come together like this already showed Loretta they were well on their way to being the three sisters who would do anything for one another and their family.

All Loretta could do for now was hope that they would be able to accept the changes coming their way and look to the future rather than the past.

Chapter Fifteen

Fern

Fern finished talking to Cooper on the phone. She couldn't remember the last time her eldest son had made her laugh so unexpectedly. She was in a little café in Butterbury with a mug of tea in front of her, a book beside her, taking a break from working on the quilt squares, but all of a sudden she'd felt an overwhelming urge to speak with the three main men in her life. Up until now conversations had mostly been with Everett, but today the boys were more forthcoming. Usually Cooper was only really interested in drawn-out conversations with his mates and their exchanges would happen in the car on the way to hockey or while she was making dinner or trying to hurry them out of the door.

When Everett came on the line she was smiling. 'Cooper told me what he did.' According to Cooper, he'd come out of his swimming lessons and in the dark, thought he spotted his dad's car, opened the boot and thrown his bag inside when the parent had turned around from the driver's seat and asked what on earth he was doing.

'I actually cried with laughter,' Everett told her, voice wobbling as he remembered. 'I was in the car behind and thought *What the hell is he doing?* His face was a picture in my headlights when he turned around. He looked so shocked, I couldn't keep a straight face. He dived into the passenger seat and sank down really low and told me to just drive.'

It felt good to be laughing with Everett. Along the way they'd almost forgotten how to do that. 'Let's hope he doesn't bump into the parent too soon, he'll be mortified, I'm sure.'

'Oh, I think that ship has sailed. We bumped into Leanne at the shops.'

'Leanne?'

'Niall's mum, she's nice, you'd like her. And her husband came in on his way home from the station so I met him as well. He seemed all right.'

'Listen to you getting to know the parents.' She wasn't sure why but she felt strangely put out. They'd always co-parented but still, it felt odd that she, the mother, had never met many of her boys' friends' parents.

'Leanne and her husband will both be at the carol concert tonight.' Everett's voice brought her back to the present. 'We're meeting for drinks first, that'll help me survive it, I guess.'

'The school carol concert?' They had one every year, but Everett and Fern never went.

'Jacob persuaded me to get tickets, I think a few of his friends are being dragged along with their parents. He wants to check it out, I suppose, although no such luck with Cooper, he was a flat out no.'

'What's Cooper doing instead?'

'Homework, which means TV.'

'He's staying home alone?'

'He's fifteen, Fern. And the school is around the corner,' he sighed. 'He'll be fine.'

'Well I guess I'd better let you get ready then.'

'Don't be like that, Fern.'

'I'm not being like anything.' She tried to put her coat on one-handed without putting down the phone. 'I've got to go, we'll talk later. Enjoy the concert.'

Discombobulated at how relaxed Everett sounded now she was away, Fern pushed the tepid tea away from her. She didn't want it now. She looked out onto the street. The rain had begun to lash against the windows of the café and she didn't even have an umbrella.

'Whoa, what did that pan ever do to you?' It was Daisy, she'd come home as Fern was trying to assemble a lasagne for dinner and failing miserably at something she usually did without really having to think about it. She, Ginny and Daisy had been sharing the cooking but tonight she wanted to take back a piece of control.

'I left the sauce for a second, only a second, and it bloody well burned!' Fern couldn't look at her sister. Her eyes were fixed on the marks on the pan as she scrubbed it to within an inch of its life. 'It won't come off!' She shoved the pan back into the water. 'It's ruined.'

'I would ask if everything is OK,' said Daisy, 'but I can see it's not.' She lingered a moment longer, but when Fern said nothing else she left her to it.

Fern wished she could just cry. The tears were there, waiting for permission, but she only ever cried behind closed doors. She took a deep breath, left the pan soaking and got the ingredients out again.

It wasn't long before Daisy braved coming back into the kitchen. 'Do you want to talk about it?'

Fern had expected her sister to give her a really wide berth until dinner. She hadn't anticipated the offer of a sounding board. She opened her mouth to say she was fine but closed it again. That's what she would've done six months ago, a year ago. That's what she'd always done and she was tired of it.

'Coming here wasn't only for Mum's benefit,' Fern admitted, the words rushing out before she could change her mind. 'I needed to get away.'

'Why?'

'Ever since Dad died . . . I haven't really felt in control the way I should.'

'But you're always so together,' Daisy said softly.

'I'm not sure I'm explaining it right.' She hadn't tried with Everett either, which was probably half of the problem. She didn't communicate, neither did he, so how could a marriage possibly work like that? 'I am in control, but sometimes a little too much . . . does that make sense?' She gave Daisy a nudge when her sister raised her eyebrows in a mocking fashion, which Fern knew was in support rather than criticism.

She hesitated before revealing more. 'When Dad died I felt as though I'd let something bad happen because I'd not expected it.'

'That makes no sense, Fern. Nobody knew it was going to happen.'

'See, I'm rubbish at telling people how I feel.' She groaned, covered her face. But the way Daisy was looking at her suggested she should keep on trying.

'I started to be more fastidious about everything I did.

I've always been a bit that way inclined, as you well know, but it's been getting worse over the years.'

Daisy nodded and paused before she admitted, 'I never once saw you cry, you know. Back when Dad died.' She wiped her finger through a dusting of flour that had been spilled on the worktop. 'I cried a lot, so did Ginny, but I don't remember you ever doing it. I thought you were so strong. I thought I was being so weak.'

Fern gulped. 'It's not weak to cry. And I did. I cried a lot.'

'You hugged me, I remember that.' Daisy smiled gently. 'And you talked to Ginny on the phone all the time, you calmed her down when she was upset, and I remember you helping Mum when she was at her worst in the weeks after the funeral.'

'I wanted to be there for you all, it made me feel useful.'

'As though you were in control.'

Fern nodded, exactly. 'I didn't want any of you to see me cry. I didn't want to upset you any more than you already were, so I held myself together whenever you or Ginny or Mum were around. I cried on my own or in front of Everett, but never in front of you three.'

'Fern, you do realise how crazy that is, don't you? Crying is normal.'

Fern sniffed. 'It's the onions.'

Daisy tilted her head to the meat sauce in the pan having already been simmered and now waiting to become part of the final dish. 'The onions must've been chopped a long time ago.'

She sniffed again and plucked a tissue from the box on the windowsill to soak up the tears that had spilled out already. 'Must be the flour I spilt.'

'Must be.' Daisy hesitated but then, surprising them both, came around to Fern's side of the worktop and wrapped her sister in a big hug. 'I'm glad you told me how you're feeling.'

Fern let Daisy hold her until they heard the door go and Ginny and Loretta arrive home from the shop.

Daisy gave her one more squeeze and told her, 'I'll prepare the salad.'

Fern passed her sister a chopping board. 'Thank you. For listening.'

'Any time. And if you need to talk, about anything, you know where I am.' Daisy took out the lettuce, tomatoes, cucumber, spring onions and beetroot from the fridge.

It wasn't long before the lasagne was bubbling away in the oven, and Fern felt herself relax. Nothing to see here. The house was calm, everything was under control, and with a smile from Daisy she realised how much she'd missed having both of her sisters in her life. She'd not communicated with them either and look what had happened – she'd lost her sense of self. She wasn't quite ready to talk about Everett with either of them yet, but maybe, given time . . .

The sumptuous lasagne went down a treat as the girls and Loretta talked about their day, what they'd been up to, the countdown to Christmas and how many gifts each of them still had to go and buy.

Daisy and Ginny between them took away the plates, the empty bowl that had held the salad.

'I couldn't eat another thing,' Loretta declared, hand on her tummy. 'That was delicious. But, Fern, you really don't have to cook quite so much.'

'Ginny and Daisy have been helping,' she insisted.

Daisy called over, 'Those tomatoes were chopped perfectly and the spring onions sliced to perfection.'

Fern grinned at her sister. 'I find cooking therapeutic, happy to do it, Mum.'

This time Daisy let out a laugh and told them all about the first attempt at the sauce, the lumps and the burned bits on the pan. She didn't let on that Fern had been quite upset and angry, only that the cheese sauce hadn't been perfect. It likely could've been salvaged, but Fern had been so furious with her inadequacy that she'd ditched it without even trying.

'Do you remember your dad's cooking?' Loretta asked them all.

'I remember the Christmas tree croquembouche,' Ginny called out, and they all began to laugh.

Fern covered her eyes. 'He tried, but what a disaster. The cream puffs didn't puff up enough, he got spun sugar and green icing all over the floor.'

'It looked terrible,' said Loretta, 'it didn't taste particularly good either with those cream puffs on the chewy side.'

'That's a bit polite, Mum,' said Ginny. 'I ate two to be kind to Dad but they were really bad.'

Loretta was watching all three of them and she took Fern's hands with her own. 'Don't you see? The dish you instantly remember wasn't the French toast he had down to a fine art, it wasn't the onion soup you all loved, it was the one thing he really made a mess of.' She squeezed Fern's hands and said quietly so the others wouldn't hear, 'Try not to be so perfect all the time, Fern, you really don't have to be.'

Fern leaned in for a hug. 'I'll do my best.' She smiled.

Alongside their mother, the girls finished clearing up and once the dishwasher was chugging away and everything too big to go in had been washed and dried, they took cups of tea over to the table.

Talk turned to Grandad's quilt and their progress so far. They had a few squares sorted and Fern knew she was pretty slow but at least she'd begun to contribute. That in itself gave her a lift and she was almost looking forward to carrying on with it.

'How's the Christmas shopping going?' Loretta asked her.

'I still need a couple of stocking fillers so I'll drive into Tetbury and have a wander around before I do some more work on the quilt. I might have a look in a couple of charity shops for more material too. It's fun finding things that'll mean something to Grandad, and we've got lots to play with now.'

Daisy agreed. 'I've done a couple of squares, Ginny has done five already.'

'I've been doing some late in the evenings,' Ginny confessed. 'It's relaxing before bed.'

Talk moved on to what to buy their grandad this year. They were giving him the quilt between them but each wanted to get him a gift to go with it too.

'I got him a personalised case for his reading glasses,' said Fern.

Ginny was next. 'I found him a tin of his favourite clotted cream fudge along with a retro container for keeping either that or his favourite biscuits in.'

'I've ordered him some books,' said Daisy. 'I'm waiting for them to come in at the bookshop, which will hopefully be any day now.'

'He seems to keep himself busy up there at Butterbury Lodge.' Ginny finished her tea.

'He has company and so much to do, I'm not surprised he didn't want to live with us,' Loretta agreed. 'And talking of the lodge, Daisy, a little birdie tells me . . . well, not a little birdie, but Mrs Ledbetter . . . she told me someone asked to buy one of your photographs.'

'That's amazing, Daisy.' Fern smiled. 'Tell us what happened,' she urged.

Reluctantly Daisy explained how she'd been taking pictures of the residents when they didn't expect it. 'I walk around the room and get natural shots, not posed for. Betty's son saw the photograph I'd taken of his mum and liked it.' She shrugged as though it was no big deal. And then she changed the subject back to Grandad's Christmas quilt and was the first to head to the sitting room to get going with it again.

'The measurements for each block are written on that piece of cardboard on the mantelpiece,' Loretta told them once they were all ensconced and ready to get to work. 'I've already built in the measurement for seam allowance.'

'And don't forget,' Daisy grinned, 'measure twice—'

'Cut once!' Fern and Ginny chorused with her, laughing as they did so and bringing the atmosphere back to what it had been earlier.

'At least I know I taught you all something,' Loretta said, shaking her head but smiling at their repetition of the advice she'd given them right from the very start. 'I will never forget your little face, Daisy, when you wanted to use the beautiful fabric with sailing boats on it for your quilt and thought you'd measured it correctly but when you cut it you realised you hadn't. You were devastated. I'd picked that fabric up in the charity shop and we didn't have any more.'

'I was gutted,' Daisy recalled. 'At least I got to use it – that's why it's cut on a diagonal with a plain piece of pale blue,' she told her sisters. 'It looks good so I got over it, but I tend to remind customers now that they must ensure to measure correctly.'

'You're good with the customers,' her mum encouraged. 'They adore you.'

'Mum . . .' Daisy flitted away the compliment but Fern knew she was right. Daisy had always been a people person, always able to go up and talk to anyone.

'Who's that?' The doorbell rang soon after they'd settled down and Daisy got up to answer it.

When Fern leaned around the door jamb she saw it was Carrie. 'The cavalry has arrived!'

Carrie didn't seem any more relaxed than the last time they met, but then she was so much younger than the rest of them. Fern asked her all about school, which proved to be an ice-breaker rather than the conversation stopper it often was with her sons. And Ginny soon got her talking about materials, textures and designs.

'Carrie, you're way better at sewing than I am,' Fern concluded, watching Carrie stitch three different-sized stars to a midnight blue background. Ginny was already cutting out a crescent moon to add on with it.

Fabric was spread across the floor right up to the Christmas tree and Fern teased Carrie. 'I'd watch your clothes, if I were you.'

Confused Carrie stopped stitching for a moment. 'Why?'

'Tell her, girls. Mum likes to cut up our clothes and use them on quilts.'

Daisy nodded. 'Yep, even cut the shirt I was wearing once.' When Carrie gasped she grinned. 'I can't do it, Fern, I can't wind up the person who volunteered to help us in our hour of need.'

Fern apologised. 'But Mum did do that, although only with old clothes. It made the quilts all the more special though. What made you want to learn to sew and quilt, Carrie?'

She spoke softly, blonde hair falling in front of her face every now and then until she pushed it away. 'My best friend says it's a good escape from school work.' She smiled. 'She's very talented and wants to study fashion, she makes her own clothes already.'

'Ginny used to do that,' Daisy informed her.

Ginny nodded and told Carrie all about the things she'd made over the years. And as they talked, they sewed, they discussed ideas, worked on new squares for the quilt, thought about what Grandad would think of their ideas, how this was going to be the best Christmas present ever.

As Fern helped Daisy by holding a piece of fabric straight as she cut out a shape, Fern glanced over at Ginny to see her sister's face lit up in a similar way to their mother's as she worked. The flecks of light in her eyes took on a sparkle and Fern wondered about the pink sewing machine relegated to the loft and why it was still there when looking at her sister now, Ginny was more in her comfort zone than she'd seen her in a long time.

Daisy picked up a neatly cut piece of material. 'This is one of the shop's newer fabrics, isn't it?'

'I couldn't resist,' Loretta admitted. She'd come back into the room and had already had a quiet word with Carrie. Fern hadn't been able to hear what she said, perhaps she was making sure the three sisters were behaving themselves.

Fern picked up one of the bundles made up of materials in different patterns and tied together with a ribbon. The top design had cats printed on it, each animal hiding behind colourful parcels and little white mice cheekily twitching their whiskers. 'This cat looks exactly like Horatio.'

'He does!' Both Ginny and Daisy agreed.

Ginny turned to Carrie. 'Grandad had a cat called Horatio and he had the same mischievous twinkle in his green eyes.'

As they pulled pieces of material together to see what worked well, Daisy wondered, 'What colour will we have on the back of the quilt?'

'I'd say either will go.' Ginny got up, retrieved the rolls of fabric in cream and red that were leaning against the wall beside the tree, and brought them closer. 'They're both equally as soft but durable enough to hold the batting in between. What do you think, Carrie?'

'Oh no, it's your decision.'

'I asked because I want your opinion.' Ginny was looking from one roll to another.

'I've got no idea,' said Fern.

'I like them both,' said Carrie, getting a *me too* from Daisy.

The sitting room had become a mini workshop with the items they needed strewn across every available surface – quilting rulers, packets of needles, thimbles lined up on the mantelpiece above the fireplace, a plastic tub on the floor containing threads in all colours – red, green, white, gold. They'd set up a board to cover the coffee table, which would do for measuring and cutting material to size, and at the very edge of that were pots holding scissors, rotary cutters, pencils and a couple of steel rulers. Fern remembered the rotary cutters and the warnings that had come every time one of them used it – they could slice through fabric incredibly quickly they were so sharp. She remembered Grandad making a slicing movement with his hands, the swishing sound from his lips, shocking them all into being careful.

Fern watched as Ginny issued Carrie a similar stark warning. Fern had been resistant to the idea of Carrie helping out when it was first mentioned, but now? Now she watched the young girl laugh along with Daisy when she narrowly missed cutting her finger and had them all hold their breath, and she decided perhaps Carrie coming their way had made this all a little easier. Rather than only having each other, they had someone else to involve, and it shifted their focus. Rather than thinking about themselves and any bickering or animosity raised over the years, they chatted with Carrie, who was beginning to talk more as she told them all about her school, her friends, and the happy home she'd been living in with her auntie since her mother died.

In the corner of the room was the ironing board and Fern's mind wound back to when her mum had stood ironing the scraps of fabric as each of the sisters selected the next piece they wanted to use. She'd iron them, rid them of the creases first, then hand them back, each piece of fabric with a soft comforting warmth. Fern had never had a passion for quilting or sewing, but what she had loved back then was all of them sitting down and working together on something unique. And now, those memories were coming back. Perhaps they were even beginning to make some new ones.

Fern's body started to ache from sitting on the floor so long so she volunteered at the ironing board. 'Pass your fabrics up here one at a time, I'll iron them. Carrie, you first.'

Carrie obliged, passing up the square of midnight blue she'd sewn stars onto. Once it was ironed it would be put aside ready for piecing the quilt together.

Daisy was wading through a tub with strips of ribbon, Ginny was concentrating on embroidering on a Father Christmas figure to another piece of material, and Loretta had Busker at her feet while she watched them all.

Daisy must've noticed Carrie looking a little lost, picking up pieces of material here and there but not daring to start anything. 'Pick whatever you like,' she said.

Ginny weighed in. 'Why don't you do a simple block, one of the gorgeous Christmas fabrics. Anything goes when it comes to Grandad and Christmas.' Carrie seemed relieved as she listened and Ginny picked up a collection of material tied together neatly with string. 'Here's a fat quarter bundle. It's themed so that each material complements the other,' she added, freeing the fabric from the string and separating them out. 'See how they work together?'

There was a pale blue fabric with angels printed on, another fabric in white depicting holly berries and ivy leaves, a forest green with Father Christmases on sleighs containing coloured gift parcels and gold bells dotted across. And when Carrie unfolded the fabric in pine green with large white snowflakes interspersed with red, white and green candy canes all tied with delicate gold bows, Fern stepped out from behind the ironing board.

'He'll love having that design in the quilt.' Her sisters didn't seem to understand why and Carrie certainly wouldn't. 'Ginny and Daisy were little but accepted we didn't eat candy canes . . . ever,' she added dramatically, hands up, fingers spread wide.

'Why not?' Carrie asked. 'Not that I like them. I had one last year and it was like wiping a stick of sugar around my teeth.'

Fern smiled. 'Grandad broke two teeth on a candy cane, and from that moment on he declared them "lethal" and that was that.'

'It's no big loss,' said Daisy. 'You're right, Carrie. They *are* like sucking on a big bit of sugar.'

'Pretty on the fabric though,' Ginny concluded, back to the task in hand. 'What about sashing, Mum?' Ginny wanted to know.

Loretta went and retrieved three more rolls of material from the cupboard in the hallway. 'I brought these home from the shop, so it's up to you, girls.' There was a white fabric, a soft green, a vibrant red.

'I might be able to answer if I actually knew what sashing was.' Fern grimaced igniting a giggle from Carrie.

Ginny explained, 'You have all your blocks, your pieces, in whatever designs we do, and the sashing will bring all those parts of the quilt together and make it pop.'

'Yeah, still no idea,' Fern concluded.

Ginny grabbed a piece of paper and a pencil and began to sketch it out, a rectangle and then squares across it and down. She pointed to the areas between the squares. 'This will be what we call sashing. It kind of separates the blocks, I suppose, but also brings the whole thing together, does that make sense?'

Carrie said that it did. Fern merely shrugged. Whatever it was sounded good and she'd let her sister lead the way if she thought it was best.

Ginny pointed to the outer area of her sketch and then one closer to the blocks. 'This is the outer border, then the inner border, and at the very outside, of course, we have the binding, which is the strip on the very edge.' She picked up the white fabric and the berry red that Loretta had just shown them. 'How about a strip of the snowy white and at the end of the strip a square of the red. The red will almost look like little quilted squares when the sashing is fixed on. Then I think a red backing for the quilt would be perfect, and it's more forgiving than white.'

'You really have thought about this,' said Fern. She had wondered whether Daisy would be put out, given she was the one in the shop every day and doing this sort of thing more than either of her sisters, but she looked just as content as Fern with the way things were playing out. 'May I ask why don't we just sew all the squares together?'

'That's one way of doing it,' said Loretta. 'Would you rather do it that way, Fern?'

Fern clasped a hand against her chest and laughed. 'Don't ask me, I don't want it ruined.'

Carrie dismissed the suggestion she get involved in the decision making. 'Both ways sound good to me.'

'I tell you what,' said Loretta, 'make the squares, lay them all out and then decide whether we want sashing or not.'

But Ginny was more decisive. 'The pieces are going to be so different we'll need sashing to bring it all together. And the snowy white will make the other fabrics shine.'

Fern wasn't going to suggest differently and they pressed on.

Carrie looked at the collection of blocks they'd made so far, piled up on the table. 'What happens when we have enough?'

'Then we lay them out how we want them,' said Ginny, 'and after that we pin them all together and, using a sewing machine, fix them together properly. After that we add the batting, which is the layer of insulation between the fabrics, if you like, and it makes the quilt warm and heavy. We add the backing as the third layer, pin all three together, and then it's back to the machine again.'

Daisy had finished working on a block of material covered in images of thimbles, balls of wool, a sewing machine and a mannequin. She picked it up along with a piece of plain red material and lay them next to each other.

'I hope I don't mess any of this up,' said Carrie. She seemed to waver between being a part of it and realising she was an outsider and panicking that she wasn't doing things right.

Ginny stopped measuring the fabric she was going to use. 'Grandad will love it all, I guarantee you. Quilting is about so much more than perfection.' She reflected on their quilts upstairs.

'She's right,' said Fern. And she had an idea. She went

upstairs and came back with her childhood quilt, she held it high in the air and from behind the material said, 'Look at the denim square with lace.' She waited a while and then when Carrie announced she'd found it, Fern leaned her head around the quilt and declared, 'The most terrible example of needlework, I think you'll agree. I got so flustered with that square, insistent I fixed the lace on so there was no danger of it falling off – it came from one of my grandmother's dresses – that I used way more stitches than it really needed. It shows, but Mum never fixed it up, because it didn't need mending just because it wasn't perfect.' Fern gulped, thinking of her conversation with her mum after dinner, and when she looked at Loretta she realised her mum was thinking the same.

How had it taken Fern so long to see what was so obvious?

Ginny added, 'If the quilt was perfectly stitched Fern might not remember how much that piece of lace meant to her. The way it is, still, has a strong memory attached at her determination to never let it fall apart.'

'Relax,' Daisy told Carrie. 'Messing the quilt up is pretty much impossible.' She picked up another container. 'Don't forget we have these stencils. There are some good shapes in here.' She indicated that Carrie should go ahead and rummage. 'You can add buttons, ribbon, whatever you can find. Although not too girlie, this is Ivor we're talking about.'

Carrie pulled out a stencil of a gingerbread man. 'Does he like gingerbread?' she asked.

Ginny gave a whoop of joy and grabbed a piece of shiny bronzed fabric. 'Use this, and he loves gingerbread men. In fact –' she nudged Carrie '– Fern was once the gingerbread queen. All of us, especially Grandad, devoured her gingerbread.'

Daisy shared with Carrie how Fern had bought gingerbread men from the Lantern Bakery every day for a month.

Fern felt herself flush. 'I wanted to recreate the recipe myself, at home.'

'You should make some this Christmas,' Ginny suggested.

'I wouldn't even have the recipe,' said Fern. 'And I'd need it because it took forever to perfect.'

'You did experiment,' said Ginny with a grin. 'And we did eat, oh yes, did we eat.'

'There were no complaints from me,' Daisy called over her shoulder before turning back to the table and concentrating on running the rotary cutter along a piece of material to make a triangle she was teaming with the other two pieces she'd already cut to size. 'Come on, Fern, you must. Carrie hasn't tried them yet.'

Carrie smiled over at her as Fern recited all the little tips and tricks to get the gingerbread just right. 'You mustn't over-beat the sugar and the butter, you shouldn't over-knead the dough once it is formed. Then there's how long to let the dough rest before cutting the shapes, whether it should be rested in the fridge overnight.'

Could she still remember how to make them if she really put her mind to it?

'They were soft on the inside and crisp on the outside,' Ginny recalled as she cut out the snowman she'd stencilled onto a piece of white fabric. The black silky scrap was beside her knee ready to cut and use to sew on a hat and buttons. 'And now my mouth is watering.'

'Mine too.' Carrie smiled.

Fern waited for her turn to use the quilt measurer and scissors and as she waited, knowing she'd check her measurements three times, as twice didn't seem enough for her, she watched Daisy and Carrie getting stuck in with designs, Ginny's look of concentration as she focused on her own work. Loretta was sitting on the same sofa Fern had cuddled up on with her sisters and their dad on movie night. It was still in the same place it had always been, its upholstery tired but loveable. The coffee table they'd moved aside still had the dent in one of its legs where Daisy had once rammed her little trolley filled with wooden blocks as a kid. One of the tiles on the fireplace surround had a chip Fern had made when she'd accidentally knocked it with the poker one evening as she got the fire going in the open grate.

Fern would've given anything for her dad to be there with them right now, sitting with his newspaper, pretending to read but really watching his girls pulling together something that would certainly be colourful. Something special, something to treasure.

Chapter Sixteen

Ginny

Working on the quilt for Grandad last night had been surreal. Ginny had become absorbed in the task, more than she'd thought she would, as though being together and doing this for a member of the family was all the permission she needed to go back to the one thing she'd adored as a child, a teen and then an adult.

Ginny had loved everything about needlework and quilting growing up but then, seeing Fern make her own way independent of the family business, had triggered something inside of her. Ginny had always been independent too and hadn't been sure she wanted to take on the shop, and so she'd found midwifery, a joy helping people and a career she had a passion for. It was only when Daisy took on the responsibility of the shop with Loretta that Ginny had realised she might well have wanted it deep down. But by then she felt her path had already been set and she'd done what she always did – she didn't make a fuss, she got on with the choices she'd made. When her mum had asked her where she was travelling to next and then whether she'd consider coming back to Butterbury, Ginny had almost admitted that she would love nothing more. But could it ever happen? Could she really make a life back here now after all this time?

With lunch with Grandad on the agenda today, Ginny had already worked on another quilt block for Ivor's gift and she decided to get outside for a long walk while she had a chance.

Butterbury held her in its winter embrace as she made her way towards Lantern Square. Frost clung to branches, lined the tops of walls and the odd patch on the pavement, yet something about this village warmed her right through.

She bought a churros from the takeaway cart set up in Lantern Square run by sisters Annie and Ellen. It sold doughnuts too, and the sweet treats scented the air, drawing in customers unable to resist.

Ginny had just taken a big bite of churros when she heard a thick, velvety voice behind her.

'I hope you dipped that in chocolate.' She turned to see Lucas, the collar of his donkey jacket turned up as the wind lifted around them, sending stray leaves scuttling across the concrete paths and onto the green spaces, into the flowerbeds.

She finished her mouthful. 'Of course.'

He reached out and ran his finger across part of her bottom lip and smiled when he held it up to show her he'd wiped away the tell-tale signs of the sweet treat. Eyes, soft brown like a liquid caramel, refused to look away. 'You always did like your chocolate.'

She was still frozen in place at the way he'd reached out and touched her as though they still did that sort of thing all the time. 'Who doesn't?' Her voice wasn't much more than a whisper as she saw him register his over familiarity too and they stepped out of the way of others queuing.

She tried hard to squash down the jittery feeling his touch had given her so unexpectedly, the conjuring up of memories of the heady days when they'd first got together, when even holding hands had ignited a spark that had the power to make her feel dizzy.

He fished in his pockets and pulled out some cash before he joined the back of the queue at the cart. 'You've done it now, I can't resist. I'd hate you to feel like you had to offer me any of yours.'

'Not a chance,' she smiled.

When he joined her and she'd almost finished her churros while he began his, she asked why he wasn't working today.

'I am, but this is my break. I started at five this morning.'

'Wow, that's early.'

'It's not uncommon.' He bit into his churros and groaned with pleasure. 'There's always something that needs doing. This time it was the heating in the greenhouse – it went on the blink so I was fixing that first thing.'

'You always were good with your hands.' She realised she'd voiced that out loud but there was no way to backtrack. 'You know what I mean.'

He was honourable enough not to make her feel any more uncomfortable than she already did and simply smiled at her remark. And as he talked about the farm and what his days involved, she watched him. At well over six foot Lucas had always been what her mum had called a gentle giant. He'd shot up in high school well before anyone else, something that gave him the ability to see to the ends of the corridors at school over the sea of heads bobbing along and warn when a teacher might be coming their way. The skill had come in handy as a teen too. He and Ginny had gone to Glastonbury one year and he'd been able to see over the heads of the crowd right to the stage, something nobody else in their group had been able to boast about, and as an adult he said it ensured he did his bit for the community because he was frequently asked, when in a shop, to reach items from the highest shelves.

Ginny balled up her napkin and pushed it into the nearest bin, putting her hands straight into her pockets afterwards. 'Do you think it'll snow this year?'

He was a much quicker eater than her and when he'd finished his final mouthful he got rid of his napkin in the same way. 'I hope so. There's nothing like Butterbury with a covering of snow.' They'd begun to walk away from the cart, along a pathway in the square, and he indicated the bench.

'I think I'll get too cold if I sit still,' she told him, although she really didn't want to say no. She'd avoided him for so long that at times like this she wondered why. There was a familiarity, a warmth that came from being near him, the man she'd thought was in her past and never likely to move back to her present ever again.

'How about I get us each a hot chocolate?'

She didn't answer, she didn't need to, the agreement was unspoken and so she sat down on the bench before anyone else thought to do it first.

Once he'd handed her the hot chocolate and it was clasped between her gloved palms warming them through, she asked him more about the family business and she could sense the passion oozing in his veins when he talked about the physical labour, the organisation of it all, the different produce, growing and harvesting schedules. It was hard to believe this man had ever thought of doing anything else.

'Do you ever clash as a family?' She wanted to know more about his life. It was as though somebody somewhere had hit a pause button between them and this year it was begging to be released.

'We get on well . . . most of the time.' His forearms rested on sturdy thighs, his cup between his palms. 'The way I see it is you might not get on with your boss no matter who they are, but when it's family, you have this obligation to make peace at the end of the day no matter your grievances.'

'You're right, but that makes it tough sometimes.'

'Sure does. I'll bet Daisy and Loretta clash.'

Ginny laughed. 'All the time apparently. Mum often complains in our phone calls, but it's only ever about little things, like Daisy texting on her phone, or leaving the dirty mugs in the sink and forgetting about them, nothing huge.' When Daisy had first taken on working in the shop Ginny had predicted she and their mother would fall out big time. Ginny had had visions of Loretta calling her to say she simply couldn't do it anymore. But it was as though Daisy had adopted a determination so fierce that she never strayed from the boundaries. Ginny wasn't so sure that was the best thing for her little sister who had always been so free-spirited, at least right up until a year or so before their dad died, when everything had changed and she went off the rails.

'Mostly we work well,' Lucas went on. 'We share the jobs around, the good and the bad – you know how I always hated paperwork, but I accept it's a part of the job so I'll do it. Dad's always saying "big red bus".'

'What does that mean?'

'He says we all need to know each facet of the job in case one day one of us is hit by a big red bus.'

'Sounds a little morbid, and I don't see many big red buses in Butterbury.' She grinned. 'But I kind of see his point.' Her hands were toasty warm by now on the half-drunk cup of hot chocolate. 'Do you ever think about what life might have been like if you'd carried on with marine biology, the diving you loved?'

He leaned back against the bench and looked at her honestly. 'Sometimes.' She got the impression he didn't admit that to many people. 'But that's human nature, isn't it? To wonder what might've been.'

'You could've been still living in Florida.'

'Away from the cold?' he said with a shiver she wasn't sure was completely put on. 'How could I give all this up?'

'I like a bit of winter, it's pretty on days like today.'

They let the words settle between them until Lucas spoke up. She wondered if he had been wanting to say it for a while when he told her, 'I'm sorry I hurt you when I left.'

Addressing it after all this time took her by surprise. She hesitated, wanting to express herself the way she needed to. 'You were right to go.' He looked shocked. 'I wasn't in a position to go with you, so you did what was best for us both.'

'I never—'

'You never expected me to say that?' He shook his head. 'I'm just glad you were by my side when Dad died, you were there for me, and I'll never forget that.'

After her dad died Ginny had found it hard to compartmentalise things in her life. There didn't seem to be room for anything other than her career and her own survival, and even though it had been Lucas's decision ultimately to break up, she'd known deep down that it was the right thing to do. She was in a strange place, on some days she didn't think she deserved happiness, her head was a mess and she hadn't the time to think of anyone else. And she hadn't wanted to inflict her misery on Lucas, she wanted him to live his dream, whatever that might be.

'Florida was one of the best experiences I've ever had,' he confessed. 'All that sunshine, the ocean, the surfing, the diving. It was a freedom I can't explain. And I loved it. Travelling is an adventure, right?'

'I'm glad I've been able to do so much.' It didn't matter whether she'd avoided him on her visits home, Butterbury was small enough that he would've heard about her travels, from his parents, brother, or her family.

'The word adventure takes on different meanings over time.' He turned so his body was almost facing her and suddenly he felt so much closer. 'I'll never regret studying marine biology or moving to Florida for a while, but I reached a point where I saw my next adventure as the family business. I wasn't obligated to take it on, you know that as well as I do. I was encouraged by my parents to go and do something else, as was Joshua. Maybe part of their thinking was that by urging us to do so to ensured we saw a different life so that we would know 100 per cent what we wanted. Joshua did his management degree but like me, he ended up still wanting the farm even after leaving it behind for a while.'

'I'll bet your parents were pleased.'

'Actually, they really were.' He held her gaze. And it seemed he didn't want to talk about him, the farm, or his family. 'I knew you were hurting over your dad and I knew you were in a place I couldn't reach. On some days you were so distant I thought I'd lost you. Perhaps it was cowardice on my part, ending it before you did.'

'I never thought of it that way.' With so much serious-ness she moved the conversation on. 'Do you think you and Joshua will fight over who gets the farm in the years to come?'

He shook his head. 'I think we both quickly under-stood we both want it so it'll be a joint venture. I'm happy with that.' They both smiled at Annie who walked past to take a bag of doughnuts over to a family at the bench opposite. 'What about you three? Ever think you, Daisy and Fern will run the shop together?'

'Could you see us doing that?' She liked the way he was smiling at her, showing he knew her and her family on a deeper level. 'Fern would go crazy and she'd be sitting in one of the upstairs rooms studying the figures constantly, then bossing us about telling us we had to this, that and the other to increase turnover. Daisy would hate being ruled by Fern after Mum treating her as more of an equal.'

He nudged her. 'You didn't mention yourself in the equation.' And when she said nothing he carried on. 'I always thought you'd be the one to take on the shop.'

'You and me both,' she sighed. All three sisters had worked on quilts together but it was Ginny who'd lost herself in the task, she who carried on long after her sisters finished up on the days they'd sit together. Ginny would take material to her bedroom and she'd make things on her pink sewing machine. Her blue and white cushions were still on the sofa in the kitchen, the hand-stitched teddy bear still dangled from her mum's house keys, the rainbow-coloured hot water bottle cover she'd made was still in the cupboard in the utility room, a little frayed, but ready for when she needed it.

'Even though I ended things, I still wanted you, Ginny.' He looked at his polystyrene cup, his declaration out in the cold open air. 'This hot chocolate must be making me way too honest.'

'Chocolate does have magical powers.' The fluttering she'd felt when they first started dating had settled over time but it was as though his words awakened those feelings all over again.

He couldn't take his eyes off her now. 'You seem happy. Are you?'

She shifted uncomfortably. 'I'm fine.' Did he mean here in Butterbury? Being with her family? With her job and her travels? Or was he asking whether she was happy to be with him after all this time?

Instead of asking she got up from the bench. 'I'd better keep walking, this is my only chance of freedom before lunch with Grandad.' And after that she'd be hard at work on their quilting project.

When her phone buzzed she pulled it out to find a text from Fern who asked whether she'd have a chance to grab some cranberry sauce because she'd already left the shops and had totally forgotten to get any. Ginny almost looked to see whether Fern was watching her standing here with Lucas.

'What's up?' Lucas enquired.

'Nothing, it's just Fern letting me know about picking something up for lunch.' But her grin gave it away that it was more than that. 'Apparently she forgot the cranberry sauce.'

'She must know I make it up at the farm.'

'Of course she does.'

Lucas pretended to look over Ginny's shoulder, first one and then the other. 'Where is she? Is she watching?'

Ginny laughed. 'Exactly what I wondered. I wouldn't put it past her.'

'So how about it? You could head up to the farm with me now.'

She held his gaze. 'I suppose I could.' And she tilted her head in the direction of the path that led them out of the square.

As they walked, Lucas turned the conversation back to her family. 'Your mum mentioned that this is the longest you three have all been home together for a while. Certainly for Christmas. Why the change this year?'

'I'm not entirely sure. Mum summoned us home, she's starting to worry it might be Grandad's last Christmas.' A lit-up squirrel in the flowerbed looked up at her as they passed the end of the square and crossed the road.

'He's not sick is he?'

'No, he seems fine. More than fine actually.' Lucas and Grandad had always got on well. Lucas had taken him fruit and vegetables at the end of the day twice a week long after he and Ginny split up. 'Fern and I think Mum might be hiding something.'

'Your grandad would tell you if he was sick,' Lucas reassured her.

'I happen to think you're right.'

He surprised her by reaching out a finger and touching her forehead briefly as they walked. 'Then why the frown?'

She tried not to make it obvious the effect his touch had on her, the same it had when she'd got chocolate on her lip. It was as though he couldn't stop doing it and she found herself not minding in the slightest. 'I'm worried Daisy might be up to something too. She seems to spend a lot of time up at the lodge.'

'You don't think she's going where she says she is?'

Ginny frowned. 'Well no, I think she's there, but . . . Oh I don't know, maybe I'm reading too much into it.'

'She was always wild, your sister. But . . .'

'So you think I should trust her, let her be an adult?'

He shrugged. 'She's a lot calmer these days. I don't know if hearing that from me helps you or not.'

He'd always been able to reassure her, be a voice of reason. 'Actually it does.' Perhaps it was time to give Daisy the benefit of the doubt, something neither she nor Fern had managed in a long time. 'It's probably nothing.' It was more likely that she was on high alert just waiting for something to go wrong.

As they reached the farm gates she felt a rush of nostalgia. 'I'd forgotten how beautiful this place is.'

'Florida had its blue skies but you can't beat the British countryside, no matter what time of the year it is.'

Beneath the clouds and despite the lack of sunshine to highlight its best features, the farmland spread out before them, the dips of the undulating land took your mind on adventures and the sound of farm equipment or voices calling out were all a part of it.

Lucas pulled his key out of his jeans pocket as they neared the farmhouse and nodded over at his dad who waved at him and Ginny. If he was surprised to see Ginny up here after all this time he didn't show it. He just took her presence in his stride. He was one of those men who'd found his place in life and drew happiness from those around him. She'd not seen it before but Lucas appeared to have fallen into the same role after all this time. Perhaps his parents had been onto something sending their sons away to see what another side of life was like. And perhaps getting away from the shop and Butterbury had worked in the same way for her.

Lucas's mum was less reserved and beamed at Ginny before racing over to kiss her on both cheeks. Her own cheeks were rosy in the cold and she wore a purple beanie on her head and matching fingerless gloves. She told her son they were down to their last twelve jars of cranberry sauce.

'That's what I've come for,' Ginny confessed.

'Everything's weighed out in the kitchen, cranberries are washed and ready to go. Make some more, would you, Lucas?' she said before squeezing Ginny's arm and hurrying back to the shop.

'Shouldn't I grab a jar now before they sell out?'

'I've got a few inside, you can have one of those.'

When they stepped into the kitchen Ginny was enveloped in a feeling she hadn't expected after all this time, a feeling of belonging that emanated from the walls of the home she'd been in more times than she could remember. What with the Christmas tree already in situ in the corner, the smell of lemons from the bowl on the side nearest the door, and the sounds of a busy farm beyond the windows, this place had always had a way of drawing you into its heart.

Lucas wasn't in any rush to find her a jar of sauce and instead took out some orange juice from the fridge to add to the line-up of other ingredients – brown sugar, white sugar, a colander filled with cranberries.

'Watch, and learn.' He pushed up the sleeves of a denim-blue shirt to expose strong forearms and hands she remembered touching her in a way that would make even the reddest cranberry blush.

Lucas turned on the heat beneath a pan and threw in the sugars, some water and the orange juice. Ginny joined him and took the spoon to stir it all while he made sure the cranberries were definitely as good as his mum had claimed. 'My reputation is on the line,' he said when he saw her watching what he was doing. He looked so serious she thought he meant it until his expression creased into a smile.

As she stirred the pot, Ginny thought about some of the things Lucas had done for her over the years when they were together – the time they went sledging in the fields near Butterbury and he bought her handwarmers for her gloves because she hated it when her gloves got wet and her skin turned red. Or the day he'd turned up to see her on her birthday even though getting there from his university had meant a long and uncomfortable coach ride for the sake of one day, after which he'd had to get up in the middle of the night to go back ready for a test. It was her first birthday without her dad and he'd gone to all that effort to make sure she didn't spend it alone.

'Penny for them?' he asked.

As she reminisced she'd gone into a daze stirring the dissolving sugars but she wasn't about to share her thoughts out loud, the way she remembered how kind he was, how gentle and thoughtful, how she wondered whether she'd been crazy to ever let him go. 'I was just wondering . . . what made you Mr Cranberry Sauce?' she said, glossing over what had really been going through her mind.

He went over to one of the wider cupboards to find the ramekins to pour the sauce into while it cooled down. 'I should get a T-shirt made with that caption.' He brought back eight ramekins, all nestled in his strong palms, and slotted them onto the worktop before setting them out one by one. 'The task fell to me the first year I was home for Christmas. Mum had the flu, Dad took charge of the turkey, I went for the cranberry sauce. Can't remember why now but after that I offered to make it in bulk, put it in jars, and we could sell it around Christmas time.'

He leaned closer, his breath on her cheek as he said, 'Time to throw in the cranberries.' He did the honours now the mixture was bubbling and took over the stirring.

She peered into the pan to see the berries slowly disappearing. 'I hope you don't mind me saying but it's a bit thin.'

'You're trying to tell me how to make my own cranberry sauce?'

'Well when you put it that way . . .'

He lifted out a spoonful. 'Blow on it first, then tell me what you think of the taste.'

Conscious he was watching her lips as she blew gently across the mixture on the spoon she tentatively let the flavours explode on her tongue and nodded her approval. It was sweet but not overly so, with the right balance of the fruit coming through.

'It'll thicken up once it cools.' He poured it into the awaiting ramekins. 'Then before it gets too thick I'll put it into the jars and pop it into the fridge to finish setting.'

He went over to the fridge and took out a jar. 'For you.' When he handed it to her his fingertips ran across part of her palm and she shivered.

'We're making sliders.'

Puzzlement crossed his face. 'Sliders?'

'For lunch, today I mean. That's what this is for.' She stumbled over her words, holding out the jar he'd just given her. One minute she was relaxed in his company, the next she remembered they weren't the Lucas and Ginny from all those years ago.

'Well I've not had it with sliders but I'm sure they'll be good. I hope you like it.'

'I'd better go.' She debated grabbing her coat first or putting down the jar first and eventually did the latter. And once her scarf was looped around her neck, she held the jar up again and escaped out of the farmhouse into the cold.

'It was good to spend time with you, Ginny.' When she turned back to face him his body filled the doorway, his arm reaching to the top of the frame resting on it casually. 'Send my regards to your grandad, I'll pop in again soon.'

'Will do, and thank you for the cranberry sauce.' And she rushed away, only daring to take a breath once she turned out of the driveway and onto the pavement of the main road.

'You girls have spoiled me rotten,' said Ivor. 'And I love every second of it.'

They were sitting in the residents' lounge and the spread the girls had brought along with them – including the delicious cranberry sauce from the Abneys' farm – had tongues wagging and envious comments coming their way, much to Ivor's amusement.

'You're lucky to have such good friends here, Grandad.' Fern smiled.

'I am indeed. And at my age making new friends is a hard thing to do.'

'Were you worried about coming here and not knowing a soul?' Ginny asked.

'Not worried. A little anxious maybe, but mostly excited. Your mother wanted me to go and live with her but that wouldn't be right.'

'We might've had fun,' Daisy protested.

'That's as maybe, but no. Loretta has her own life, although she could do with getting out and about a bit more.'

Fern laughed. 'I dare you to say that to her.'

'Don't you worry, I have and I will continue to do so. After your dad died she never dated anyone, and that is very sad.'

Ginny hadn't ever thought much about it before. 'Did you date anyone after Gran?' she wondered.

'I didn't, but I was much older than your mum when I lost Rebecca.' He sighed. 'But I suppose I can understand it with Loretta. Like me, she had the love of her life in Harry.'

Ginny smiled, understanding, so did Fern. But when Ginny happened to glance Daisy's way their younger sister had a totally different expression on her face. There was doubt there, suspicion, Ginny wasn't sure quite how to take it. Had Loretta found someone else, perhaps? Was that what Daisy knew and hadn't shared?

'You don't think she's happy?' Fern asked.

'She's content, and that's a good thing. But now and again, try and persuade her to do something different, would you?' He was looking at each of them and they all nodded or murmured their assent. 'That sewing shop was my own mother's true love alongside my father, then it became mine and Rebecca's, but it's different when Loretta has nobody at her side. It breaks my heart to see her lonely.'

Maggie brought around cups of tea and they settled into more chatter before Daisy announced she'd have to get going back to the shop. Before Daisy left she shared a hushed conversation with a man who'd passed her in the doorway but when Ginny remembered how Lucas had told her that her younger sister had calmed down a lot, Ginny turned away rather than scrutinising Daisy's every move. It was time to let Daisy be an adult, to not worry about her without good reason.

After another hour up at the lodge Ginny and Fern left Grandad with Flo for company.

'What do you think is going on with Daisy?' Ginny asked as Fern shut the little wooden gate at the front of the path to the lodge and they made their way down the hill back into Butterbury and towards Lantern Square. 'Did you see the way she reacted when Grandad talked about Mum and Dad and how in love they were?'

Fern shook her head. 'I can't say I did, no.'

'You don't think . . . you don't think Mum has a boyfriend, do you, and that's why Daisy is acting so weirdly?'

Fern's coat, long and business-like, flapped until she did the rest of the buttons up. 'I don't think so, like Grandad says, Mum is always at the shop. It would be impossible to have a secret lover without us finding out.'

'Unless he went to ground because we're here and she's waiting to tell us.'

Fern seemed to be thinking about it. 'I don't know. Maybe.'

A moment passed between them. 'Actually, I don't think that's what it is,' said Ginny. 'But we can't confront Daisy because she'd think we're ganging up on her.' There was a fine line between taking an interest and interfering.

'You're right.'

'Where do you think she's been going when she nips out?'

'You've noticed it too?'

'I have, and so has Mum, although she seems to have something else on her mind, something that clearly takes priority and isn't allowing her to question Daisy. There was a time when she would've simply asked her outright.' It was true. Loretta hadn't tiptoed around the youngest sibling when she had gone through a phase of getting into trouble – drinking stupid amounts, staying out beyond curfew, answering back, skipping school. After it all came to a climax Loretta had been on top of it. She'd not let her youngest daughter leave the house unless she knew where she was going, who she was with. And after that Daisy hadn't dared to come home late or do anything that strayed beyond normal behaviour. Dad had died soon after and Daisy, to her credit, had pulled herself together from that moment on, enough to not repeat her behaviour.

'We should trust Daisy for once.' Fern smiled at Ginny's inability to hide her shock. 'Well we did agree to try.'

'We did.'

'Maybe it's being a mum that has made me see things a little differently. Motherhood is hard work mentally as much as anything else – trying to second guess hidden meanings, gauge moods, manage children by saying the right thing and knowing when to keep quiet. Half the time I think I do a terrible job so I can't criticise Mum for how she is with Daisy, or how she is with anyone for that matter.'

It was rare for Fern to open up let alone admit to anything less than perfection. 'I doubt you're doing a crap job.' But when her sister sighed again Ginny realised how tired she looked, even when she appeared so together on the surface.

'In order to keep the peace I think we should stay out of it, at least for now. I know I've bossed her around – I bossed you about too, over the years. She's obviously a grown woman and perfectly capable, so perhaps I need to readjust my thinking and stop assuming she isn't.'

Two admissions from Fern that she was less than perfect, in under ten minutes? This wasn't like her at all. 'We need to forgive her too.'

Fern didn't have to ask what for. 'I have already.'

'That's good, but Daisy doesn't realise we have.' And neither of them knew what to do about that. 'We gave her hell back then.'

Fern winced. 'It came from a place of pain, that's why. It was about losing Dad, something else taken away. It was about so much more than a missing quilt.'

Their dad had sat with his daughters every Sunday night for movie night – pyjamas, popcorn and pillows, the three p's he'd called it. One Sunday afternoon after he came home from a run and they'd been sitting with their mum in a circle, pulling together pieces of material for another project and talking about what to make next, he'd suggested they make a movie quilt for their movie nights. Daisy had said they'd never have it ready in three hours. They'd all laughed and said it wasn't necessarily for that night. But they'd all fallen in love with the idea and so they'd made a start and in the weeks afterwards the sisters had committed their time to the task. They'd worked on it when they came home from school, they'd carried on at weekends, their dad supervising when Loretta was at the shop and laughing at his own inability to stitch anywhere near as well as his girls. But what he lacked in skill he made up for in enthusiasm. He'd had the idea to have each of their names embroidered onto a block in their favourite colour – lilac for Fern and her name stitched in white, emerald green for Ginny with her name stitched in gold, red for Daisy with her name stitched in bright yellow like the centre of the flower. Between them they'd decided on the other blocks – some in solid colours, others with favourite patterns, and each of them had selected one that related to their favourite book. Loretta had ordered a lot of fabric into the shop to specifically make kids' book-themed quilts and so they had their choice of material – Fern chose the one peppered with characters from *Alice in Wonderland*, her favourite when she was really little and before she moved on to more teenage reads, Ginny had opted for a Peter Rabbit design, the first book she'd been given as a gift one year and still treasured. Daisy had been a good reader from a very early age and although not quite up to speed reading the story herself had loved *Charlotte's Web* and so her choice of block was in a fabric covered with Wilbur and picket fences, spiders hanging from their webs. Fern always insisted that block of the quilt was never near her when they sat in a row, all four of them, for movie night, as if the spiders might actually be real.

Their project was a success and by the end of it they had a quilt the size suited to fit over a double bed and plenty big enough to cover their laps as they sat in a row on the sofa to watch a movie. Fern was much older than Daisy by then but none of them cared about age difference, Fern was always happy with a Disney movie, because it was about so much more than the film. They'd spend all of Sunday with their mother and she'd have Sunday nights to herself with a long, luxurious bubble bath while their dad took over with his daughters. The quilt had remained special to all three of the Chamberlain sisters. And when Daisy got into trouble one thing led to another and they never saw it again.

'Grandad loved today,' Fern smiled as they walked past Lantern Square to head for home. 'And he's going to love his Christmas quilt.'

Ginny couldn't agree more but she was distracted when she spotted Lucas coming out of the post office. She upped her pace before her sister said hello to him, or worse, picked up on how uncomfortable Ginny felt around him.

Fern made an impromptu move, taking Ginny by surprise by linking her arm through Ginny's. 'This is nice, chatting properly.' But she hadn't finished. 'And don't think I didn't spot Lucas. He's so interested in you it's not funny. He's still single, by the way. You know, if you were wondering. It's my big-sister duty to know these things. And I've subtly been asking around town about the Abney boys.'

'You're shocking, you know that.' But Ginny was grinning. She couldn't deny it. Her feelings for Lucas Abney were still there and it would be easy to fall in love with him all over again.

The question was, did they really have a future together?

Chapter Seventeen

Daisy

'Are these a gift?' Doris, the owner of the bookshop, admired the two books Daisy had arrived to collect – the latest Agatha Raisin mystery in hardback, and a beautiful book about the history of quilting. 'Must be for the family.' She smiled knowingly.

'They're both for Grandad. He's addicted to the Agatha Raisin stories and you know what he's like when it comes to quilting.'

'I wish my husband could take an interest.' Doris shook her head and rang the order up on the till. 'He has me sew on a button if it falls off, fix a cuff if the seam unravels, turn up trousers that are too long.'

'Well send him our way or to Miriam's haberdashery if you get tired of doing the repairs.'

'I probably should.'

Daisy put the books into her bag, looking over at the man in red by the far wall and a line of excited kids queuing up for their turn. She fondly remembered the times they'd come here as girls and done the same.

Butterbury's bookshop was bigger than most in the other little surrounding villages, they were lucky. It had been two buildings that were knocked into one and with a lot of floor space, which meant a lot of choice. But Daisy went straight for the section she really wanted to check out.

The photography section.

She flipped through a book about using lighting techniques to your advantage. She found a book filled with photographs from Egypt with each one reviewed to detail what had worked and what could be improved. And the minute the oversized upholstered patchwork chair in the corner became vacant she took a book about twilight photography and sat down to devour it. Even though she knew she was going to buy it, she wanted to look at it there and then, with nothing else to demand her attention.

Daisy had been sitting for some time and only looked up once when Father Christmas walked past and winked at her.

She felt like she was five years old all over again the way she giggled.

Daisy took the book to the counter where Doris was taking a phone call. After Doris had hung up, her murmurs of *oh no,* and *but what am I going to do?* had Daisy concerned. 'Everything all right?'

'Not really,' Doris sighed. 'I had this whole promotion thing planned with the local newspaper. They were sending a photographer to take pictures of Father Christmas and the kids as well as the bookshop and it was going to feature in a week or so. It would've drummed up a lot of business.' She leaned in conspiratorially. 'I don't mind telling you that the kids' story corner makes up a huge proportion of our sales at this time of the year. Parents spend a lot on their offspring when it comes to books – something I wholly approve of – but I need publicity every now and then to remind people we exist. Many don't realise the stock we have here in a quiet Cotswold village and they go to the bigger retailers or order online.'

'What happened with the local newspaper? Did they cancel?'

'Their photographer has come down with a tummy bug so the journalist can do the write-up but without the pictures, it's not the same. They don't have anyone else as they're all on other assignments.' Doris sighed. 'She's coming by in half an hour to do the story anyway, the photographer will be at a later date, which means we might miss the Christmas peak period.' She picked up a pile of brightly coloured books and shook her head. 'Nothing I can do.'

'Wait,' said Daisy before Doris could head over to the children's section. 'I'm not bad with a camera.'

Doris's brain seemed to register the purchase Daisy had just made. 'That's true, and I have seen you around Butterbury taking pictures.' She lowered her voice again. 'They selected this particular photographer because he had experience working with kids.' Daisy had to lean in when she whispered, 'Between you and me, they can apparently be a little difficult.'

'I'm sure I could handle it.'

'Oh Daisy, it's a big ask, and I couldn't take you away from your own job.'

Daisy was surprised by how much she wanted to do this. 'Why don't I go to the shop and check with Mum that she can spare me for a couple of hours, grab my camera from home and come back. I'll take the photos while the journalist does her observations and makes notes, interviews you and whatever else she's going to do, and then if you don't like the pictures I've taken and she has no interest in them either, no harm done at all. The professional can come whenever and the newspaper coverage will still happen.'

Doris pulled her against her ample bosom and squeezed her tight. 'Daisy, you're a wonderful girl, a credit to your family.'

'So that's a yes?' She was laughing at the surprise gesture that almost bowled her over.

'Go!' she said with a flourish. 'Go get your camera!'

Loretta had no problems with Daisy helping Doris. The pair had known one another for years and when Daisy told her mum that Doris needed to keep business booming if they all wanted the bookshop to be around in years to come, Loretta hadn't hesitated, especially when Ginny said she could stay and help out in the shop as long as was needed.

Daisy started by taking pictures of the bookshop from the outside, of the bookshop's beautiful mullioned glass and curved bay windows with low lighting, picturesque with the frosted effect Doris had had going since the start of December. In the window on one side of the front entrance was a book tree with colourful spines, on the other was a real tree with book-related ornaments that were on sale inside the shop, and when the pavement was clear of passers-by Daisy got a wonderful wide-angled shot of the frontage in all its splendour.

Inside the shop she put her coat and scarf out at the back and got ready to meet the kids, plenty of whom were swarming with excitement already. She hadn't photographed many children but she had been asked to take the odd picture of grandkids visiting their elderly relatives at Butterbury Lodge – her grandad had volunteered her services more than once – and she'd actually enjoyed the challenge. What she'd found was that she had to throw all the rules about poses out of the window because kids were better in candid, natural shots, and when an adult was around they took a while to act the way kids should act. The trick was to give them some time to get comfortable with your presence, let them ask questions about your camera, settle their curiosity, and once they'd heard enough, got a bit bored of you and moved on to thinking about the next thing, it was time for you to move around freely.

Doris had put a big sign up to say there was a photographer in the shop this afternoon and Daisy could hear her briefing parents who could choose not to have their child included if they preferred, although most were local and more than happy for them to go ahead. As the journalist chatted with Doris, Daisy approached the kids' corner where Father Christmas was sitting with a little boy talking about trains. Two little girls had spotted her and her camera and came straight over. She got down to their height and as a couple of others flocked her way she explained that she wanted to take lots of pictures for Christmas and that an article was going to appear in the newspaper. This made their eyes go wide and they followed her around for a little while, she took their pictures whenever they wanted her to so they could see themselves in the screen on the back. And as predicted their curiosity soon waned and they were back to the book and toy areas.

Daisy captured the nooks in the bookshop and the displays, some with fairy lights strung along the wood.

She doubted the newspaper would want too many photographs with the article but a nice variety was a good idea. Her stomach churned at the thought that this could be real. A photograph of hers might be used for publication. And that was something she hadn't imagined in a very long time. She'd shut the feelings down a long while ago, but showing Joshua all those photographs in the pub that night, having the man at the lodge compliment her on her talent, had stirred up her passion all the more.

Slowly Daisy made her way over to the corner where Father Christmas sat on a huge chair in his red suit teamed with shiny black buckle boots. She was patient with curious kids' questions but managed to get a few really good shots as they had their turn with Father Christmas and when she was done she took her camera over to Doris and the journalist, who was formally introduced as Sally.

'Let's see what you've got?' Sally, also disappointed the photographer couldn't make it, viewed the shots once Daisy rested her camera on the counter, their backs to the rest of the shop. 'I'm not a photographer myself, especially when it comes to children, but I do have an eye for what works.'

Daisy was getting worried when Sally had scrolled through most of them and not said much at all. 'It's fine if they're no good,' Daisy dismissed. 'I just thought I'd try and help.'

Sally began to laugh. 'You're mistaking my silence for something else. These are great!'

'Really?'

'When Doris told me a local volunteered to take some pictures I thought it would be a friend of hers with their phone. I never expected anything like what you've shown me. You've got a real eye for detail. Your subjects are captured perfectly – some of the expressions on the kids' faces are delightful. What about permissions?'

'Doris did inform anyone coming in and I think she may have had them sign a waiver if they don't mind their kids appearing in the media coverage.'

'OK, you're impressing me all the more.' Sally went through the shots again, stopping at any she really liked. 'This one of the little girl is perfect, look at her face as she gazes at Father Christmas, and she's clasping the book, the shelves behind her add a colour that . . . well it works, Daisy. What you've done with all these photographs is helped me to deliver the right message – it's a quaint Cotswold bookshop, has a vast selection of titles, but more than that it's a place to come and enjoy.' She lingered on the picture of two kids squeezed together on the brightly coloured chair, concentrating as they flipped through a book each, with the backdrop of books and twinkly lights. 'Will you send them all to me via email?'

'Of course.' Daisy did her best to sound professional rather than too excited.

'We'll use them, the article should appear in a couple of days.'

Her heart thumped harder and when Doris went back behind the till, Sally pulled a business card from her bag and handed it to Daisy. 'If you're interested in more work as a freelancer, give me a call. We could use someone like you. You have talent and a knack with your subjects. Call me,' she urged before she rushed off and left Daisy standing there open-mouthed.

She turned as Father Christmas appeared behind her. 'Sounds like someone was impressed,' he boomed, nodding to the door where Sally had just exited.

'You don't need to put the voice on for me, you know, I'm a grown adult.' She grinned, because she'd suspected his true identity when she was busy with her camera, and now he was closer she knew for sure. She whispered to him, 'I repaired those trousers myself, remember?'

'I don't know what you're talking about,' he said, his voice still in character, although his eyes danced. 'Mrs Claus sewed up my trousers after I tore them in the workshop trying to get all the presents into the sack.' She saw him do a quick head tilt and she realised there must be a young pair of ears close by.

Daisy clocked the little girl doing her best to surreptitiously eavesdrop. Time to think fast. 'I must be mistaken. They're very much like a pair I worked on recently, although I'm sure Mrs Claus did a much better job than me.' She sneaked off out to the back, leaving Joshua to deal with the kids, and collected her belongings.

She'd just put on her coat and wrapped her scarf around her neck ready to set off for the Butterbury Sewing Box when Joshua came behind the curtain that masked the rear of the bookshop from the customers and pulled down his beard. 'That was a close one, Mrs Claus.'

She prodded his bulging belly, for some reason it was difficult to resist. 'What's it made out of?'

'It's foam and it makes the costume really hot. Kind of a good thing when I'm up at the farm, it's drafty inside the barn, but in here it's a different story. I can't wait to take it all off, to be honest.'

Daisy ignored the flip in her tummy at the thought of

those jockey shorts she'd seen, the muscular thighs. She cleared her throat. 'You're really good with the kids.'

'You seem surprised.' He checked the curtain was still closed and pulled his hat off for a bit of respite, running a hand through the peak of his fringe. 'And you were pretty good with them too, I noticed.'

'They're fun to work with.'

'So you're thinking about the job offer from the journalist?'

'It was hardly a job offer.'

His eyes pinned her to the spot and danced dangerously. 'Yes, it was. The question is whether you're going to go for it?' He didn't look away. 'A photojournalism job in Butterbury . . . next stop the big smoke. You could go to London, hit the big time.'

She was well aware of him standing so close, the way she could see the rise and fall of his breath even beneath the costume. And unsettled by his intuition, how much he had to know she wanted this, she took hold of his beard and lifted it back into position for him, never breaking eye contact. 'We'll see.'

'Doris said you were amazing,' Loretta told Daisy the moment she got back to the Butterbury Sewing Box.

'How would you know?' Daisy hung her coat on a hook.

'Doris called me the minute you left, extolling the virtues of Butterbury's new photographer. May I see the pictures?'

'I dropped my camera in at home, I'll show you later. Where's Ginny?'

'We were quiet so she's gone up to see your grandad.'

As Loretta served a customer, Daisy's mind wandered to Sally's business card that was burning a hole in her purse. She thought about Joshua and how he'd told her she was good at photography, how he didn't seem to harbour any doubt that the job offer was there because of her talent.

She thought too about the way he'd looked at her today, but still not made a move. She'd resisted so long, perhaps he was giving up, but that kiss in the pub must've told him exactly how she felt. Hadn't it?

When Fern and Ginny returned from Butterbury Lodge, Ginny wasted no time settling down on the stool beside the Christmas tree after taking out the block she was working on for Grandad's quilt. Fern leaned against the counter while Loretta rewound a reel of ribbon she'd shown a customer who couldn't decide between the forest green, the lime green and the bottle green. Sometimes the indecisive customers drove Daisy nuts, but she'd learned patience and she certainly hadn't had a problem with tolerance at the book shop today when anyone else might have been tearing their hair out with those kids. Joshua was good with them too, he was a natural.

When Daisy's phone rang she snatched it up seeing it was Maggie from the lodge. They were two nights away from executing their plan for the secret project and she didn't want to blow their cover now.

She took the phone away from the counter and out to the back. Maggie had called to confirm they had all the necessary permissions for the planned activity and that they were all set. She was so excited, she couldn't wait to be a part of it, and she'd arranged the staff rota so they'd be able to bring a minibus of residents into Butterbury at the allotted time and ensure nobody was cold, none of them were unattended, and that they were all safe.

'This is going to be amazing.' Daisy kept her voice low as she talked with Maggie, excitement bubbling away. 'You wait until people see the effects of the bombing.'

And when she heard a shuffling noise behind her she hung up the call and got back to work, avoiding her mum's suspicious gaze or apparent desire to quiz her on what she was up to.

Chapter Eighteen

Loretta

Loretta's heart pounded as she watched her youngest daughter put her phone into the pocket of her jeans and go back into the shop. *Bombing?* Had she really heard that word on Daisy's lips? Surely not, it made no sense at all.

She tried to put any panic out of her mind. Daisy was level-headed now, she wasn't up to anything untoward, she couldn't be. 'It's looking wonderful,' she said of the block Ginny had almost finished working on. Ginny had chosen to add a candle holder patch to the quilt because it reminded her so much of her grandad's favourite nursery rhyme, 'Wee Willie Winkie'. Ivor had told each of her girls the rhyme during their childhoods and it had brought back so many memories for all of them. Loretta loved the rhyme's imagery, its personification of sleep, and this block was perfect for his Christmas quilt.

With every thought and every detail that went into the Christmas quilt, Loretta felt the fabric of her family settle a little more around her. Her girls were as strong as they'd always been, they were beginning to find one another again, and it gave her hope that when the truth finally came out, they'd all get through it together.

'You really should plan a holiday next year, Mum,' Fern said when the lady who'd wanted some Christmas-themed fat quarters went on her way. Fern had finally sewn most of the way around the gingerbread character on the cream material block and seemed satisfied with her progress.

'Haven't we talked about this already?'

'We have. But you really could do with a break,' Fern went on. 'Everyone who has a job has holidays.'

'She's right, Mum,' Daisy joined in.

'I don't even know where I'd go.'

'Anywhere!' Ginny interjected.

'Why do I get the impression you're all ganging up on me?' Although she kind of liked it, it meant they were drawing closer together, precisely what she'd wanted. 'I'll think about it.'

As she left the girls to their quilting she took the opportunity to unpack the box of angora wool in the most beautiful lavender colour down the farthest aisle, next to the window. Her hands relished its softness as she pushed each ball of wool onto the shelf section and she thought about Harry as she often did when she was in here among the beautiful fabrics and textures, when she caught sight of his photograph on the wall, and when she had time for her mind to wander.

Harry had had the kindest eyes and a smile so big it lit up his whole face. He was a brilliantly minded mathematician and she'd been drawn to his intellect, adoring the way he could get so immersed in a topic he barely came up for air. When Harry reached his late forties and needed reading glasses the sexy professor look had only added to his appeal, and that was how she liked to remember him, looking up at her from whatever he was focusing on, giving his kind smile that told her *I know you.* On the whole Loretta and Harry had had a good marriage, besides the normal ups and downs, and despite one very big down she hadn't been sure they'd get through at the time. Harry had been in the wrong, but then so had she. Both of their actions had nearly broken their marriage apart, but it was as though from their lowest point they had begun to rediscover one another. They worked through everything that had happened. He told her she had forgiven him on a deeper level than he could ever imagine, he was willing to walk away for what he'd done and wouldn't blame her for wanting him to. But Loretta had known, and admitted, that the part she'd played had been more subtle but no less damaging. Her passion for the business combined with motherhood left little time for anything else and along the way, unintentionally, she'd shut Harry out. He'd offered to look after the accounts and manage the shop's finances when she was struggling so much she was worried she'd lose the Butterbury Sewing Box. He'd offered to take the reins with the accounts and free her up to deal with the part she loved, but Loretta had wanted to do it all herself. She guarded the shop that had been in her family for years as though letting anyone help take the strain might take a piece of it away from her. She felt it was solely her responsibility to save it and get on top of the financial difficulties. She didn't want to burden her husband when really she should've recognised that as a family business, that's exactly what she should've done.

Loretta had always given her all to the Butterbury Sewing Box. Even when Daisy was very young Loretta had worked long hours and juggled parenthood as though she was the star performer in a circus, she'd left little time for anything else. And in her late forties when she began to feel so low, so exhausted and drained of energy with sleepless nights beginning to take their toll, her doctor had put her on a course of antidepressants. But the tablets hadn't done much at all and she'd continued to push Harry away. Things had got so bad between them that Loretta eventually asked Harry for a trial separation, she couldn't bear to be around him, she hated the way she was being so awful to him and treating him as though he was in the way but yet she couldn't stop what she was doing. And the way he looked at her all hurt and distraught that his wife was falling apart in front of his eyes made it even worse. She felt like a total failure. With the business, with him. Harry had agreed on the trial separation and before long separation led to talk of divorce.

Both Harry and Loretta had worried about their girls, they'd been the priority no matter what. Neither of them wanted to hurt Fern, Ginny and Daisy and so they'd told their daughters that Harry would be working away during the week and home at weekends. Then at weekends they'd done their best to pretend everything was normal. Harry had begged to come back permanently but Loretta had told him no. Their conversations became scant and when they did speak it got them nowhere, over and over again. Loretta reached the point where she barely knew herself anymore and bit by bit she was falling apart, but on the surface she was trying to prove to the rest of the world that she was fine.

If only she'd let Harry in sooner, if they'd communicated with one another they might never have reached breaking point. They might never have wasted all that time apart.

Loretta eventually made an appointment at the bank and with finances in both names, Harry came too. After the appointment to secure a small loan to tide her over for a while, she and Harry sat in a café. It had been pouring with rain that day, the sort of rain that pelted the windows with such ferocity that all you could see was water running down the glass.

That day she'd told him everything – how the shop had had a quiet spell, how the repairs they'd had to do to the roof had used up most of the spare cash, how she'd forgotten to reorder stock more than once and hadn't had the energy to secure big discounts the way she might once have done. And as it all came tumbling out she'd realised what a weight she'd been putting on her shoulders without letting anyone else help at all. She'd looked across at Harry, her poor husband, who was being so patient with her when she was the one who'd instigated the separation, she was the one who'd been the most distant and it was she who mentioned the word divorce. She apologised for how awful she'd been to him, how she'd held him at arm's length. She wanted him in her life and she was terrified that it was too late.

She begged Harry to forgive her and please come home. But when he did, his truth had come out, and that had been something he didn't ever expect her to forgive. He felt sure she'd want to go ahead with the divorce and he said he wouldn't blame her if she did.

When Daisy went off the rails when she was fifteen, something neither she nor Harry had ever determined the cause of, and had put down to her hanging out with the wrong crowd, Harry had been a tower of strength. The counselling they'd already been through as a couple had made their bond stronger than ever and Loretta was thankful they'd been able to support their youngest daughter. When Harry died, Loretta had wondered whether Daisy would fall apart and history would repeat itself, but something in Daisy had made her stand up tall, pull herself together, stop living as though she was invincible. Daisy had been there for Loretta every day since, when it should've been the other way around. Loretta should've been the one encouraging Daisy to live her own life, which may or may not be in Butterbury, she should've been the one to support Ginny who had fallen apart in a quiet way, and she should never have left it up to Fern to provide so much support for her sisters. She imagined Harry looking down at her, shaking his head at the way she was handling all of this. She'd always feel guilty for not being stronger back then. And it was time she told her girls, apologised for not being there in the capacity she should've been.

Loretta looked at her daughters now, all three of them sitting around the Christmas tree in the Butterbury Sewing Box, working at their own blocks, helping one another or passing opinion as though this was what they had always been like. Loretta wished Harry could see his girls now, he'd be so proud. And she wished he was here to share the worry too, about what she had to tell all three girls, and about what to do about Daisy.

But he wasn't. And this time she was going to have to handle it properly on her own.

Chapter Nineteen

Fern

Fern emerged from her bedroom wrapped in her quilt as usual. With only three sets of silk nightwear to choose from and the house holding onto the winter chill the best it could, perhaps having Everett here would at least keep her warm. Everett and the boys were scheduled to arrive on Christmas Eve and Fern had begun to get strangely anxious about seeing them.

'Where's Daisy?' she asked her mum as she joined her in the kitchen and nodded to the offer of a cup of tea.

'She's out walking Busker.' Loretta put the kettle on. 'How are Everett and the boys?' She must've heard Fern talking on the phone already this morning.

Fern recapped on their news, school wrapping up, Everett looking forward to time off, and told her mum they seemed to be coping absolutely fine.

The kettle had boiled and Loretta filled the mugs before bringing them over to the sofa at the end of the kitchen past the table. 'What did you expect them to do, fall apart?'

'No . . .' Fern reached out to take a cup of tea and then, noticing her mum looking down at her over her glasses, smiled. 'Well yes, a bit.'

Loretta sat down beside her. 'Everett is a grown man. And your boys are growing up too, they'll be men before you know it.'

'Time goes way too fast.' Fern blew across her tea.

'I can't wait to see them all again.'

'Me too,' smiled Fern. 'But I've needed this time away. Does that make sense?'

'Perfect sense and don't feel guilty for admitting it. Motherhood is hard. Add in work and running a household and it's a recipe for exhaustion.' She paused. 'I should've taken a break back when you were little, never mind now. I never did, but it was a mistake.'

Fern let the warmth of her tea slide down her throat, comforting in its ritual as much as the taste. 'I'm glad you had us come home for longer.'

'You are?'

'I am, but I get the feeling this visit isn't just about Grandad.'

Loretta, dressed in jeans and a soft plum-coloured cashmere jumper, pulled a section of Fern's quilt across her knees too. 'No, it's not.' She reached out and toyed with a lock of Fern's hair, loose rather than in its usual efficient ponytail. 'I've been worried about you three.'

'We're grown women.'

Loretta's head tilted to one side. 'And you'll forever be my three little girls. You've all been through so much but you've drifted apart.'

'So throwing us together in the house is an attempt to get us back to who we once were?'

'It's not as simple as that. Years of problems lacing themselves together, layering up bit by bit, miscommunications for years, they're not simple to sort through.' She set her mug down on the side table. 'I need to apologise to each of you. I should've done it a long time ago.'

'Apologise. What for?'

Loretta took a deep breath. Whatever she had to say wasn't coming easily. 'When your dad died I fell apart and my role as mother was somewhat blurred.' She shook her head, frustrated with herself. 'I didn't have the strength back then and I should've found it from somewhere. But before I knew it Daisy had settled into the shop, Ginny was off travelling, you'd gone back to work. I let everything evolve, move forwards.'

'And that's a bad thing?'

'It was, because you three were never the same again.'

'We're doing all right, Mum.'

Loretta smiled. 'You seem to be.'

Fern sipped her tea. 'You had a lot to cope with when Dad died. You were only in your late forties . . . I can't imagine what it would do to me and the boys if we ever lost Everett.' A shiver ran through her at the very contemplation.

'I lost my husband too soon.' She put a hand on her daughter's. 'And you lost your father, yet you scraped me off the floor when he died.' Fern's eyes pricked with tears because her mum was right. 'It was you who comforted both of your sisters and had them cry all over you, it was you who closed the shop for a couple of weeks but made sure it was ready for me to get going with after the funeral. You did the funeral arrangements pretty much on your own, chose the hymns, the poetry, you left me list after list to help me function. You had the control I'd always had but lost when Harry died.'

'You needed help.' Her voice caught.

'I did, but I'm ashamed of how bad I was, how it was you who had to help me. There you were on the days I couldn't get out of bed, bringing me breakfast when I said I didn't want to eat, talking to me when I wanted to close the curtains and block out the world. It was too much to expect from a daughter and it's something I've never forgiven myself for.'

Fern put down her mug of tea and swiped at the tear that slid down her cheek.

Loretta put down her mug of tea too and grabbed hold of both of Fern's hands. 'You still worry me.' She hooked Fern's hair behind her ear on one side and then the other. 'Both of your sisters fell apart, they cried their tears, Lord knows I did too. But when did you ever cry? Behind closed doors, I'd hear you. I'd go to knock on the door and my hand would stay raised, I couldn't do it. I didn't want you to feel exposed in the way I was. I thought that you had decided to cry away from the rest of us and that was your way of coping. But it was wrong of me. You should've been grieving along with the rest of us, together. We should never have let it turn out the way it did with you being the strong one the whole time, never allowed to show any weakness.'

'I coped.' Shutting herself away stopped her inflicting her suffering on anyone else, she didn't think they needed to see it, she wanted to be relied upon, to help, to mend their splintered family.

'Don't you see, Fern? You do cope, you always have.' She put a hand to her daughter's cheek, wiping her tears away with the pad of her thumb as they fell openly for the first time in forever. 'It's a strength, but sometimes it's also a weakness.'

'I know.' And she did. She'd been doing it too long and only now, away from her everyday life, had she begun to see it.

Fern let herself be held, wondering why she'd resisted it for so long, thinking she didn't need the extra comfort, that it was she who had to be the pinnacle of strength.

'At the time I think helping you out was my way of coping, of processing what had happened,' she admitted, glad Ginny was still in bed sewing, and that Daisy was out. She wasn't sure she could be so open with anyone else watching, at least not yet.

'You're a strong woman and I'm proud of you, Fern. But promise me from now on you'll try to let us all in a little bit more.'

'No man, or woman, is an island, right?' They both laughed. 'I'll try, Mum.'

Loretta sighed. 'Do you think Daisy's way of helping and therefore coping was to leap at the chance to take on the shop alongside me?'

Fern had been wondering the same thing recently. Back then she hadn't questioned it. 'All I know is she was dead set on the idea and I think a big part of it was that she'd had enough of being the youngest sibling, the one who had got into trouble the most. I think she still thinks we all see her as unreliable, but Ginny and I have talked. We're doing our best to show her that's not what we think at all.'

Loretta looked relieved but sad at the same time. 'So she stayed at the shop with me just to prove a point?'

Fern pulled a face. 'It sounds terrible putting it that way. But kind of, yes. Although I also think for a time she was happy with her decision and I think she needed to be with you too.'

'I hope so, I really do.' She shook her head. 'I was only glad she wanted to channel her energies into something that wasn't going to get her into trouble. I had visions of that happening when your dad died. I dreaded it. And then all of a sudden she came out with the offer to give up her university place and stay behind in Butterbury. She insisted it was what she wanted for herself, to be a part of the family business, and my relief let me think it was the right decision for her.'

'Don't beat yourself up about it, Mum.' She squeezed her mum's hand. 'Like I said, I think she needed it at the time.' With her sister still upstairs she confided, 'I always thought it would be Ginny to take over the shop.'

'Me too.' And with a smile Loretta told her, 'She's always the first to volunteer to help at the shop when Daisy wants or needs some time to do something else, she's done more blocks for the quilt than anyone else and doesn't show any signs of slowing. When she put the pink sewing machine up in the loft I thought she'd moved on to the next thing. She was happy following the path to midwifery, she seemed content, I assumed she didn't have much time outside of that to have a hobby. And then of course she took to travelling.'

'I'll bet she's a good midwife.'

'She's got the patience.'

Fern nudged Loretta's elbow. 'I think we've all turned out relatively OK.'

'The three of you are wonderful, beautiful, capable girls.' Loretta's frown deepened. 'But I wish I'd gone the extra mile back then to make sure you *all* got what you wanted and needed.'

'You did all right, Mum. You did your best. That's all anyone can ever do.'

Fern took the mugs away and poured the dregs into the sink and when she sat back down she knew her attempt at distraction hadn't worked when her mum said, 'I'm worried about you and Everett.'

Fern almost insisted she was fine, that her marriage was as strong as it always had been. But she couldn't do it. 'I needed to come here to Butterbury, not just for you but for me, for us as a couple.'

Loretta nodded as if she'd known all along. 'Time apart in the short term can be a tonic, as long as you address what's wrong and try to put it right.'

Her eyes had already filled with tears. 'I feel like I've always been strong, always been able to juggle whatever comes my way, but lately . . .'

'You're not superwoman.'

'I'm beginning to realise.' In the same way she'd shut herself in her bedroom to cry when her dad died, she'd shut Everett out, and he'd done it with her too. 'I don't know when it happened – partly it was after Everett's mother died, but it was happening even before that. Along the way we got busy with the boys, gave our careers our all, and we stopped talking. I threw myself into running the household, Everett put even more hours into his work than I did. It feels like it's been years since we were those two people who fell in love.'

Loretta put a hand to Fern's cheek. 'We're often our own worst critics. Talk to Everett when he gets here. Tell him how you feel. I mean how you *really* feel. I bet you haven't done that for a long time, have you?' One look from Fern and she knew she was spot on. 'I suspect he hasn't either. I did the same with your dad and it didn't work. In fact it very nearly broke us and I'd hate to see that happen to you.'

When Daisy bundled through the door calling out to Busker, telling him in a low tone to drop the stick, Fern quickly kissed her mum on the cheek as the stick landed at their feet. 'Thank you for listening.'

'Any time, Fern, you know that. And thank you for hearing me out too.'

She hugged her mum to say it was OK, she understood, pulling apart before Daisy came in and picked up that anything was wrong.

When Ginny shuffled into the kitchen in her pyjamas Fern reminded her, 'Your turn to do the advent calendar this morning.'

With a cheeky smile Ginny went back out to the hallway and her sisters hovered as she pulled the reindeer face from one of the pockets and hung it on the embroidered tree. Fern had had her turn yesterday.

When the letterbox went all three girls saw the newspaper drop onto the mat and Daisy lunged for it first.

'Show us, Daisy!' Ginny was impatient.

'She will in her own time,' said Fern, although she wanted a look too.

Daisy hugged the newspaper against her chest, eyes welling. 'My photographs are on the front page.'

'Daisy . . .' Ginny said, a beaming smile for her sister as she held out the newspaper for them both while she put a hand across her mouth to pause the emotions.

'This is beyond amazing.' Fern grinned, hugging Daisy.

And when Loretta took the newspaper next her eyes

welled with tears. 'We'll have to frame this.' She gave her shoulders a squeeze. 'Your first article.'

Between them all they looked at the photographs over and over again until Daisy told them they'd ruin it with their paw prints and went to stash it in her bedroom.

When Daisy eventually came back downstairs the girls filed into the sitting room to get going with the quilt again. Loretta had given Daisy the day off, she refused to let Ginny anywhere near the place, and she'd even supplied them with mince pies from the bakery to keep them all going for a while.

Fern was completely on board with her mum's tone, which brooked no argument. 'I'd better get dressed then.'

'Before you do . . .' Loretta held up a finger to stop Fern in her tracks, disappeared for a moment and then came back brandishing a parcel wrapped in pine green with a darker satin bow. 'I know it's not Christmas yet but this is ridiculous.' She took the quilt Fern had wrapped around herself again so she could undo the gift. 'I'll get you a little something else for beneath the tree, but you have to have this gift now.'

Fern tugged the end of the bow and tore off the wrapping paper, laughing when she saw the pair of neatly folded brushed cotton pyjamas in midnight blue with gingerbread men printed all over. 'They're brilliant.'

'Put them on,' Loretta insisted. 'Stay in them all day. Relax, no rules, enjoy yourself.'

Fern raced up the stairs, showered, and then dressed in the brand new pyjamas that were cute, soft and, more importantly, warm. And by the time she came back downstairs Daisy had put a pair of pyjamas back on so she wouldn't be the odd one out, and Ginny had a shower and picked out her favourite pair too.

The girls worked through the day, past lunch, which was a snatched snack of mince pies followed by toast and cheese eaten from plates on their laps, and well into late afternoon. They chatted as they worked and the longer they were in the sitting room together, the more Fern found she was enjoying the creativity. Talking with her mum had released plenty of emotions and Fern suspected that had a lot to do with it too. She was able to focus, laugh with her sisters and there was certainly a lot less tension than there might have been a couple of weeks ago. Fern hoped that she'd be able to open up to Everett when he was here soon, that they could both find a way to move forwards.

Fern sighed and turned her neck this way and that to release tension caused by leaning over the fabric for so long, added her latest completed block to the rest, and Ginny counted them all up.

'I think we've got enough now to lay them out and arrange the quilt ready for piecing and sashing,' Ginny declared.

'At last,' groaned Daisy, standing up and bending over to stretch out her body.

'Mulled wine, anyone?' Fern offered. 'We've earned it.'

Daisy checked her watch. 'I'll pass.'

'Got somewhere you need to be?' quizzed Ginny.

Daisy hesitated enough for both Fern and Ginny to realise she certainly did and she would not be sharing the details with anyone else.

'We've had a lovely day, don't spoil it by being

suspicious,' Daisy scolded, but she didn't seem to be as defensive as she might once have been.

'Daisy, sit down. Now.' Ginny said this so forcefully that it even took Fern by surprise.

'Bossy,' grinned Daisy, flopping down onto the carpet. 'And I *was* kidding, it was meant to be a joke.'

'Neither of us are being suspicious,' Ginny began, ignoring her claim. 'Well, we are, but only in a we're-interested-in-what-you're-doing kind of way. Which is normal sisterly behaviour.' Ginny clearly wasn't about to let Daisy get a word in until she'd finished. 'Fern and I were horrid to you about a past mistake that was just that, a mistake. Your crime was to go out and get drunk, and we might not understand what made you do it or why you hung around with those girls who were so unpleasant. We might not get what made you drink so much you were unbearable to be around at times and your drinking culminated in a trip to A & E—'

'This is making me feel so great,' said Daisy with an air of sarcasm.

'But . . .' Ginny went on, 'we *are* sorry we made your life so difficult. It was wrong.'

Clearly Daisy hadn't expected the ending to the speech, especially from Ginny. 'It was my fault the quilt went missing.' She looked down at her hands, fingers clasped together, one palm on top of the other. 'You should be angry.'

When Fern had seen the unsavoury characters Daisy was hanging out with as a teen she'd warned her sister to stay away, suggested she make other friends. But the more she'd offered her advice the more Daisy had pushed against it. Instead she'd hung out with them all the more and the drinking got out of hand. One night Daisy had mixed vodka, gin and goodness knows what, and after a night of partying ended up in the hospital. The doctors had called the house. Fern and Ginny were there, it was a weekend and they'd both come to stay, and Fern would never forget how their dad's face had drained of colour, how his voice shook when he spoke and told the doctor he'd be there as soon as he could. He'd grabbed a bag with some of Daisy's things after the doctor suggested she'd be kept in overnight.

Their dad had returned home from the hospital exhausted. Daisy had had her stomach pumped but she was recovering well. Harry and Loretta went back the next day and the day after that their dad had gone to collect Daisy and bring her home. He'd taken the special quilt he'd made for all of them to curl beneath on movie night, something that had fallen by the wayside since Ginny and Fern moved out and Daisy got other interests. Presumably taking the quilt had been a vain attempt to provide comfort to his youngest daughter and remind her she didn't need to be doing these things, that she had a family who loved her and always would. Nobody gave much thought to the special quilt after that, Daisy was getting better and seemed to have been shocked into behaving herself, and Ginny and Fern both went back to their own lives.

A couple of months later, tragedy struck and their dad was taken from them after a sudden heart attack. The family focus had shifted, nobody questioned where the quilt was, their lives became all about survival and holding themselves together the best they could. It was only when Fern was putting Harry's car up for sale, her mother incapable of much at all, that Fern realised she hadn't seen the quilt in its usual place, folded up on top of the trunk in her parents' bedroom. She'd assumed it was still in the car, having been taken to the hospital for Daisy's homecoming, but it wasn't there either. And when she'd asked her mum about it, it had been fruitless, because Loretta was in no fit state to think about much at all, let alone a quilt they hadn't used in years. And so in their grief, Fern and Ginny, rightly or wrongly, had both firmly laid the blame at Daisy's feet for losing something so precious to all three of them. Fern had yelled at Daisy that day. She'd kept her cool up until that moment, shielded her sisters from her own grief, but the additional loss of something that meant so much was too much to process. *If you hadn't been pissed out of your head, we wouldn't have lost something so special, so fucking irreplaceable,* she'd yelled at her sister. Daisy had covered her ears, rocked back and forth, the hurling accusations topping up her own grief. *I'll never forgive you,* Ginny had shrieked, venom lacing her voice, not the way Ginny ever was to anyone, let alone a member of her own family.

Fern sunk down on the sofa in the sitting room now, next to her youngest sister. 'It wasn't really your fault, you didn't leave the quilt anywhere. Dad took it out of the house, it just never found its way back to us. And Ginny and I were both wrong to take our hurt out on you. I'm only sorry it's taken us until now to really get this out in the open.'

'Don't tell me, you were worried I'd overreact?' said Daisy, her comment silencing them both.

But then Daisy smiled, even though she sniffed at the same time and the tears began to flow. 'I've changed, I'm not that irresponsible little sister anymore.'

'I know,' Fern insisted.

Ginny crouched down in front of Daisy. 'I know it too, Daisy. Grief affects us all differently. My anger towards anyone at that time came from a place I never really knew existed. Unfortunately all three of us let our grief swallow us up whole. We all did it in different ways and didn't turn to each other the way we should've done. We certainly never talked like we're doing now, did we?'

When Daisy shook her head Ginny told them both, 'I was angry at myself.'

'For saying those things to me?' Daisy wondered.

But Ginny shook her head and her voice wobbled. 'I was angry at myself . . . because I wasn't there.' No matter how much she bit down on her lower lip she couldn't hold back the tears now.

Fern put a hand on her sister's shoulder. 'What do you mean, you weren't there?'

'I was swanning around Europe on holiday. When Dad was taken to hospital I was off having a grand time. I've never forgiven myself that I wasn't here to kiss his cheek, tell him I loved him one last time. You both did. I didn't. And I've never got over it.' She sucked in air, trying to get the words out, and Fern wondered how much of her grief she'd held in in front of everyone else back then, the same way as Fern had.

Daisy launched at her first, then Fern, both hugging their sister so tight she toppled over with them on the floor and tears became mixed with laughter. It was a gesture that hadn't happened quite like this in years, but it felt right, it felt natural. It was as though with all of them being here in the family home something had at last unlocked and Fern knew they had their mum to thank for that. They didn't like it when she meddled, but Fern was sure all three of them were eternally grateful she had this time.

When they pulled apart Ginny dried her eyes and plucked another tissue from the box, just in case. 'You know, I think if Dad hadn't died I might have come back to Butterbury and become a community midwife.'

'I could kind of imagine that,' said Daisy.

'Instead I found it painful to be here for too long, remembering what we'd all lost. I protected myself by being elsewhere and travelling.' She looked at each of them in turn. 'And that's why I packed up my sewing machine.'

'Because you couldn't take it in your backpack?' Daisy asked.

'That's not quite the reason,' Ginny laughed. 'I grew up loving anything to do with sewing and quilting, you both know that, but then I found out about midwifery and I found I really wanted to explore something totally different. I wanted to forge a career for myself, get away for a while and try something completely different, but I know if Dad hadn't died I would've kept up with my hobby at the same time and perhaps eventually followed in Mum's footsteps at the Butterbury Sewing Box.' She shrugged. 'I always knew Fern never wanted the shop, I didn't really think about whether you might, Daisy. I can see it's working really well, you know your stuff, you're good with customers, it all worked out.' She gave her younger sister a reassuring nod. 'It's just that I'd always assumed at some point Mum would bring us together and ask the question. That was until everything changed. We lost Dad, I stopped sewing, and here we are.'

'I always knew you wanted the shop,' said Daisy. 'But

then you chose a different career. I didn't think I was treading on any toes when I was the one to take it on with Mum.' She pulled a face. 'Actually that's not strictly true . . . I did it partly to prove a point to you both, that I could cope and be responsible, for once in my life.' She sighed. 'I wish you'd said something before.'

One by one they all moved from their positions on the carpet over to the sofa. Busker snored from his position curled up beside the tree.

'I couldn't,' said Ginny. 'I couldn't say anything because I didn't know I really wanted it. I found so much joy in the shop, in the fabrics, in the creativity. I'd sew in my spare time despite studying something totally different. But when we lost Dad I questioned how I could justify making such beautiful things and feeling so happy surrounded by so much colour when life could be so terrible.' She hung her head as though ashamed she'd blown it out of proportion. 'Then I thought the best thing to do was keep moving forwards with the choices I'd made.'

'I was happy in the shop for a while,' Daisy admitted. 'I still am. I have a job, I'm with Mum, I don't hate it.'

'But you don't love it,' Fern finished for her.

'No, I don't. I gave up on my own dreams to be the one to step in for once and mend things rather than make more of a mess. I'm glad I did it, I think I needed to for a while, but now? Especially after seeing my work in the newspaper, which I still can't quite believe, perhaps it's time I thought about what I truly want to do with the rest of my life.'

They'd all reacted differently to their dad's death. Ginny had left, Fern had organised everyone, Daisy had changed her plans. 'I wish we'd aired all of our feeling back then,' said Fern. 'We could've saved ourselves a hell of a lot of pain.'

Ginny braved a question, looking Daisy's way. 'I'm not saying this to upset you, Daisy, but may I ask why you were so wild back then?'

Fern knew it was usually her who would be blunt, but she was glad Ginny had been the one to ask the question she wouldn't mind knowing the answer to as well.

When Daisy stayed quiet Fern prompted her. 'Was it a result of the tumultuous teenage years – which, by the way, I'm constantly on standby for with my boys?'

'Good luck with that,' Ginny grinned.

Daisy took the question in her stride, staying beside her sisters and not storming away and thinking they were trying to make her feel worse again. 'It was a little bit more than that,' she offered, but then quickly stopped as though she'd already said too much. 'I'll tell you about it sometime, but not tonight, yeah?'

'Whenever you're ready,' Fern forced herself to say when all she really wanted was for Daisy to tell them everything right now.

'Thank you.' Daisy looked to Ginny. 'I wish I hadn't been so messed up that you couldn't talk to either of us about Dad and how upset you were at having not been with him when he died.'

'He knew you loved him, Ginny,' Fern assured her. Their dad had been in hospital following the heart attack, survived almost thirty-six hours, long enough for Loretta, Fern and Daisy to say their goodbyes, but not long enough for Ginny to get home to England and do the same. 'I saw him in the hospital, but it wasn't the man I want to remember. It wasn't Dad, it was a shell of him, a version, but not the one who laughed with us, who made that quilt with us and held our hands and told us off, not the man who was proud of each and every one of his daughters.'

Fern looked at Daisy then. 'The quilt *was* special, nobody can deny that. But while we are all gutted that it's gone, it was never as special as the memories we have. Nobody can take those away from us.'

They sat in quiet contemplation, in a row on the sofa, hands linked together, until Ginny blurted out, 'Personally I think I need a mulled wine now.'

'Daisy?' asked Fern, before remembering her sister hadn't wanted any when she offered earlier. 'You still haven't told us where you're off to later.'

Daisy grinned as though she really was up to mischief. 'I tell you what . . .' The look on her face reminded Fern of when Daisy was a little girl, ten years her junior, with all the innocence of childhood and the sense of adventure. 'If you get your pink sewing machine out of the loft, Ginny, and set it up ready to use it to piece together Grandad's quilt, I'll tell you where I've been sneaking off to.'

'Where are you going?' Ginny asked when Fern leaped up first.

'To the loft to get the machine! No way are we missing out on some gossip!'

And just like that there was a sense of being equals, sisters, with roles that had ever so subtly evolved over time.

Chapter Twenty

Loretta

Loretta arrived home from the shop to find her three girls not only together, but laughing. She lingered in the hallway for a few minutes longer than it took to remove her coat because the sound was something she'd yearned to hear once again. A few more minutes listening to her beautiful girls was to be savoured.

When she opened the door to the sitting room they were all on their hands and knees. And Carrie had joined them.

Carrie stood up. 'I hope this is all right.' She had a tub of pins resting in her palm.

Loretta's eyes misted but she managed to get out the words that it was fine, the more the merrier.

The coffee table had been moved out of the way, the sofa and armchairs pushed back as far as they would go, the rug rolled up and leaned against the wall in the corner. Each block of the quilt that they'd worked tirelessly on was on the floor in the pattern they were currently debating, with Ginny running the show talking about colours complementing one another and shuffling things around in a way she hadn't ever done before. Loretta spotted the pink sewing machine set up in the corner too and when she spoke she fought to keep the emotion from her voice. All day she'd been itching to pick up the phone and check on them, expecting one of them to at least appear any moment and insist they had to have a break. She'd never expected this, all of them along with Carrie working away as though they'd been born to do it.

'What do you think of the layout, Mum?' Ginny stood back, hands on hips.

'It looks like a fine quilt to me.'

'Just wait until we piece it together and add the sashing, the backing and the batting,' Ginny enthused as she directed Carrie over to the section in the corner of the design ready for pinning.

Loretta pointed to the pink machine. 'Does that thing even work?'

'Tried and tested,' said Fern, looking up from the gingerbread block she was pinning against another colour. 'Almost ready to use it to piece the quilt together.'

Carrie finished helping Ginny pin the blocks at the corner. 'I need to get going, up to the lodge.'

'So soon?' Fern asked. 'You're such a help, you really can't stay?'

Carrie looked at Daisy. 'I said I'd help Victor.'

Daisy seemed to know what she meant. 'Yes, off you go, don't keep him waiting. I'll see you later, yeah?'

Loretta presumed they saw one another at the lodge often, given Carrie sung with the choir and had begun to volunteer to keep residents company. 'I'll show you out,' she told Carrie, 'you girls keep working.' She ushered them on with a wave of her hands and closed the sitting room door behind her.

'Loretta, I—'

She put her hands on Carrie's shoulders. 'Don't apologise, you've nothing to be sorry for.'

'You're not angry I ended up helping? That I've come here to the house?'

'Not at all.' She had never been angry. Worried perhaps, but never annoyed.

Should she tell Carrie she was going to talk to the girls now? She hadn't intended it to be tonight but seeing Carrie here with them all, hearing the laughter and chatter when she came through the door and the warmth in the atmosphere when she saw them all working together, she knew it was time.

But when Carrie gave her a hug goodbye, Loretta said nothing. She'd talk to the girls first, then take it from there. And she didn't want Carrie worrying herself silly. She seemed to have a habit of doing so and Loretta couldn't stand the thought of her in turmoil. It was bad enough when it was her struggling with what to do, what to say, how to handle this.

Loretta took a deep breath. She opened the sitting room door and as Ginny finished pinning two blocks, Fern another and Daisy got up from the floor, she asked, 'Could you all come into the kitchen please?'

'What is it?' Daisy was alert to something off.

But Loretta had already disappeared back along the hallway calling over her shoulder, 'I'll make us some tea.'

Loretta's hands shook as she took out the mugs, her mouth went dry. She must've looked so worried that Fern took over making the tea.

Ginny was the last to come in but once they were all there, all with a cup of tea in front of them, it was time to tell them the real reason she had wanted them home in Butterbury. She only hoped her thoughts and words wouldn't be too muddled as they tumbled out and that they would understand why she hadn't told them straight away.

'Mum, what's going on?' Ginny prompted. 'Is this about Grandad?'

Loretta realised they all looked worried and likely for the same reason. 'Your grandad is absolutely fine, I promise.'

She waited for relief to calm each of them, prepare them for what came next. 'I know how much you all adored your father,' she began. 'So did I. He was and always will be my one true love. We had a good marriage on the whole. But we had ups and downs too, and parents don't always share those with their children.'

All three of them looked like they had no idea where this was going. Harry had been gone for so long that addressing problems in their marriage would be the last thing they expected to hear. But Loretta wanted them to pull together and lean on each other for support, and she wanted them to still love their dad as much as they always had, to judge him for more than this one mistake. And she wanted them to welcome the changes ahead.

'Your dad and I went through a very tough time and I'm afraid to say we both did things wrong, it wasn't all one person's fault.

'I was going through a terrible time – business was slow, I got in a muddle with my finances because I couldn't focus on everything, and I turned down your dad's offers of help more times than I would like to admit. I became closed off. Do you remember when he worked away for a while?' They all nodded. Her voice was barely above a whisper and she forced herself to look at each of them. 'He wasn't really working away. I asked him to leave. It was a trial separation and we were talking about a divorce.'

Ginny's mouth fell open as Loretta's words tumbled out. 'Divorce?'

Fern was too shocked to say anything.

And Daisy looked uncomfortable as though remembering all too well the time her dad had left. Daisy would've been fourteen at the time and it must've been incredibly difficult to be around when her parents' marriage was falling apart.

Loretta toyed with the handle of her mug. 'We were in a mess and separating seemed the only way out of it. I felt as though I barely knew myself anymore, your dad didn't know what to do, neither of us did. And so he left and we decided for a while we'd pretend he was working away. We never wanted to hurt any of you, believe me, that's why we never said anything.

'Whenever your dad was home at weekends it wasn't nice for either of us, pretending everything was normal, being polite but not wanting to be near each other.'

Fern spoke up. 'I had my suspicions something wasn't right.'

Tears in her eyes, Loretta admitted, 'It wasn't right for a long while. It all came to a head when my financial difficulties got so bad I had no choice but to try to seek help. I had a meeting at the bank and with the accounts in our married names both of us were there.

'After the appointment I admitted everything to your dad. I told him how much trouble I thought the shop was in, that I was terrified I'd lose it.' She smiled then, remembering their closeness that day, that had come unexpectedly at the perfect time. 'We were sitting in a café, rain pounding against the window, and it was the first time we talked for that long in years. It reminded me of the early days when we were dating, when talking never stalled, when we saw each other for who we were.'

'And they all lived happily ever after,' said Daisy, but a bitter tone lacing her voice had her sisters looking at her bewildered.

Loretta's heart broke that little bit more that for Daisy being so young this must have been the worst for her. 'I asked your dad to come home, we both wanted to try again, and he agreed.' She paused. 'He was also honest.'

'What do you mean, honest?' Ginny wondered.

'He'd been away for over six months, we'd talked divorce. And during that time he met someone.'

'Dad had an affair?' Fern swore when she slopped her tea and Daisy passed her a piece of kitchen towel.

'He did. But it was only one night.' She hated saying it. Nobody ever wanted to know about their parents' sex lives, especially in the form of a one-night stand, which made it sound sordid as well as wrong. 'He was incredibly sorry, crying, he offered to move out and still go through with the divorce because he didn't expect my forgiveness.'

'Yet you took him back?' Ginny asked, face paled with the shock.

'Not straight away, but yes, I did. Marriage is complicated and there are always two sides. I'm not excusing what he did and he never tried to either, but I could see how it had happened. I'd batted him away at every opportunity during those six months we were apart, I didn't want to talk about saving our marriage, I felt as though I was buried under rubble with the shop's finances, trying to find a way to simply breathe. And that became my only focus.

'We talked more and more after he admitted what he'd done. He told me it was a big mistake, that as soon as it had happened he'd realised what he wanted was me, us, our marriage and family.'

'How could he do that to you?' Ginny shook her head, tears streaming down her cheeks at the revelations about this man they'd worshipped.

If she hadn't had to, Loretta never would've shared the whole truth with her girls.

'I'm grateful he told me,' she told her daughters. 'I think I needed to realise what I'd almost lost.' Her voice wobbled, because she had lost him in the end, but maybe what he'd done had also brought more love into her life and it would be the same for the girls.

Loretta looked at each of her daughters, Fern's quiet acceptance beginning to replace the shock, Ginny's watery eyes and the way she was leaning towards Fern as though she needed the comfort of a sibling. And then she looked at Daisy and there was something in her expression that warned everyone to give her space.

Daisy stared into her mug and slowly everyone's eyes had fallen on her as though they were waiting for her to explode.

But she didn't. She looked up and all she said was, 'I knew.'

Silence washed over all of them.

'I've known for years,' sniffed Daisy.

'Daisy, how could you know?' Ginny asked.

'Did Dad tell you?' Fern demanded. 'Did you overhear a conversation?'

'I saw him.' Daisy's voice came out small, as though she was the one who had to confess to a sin. 'I went to see him, I missed him, and I knew the hotel he was staying at. I got all the way to the front steps and I saw him with a woman, they were kissing.' She looked up, eyes full of tears, her expression a mixture of anger and utter despair. 'I ran home and never said a word. Not to him, not to anyone.'

Loretta didn't wait for permission, she went around to her daughter's side and hugged her tight. She felt Daisy grip onto her arms, hold on for dear life.

'Why did you never say anything?' Loretta kissed her head, the softness of her rich chestnut hair, so much like Harry's had been many years ago, reminding her of simpler times and cuddles on the sofa, when they didn't have an ocean of secrets between them.

Daisy's voice shook. 'I never wanted you to feel the way I did when I saw him. And two weeks later he was home, you were going to counselling together and I thought whatever it had been was over. I tried to be mature and think about adults' lives. I read magazines about it, about affairs, about marriage, I told nobody, but I watched you both and I watched him. I didn't trust him, Mum.'

'Oh, Daisy.' Her heart broke a tiny bit more for her youngest daughter.

'I followed him more than once.' Her daughter's curious coffee-coloured eyes looked directly at her. 'I even bunked off school to do it.'

'I'm sorry you had to carry that with you for so long.'

But Daisy didn't look at all relieved she'd shared after all these years. 'Mum, that's not all . . .'

Loretta's insides plummeted because it was then she realised Daisy knew the whole truth. She had to. It all fell into place. Daisy's lack of focus at school, the trouble she got into, the way she went wild and there was no getting through to her. The timing fitted. And her daughter had carried that secret without talking to a soul about it.

'I know it's not,' Loretta said calmly, because she needed to be strong for all of them.

'You know?' Daisy swiped her tears and Ginny passed her a tissue.

'Are either of you two going to tell us what's going on?' Fern asked, shaking her head, confused.

Loretta took a deep breath. 'A year ago I was in the shop on my own – Daisy was away on a hen weekend, it was a slow day, and a girl who'd been in a couple of times before came in again. She was so jittery I wondered for an awful moment if she was on drugs. She'd been in an hour before that and bought three balls of wool and a crotchet needle and here she was, back again, choosing a bunch of fat quarters. I was at the counter, letting her make her own way around, and she kept looking at me. Eventually she brought a packet of two zips over to the till and when I asked if I could help her with anything else, she started crying.

'I thought I was going to have to get her a paper bag to breathe into, she was in a state, kept saying she never should've come. I asked her, come where? To Butterbury? I thought maybe she was on the run from a man, perhaps she'd had a row with a friend or her parents. I made her a cup of tea and everything came tumbling out. Her mum had died, she was devastated, and then she told me her dad died too.

'My heart went out to her at the loss she'd suffered.' Loretta willed herself to carry on. 'It was then she looked me right in the eye and told me, "My dad was Harry".'

Ginny and Fern didn't utter a word, Loretta saw Daisy's hand reach beneath the table for Fern's and across the table with her other hand, she took Ginny's.

Loretta almost wept. She wasn't sure whether it was because they knew the truth about their dad or because they were doing exactly what she wanted, they were there for one another in a way they hadn't been for years.

Fern's voice, usually strong and collected, was timid and raw. 'Did Dad know about her?'

'He knew.' Daisy's voice was like a lightning bolt, striking before Loretta could say a word.

Loretta knew she'd failed Daisy, that if she hadn't then her daughter might've turned to her, but she'd been weak and a mess when she lost Harry. And now she owed them all the absolute truth. And so she continued. 'The girl in the shop told me that her mum, the woman your dad had an affair with, wrote to Harry after the baby was born, she told him she thought he had a right to know about the baby, but that she didn't want any help. She didn't want to break up a marriage or a family.' She looked at all three of them. 'Knowing your dad he would've been wrangling with how he was going to tell me, how this would impact on all of us, and there's no way he wouldn't have offered support. I don't think he ever had a chance to tell me or to offer his help.'

The reality sunk in with all three of them until Ginny asked, 'Mum, why do I get the feeling there's something else?'

Deep breath. Here goes. 'The girl's name is Carrie.'

It felt like she'd thrown everything at them now, that the girls would either swim among the facts or sink beneath the weight of it all.

Fern spoke first. 'So she's been getting to know us without admitting who she is?'

Neither Loretta nor Carrie had meant it to happen that way. 'You have to know that it wasn't our intention to deceive anyone.'

Fern's nod of approval told Loretta that she understood or at least she was trying to. Fern had always been protective, in charge even when she didn't need to be, and Loretta sensed that Fern might be particularly sympathetic to Carrie given her eldest wasn't too dissimilar in age.

'Carrie and I met up several times in the village where she lives,' Loretta explained. 'We talked at length, I got to know her, and then I was happy for her to stop by the shop. I was pleased she wanted to learn to sew or even quilt. And slowly, I started to enjoy her company. Then Daisy suggested she help with the quilt and I couldn't very well disagree.'

Loretta took in their shock, their need to hear more. 'I couldn't tell any of you at first, I needed time to get my own head around the facts. And you three have been through so much.' Their silence was their acknowledgement. 'But so has Carrie. She's never known her own father. Carrie's mum took Harry's silence as a sign he was happy not to be involved and so she moved on with their lives without his involvement. She had no idea that he'd died.

'Carrie never intended to spend time with you all the way she has. She was singing with the choir long before she knew Ivor was up at Butterbury Lodge and then she volunteered up there. She said Daisy had been friendly to her one day and she'd grasped onto it. Not having siblings of her own she admitted to me that it felt nice. And when Daisy asked her to help with the quilt project she didn't want to say no. She told me soon after that she was upset at how she'd got involved without intending to and without any of you knowing the truth. She offered to step back, but it was me who said not to. I could see how much she wanted to be a part of something, she had the best of intentions. She's only a teenager, it's a hard age to feel so lost.'

Her words seemed to have an effect on Daisy in particular. 'We've enjoyed her company.' The others didn't disagree and Loretta hoped it was a good sign.

'I'm sorry you all had to find out this way. I intended to have you come home, for you to realise you wanted to be sisters again in the truest sense, there for one another no matter what, and then I was going to tell you, introduce Carrie, if that was what you all wanted.'

Fern looked at Daisy, her brow creased in confusion. 'How did you know about the baby?'

Loretta tried not to read too much into the way Fern referred to Carrie as the baby, when now she had a name, an identity. All of this was going to take some getting used to.

'I found a photograph of a baby tucked inside a book in Dad's study. It had a date on the back, the name Caroline, I knew that the date was around nine months from when I saw him with that woman.'

'So Caroline is Carrie?' Ginny asked Loretta.

Loretta nodded. 'She's been Carrie ever since she started school.'

'There was a note with the photograph,' said Daisy, 'it said they were both doing well and she didn't want anything from him, she would stay away for the sake of our family.' Her voice wobbled. 'I hated her. I hated him, for what he'd done. But I loved him too.'

'Oh, Daisy.' This time it was Fern going round to her sister, holding her tight, rocking her back and forth. 'You never said anything to anyone. I wish you'd said something to me, or to Ginny.'

'I couldn't,' she sobbed. 'I loved Dad, I loved you all, I didn't want our family to break apart.'

Ginny's eyes widened as she pieced it all together for the first time. 'This is why you went so crazy. This is why you went out and got drunk all the time, this was why you went through a phase of being rude to Dad where he couldn't do anything right. And this is why you stayed at the shop with Mum, to look after her and make her happy, instead of going to university?'

'Daisy?' Loretta hardly knew what was true anymore. 'Is that why you stayed with me?'

'I didn't want anything to hurt you again, Mum.' Her voice shook. 'I'd played my part in that by never telling you what I saw, Dad had been the one to cheat, and then when Fern and Ginny looked at me like I was the mess that I was, I needed to prove to myself that it was me who could hold us together, me who could protect our family and you from hurt. You fell apart when Dad died and I couldn't bear to think what it would do to you if you found out about the affair and about the baby.'

'Oh, Daisy, that wasn't for you to carry on your own.' It almost broke Loretta that her daughter had carried this for so long.

'It must've been a shock to have Carrie turn up, Mum,' said Ginny.

'I took a while to get used to the idea of her, this person who might well come between me and you three, who might come between each of you. After the initial shock, however, I began to see things from her perspective. She told me she got curious about her father after her mum passed away and wanted to find out more. I think she feels confused and a bit alone in all of this and she's still trying to make sense of everything.'

One of the strangest things had been picking up on the odd reminder that Carrie was Harry's child. She had his kind eyes, the gentle way of tilting her head to listen. And slowly over time Loretta had begun to enjoy her company.

'Carrie came to Butterbury to see for herself where Harry had once lived,' Loretta explained. 'But she hadn't intended to share her identity with any of us, she didn't want to ruin anyone else's life, she just wanted to find a way to connect with Harry and had no idea how to do it. She said she'd gone into the shop out of curiosity about us all and then when she saw me she said she felt overwhelmed, torn as to whether to tell me the truth. And then it all tumbled out.' She looked at her daughters warily, unable to read their expressions or perhaps not wanting to. 'In all of this Carrie assures me that the last thing she ever wants to do is hurt any of us. She shared the truth with me and would've been happy to keep it between us if that was what I chose.'

'But you didn't,' said Fern.

'She's our half-sister,' Daisy muttered, not really to anybody. She wasn't looking at Loretta either.

'Nothing can change our history,' Loretta assured them.

'Harry was your dad, and me and you three girls – that's been our family, with all its imperfections.'

'Imperfections?' Ginny grinned. 'We are perfect.' At least she got a laugh.

'The bad time me and your dad went through overshadowed everything back then, especially what was going on with you, Daisy.' It was no use wishing Daisy had told them what she'd found out. They couldn't change it now. 'We were in survival mode. And Ginny . . .' She looked at her middle daughter. 'I know you were lost along the way – not the eldest, not the youngest, and I feel I've failed you too.'

'Oh, Mum, you haven't failed any of us.'

She gulped. 'I saw that pink sewing machine tonight, I think about you doing the quilting, and I know now that a part of you wanted a different future but somehow you never got to have it. I know you almost broke not being here to say goodbye to your dad too, but I was such a mess I couldn't help you through that.' She let Ginny squeeze her hand in reassurance but she felt she had to carry on, she had to let them know how sorry she was for every wrong decision she'd made, every time she hadn't handled things the way she probably should have. 'And, Fern, we've talked, and you know how sorry I am that I let you carry the burden, that it was you who had to look out for your sisters when I was a mess.'

'Mum . . .' Ginny interrupted, coming to her side. 'You're recounting every single thing you ever did wrong. What about everything you ever did right?'

Daisy nodded her reassurance along with Fern. 'She's right.'

'We were safe, we were loved, we had security,' said

Ginny. 'We have plenty of special memories and part of us not being close boils down to ourselves, we're equally to blame for not trying harder. We're grown women!' Ginny was laughing now through a few tears. 'Maybe we should've tried harder with one another rather than have our mother have to summon us home to sort us out. And that's on us. You've carried the weight of secrets that I can't even imagine having to keep and here you are again, trying to fix everything for everyone else.'

'She always was good at fixing.' Fern smiled.

'I should've told you what I'd discovered,' said Daisy. 'Burying the secret for so long was probably the worst thing I could do.'

'I'm relieved this is why you got us home, Mum,' Ginny confessed. 'Finding out about what happened with Dad and discovering we have a half-sister is way better than what I assumed was going on – I thought perhaps things were really bad with Grandad, that he really was sick.'

'Your grandad will go on for years yet,' said Loretta with a dismissive wave through the air. 'Although you should know it was his idea to have him as the excuse to bring you all home.'

'Might've known.' Fern laughed.

'The sneaky old thing,' grinned Daisy.

Ginny realised something else. 'I'll bet he doesn't even need a Christmas quilt either, does he?'

All three of them were looking at her and Loretta admitted, 'We talked about how you girls used to work together, so very happy, and it was his idea to pretend his quilt was ruined in the wash. We didn't intend to involve Carrie though – she overheard us talking about the special quilt and then she ended up telling Daisy.' She shook her head. 'I feel terrible making up all these lies.'

'You did it for our own good,' said Fern, surprising everyone.

'I like Carrie,' Ginny said all of a sudden. 'But knowing the truth does explain a lot.' She told Loretta how jumpy Carrie usually was, how unsure of herself.

'I'm glad you've all made her feel welcome so far,' said Loretta tentatively, because she wasn't sure what would happen now that they knew the truth. She stood up. 'I'll leave you three to talk, without me. I'm taking Busker for his walk.'

As Loretta shrugged on her coat and pulled on her boots, Daisy posed the question Loretta had been waiting for, the question each of them had probably wanted to ask for the last half an hour as the truth came tumbling out.

'Where does this leave us, Mum?' Daisy wondered. 'What about Carrie?'

She grabbed Busker's lead. 'That, my girls, is up to you.'

Loretta arrived home with Busker and from her position in the hallway she could see her daughters were back in the lounge at the far end of the house, all down on their hands and knees, working away to finish pinning the quilt. 'So far so good,' she whispered to Busker as she ruffled the fur on his head. 'They haven't all packed up and left the house.'

But Loretta had only just unlooped her scarf from her neck when she heard the girls talking and the unmistakable word *bomb* from Daisy's lips.

She didn't pause to take her coat off. Instead she burst into the lounge.

'Mum!' Fern clutched a hand against her chest. 'You scared me, I didn't hear you come in.'

'Daisy, what's going on?' She put up a hand before her youngest daughter could say anything. 'I've respected your privacy, tried to trust you, but when a parent hears the word *bomb* and her daughter has been sneaking off at every opportunity, it wouldn't be right to leave it.' She waited, tipped her head to let Daisy know she could speak.

Daisy didn't deny it but she did smile and tell her mum, 'Keep your coat on.' She secured the last pin to fix the snow-white block against the bright red block with a Father Christmas figure and a sackful of presents, a candy cane bulging out of the top.

Judging by the way Fern and Ginny were grinning conspiratorially as they went to grab their own coats and shoes as well as hats and scarves, constantly giggling because Loretta was the only one still in the dark, Daisy's sisters were in on this.

Before they filed out of the door Loretta pulled Fern back. 'Please tell me we're not going to a protest or anything like that.' She had visions of paint bombs being slung at businesses or politicians as they protested the cause.

But Fern's reassurance that this was a good thing had Loretta believing in all three of them. Because seeing Fern, Ginny and Daisy pull together on anything was exactly what she'd wanted this Christmas.

Telling them about Carrie hadn't broken them, it hadn't driven them running off to their own lives and ripped another seam that barely held tight enough to keep them attached.

And that was all she could really ask for.

Chapter Twenty-One

Ginny

Ginny, Fern, Daisy and Loretta headed towards Lantern Square, Loretta questioning them all the way but none of them letting her in on the secret. It would be far more powerful when she saw what they were doing, and more so when she was a part of the shenanigans.

The shops in Butterbury were all closed, the streets next to empty, and they passed Lantern Square and turned onto a quieter street where Miriam's haberdashery stood beyond the post office. And there they waited, Fern and Ginny linking their mum's arms, one on each side. Daisy was keeping a look out, a big bag looped over one arm – a bag that their mother continued to try and check out but couldn't while she was anchored to her two eldest daughters.

Ginny was still trying to get her head around the idea that her parents had almost divorced, her dad had had an affair, and they had a half-sister as a result. In her work she'd met so many different women, plenty of single mums too, and she'd wondered about their stories. Were they women like Carrie's mum? Where was the father and did he even know? Now, she understood all the more how easily it could happen. Relationships were difficult and even the sturdiest of marriages came up against hurdles. Had her and Lucas hit a very big bump in the road that at the time was insurmountable? And did that bump really have to be the end?

When Ginny confided in her sisters about her pain at never having been able to say goodbye to their dad when they'd both been at his bedside, it was like something unlocked inside of her. The tears had fallen, but more than that the guilt had been shed like an unwelcome cloak from around her shoulders. And when Daisy had broken down about the special quilt and was honest about how she felt too, Ginny had seen that in their own way, they were all in pain. They'd all carried the weight of their father's death alone and, sure, Fern had comforted Ginny and Daisy when they cried, but they hadn't been there for her, and holding it together for others must've affected her in a way she never shared either.

When Loretta had taken Busker out for a walk earlier the sisters had really talked, mostly about their disbelief over their parents' troubles, but also about Carrie.

'She's such a lovely, kind girl,' Fern had said.

'I suspected she was holding something back,' Ginny admitted.

'I always thought it was because she was so young,' said Fern. 'I thought perhaps her age made her feel awkward around us.'

Daisy put the last mug into the dishwasher and started its cycle. 'Being a teenager is tough sometimes.'

'Mum's right though.' Ginny looked at both of her sisters. 'Carrie hasn't done anything wrong. Not really. Her intentions have been good, and, Daisy, wasn't it Carrie who encouraged you to ask us to help with the quilt?' When Daisy nodded, she added, 'The way I see it, she did us a bit of a favour, pushing us together.'

'Could've easily backfired.' Fern grinned. 'And perhaps we should see Carrie's involvement as a good sign of things to come between us.'

'How's that?' Daisy asked.

'Carrie came back to spend time with us more than once – clearly we're not that terrible.'

'Good job she met us now and not a couple of years ago when we didn't have anything very nice to say about each other,' said Ginny.

Daisy whipped her playfully with a tea towel. 'We weren't that bad.'

Fern took the tea towel from Daisy and hung it up. 'We were, but we're good now. Aren't we?'

Ginny put an arm around Daisy's shoulders, her other around Fern's. 'We are good. But what do we do now, about Carrie?'

'I think we just need to try to include her for a while,' said Daisy. 'We don't have to go over the top, talk on a deeper level, that will come later I expect. For the moment I think we should all just try to be her friend?'

As they waited outside in the cold now, Ginny listening to Loretta persistently quizzing them about what was going on, Daisy telling her to be patient, Ginny thought about her mum's plan to get them all back together and working on a quilting project like they'd done all those years ago. Without knowing it Loretta's plan had done more than bring the sisters together, it had made Ginny realise how much she wanted a different future, how much she really wanted to take over the shop.

Her insides fizzed with excitement at the thought. As

a little girl she'd imagined standing behind the counter and cutting exquisite fabrics for a customer, wrapping purchases in brown paper bags and handing them over for another project to start. She'd gone to the Butterbury Sewing Box after school on more occasions than she could count to help her mother out, but as she got older schoolwork came first. Life evolved. Ginny showed an interest in midwifery, and thinking her mother's retirement and the shop passing down a generation was a long way off Ginny hadn't thought a second choice of vocation would change much at all. She'd thought she had all the time in the world to make her choice. But perhaps Daisy had needed to be with Loretta in the shop as much as Ginny had needed to get away for a while. And maybe now Daisy could see she might too be able to take her life in a different direction.

Working in the Butterbury Sewing Box to help out over the last week or so had been a pleasure for Ginny. And it had been all she'd needed to remind her of the dream she'd once had as a little girl, the dream that was still on the periphery, knocking ever so gently to remind her it was time to let it back in. When the pink sewing machine had come down from the loft earlier it was like time flashed before her, all the evenings she'd worked in her bedroom by lamplight until one or other of her parents had rapped on the door and told her it really was bedtime. And now the machine was ready and waiting at the house, in position for them to sew together Grandad's Christmas quilt they'd all worked so hard to get ready in time.

Ginny looked at her sisters now, laughing and huddled together as they waited. They were a work in progress and who knew where Carrie would fit into their world.

'Right, it's freezing cold, girls,' said Loretta, authority in her voice. 'Whatever is going on?'

At that moment Daisy jumped on the spot and let out a squeal. 'They're here!'

A minibus trundled around the corner and came to a sedate stop before Maggie from Butterbury Lodge climbed out and slid open the side door.

Loretta immediately stepped forwards. 'Dad? What on earth are you doing here?' She meant it collectively, of course, because inside the minibus was Ivor, Mr G, Flo, Ernest, and three other elderly residents Ginny had seen in passing but couldn't put names to.

'So the secret is out,' said Ivor, giving his daughter a hug, but he kept his voice low. 'Nobody else, OK?' He put a finger over his lips to let Loretta, Ginny and Fern know this wasn't to go any further. 'Daisy and I have been planning this for almost a year, the village is in for a real treat.'

'Daisy?' Loretta looked at her youngest daughter, still desperate to know what was going on.

'Gran would've loved this,' Ginny told Ivor.

'She would.' He hugged her, then Fern and then Ginny as Maggie helped the other residents out of the minibus and made sure they were wrapped up adequately for the cold winter's night. 'She would've loved the secrecy, the adventure.'

When Ginny looked up one more person emerged from the minibus. Carrie.

All three sisters quietened and Carrie looked as though she wanted to dive right back in and hide until all of this was over.

Fern beckoned her go join them. 'Carrie, you've come to help?'

Carrie nodded. Perhaps they'd wait to tell her they knew everything at long last. Perhaps a joint focus might go some way to making it easier all round until they did.

And now Loretta's impatience began to show through some more. 'Is anyone going to let me in on what on earth this secret is?' The chopped long layers of her hair poked out from the sides of her charcoal woollen hat. 'I feel like everyone else knows something I don't.'

Carrie beamed a smile at Loretta that left Ginny dumb-struck because in that moment she looked so much like Harry, the man who'd made this connection between the women forever.

Daisy took over the announcement. 'Tonight, we are going to yarn bomb Butterbury!'

Loretta's smile spread wide, a hand against her chest. 'I'm a little relieved, Daisy, I have to say.' And as her daughter gave out instructions to everyone gathered she asked, 'Is this even allowed?'

'Daisy got the relevant permissions with the council and shop owners,' said Ginny, 'don't worry.'

'Let's get going then.' Fern wasn't one for standing around in the cold without doing something and had already taken possession of a big bag of colourful wool designs. 'Come on, Grandad, you're with me, the tree outside the post office is our first target.'

Ginny was impressed. The residents from the lodge were accompanied by helpers and everyone seemed well informed. Daisy must've done a stellar job with the organising of all of this. When she'd told her and Fern what she'd been doing up at the lodge for so long they'd surreptitiously exchanged a glance to say this is Daisy, the woman she is now, so very different from back then. And now they knew everything the family had had to contend with, especially Daisy, they couldn't be more proud.

'Carrie, come help me and Ginny,' said Daisy, handing her a bag of colourful yarn with another in her own possession.

Daisy, although a lot older than Carrie, seemed to gel with her easily and for now Ginny knew it was baby steps. For all of them. But for once she truly believed that they could get there together.

Armed with the creations, Daisy, Ginny and Carrie secured a white knitted snowman with a black hat and a chunky red knitted scarf protruding outwards up against the bark of a tree. They moved to do the posts on either side of one of the iron gates leading into the square, decorating both in red wool they wrapped around and fixed together quickly and efficiently with the ties they'd sewn in. Each post became a Father Christmas – red wool with white yarn trim for his coat and a big white beard. They decorated trees in Lantern Square, one with a knitted reindeer, which looked as though it was galloping upwards towards the sky, and when it's knitted red nose fell off Carrie brushed the dirt from it using a tissue in her pocket, smiled and handed it to Ginny. Ginny quickly saw to it that it was stitched tightly back on.

They hung knitted stars and snowflakes from branches of trees, decorated the railings beside the illuminated fox in a flowerbed with knitted baubles, they added miniature snowmen to a bench seat near the tall village Christmas tree, Carrie grabbing Ginny's hand and pulling her behind the bench when a man walked past with his dog, whistling and in his own little world.

'Almost sprung,' winked Ginny, before they got back to work.

Carrie went to help out one of the residents who was having trouble fitting yarn around the bark of another tree.

'Fix it on tight,' Ginny called over to them. 'We don't want it to flap around in the wind remember.'

Carrie, relaxed this evening without any of them uttering a word that they knew who she was, was a real part of this too and Ginny could already feel her guard coming down. Even Fern seemed open to the idea of a half-sibling and Ginny knew if they'd been thrown this curve ball a while back, they might have handled it very differently.

They worked quickly and Ginny felt immensely proud of Daisy when her younger sister stopped all of a sudden as if immersing herself with this creative secret had given her the confidence to speak up at long last. 'Mum, remember when I was at the bookshop that day?'

'Taking the photographs of Father Christmas and the children?' Loretta asked. 'Of course.'

'Well the journalist at the newspaper gave me her card.' She paused and Ginny nodded excitedly for her to keep going now she'd started. It all came tumbling out, her admission gaining momentum. 'She loved my work. And tomorrow I'm going to get up at the crack of dawn, come down here and take more pictures as daylight breaks. I want to capture people's faces and reactions. I'm going to do a write-up too and send it straight to the local newspaper.'

Ginny wanted to cheer. Her little sister had finally said what had probably been on her mind for so long she'd lost the ability to voice it.

'Well it's about time!' Loretta clapped her gloved hands together.

'You don't mind?'

'Daisy, I want you to be happy.' Loretta clasped her daughter's face between her palms. 'That's all I've ever wanted. You always protested you were happy with me at the shop and I let myself believe that was true without questioning it. I've loved having you by my side. But now it's time to do what's right for you.'

'You really don't mind that I don't want to work at the shop?'

'Daisy, my happiness comes from my children, not just in the things that they do for me but also in the things they do for themselves. I can't even begin to tell you how it makes me feel to see you happy and it breaks my heart that you made your world smaller to accommodate me.'

'I'll never regret my decision, you know.'

'I'm glad. Now can we get on, it's freezing out here!'

They met up with Fern and Grandad who, along with a smiling Carrie, were finishing fixing a Father Christmas and a pile of knitted gifts to the bottom of a tree in a flowerbed that might ensure it was safe from being trampled on.

'What happens if all of this gets wet?' Loretta asked.

And almost as though the roles had already switched with her younger sister, Ginny explained, 'Daisy made sure they used the most appropriate yarn, she's had it all sorted from the beginning.'

Daisy added, 'And the weather forecast from now until Christmas is favourable – cold, but dry. Fingers crossed it stays that way until New Year's Eve so this yarn bombing looks as good as it does now.'

'You've done very well with all of this, Daisy.' Loretta brushed a twig from the bottom of her coat as they emerged onto the street again. 'But one more thing . . .'

'Yes, Mum?'

'You're fired.'

Daisy grinned and gave her mum a big hug. They admired some of their handiwork that could be seen in the light of the street lamps, with the help of the moon from up above. Around the tree closest to the post office were reds, greens, mustard yellow, snowflakes knitted in to several places. The knits had been made oversized so that they could easily be wound around the misshapen trunk that didn't allow measurements to be that accurate and had been quickly stitched in place. In front of the post office on top of the postbox was an open-weave crocheted white topper. On top of that was green knitted holly to adorn the circumference at intervals with bright red knitted berries and in the centre a cleverly knitted snowman beside a couple of reindeer and a knitted sleigh. Daisy had told Ginny they'd used foam to get the shape of the sleigh and pulled the yarn around that and it worked well. On top of a parking post, which had been wrapped with a series of green knitted squares, was a collection of three knitted presents, using foam for their internal structure too, and on top of the next, which was also wrapped in green, and running down the sides were knitted figures – wise men, an elf, baubles and a star – as though the post were a Christmas tree. The railings surrounding the square hadn't missed out either because right beside the gate was a rectangle of midnight blue upon which was a knitted Christmas tree, flat faced with coloured baubles, all done in thread, a skilled project mastered by two ladies up at the lodge.

Grandad and Carrie joined them and Ivor pointed out the midnight blue rectangle up against a tree with a characterful snowman on its front complete with red scarf and black hat. He and Flo had been in charge of that one. He pointed too to the lamp post they'd just been in charge of bombing. Now it was wrapped in a deep forest green and had Father Christmas figureheads knitted on it, each with a white ball sewn on as the bobble for their hat.

'Spot the odd one out,' Carrie giggled. 'Flo made it and I think it's the star of the show.'

Ginny had to move a bit closer across the street to see and burst out laughing when she did. 'What happened there?' The Father Christmas Flo from the lodge had knitted was a great deal fatter than all the others, with rosy cheeks and a winning smile.

'She wanted it to be different, I think,' said Carrie.

'It's good to be different,' Ginny agreed, and if Carrie had any inkling she knew they were well aware of who she was, she didn't say.

Loretta hugged Ginny as they turned to look in another direction past the square. She pointed over to the railings closest to the pub. 'How did they get those yarn bombings fixed there without anyone seeing them, I wonder?' The pub was pretty much the only place tonight that had people coming and going, but somehow, someone had fixed elves on the bench on the pavement across the road, directly opposite. The elves were along the back of the bench, some sitting, others lying, all looking mischievous.

'Perhaps the punters have drunk a bit too much and assume they're seeing things.'

Loretta chuckled. 'We might well be responsible for a few calls to the doctor tomorrow.'

'Or the optician,' Ginny laughed, pointing out the row of knitted reindeers on one of the benches just visible in the square itself as they peered over the railings. Beyond was the village Christmas tree at the opposite end, but it stood so tall they could see it from here. Christmas in Butterbury had always been wonderful but this year was extra special.

They gathered on the street ready to help everyone back onto the minibus. Maggie from the lodge had done a head count more than once to ensure nobody had gone astray.

'How are you all feeling about Carrie?' Loretta asked quietly as they waited. Carrie was helping Flo onto the minibus but it appeared Flo didn't want to leave, she was buzzing with excitement and hard to convince it might be time to head back.

'You'll blow our cover if you're not careful!' Ivor told her, and it seemed to have the necessary effect as Flo climbed into the vehicle.

Ginny spoke quietly to Loretta. 'We're all enjoying getting to know Carrie.'

'You are?'

'We are. And we've agreed to take it slowly, probably best all round.'

Loretta paused before she asked, 'Are you angry at your dad?'

Ginny smiled. 'It's a lot to get our heads around, but no, life's too short for anger. We love him as much as we always did.' It felt good to be talking about her sisters collectively, the way it should have been all along.

Loretta nodded. 'You've always been the peacemaker, Ginny. Even as a child you backed off, you let others around you carry on. But with Daisy finally telling me what she wants, perhaps it's time for you to do the same.'

Ginny barely took a breath before she blurted out, 'I want the shop.' She covered her mouth as though she might be saying something shocking, but when she turned to face her mum, Loretta was grinning.

'Hallelujah!' Loretta raised her hands heavenward.

'You knew?'

'I had an inkling, we both did . . . your dad and I,' she clarified. 'But when you were happy with your choices we weren't going to dissuade you.'

'I've loved being a midwife.' It almost felt a betrayal to leave her career behind, but it was time.

'I know, and that's why I never pushed it. Your dad didn't either when you told us what your career plans were. But we did both wonder how long it would take you to come back to this place.'

'How did you know I ever would?'

'I didn't, not for certain, and I didn't want to ask you about it because you were so independent, I knew that for it to be the right thing for you, you had to come to the conclusion yourself. And when Daisy said she'd stay on and be with me in the shop, that she wanted the family business, you didn't protest. I thought that perhaps your dad and I were wrong about you all along. It wasn't until you came back to Butterbury this time and I saw you in the shop or working on the quilt that I realised you hadn't looked so happy since I'd seen you working late in your room on that pink sewing machine of yours.'

Ginny gave her mum a hug. 'I think we all need our heads banging together, you know. We should've talked from the start.' Everyone who needed to be was in the minibus ready for the off and Maggie closed the sliding door.

'No,' said Loretta, laughing, 'we might have been looking at a war if we had. Sometimes it's best to let these things emerge.'

'A bit like Carrie.'

Loretta hesitated. 'Yes, a bit like Carrie has.'

And Loretta still had Ivor in her life, the three sisters had Loretta and their grandad. Carrie had nobody, and it made Ginny realise how lucky they all were. 'For what it's worth, I think Dad would've told you about her. He was probably trying to find the right time.'

Loretta squeezed her hand in agreement as Daisy came towards them with her camera in her hands, the strap around her neck.

'I've taken loads of pictures already,' she enthused. 'More in the morning, but I've got some cracking shots with the Christmas lights and the tree in the background, the colours beneath street lamps. Sally will have a whole selection.'

'Pub?' Fern asked her sisters. 'I've not got many more nights of freedom, what do you say? Mum?'

Loretta closed the minibus door for Maggie. She leaned in to her daughters. 'Not for me, I've volunteered to head up to Butterbury Lodge with Maggie, make hot chocolates for this lot, deal with the euphoria so they eventually settle down a bit.'

In the Butterbury Arms Ginny leaned back against the wall as Daisy and Fern went to buy a round. She didn't open her eyes until a Baileys Irish Cream had been set down in front of her – double measure, oodles of ice, the way she loved it.

They all raised their glasses and quietly Daisy whispered, 'To the Butterbury yarn bombers,' and she put a finger across her lips.

They went through the photographs Daisy had taken, careful not to let anyone see what they were up to. 'It's amazing.' Ginny beamed. 'Thanks for including us.'

'You weren't going to let me keep it a secret any longer.' Daisy smiled, but there was no anger behind her comment, no resentment that they'd wanted to be a part of what was going on in her life like there might once have been.

'You're a wonderful photographer, Daisy. You have a way of capturing your subjects, showing the emotions.' Ginny swilled the ice in the bottom of her glass and took a deep breath. 'I owe you an apology.'

'Whatever for?'

Ginny looked at her younger sister. Fern was quiet, waiting to hear what came next. 'For tearing up the photograph you took of me after Dad's funeral.'

Daisy looked into the contents of her own glass.

'I'm really sorry I did that.'

Daisy shrugged. 'It was insensitive of me.'

'I overreacted,' said Ginny.

'I took it because you looked like you always had, the one who was calm, the one who always knew what to say. I took the picture because it made me realise I didn't have to be alone, I had other people I could share a burden with.'

'Except you never did,' said Fern and covered her hand as each of them accepted the acknowledgement of what had gone before, what couldn't be changed but could be learned from.

'It was nice to spend more time with Carrie tonight,' said Ginny, glad she'd finally cleared the air with Daisy. She'd never forgotten the distress on her sister's face, the emotions she'd caused by tearing up that picture. But now Daisy had to know how proud she was of her.

'It certainly was.' Fern nodded. 'It must be terrifying being the outsider.'

'You are pretty scary,' Daisy teased and got a nudge in return.

'I'm serious,' said Fern. 'I was watching her this evening and I kept trying to put myself in her shoes, wondering how she must feel.'

'She was brave to come here to Butterbury,' Ginny agreed.

'I think it's going to take time, on all our parts,' added Daisy.

Ginny nodded her agreement and took another gulp of Baileys. 'Why is this so good?'

Fern pulled a face. 'What I'd like to know is why it takes mere seconds to drain a glass?' She held up her empty vessel, ready for another.

Ginny picked up Daisy's camera again and flipped through more photographs, this time those of one of her camping trips. 'Where's this?'

'Northumberland.'

'It's beautiful, I'll give you that, all those wide open spaces. It proves you don't always appreciate what's on your own doorstep. But the camping?' She shook her head and looked across at Fern.

'Never a truer word,' said Fern with a weird look on her

face before she beckoned Daisy to go get another round in with her. 'We'll get doubles again,' she winked.

Ginny's puzzled glance at her sisters who were clearly conspiring was replaced with a smile when Lucas came and sat down in front of her.

You don't always appreciate what is right in front of you either, she thought to herself. Here he was, so close, soft brown eyes fixed on her, hair that in the summer went from its mid-brown to a dirty blond. And it was as though they were two twenty-somethings all over again.

She caught sight of her sisters watching them and wanted to swat them away. Lucas had noticed them too and grinned.

When he offered her another drink she shook her head. 'How about we walk instead?' She needed to escape if they were going to be able to talk properly. And she desperately wanted to know whether his feelings were as strong as hers.

He downed the remains of the pint he'd brought over with him and picked up his coat. 'Sounds good to me.'

As they walked over to Lantern Square Lucas spotted the yarn bombing and Ginny did her best to act surprised too.

'You, Fern and Daisy seem to be doing all right,' he said as they headed for one of the benches.

'We're getting there.' They sat down on the bench that had the knitted reindeers across the back. 'We've had a bit of time to talk, properly I mean. It's something I think we all neglected and somehow let things come between us.' She wasn't going to share all the details just yet, and she was conscious Carrie might want to take things slow too. She might not want everyone to know how she was connected to the family until they'd all got more used to the idea themselves.

'I'm happy for you, Ginny.'

It was cold but they were sitting close enough that she had a bit of warmth from his proximity. 'Do you remember when we last talked and you said you thought I'd take on the shop?' Ginny smiled.

He nodded, knowing what was coming. 'I wondered how long that would take. You finally told your mum and Daisy how you felt?'

'I did, and more than that, Daisy wants to do something entirely different anyway.'

'Don't tell me, there's a camera involved? Joshua has mentioned once or twice – or was it several times – how talented she is.'

'She wanted to study photojournalism at university but never did, because of Mum, because she felt she needed to stay here.' Her heart was thumping as she delivered her explanation when all she wanted to know was whether they stood a chance together.

'While you needed to get away.'

She explained what she'd told her sisters, the guilt at having not been there for her dad, the pain at not saying goodbye to him. 'I didn't think I should be happy.'

'You know that's crazy, don't you?' He hesitated and then, looking away and into the wintry sky, said, 'I'm truly sorry I hurt you, Ginny. Ending things was something I never thought of when we were so good together, but then . . .'

'I know, we both changed.'

'We both grew up.' He looked at her and managed a smile. 'For so many years I'd been in Butterbury in my

309

comfort zone. Even when I was at university I knew I had this buffer, that the family business was here if I needed it, and I can't explain it but that got to me. I saw the way you'd found a career and a passion and despite everything that had happened to you, you had found a way through it. That strength – which I think all you Chamberlain girls have, by the way – is something I wondered whether I had deep down. When I was offered the job in Florida I didn't think I should burden you with a choice to come with me or not. You needed your family, even though you didn't really see it at the time. And there's a difference between going off travelling and moving to another country. At the time I was open to staying out there. I couldn't do that to you.'

'I would've come with you.'

He went to lay an arm across the back of the bench but the reindeers were in the way. He clasped his palms together again, leaning forwards. 'I know. But we both had to carve out our own paths, move forwards, learn, grow up some more.' She couldn't deny it. Even now, the attraction so strong, she knew it was right they'd had time apart. And she was only glad he'd had the strength to be the one to make the decision for them. 'It took me a while but I eventually realised that Butterbury and the farm were what I wanted in my future despite having other options.' He harrumphed. 'I also naively expected you to run back into my arms. I thought we'd see each other here in the village and that would be it.'

'I avoided ever bumping into you once I knew you were back,' she admitted.

'I know, and I was gutted. But I told myself you were probably happy, I accepted it and tried to move on.' He put a hand over hers. 'We were both so young when we got together, we had so much to learn.'

'I learned I love train journeys.' It got the laugh she'd anticipated. 'I'm serious. Especially the Eurostar . . . you leave London behind and sit in darkness whizzing through a tunnel that spits you out into another country. The first time I did it I was in awe, I think I still am really, to be travelling beneath water for all that time to reach another place entirely.'

'I learned I hate the middle seat on a plane.' It was his turn to make her laugh. 'I mean it, it's the worst seat ever. I'm tempted to book a spare seat next to me next time I fly.' Neither of them said it but she felt sure he must be wondering whether she could be the one to sit in that seat instead of having it empty.

'I learned I love meeting new people and the challenges of new environments.' She sighed and almost leaned her head against his shoulder. 'But I've also learned how much I love this village. I've been to some stunning countries, towns and villages, I've seen so much, but this is where my heart is.'

An unspoken understanding passed between them when she turned to face him.

Lucas twirled the ends of her hair that were poking out from beneath a woolly hat. Their separate experiences, paths and the years apart had brought them to this very moment. And what he said next made her breathless. 'I've learned I don't want to be without you for a single day, Ginny Chamberlain.' He looked so vulnerable in this moment. He exuded the gentleness and kindness that had always made her feel like she mattered to him more than anyone else.

She shivered and a sigh let her breath puff out against the cold. Even in the dark you could see it. 'You're a good man, Lucas.'

'So I'm told.' She wasn't looking at him but she knew he was smiling.

'Are you happy here in Butterbury, at the farm, for good?'

He slotted his fingers between hers. 'I'm happier now that you're here. Don't get me wrong, I've had a life, I've had girlfriends since you and I split up, but I've never found someone who really fit, someone who wants the same things, someone who loves life in an English village not quite as hip as some, but just as quaint as others.' He looked into her eyes. 'You'll be coming back to Butterbury for the shop.' It wasn't a question. 'I guess I'm wondering whether you'll be staying here in Butterbury for another reason.'

Her heart thumped. This was it. With his words he'd given her the answer to the question she'd been asking ever since she realised their connection had never truly been lost. 'I think I might be, yes.'

'Well it's about time,' he murmured, voice low, teasing and laced with promise as he leaned his forehead against hers and the warmth drew them together in body and in mind. She no longer felt the shiver of cold when he drew back and his gaze fell to her lips.

'We haven't kissed for over a decade.'

'Maybe we won't remember how to do it,' he said, their lips almost touching as he inched closer.

'Maybe . . .' But she didn't get to say anything more because his lips were on hers, and they fitted every bit as well as they used to.

Chapter Twenty-Two

Daisy

Daisy was manning the shop while her mum took care of some last-minute Christmas shopping in Tetbury. Loretta had tried to persuade Carrie to come into the Butterbury Sewing Box and keep Daisy company now that the girls knew all about her. But she'd been wary and made her excuses. Daisy couldn't blame her. There were three of them, one of her, and being the one who felt like they were on the periphery wasn't easy. But given a chance, they'd all prove that wasn't how it had to be and they'd show her how much they wanted to get to know her and perhaps make her a part of the family, if that was what she wanted.

Daisy yawned again. It had been an early start this morning following a late finish last night, charged with Baileys and watching Ginny and Lucas out of the window of the pub, both Daisy and Fern cheering them on when they kissed at last. Even Colette had stopped collecting up the empties from her pub tables and come over to see what the girls were gawking at and let out a cheer, proving there were plenty of people who'd hoped that the two Butterbury locals would one day find their way back to each other.

Daisy had walked Busker this morning and he'd done well, sitting when told, not wandering off even though she wasn't clutching his lead but instead taking photographs of the yarn bombings in the daylight. She'd captured local retired judge Mrs Addington posting a silver-enveloped Christmas card in the postbox with the yarn on top, her smile a festive beam she was happy to have appear in the newspaper. Daisy had interviewed her to find out her reaction to the yarn bombings, she interviewed Miriam who'd arrived back late last night to see the bollards near her haberdashery looking spectacular. Miriam had told Daisy it was the best welcome home she'd ever had and Daisy got the impression it had been tough going with her family so she was doubly pleased she'd been a part of bringing her some much needed festive joy. Daisy had also spoken to Dawn and Troy who owned the Lantern Bakery and they'd agreed that the colours brought something new to the village and had created a buzz that had more and more people coming out of their houses and talking to their neighbours as they speculated as to who had done this wonderful thing.

Daisy had sent each of her photographs from this morning and last night along with a write-up she'd typed in record time to Sally, and Sally had promised to get back to her ASAP. Daisy knew she was going to have to fight the urge to check her phone every five minutes while she was working in the shop and when her next customer came in she shoved her phone beneath the counter in an effort to resist looking at it.

Daisy picked up a dry leaf that blew in as a customer left and as she shut the door again another customer appeared, this time a man slightly older than Loretta, small wire-framed glasses that had steamed up upon meeting the heat of the shop, and a big bag in tow. He'd probably come to donate some material – it happened with regularity and sometimes the best treasures were found in what strangers brought into the shop.

'Are you Fern?' the man asked. And before she could answer added, 'Or Ginny, or Daisy, or Loretta?'

'I'm Daisy.' She smiled. 'And you are?' They were well known locally and it wasn't unusual for people to know their names when they came in to the Butterbury Sewing Box.

He took his glasses off and gave them a wipe before loosening his burgundy scarf. 'It's lovely and warm in here.'

'You can take your coat off, have a browse if you like.'

'Actually I have something for you.' He indicated the bag he had with him, a bulging bin liner. 'It's a long story.'

Something else customers did – something Ginny would probably be fascinated by when she took over full-time – was to share where their material had come from, why it was special to them, why they were parting with it. Loretta said it always made it that bit more special to use.

'I've been looking for you for a while,' he went on.

'Well now you've found us.'

'I had thought if I'm after a haberdashery in Butterbury, it must be the one down past the post office. I heard the owner was on holiday so I've been waiting for her to return. I didn't even think there might be two sewing shops in the village. I'm not exactly local, you see. Anyway, the owner, Miriam, sent me this way, and I must say I'm pleased to get this to you before Christmas.'

'Right.' She indicated to pass her the bag.

'My late wife was in a terrible car accident many years ago.'

'I'm so sorry to hear that.' Daisy had had plenty of customers in desperate need to offload their worries and talk to another human being. And she never minded at all. It had become a regular part of the service you got from a family-owned business.

'Oh she didn't die,' he explained. 'Not then at least. She lived many happy years right up until fourteen months ago.' His bottom lip quivered but only momentarily before he patted the bag he had with him again. 'This has been in our attic since the car accident. I'd forgotten about it, to be honest. It got pushed aside in the busyness of life and it was only when my son helped me to clear my house out that at long last I found it. I always knew it must be special.'

'May I?' She indicated the top of the bag, wound tight and secured with a rubber band. She was parched and the sooner she saw what was in the bag, the sooner they could move the conversation on. She was happy to sit and listen to him talk about his late wife, she just wouldn't mind doing it over a cup of tea.

He opened the bag up for her and she wasn't sure what she'd been expecting – a wedding dress in beautiful lace, a garment his wife had made by hand perhaps, a blanket they'd owned for years and he was finally getting rid of.

She definitely hadn't expected this. And all at once her past rushed at her.

At fifteen years old Daisy had been what you might describe as wild, all over the place, vulnerable and in with a bad crowd. She hacked off her hair and turned the luscious chestnut locks into a harsh mess in desperate need of attention, she bunked off school as much as she could get away with, she was rude to her teachers, resulting in several written warnings home. She had a fake ID, got into nightclubs and danced until the early hours, breaking all the rules at home. She started drinking alcohol underage, it helped her to forget or at least numb the pain of what she'd discovered about her dad.

One night Daisy had been in cahoots with Sinead, a girl who hadn't seen the inside of a classroom in months and seemed glad to have a partner in crime in Daisy. They made cocktails with Sinead's boyfriend and all of them, including Daisy, were knocking them back. Most of the time Daisy hadn't had any idea of the contents in her glass apart from a good dose of gin and anything else they'd stolen from Sinead's parents' house. The evening started out much like any other, drinks followed by a nightclub and a lot of dancing. Daisy remembered feeling like she wanted to be sick, she vaguely recalled slumping in a corner and sitting on the sticky floor watching people's feet going this way and that, barely able to lift her head. A bouncer had found her collapsed in a corner, called an ambulance, and somewhere in the mayhem the hospital had contacted her dad. Daisy had had her stomach pumped and could remember her dad coming, her feeling safe and warm as he wrapped the special quilt they'd made for movie night around her as they walked out to the car when it was time to go home. Daisy had never been so ashamed as she was that day. She couldn't believe the mess she'd made of herself, the embarrassment she must've caused, and she kept out of everyone's way as much as possible when she got home.

That was the last time Daisy ever saw their special quilt too. And when Harry died and it became apparent that the quilt had gone missing, that she was the last one to have it, it had instigated both of her sisters hurling terrible insults her way, fuelled by their pain. *You're selfish! It's your fault! You destroyed something special to us!* they'd said. And up until recently, until they'd talked to each other properly, Daisy had thought she deserved the way they'd blamed her and taken their grief out on their youngest sister.

Now, in the shop, Daisy pulled the quilt out of the bag the man had handed to her. Her voice shook. 'Where did you get this?'

'If you don't mind me saying so, you look a little pale, my dear.' He guided her over to the stool beside the Christmas tree where she sat down, still clutching the quilt in her arms. 'I hope I haven't upset you.'

Eyes swimming, tears spilling over, she managed to say, 'I promise these are happy tears.' She sniffed and took the tissue he handed her from his pocket. 'Where did you find it?' She couldn't take her eyes off the quilt in her arms, she couldn't let go, as if knowing her dad had once touched it and worked on it with his daughters and his wife made a connection she'd thought was gone for ever.

'Might I suggest a cup of tea,' the man said softly. 'Or I can go, leave you to it.'

Daisy didn't want that. 'Please stay a while.'

'Very well.'

'I want to hear more.' She squeezed hold of the quilt more tightly. 'I need to.'

'I'm Anton, by the way.'

'Daisy. But you know that.' She laughed.

318

'I do. And I'm glad I found you, Daisy.'

She took a deep breath, he waited while she ran her hand across the quilt reacquainting herself with its familiarity, the stitching and designs they'd carefully thought out and worked on diligently.

And then with the quilt in her arms she stood up. 'You're right. I think we need a cup of tea.' She wanted to know everything, to process how the quilt was still in one piece, how it had found its way home after all this time.

'I never say no to a good brew.' He smiled.

She folded the quilt carefully and although it was hard to let it go when she'd only just got it back, she set it onto the counter. And with mugs of tea made and a chair brought out from the back for Anton, they sat beside the tree and she listened as he told her everything.

'When my wife had her car accident it was bad,' Anton began in a soft voice she could've listened to for hours. 'She'd gone through the window, was lying on the ground, the car upside down. A good Samaritan stopped, called an ambulance, and waited with her, talked to her even though she was unresponsive. He covered her in a quilt.' He waited for Daisy to realise what his words meant.

Daisy's voice wobbled. 'My dad was the good Samaritan.'

'Yes,' he nodded. 'The quilt went with my Lily in the ambulance, the paramedics must've thought it belonged to her. And when Lily came to in the hours after the accident and saw the quilt on the back of a chair I told her what had happened. She was desperate to find the person who had helped her. We asked questions but all I could find out was that it had been a man, that he was local, and other than that I couldn't get any more details. I don't know if it was confidentiality or because they didn't know who he was, but we just knew the quilt was very special to someone out there. Handmade, am I right?' He took in the view of the interior of the shop, the quilts on display at the far end.

'We all worked on it – Mum, Dad, us three girls. It was a special quilt for us to snuggle under for movie night. Every Sunday.' Her voice drifted off.

'When we couldn't get the answers we needed,' he explained, 'we had the quilt cleaned and put it in a bag for safe keeping. I put up photographs in the local community centre, I asked around, but nobody knew where it had come from. And I'm sorry to say that after a while, it was forgotten about and pushed aside.'

Daisy held onto her mug of tea more tightly as details came rushing back at her. 'I remember the night it happened.' She shook her head. 'I hadn't thought about it until now.'

Daisy had been at home every day since her stint in hospital, ashamed of how she'd acted, wanting to find a way forwards but not knowing how. One evening Harry had been home late from work and she'd hung back from going downstairs because she could tell something had happened. Loretta was hugging him tightly in the hallway and Daisy had wondered whether he was going to confess everything to his wife. She'd crept along the landing and halfway down the stairs to listen.

'Dad told Mum how he'd seen an accident,' she said to Anton, 'how he'd stopped and seen a woman badly hurt. He was devastated that the hospital wouldn't give him any details about whether the woman was all right.'

'The not knowing is often the worst part,' Anton agreed. 'If your dad hadn't been there to call the ambulance and keep her warm until help arrived, she might not have made it home at all.'

'How did you find us in the end?'

'My daughter, Fay, wouldn't let it rest. She remembered Lily and I talking about the good Samaritan, about the quilt and how special it was and when she saw the quilt once it was out of the attic she burst into tears.' He grinned. 'She's just had twins, and by her own admission is a bag of hormones and emotions. And she told me she was crying at the thought of having something so special for her own little family and losing it in a moment. Fay suggested we use social media and cast our net a little wider. She put up a post with a picture of the quilt and we knew the three initials, F, G and D, had to mean something, so she asked if anyone knew somebody into quilting with sisters or daughters or best friends with those initials. We said they were most likely, but not definitely, going to be living within a ten mile radius of where my wife's car accident happened, although of course we weren't sure, it was a long shot, but we listed all the towns and villages and that included Butterbury.

'Fay had several responses about the quilting but none specific for the initials until one reply that said there was a sewing shop that sold haberdashery items, quilts and quilting equipment and that it was run by a lady who had three daughters. They didn't know the names but a week later several others had seen the post and we had our F, G, and D. Fern, Ginny and Daisy. It still feels strange –' he smiled '– after all these years to finally put names to the initials and now a face to one of the names.'

Daisy picked up the quilt again and hugged it to her. 'Thank you, from the bottom of my heart. You have no idea what this means to me and my family.'

'I think I do,' he said. 'That's why I'm here after all.'

Anton didn't go straight away. He'd asked her to thank Harry for him and she told him Harry had passed away soon after the accident. She'd managed not to cry though and instead between them they'd opened the quilt up on the counter and she talked Anton through the squares. She told him how Fern was into mathematics, she was a keen photographer, and it had been Ginny who was the most passionate about sewing. She talked about how Harry wasn't too good at any sort of needlework and that he always complained his fingers were too fat. And when Anton said he had to go she almost didn't want him to.

Fern burst through the door before Anton had a chance to do up his coat. 'Daisy, I've discovered the best gingerbread ever!' She had a brown paper bag in hand. 'Oh, excuse me, sorry, customers.' She pulled a face.

'Which one's this?' Anton beamed and Daisy wondered whether this might be a process that had brought him some comfort, honouring his wife's memory by returning the quilt that had helped her on that dreadful night.

'I'm Fern.' Fern smiled, extending the hand that wasn't clutching the bag of gingerbread.

'Anton, pleased to meet you.'

Daisy grinned and pointed beyond the door. 'And that lady out there is Ginny, the middle sister.'

'The one in a lip lock with the young gentleman?'

'That's the one,' Daisy grinned, both her and Fern laughing at her sister's blatant public display of affection, which was so unlike her.

'A Christmas romance is always special,' Anton approved. 'Now I must go. Thank you for the tea, Daisy.'

'It was my absolute, absolute pleasure,' she answered, puzzling Fern.

When he was gone, Ginny came into the shop and the waft of gingerbread held them captive until Fern spied the quilt laid out on the counter. Her face fell, Ginny's too. They were both staring at it, mesmerised, silence.

Fern covered her mouth and began to cry.

Ginny put an arm around Daisy and an arm around Fern as they all looked at the quilt, its blocks of fabric, decades old and still as strong as the memories that came with it, and Daisy finally managed to say, 'It's a long story.'

Chapter Twenty-Three

Fern

'Stop tugging the end, I'm cold,' Fern moaned. It was Christmas Eve and after the dramas of the quilt turning up at the shop so unexpectedly and Daisy sharing the story Anton had told her, none of them wanted to let the quilt out of their sight. As such they were all beneath it watching *Santa Claus: The Movie* and fighting over their special movie quilt when it wasn't positioned exactly the way they liked.

'You'd be even colder if you were still wearing those inappropriate pyjamas, Fern,' Ginny quipped, sharing a giggle with Daisy.

They watched the rest of the movie as the sun came up. It reminded Fern of when she was little, when Ginny was a baby and Daisy wasn't even a twinkle in their parents' eyes. She'd always got up early on Christmas Eve and helped Loretta with the baking, because come Christmas Day it would be mayhem with the lunch being prepared and there wouldn't be room to make anything fancy like truffles or biscuits or brownies. And it had always been nice to have the baked goods ready for the big day, tucked away in tins and containers and there to snatch whenever it took your fancy.

When the movie finished Daisy took a delivery at the front door and made her sisters promise they'd wait there until she came back.

'What's she up to?' Ginny wondered.

'I've no idea.' But Daisy soon appeared in the sitting room again and this time handed a small box to each of her sisters.

'I hate to tell you but we usually open gifts on Christmas Day,' said Ginny. 'It's how Christmas works.'

Daisy rolled her eyes. 'Just open them.'

Fern prized open the small box and inside nestled on a bed of white satin was a silver bell almost identical to the one she'd once hidden outside for Daisy to find. The sleigh bell Daisy had thought their dad had put there for her. 'Daisy, these are beautiful.' Ginny had one too.

'I didn't think they'd come in time for Christmas, I only ordered them a few days ago.'

Not only had Daisy grown up a lot, she'd matured in ways that meant she could share her feelings more easily, it seemed. Or perhaps it was because Fern had changed too. Over the last few days, with Everett's arrival imminent, family secrets aired and Carrie coming into their lives, Fern had done a lot of thinking about her marriage. And she knew now more than ever that she desperately wanted to make it work.

Daisy smiled. 'I must admit I kept thinking in some ways the bell connected me to Dad even though he was gone, because he'd been the one to leave it out for me to find. I guess I could throw it out now, knowing it was from you.'

Fern gave her a playful shove. She was holding her own silver bell. 'Thank you for this, Daisy.' It wasn't just a beautiful bell, it was what it represented – sisterhood, friendship, a fresh start for all of them at long last.

Ginny pulled Daisy in for a hug. 'I will treasure this.'

Fern was the first to pick up the ends of the quilt ready to refold it. 'Hadn't you better be getting ready for work, Ginny?'

Ginny checked the clock. 'I should. I'm out of practice! I'll jump in the shower, but not before I grab another gingerbread man.' She took one from the plate before Fern took it out to the kitchen.

'Any word from Carrie?' Fern asked Daisy.

Daisy shook her head. 'I think she's giving us and herself time to get used to the idea. Mum said that when it was just the two of them, they talked easily, Carrie opened up. I guess three of us is a lot scarier than just Mum on her own.'

'She might prefer to be with her auntie, but did Mum invite her for Christmas?' Fern asked. 'It might be nice to give her the option, let her know she's welcome.'

'Mum did invite her, so fingers crossed,' said Daisy as she plucked another gingerbread man from the plate and began to devour it, cupping her hand beneath as they left the lounge so she didn't spill any crumbs. Still in her pyjamas she seemed determined to make the most of not having to be at the shop today, being able to sit around and really think about her next step. Fern was doing her best not to interfere because it was Daisy's choice as to where she went from here, which was exactly what she'd said when her younger sister asked for advice.

When Ginny went off to the shower, Fern put the lid back on the container of gingerbread. Yesterday she'd baked five batches, trying to get close to the taste of the gingerbread she'd found all those years ago and she was sure she'd managed it. Now there were plenty of gingerbread men here for Everett and the boys too and with them due to arrive in a couple of hours Fern was restless, nervous, and excited all at once.

Daisy's phone rang and Fern passed it to her from the counter, doing her utmost not to listen.

But Daisy was almost bursting by the time she hung up the call. 'That was Sally from the newspaper,' she gushed.

'And?' Fern calmly wiped the crumbs from the kitchen worktop, but sensing her sister wanted an audience this time, wanted the focus on her and what she was doing, she put the cloth down and turned to face Daisy, whose smile was as big as it had been when she was little and came down to see that Father Christmas had left shiny and carefully wrapped presents beside the tree and that her stocking was bulging as it dangled from its hook above the fireplace.

'She loved my photographs of the yarn bombing, she's going to edit my write-up, and both will be in the newspaper in a couple of days.' Her words came out in a rush.

Fern hugged her sister tightly. Not just because of her news but because it was long overdue, and Daisy reciprocated, although she pulled away first, clearly not finished.

'She's asked me in for a discussion about getting regular work with the newspaper.'

'Daisy, that's amazing!'

'It really is. I don't know what I want yet, not exactly, but all I do know is that it'll involve photography, whether freelance or permanent.'

It was on the tip of Fern's tongue to suggest she get some formal training too, to take her to the next level, but she was learning to take a step back before she leaped in and tried to organise other people. If that was what Daisy wanted, she'd reach that conclusion by herself. And any time she wanted an opinion, Fern would share hers, but she wouldn't push. Her sisters were her equals, they were all grown ups and had their own lives. She knew she'd forgotten that somewhere along the way, perhaps moulded into the role of the protector when they lost their dad or simply because she was born first. But it didn't have to be that way. And it would work far better if it wasn't.

When there was a knock at the door, Fern's heart leaped and Daisy was onto her. 'I don't think your husband could wait any longer.'

'I'm still in my pyjamas!' And brushed cotton ones at that, she hadn't worn anything like this in years, favouring silk and sexy nightwear.

'You look gorgeous just the way you are.' Daisy motioned for her to go before Everett froze outside on the doorstep.

When she opened the front door she found it was Jacob who had been knocking, with Everett and Cooper at the car boot bringing everything out, their bags, gifts, and a few bottles, judging by the clinking sounds. And even though his brother was moaning at him to come and help, Jacob didn't miss getting the first hug with his mum.

She fell into the embrace and breathed in the smell of his freshly washed hair. 'I missed you so much.' She didn't get many of these sorts of hugs these days and she treasured it, especially given their time apart and the distance that had allowed her to see what was wrong in her life and how they could work to put it right.

'Bit of help would've been nice,' Cooper moaned as he

came through the gate laden with a bag and an armful of presents. 'Hey, Mum.' He might not be able to rush in for a hug but the smile told Fern she'd been missed more than a teenage boy might care to admit because he was grinning from ear to ear at the sight of her.

Fern put an arm around her eldest son and jostled him inside out of the cold. Everett had closed the boot, pointed the remote, which bleeped and set the alarm, before he made his way up the short front path towards his wife. He took in the sight of her in her pyjamas. 'You do realise it's almost eight o'clock in the morning, and that, a) you're not dressed, and b) you're in public in your pyjamas. Or maybe not your pyjamas.' He quirked an eyebrow.

Marianne from the post office walked by on the other side of the street and waved over. 'Merry Christmas, Fern,' she called out.

'Merry Christmas!' When she returned the greeting she realised Everett was looking at her like she'd gone mad.

'Could someone please tell me what happened to my wife?'

The box of wine beneath his arm didn't look all that secure and Fern took it but set it down on the doorstep. She took the small overnight holdall he had too and put that on top of the box before she pulled her husband tightly into a hug, this man she'd fallen in love with so quickly and so deeply it had almost hurt. And she kissed him right there and then, ignoring remarks of *eww, disgusting* from Jacob behind them and a giggle from Daisy who only had to mention gingerbread to shift Jacob's focus.

When Fern pulled away she looked up at her husband. 'I missed you.'

'The feeling was mutual. But this is a welcome I can get on board with.'

'You didn't all love me being away, not being bossed about?' She pushed against his chest when he pulled a face like he was thinking about it. 'We need to talk about that, I have some things I want to say.'

'That's fine, but can we at least go inside before I lose all feeling in my feet and hands?'

She laughed and lead him inside. With any luck they might well get snow later today and rather than moan about it like they did every year at home because it hampered their commute to work, because the boys' activities were cancelled, because driving anywhere became a nightmare, cocooned in Butterbury snow was a whole other story.

Fern and Everett headed away from the house on a walk, her arm linked through his as he said, 'Christmas in Butterbury is always magical.' He'd been brought up in a town, he'd always envied Fern this little corner of the world as the place she grew up, and for years he'd said that once the boys were older he wanted to retire here. Judging by the look on his face as they made their way from the house, through the village and towards Lantern Square with its impressive decorations and village Christmas tree, he hadn't changed his mind at all.

As they walked Everett began to notice the yarn bombings and Fern confided that it had been Daisy and Grandad's doing, a long time in the making, but the three sisters as well as Loretta had executed the plan along with a group of folks from Butterbury Lodge.

'You and your sisters?' he pondered. 'Together?'

'Surprising, I know, but coming home this time turned out to be better than I imagined.' She huddled closer to him and explained the real reason why Loretta had summoned them back to Butterbury, what had been going on since her arrival, the quilt, her sisters' revelations, their dad's past, and all about Carrie.

Everett whistled between his teeth. 'How do you feel about it all?' By mutual agreement they headed towards the mulled wine cart.

'Strangely OK.' She went on to admit, 'I'm not sure I would've been had I not had Daisy and Ginny to talk to.'

Everett stopped as they joined the queue for mulled wine. 'I never thought I'd hear you say that.'

'Me neither.'

As they waited in line he put an arm around her shoulders, his fingers toying with the free ends of her hair, loose and wavy rather than in its strict, straight ponytail. He'd always told her she should try a bit harder with her sisters, that family was too important to not want to make an effort. And as they watched their mulled wine being ladled into the awaiting cups he kissed her forehead and she leaned into the gesture, happy to have him by her side.

They found a spare bench to sit on right near the village tree. 'Tastes so much better out in the cold,' Everett declared after his first gulp of mulled wine.

'I happen to agree with you.' There was something about drinking a warm, spicy drink when the temperature had fallen that reminded them to sit back and enjoy, it was almost Christmas.

'Fern, I need to apologise to you.'

Confused she asked, 'Whatever would you need to apologise to me for?'

He briefly looked her way. 'I talked to Loretta.'

'You always talk to Mum.'

He shook his head. 'I called last week and asked her not to tell you.' He quickly added, 'I wasn't spying on you, I was worried. I knew she'd wanted you home but we've been married long enough that I knew it wasn't the only reason you left so willingly for an extended festive break.' She didn't deny it. 'Your mum told me that like you she'd always been one to protest her strength, afraid to show weakness.' He put a hand over his wife's to show he wasn't criticising. 'The way she talked helped me to see that you were struggling without me realising. She didn't make me feel bad, she didn't betray your confidence, but she did mention struggles in her own marriage and it was as though a light went on for me. With you away I could see we'd both let our relationship take a back seat to everything else, without even meaning to.'

Loretta and Everett had always had a mutual respect. Her mum adored having him in the family. She saw him as strong emotionally, a good match for her daughter and he fitted in as though he'd always been there.

'Are you angry that I called her?'

'No, well I might have been a few weeks ago,' Fern admitted, 'but being here has helped me realise I can't always be the one to do everything, I can't stay in control so that nothing bad will ever happen. It's exhausting. But after Dad died, that's how I coped. I threw myself into organising everyone else and being the person to turn to. And for a while it worked.' She paused, not wanting to sound accusatory either. 'You stopped talking to me when your mum died and that was hard to accept.'

He stared into his cup of wine. 'I know. But being

withdrawn, throwing myself into work, that was my way of coping. I didn't really know how to let you in, so I guess I just didn't. And somewhere along the way we stopped investing time in our relationship with one another. It was all about the kids, about work, about anything other than us.'

She nodded in agreement. 'I see that now too. When Mum told me she and Dad nearly got a divorce it was like a punch in the stomach, not just because of what it would've meant for our family, but because it made me see how easily it could happen to anyone. It could happen to us, Everett.'

'That's not what I want.' He leaned over and planted a kiss on her lips, warm, firm, sure, and a forever promise that whatever challenges they were up against, they'd work through them together. 'I know you'd like me to always be the man you met that day in the Underground, that you want to be the woman I fell in love with. And we'll always be those people, but we've evolved, Fern, it's the way of life. I'm more in love with you now than I ever was.'

She put a hand to his cheek. 'I was jealous of you and the boys when I first called to see how you were. No, let me finish,' she added before he could ask why. Part of letting go of control was admitting things that she previously might have kept quiet about. 'You were all having a great time, coping without me. It was really hard to suddenly become aware that you could. Part of me felt redundant, but over the time I've been in Butterbury I've begun to see it a different way. We're a family and we're all changing as the years go on, and I don't need to fight it.'

'You don't. And you don't need to do it on your own. Once in a while, try not to worry that the boys will do themselves a disservice by not getting their five a day. Let them eat pizza occasionally, buy your own tomatoe sauce rather than slaving away making your own sauce, keep your hair like this,' he added with a twinkle in his eye, he'd always loved it especially at the start of their relationship when they'd make love and her hair would tumble over him. 'And occasionally maybe I make you a coffee for you to take on your commute to work.'

She nodded and he smiled the smile that had almost floored her the first time she saw it.

'Did you hope we'd all have a miserable time and fall apart without you, beg you to come home?'

She wrinkled her nose. 'A tiny bit, yes. I got used to wanting and needing to do everything myself. Did you resent it?'

'Sometimes. But I never resented *you*. I've always loved your strength, your ability to be the person everyone turns to.'

'The boys are growing up fast, they won't need me for much longer.'

'They'll always need you, except maybe not in the same way.' He clutched her hand. 'And I'll always need you, Fern.'

'Likewise.' She squeezed his hand in return.

'You need to schedule time for yourself, too. I have squash games to unwind.'

'I have cooking.'

'You need something else. Why don't you take up running again, you always loved it.'

'Maybe,' she agreed.

'And I'm not sure I heard right back at the house but Daisy claimed you'd been on your hands and knees picking vegetables up at the local farm. And she also told me all three of you will be cooking the Christmas lunch this year.'

'Correct on both counts.'

'So much has changed in such a short time.'

She hoped so. And when he pulled her against him she asked, 'Were the neighbours upset there was no Christmas party?'

'There were a few grumbles, but also a few offers to host next year. How would you feel about that?'

'Honestly?' She looked him in the eye, her gaze dropping to his lips more than once. 'More than happy.'

'So how does this work when we go home?' Everett asked, his voice peppered with concern.

'I think we start with a date night.' She'd been thinking a lot about this. 'Once a week as a minimum, just you and me. Set a day and we never schedule anything else apart from time for each other.'

'Even if you have a work meeting? Or the boys have sports?'

'We can be a little flexible.'

'There's a novelty,' he teased. 'I think you coming here has done you the world of good. I don't mind if you want to take another holiday on your own, you know.'

'Daisy suggested I go camping with her.'

He threw his head back laughing. 'I'm pretty sure I know how that went down.'

'Not a hope in hell,' she confirmed, finishing her wine and depositing the cup in the bin along with Everett's as they began to weave their way out of the square and back towards the house. 'Everett . . . if you don't mind I'd rather not go on holiday on my own. I'd quite like all my boys with me.'

He hugged her close. 'Now that can definitely be arranged.' He kissed the top of her head and lingered a while. 'A holiday for two might be an idea as well.'

By the time they reached the house, Loretta was having a lunch break. Ginny was finishing up at the shop, which would be closing over Christmas, and Everett's mother-in-law embraced him the minute Everett stepped across the threshold. Everett hadn't even taken his coat off when he was shown the advent calendar, the quilt they'd thought lost and never to be found, and then they were on to talking at a rapid rate about the bracing evening walk Loretta planned on dragging them all out on as well as the Christmas lunch tomorrow.

The boys barrelled through the door not long after, as three of them sat at the kitchen table drinking mugs of tea. They had tales of Busker chasing a squirrel up a tree as both of them went for yet another gingerbread man, asking their mum to please make these at home. Fern assured them she would and Everett whispered in her ear that they'd like them a lot more than anything wholegrain she'd tried to ply them with before. She would continue to make them follow a healthy diet but she knew sometimes she could loosen her rules for the sake of family.

Busker lapped up his water from the bowl in the corner and Fern, revelling in talk of Christmas, asked her mum whether Carrie had decided she would join them for Christmas.

'Actually she has,' said Loretta cautiously. 'Are you sure that's all right?'

Fern had hold of Everett's hand beneath the table. Now they were together again it was as though she didn't want them to be separated at all, let alone by miles. 'We would all love it, Mum. We'd like to get to know her, if she can put up with us for the day, that is.'

The boys were laughing as they stood looking out of the window and Cooper started singing 'I saw Daisy kissing Santa Claus', which of course had their attention.

'What *is* going on?' Loretta asked, following Fern and Everett to the sink, which was in front of the window, the glass just wide enough they all had a view.

'It really is Father Christmas,' mused Everett using the more common name in their household for the man in red. 'And that is your sister, right?' he asked, watching Daisy in a passionate clinch with Joshua.

'It certainly is.' Fern smiled.

'It looks like I may have competition for the spot of favourite son-in-law,' said Everett.

Fern smiled. 'And you do know Ginny just got together with Lucas, don't you?'

Everett put a hand against his chest. 'I'm going to have to up my game by the looks of things.'

But Fern just hugged her husband. 'Don't change a single thing about yourself. You're perfect just the way you are.'

Fern knew now that coming here was the best thing she ever could've done. It had made Loretta happy, Grandad too, it had given her her sisters back, and now her husband and her kids. More than that, it had given her back a sense of self by seeing that she didn't have to do it all, she didn't have to be strong all the time. And it was OK to be the person who needed help and advice along the way.

There was nothing more she could've asked for this Christmas.

Chapter Twenty-Four

Loretta

Carrie had taken a bit of persuading to join them for lunch on Christmas Day but after talking it through with her auntie she'd decided it might be a nice idea. And now here Carrie was, standing at the front door to the Chamberlains' home in Butterbury.

'I'm nervous.' Carrie held a winter bouquet that she thrust at Loretta.

'It's beautiful, thank you. And I understand the nerves.' Her voice soft, she didn't rush Carrie. And she'd spoken with Carrie's auntie Ruth already to assure her that they all had Carrie's best interests at heart, that they'd look after her. 'Remember you've met most of the family already. And everyone wants you to be here today.'

Loretta tipped her head, her arms full. 'Come on, get it over with. Otherwise I'll turn into an icicle and you can guarantee the turkey will be ruined.' Although a hard frost had made Butterbury look pretty from the warm confines of the house, without a coat on after Loretta had stepped outside to cajole their guest to come in it was freezing. 'Daisy is in charge of the turkey this Christmas,' she whispered, 'and although she has many, many strengths, I don't think her talents quite extend to turkey just yet. I don't even think she knows what the word basting means, never mind one end of the bird from the other.'

Carrie at last followed Loretta inside the house, into the warmth. She removed her coat and hung it on the banister, briefly glanced at the quilted advent calendar, and the next thing they knew Cooper was charging along the corridor after Busker. 'He took the last piece of gingerbread! That was mine!' Cooper wailed.

Loretta grabbed Busker and tugged the remains of the biscuit from his jaws before scolding him. 'I know it's Christmas but too much sugar is bad for you.' She motioned to her grandson, 'Grab him one of his own biscuits, Cooper.'

'Mum!' came Daisy's call from the kitchen. The girls had no idea Carrie had arrived – Loretta had spotted her from the top window, lurking outside, nervous as anything. 'The turkey is done too early!' came another yell of panic.

'Mayhem, that's what this house is,' said Loretta, and led the way into the kitchen. Carrie would hopefully follow.

Everett took the bouquet from Loretta. He briefly nodded to Carrie who had indeed followed Loretta and with a reassuring smile at the newcomer and a brief introduction, he went to get a vase.

'Right, Daisy, what's the problem?' Loretta peered at the beautifully golden, crispy-skinned turkey. 'Oh, yes, it certainly does look done. Did you put the thermometer in?'

'To take it's temperature?' Daisy asked as though it was the most ridiculous thing she'd ever heard.

'Sometimes it looks done but inside it's not cooked,'

Carrie volunteered, her voice gentle and giving away how big a feat it was for her to speak up. Even though she'd been with Fern, Ginny and Daisy before, this felt very different even for Loretta, and it had to be a lot tougher for Carrie. Ginny and Fern were sitting at the table, Ginny mending the end of the torn tablecloth and Fern sitting with her feet up on another chair until she was needed again.

Ginny stopped what she was doing and came over to give Carrie a hug, Fern followed soon after. 'Merry Christmas,' they both said in a way that suggested they didn't need to say much at all apart from that, at least not until they were all ready.

'I'll hug you later,' Daisy persisted with a frown as she stood at the kitchen worktop, still unsure what to do next. 'How can it be done outside but not inside?' And when she took the meat thermometer from Loretta she cried, 'I've ruined the Christmas dinner.'

'I helped my mum every year,' Carrie offered.

Daisy didn't even hesitate. She put down the thermometer, took off her apron and hooked it over Carrie's head. 'In that case, you're in charge.'

It was the best thing the girls could've done as they all rallied and Carrie's shoulders dropped a little in relief as she plunged the thermometer into the turkey. Daisy was drumming her fingernails on the worktop alongside, anxiously awaiting the verdict.

After a moment Carrie declared, 'It's perfect, Daisy.'

'Yeah?' But her face fell. 'Not much good when nothing else will be ready for ages. It'll be stone cold by lunchtime.'

'You've been thinking about Joshua too much, that's your problem,' Ginny teased.

'I was sure I'd calculated the timings right,' Daisy moaned, recounting the kilograms and time per kilogram, the estimates she'd made of when to put in the potatoes, the pigs in blankets, the stuffing, vegetables.

'Let's face it, you didn't get the maths gene,' said Ginny before adding, 'neither did I, don't worry. What about you, Carrie, are you any good at maths? Dad was a bit of a whizz. Fern is too.'

Carrie looked as though she were wondering whether it was a trick question but then said, 'I'm studying maths and economics A-level.'

Fern gave a cheer. 'At last, someone else with the family maths gene.'

'Sounds dull to me,' said Ginny. 'Give me textiles any day – if I had my choice now, that is.'

'What did you study?' Carrie wondered.

Ginny explained her career path, her love of midwifery, the change of course she'd had lately after the travel and the hopping from one workplace to another and slowly casual conversation gave way to each of them revealing different parts of themselves. 'It feels like the right time to make a change,' she finished. 'Come back home, be in the shop.'

Daisy interrupted them. 'As much as I would *love* to talk about careers and Butterbury and life choices, what about the turkey? Nothing else is ready!'

'It's best to let the turkey rest for a while anyway,' said Carrie.

'How long do you think?'

'I'd say at least forty-five minutes, uncovered so it doesn't continue to cook and the skin doesn't go soggy.'

Daisy began to smile. 'Well it sounds as though perhaps I wasn't too far off the mark then.'

'I did tell you to allow time for resting,' Fern piped up with a shake of her head. 'You wouldn't listen.'

Ginny leaned in to Carrie. 'Fern would've been happy doing all this herself, but she's not allowed to take over.'

After introducing Cooper and Jacob to Carrie, Loretta shooed the boys away along with their questions about how long until lunch, could they have another mince pie each, and complaining they'd pass out if they didn't eat soon.

Loretta found two trivets and put them side by side on the worktop. 'Put the turkey on here for the time being, Daisy.'

'I'll get the potatoes on,' said Ginny. 'Could you slice up the carrots, Carrie?'

'I'll do the stuffing,' said Fern.

Between them they par-boiled potatoes, got the carrots caramelising beautifully, lined up pigs in blankets on a tray. They formed stuffing balls and slotted them into the oven to turn them into golden morsels that paired well with the turkey, and Loretta made the gravy using the pan juices Daisy had thankfully remembered to set aside.

'I saw Mum do it once,' Daisy told them. 'I admit I didn't know why she was doing it, I thought she'd put the liquid in a bottle to throw out or something. But today I thought I might have remembered her saying something once about gravy and juices, so I kept them aside.'

'How can you not know this stuff after eating Mum's roasts for years?' Fern scolded.

'OK, Mrs Domesticity,' Daisy laughed, 'I'll get there in the end. Who knows, one year I'll have my own place and cook for you all. How does that sound?'

'As long as it's not in a tent I'll be there,' said Ginny as she spooned out the cranberry sauce she'd got from Hawthorn Lane Farm. 'Daisy's into camping,' she explained at Carrie's confusion.

'I love camping,' Carrie enthused. Her put-together appearance suggested nothing of the sort, it leaned towards a careful cleansing routine, self-care and plenty of sleep, none of the things Loretta associated with camping. That had been Harry's thing, and Daisy's.

Daisy poured the finished gravy into the awaiting porcelain jug. 'Dad used to take me a lot when I was little,' she said to Carrie. 'We could go sometime . . . if you like.' The suggestion was tentative but a good one, a more promising start than Loretta ever could've imagined, and Ivor had come into the room with enough time to overhear it. He gave her a wink and came to her side. He'd promised he'd stay in the sitting room with the boys when Carrie first arrived so the house wasn't too crazy.

'What a Christmas this is going to be,' Ivor said quietly to Loretta.

'Almost time to dish up,' Daisy announced, pulling out the pre-warmed plates from the oven.

Ginny rounded up the family and as the room filled and everyone began to sit down for Christmas lunch Carrie came to Loretta's side.

'You have a beautiful family.' Her eyes glistened with emotion.

Loretta gave her arm a squeeze. 'You're a part of it now. Come on, let's eat.'

The girls had already arranged the place settings and had Carrie sitting towards the middle, not on the end. The boys could have those spots, they wouldn't care when there was a bowl of pigs in blankets bigger than Loretta had ever seen, enough roast potatoes to feed a football team, a generous boat of gravy to drown everything.

'There is something very important we all need to know, Carrie.' Fern passed the bowl of sprouts to Ginny. 'Where do you sit on the great sprout debate?'

'You mean love 'em or hate 'em?' Carrie seemed happy with the relaxed subject matter. She put her hands together, everyone was waiting. 'Well, I would have to say . . . I love 'em!'

Groans came from Ginny and Daisy who had a mutual dislike for them. Fern and Ivor on the other hand cheered and extolled the virtues of the humble green vegetable. Everett and the boys declared they'd eat pretty much what was put in front of them.

'As long as it's smothered in gravy.' When Fern eyed Cooper's plate the teen cheekily added another slop of gravy for good measure.

Everett involved Carrie by asking her what her favourite thing about Butterbury was.

'I love that it's a village but big enough to have a few shops, the bookshop especially and the pub. But my favourite thing is Lantern Square. It's beautiful.'

'Couldn't agree more.' Everett accepted Fern's offer of more stuffing balls. 'Ever since I got together with Fern I fell in love with this village. I think we'll end up retiring here.'

Carrie asked Loretta and the girls more about their lives in Butterbury, growing up here, school. None of them mentioned Harry. Loretta sensed that would come later, either with or without her. She'd already shared a lot about her husband and the sort of man he was in the time she'd spent with Carrie. Perhaps in time the girls would be able to share with her the sort of father Harry was to them. But for now it was Christmas, a time to welcome, embrace, enjoy.

When it was time to clear some of the detritus before the Christmas pudding, Loretta and Ivor took plates and serving dishes over to the kitchen and stacked them beside the sink. And for a few moments, as the lively conversation played out at the family table, they watched everyone else.

'I'm proud of you,' said Ivor. And it didn't matter what age you were, praise from your parents was always powerful. 'Accepting Carrie into your lives is a huge step, never mind attempting to bring the girls back together. I had my doubts.'

'You never said.'

'Of course not, that's not how you parent. You offer your opinion, you give your advice, but you never assume your child will fail. Kids wouldn't ever try anything new if that was the case.'

He was right. If he'd voiced his doubts she might never have asked her girls to come home, she might never have introduced Carrie and Carrie may have thought it all too hard and walked away before she had a chance to get to know any of them. Harry would've been happy at the way things had turned out, she felt sure of that.

Loretta brought over the last of the serving bowls and set it with the others. And she wasn't sure but she thought she might have seen the first flakes of snow beyond the kitchen window. She stayed there, the noise of conversation in the background, the beating heart of her family, letting it wash over her as she waited to see whether any more flakes would appear.

Ginny's voice came from behind her and Loretta realised she must've been standing looking out of the window
for a while. 'What do you think, Mum?'

'Sorry, what do I think about what? I was miles away.'

'We all thought we should take a break and open some
presents before dessert.'

The girls were impatient. They wanted their grandad to
see the quilt they'd worked so hard on. 'That sounds like a
lovely idea.' And then she began to grin.

'What are you smiling at?'

'I think you and Daisy might need to go answer the
front door.' Lucas and Joshua were outside, clutching gifts
and making their way across from the opposite side of the
road.

'Mum, I'm sorry, I did tell Lucas to come over,' said
Ginny. 'I didn't expect us to take so long eating the
Christmas lunch.'

'It's completely fine, I love those boys, they're welcome.
And they can have Christmas pudding with the rest of us
after we open presents. There's plenty to go around.'

'Are you sure this is all right?' Joshua asked Loretta the
moment he stepped into the hallway. 'Are we too early?'

'Merry Christmas to you both.' Loretta smiled, giving
each of them a welcome hug. 'And no, you're not too early
– it's getting dark already, *we* are very late to finish.'

Joshua lowered his voice. 'How did Daisy do with the
lunch? She was really nervous about taking charge of a
turkey.'

'She did brilliantly.' Loretta smiled. 'She's a keeper.'

'Don't worry.' He smiled. 'I know she is. Took me long
enough to get her, I'm not about to let her go now.'

They all settled themselves in the sitting room – Ginny

346

snuggled next to Lucas on the sofa, Daisy knelt on the floor next to Joshua. Jacob was getting restless, Cooper was trying to act cool as though he, like the rest of the men, wasn't that interested in gifts at all.

'You're first, Grandad,' said Fern, barely able to contain her excitement as she handed over the wrapped quilt.

Hidden beneath silver wrapping paper and tied with a white satin bow, the gift sat on Ivor's lap while he did the same thing he did every year, feeling it for clues as to what it might be and throwing guesses into the air: *A dressing gown? A jumper? Some pyjamas?* He gave it a shake to see if it rattled and finally released the bow and tore off the paper.

'Well I never.' He beamed as he unfolded the Christmas quilt.

It was beautiful. The girls had all worked so incredibly hard on it and now, with the sashing that pulled it all together, it was a sight to behold. Ivor inspected the squares in turn, laughing at the one with candy canes, appreciating the cat that looked remarkably like Horatio, thanking Carrie when it was revealed she had been the one to choose the fabric with winter berries and robin redbreasts.

'I don't know what to say.' Ivor had reluctantly folded up the quilt when Jacob tried to move things along and open more gifts.

Ginny laughed. 'Come on, the game's over, Grandad. We know you didn't really need a new one.'

He opened his mouth to protest but instead said, 'Sprung.'

'I'm afraid so,' said Loretta. Although the idea had worked even better than they'd imagined.

Fern handed Carrie a gift next. 'Boys, have patience . . . Carrie can open this first.'

Embarrassed, Carrie took the wrapped rectangular present. 'But I didn't get you anything.'

'You brought flowers,' said Loretta, 'and you brought yourself.'

'This is from all three of us,' Fern added. 'And we all received the most special gift in the world this year.' She looked to Daisy who explained the quilt their dad had had them all make, how they'd all helped, how it went missing and turned up this year completely out of the blue.

'I'm so pleased you got it back.' Carrie, nervously holding her present, seemed unsure what to do with it.

Cooper lost his cool façade and encouraged her to open it quicker. Loretta had known it wouldn't be long before he gave up trying to hide his excitement. Fern had years with these boys and plenty of family Christmases before they spread their wings.

Carrie slowly tugged the green velvet ribbon undone. Loretta had no idea what the gift was because it had come from the girls, not her. And when Carrie took off the lid of a box it revealed some carefully folded lavender material, a pencil, some scissors, a beautiful grape-coloured fabric, yarn, a needle, and along with it a patch in the shape of a grand piano.

'It's everything you need to make a letter C,' Ginny explained, 'I mean, we can change the colours if you don't like them.'

'No, they're beautiful.'

'Fern, Daisy and I thought that we could find a plain square on Dad's quilt and you could, with our help if you need it, stitch on your initial and the piano symbol.'

Loretta had tried to share with her girls as many details as she knew about Carrie from their chats to give them a way to know their half-sister without bombarding her with questions for the time being.

'Mum says you like to play,' said Fern. 'Or you can choose another symbol if you prefer.'

But Carrie couldn't speak and the tears she'd done so well at holding in began to flow from the emotion of the moment, the occasion, the significant change in all of their lives. 'Thank you, all of you, for this, for today, for being so nice.'

'We're glad you're here,' Ivor assured her with everyone chorusing their agreement.

Fern went back to sitting next to Everett, their hands entwined. 'If you need help with the sewing just say . . . and by help I mean from Ginny or Daisy, unless it's calculating any measurements, I'm always happy to help there.'

Carrie nodded through tears. 'Deal.'

The boys finally got to open their presents, and when Lucas suggested a walk for anyone who needed it, surprisingly every single person said yes. Even Busker wagged his tail, not wanting to miss out.

'We won't go far, Dad,' Loretta assured Ivor as they set off from the house. 'And we can hang back. Let the young ones go further and we'll be first in line for the Christmas pudding.'

'Sounds like the best idea to me,' said Ivor once he'd convinced his daughter he was plenty warm enough.

'Thank you for always being there with your advice and your help. And thank you for always being there for my girls. It means the world to all of us.'

'It means the world to me too. And thanks to this

project of ours I got a new Christmas quilt, no complaints from me.'

The four girls were up ahead walking two by two, Everett was talking to Lucas, Joshua had somehow been persuaded to give Jacob a piggy back.

Loretta looked up into the darkened skies. 'I think it's going to snow later.'

'I hope so. We've got a bet going at the lodge. I've got fifty quid on it.'

'Dad! I didn't let you go there so you could turn into a gambler.'

'Don't you worry about me. You just keep an eye on those girls . . . all of them.'

They watched the four girls now walking in a row in the road that was deserted with it being Christmas, their arms linked together.

'You pulled them back together,' said Ivor.

'One stitch at a time, eh?'

'One stitch at a time.' He beamed as a few flakes of snow began to fall around them.

Butterbury at Christmas. There really was nothing like it.

THE END

Acknowledgements

Textiles wasn't exactly my forte at school – in fact, it was my worst subject! Therefore a huge thank you goes to my Australian friend Alison for all her help surrounding the wonderful world of quilting. She was the first port of call when I researched this book as I can remember the beautiful handmade quilts she had at her home in Melbourne. I hope with my research and my imagination I have managed to conjure up a world of quilt lovers in *Christmas at the Village Sewing Shop*, even though I found some of the terminology confusing. All mistakes are therefore my own!

A big thank you to my dad who never fails to go the extra mile as soon as I mention that I'm interested in something. This time I happened to mention I was writing a book set in a sewing shop and the next thing I knew he'd emailed me a link about yarn bombing. Of course, I couldn't resist having my characters get involved in some yarn bombing of their own! A big thank you also to anyone who has contributed to #yarnbombing on Instagram – following the hashtag was really inspiring as I wrote this book.

Thank you to the entire team at Orion who work so

hard to bring my books to readers. Particular gratitude goes to Olivia Barber, my former editor at Orion as she was the one who championed this idea from the start. Thank you Olivia, it was a joy to work with you! Thank you also to Charlotte Mursell who became my editor after Olivia. Your enthusiasm and expertise has brought this book to an entirely new level and I'm hoping readers will fall in love with the story.

Helen x

Credits

Helen Rolfe and Orion Fiction would like to thank everyone at Orion who worked on the publication of *Christmas at the Village Sewing Shop* in the UK.

Editorial
Charlotte Mursell
Olivia Barber
Sanah Ahmed

Copy editor
Joanne Gledhill

Proofreader
Laetitia Grant

Audio
Paul Stark
Jake Alderson

Production
Ruth Sharvell

Contracts
Anne Goddard
Humayra Ahmed
Ellie Bowker

Design
Rachael Lancaster
Joanna Ridley
Nick May

Editorial Management
Charlie Panayiotou
Jane Hughes
Bartley Shaw

Marketing
Tanjiah Islam

Finance
Jasdip Nandra
Afeera Ahmed
Elizabeth Beaumont
Sue Bake

Publicity
Ellen Turner

Operations
Jo Jacobs
Sharon Willis

Sales
Jen Wilson
Esther Waters
Victoria Laws
Rachael Hum
Ellie Kyrke-Smith
Frances Doyle
Georgina Cutler

If you loved *Christmas at the Village Sewing Shop*,
don't miss Helen Rolfe's next heartwarming
and gorgeously uplifting book . . .

The Boathouse by Stepping Stone Bay

Available to pre-order now!

If you loved *Christmas at the Village Sewing Shop*,
don't miss the next delightfully enchanting
read from Helen Rolfe . . .

Home is where the heart is . . .

Joy has made a family for herself. She's turned her
beautiful old farmhouse into a safe haven for anyone
who is looking for a new beginning. She's always ready
with a kind word, a nugget of advice and believes
that anyone can change their life for the better,
if they really want to.

Libby has exchanged her high-flying job in New York for
a break in the quiet Somerset countryside. She's
soon drawn into Joy's world and into her family of
waifs and strays - including Drew, whom Joy
once helped get back on his feet.

So when a secret from Joy's past threatens everything,
can the unlikely group come together to give Joy a
second chance of her own?

Available to order now!

Escape to Mapleberry Lane . . .

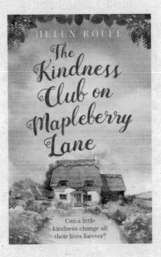

The smallest things can make the biggest difference . . .

Veronica Beecham's cottage is the neatest house on Mapleberry Lane. A place for everything, and everything in its place – that's her motto. But within her wisteria-covered walls, Veronica has a secret: she's hardly left her perfect home in years.

Then her teenage granddaughter, Audrey, arrives on the doorstep, and Veronica's orderly life is turned upside down. Shy and lonely, Audrey is struggling to find her place in the world. As a bond begins to form between the two women, Audrey develops a plan to give her gran the courage to reconnect with the community – they'll form a kindness club, with one generous action a day to help someone in the village, and perhaps help each other at the same time.

As their small acts of kindness begins to ripple outwards, both Veronica and Audrey find that with each passing day, they feel a little braver. There's just one task left before the end of the year: to make Veronica's own secret wish come true . . .

Come and find love by the sea . . .

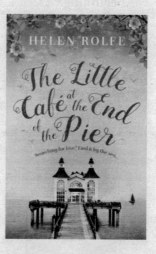

Searching for love? You'll find it at the little café at the end of the pier . . .

When Jo's beloved grandparents ask for her help in running their little café at the end of the pier in Salthaven-on-Sea, she jumps at the chance.

The café is a hub for many people: the single dad who brings his little boy in on a Saturday morning; the lady who sits alone and stares out to sea; the woman who pops in after her morning run.

Jo soon realises that each of her customers is looking for love – and she knows just the way to find it for them. She goes about setting each of them up on blind dates – each date is held in the café, with a special menu she has designed for the occasion.

But Jo has never found love herself. She always held her grandparents' marriage up as her ideal and she hasn't found anything close to that. But could it be that love is right under her nose . . . ?

Welcome to Cloverdale, the home of kindness and new beginnings . . .

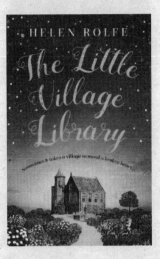

Sometimes it takes a village to mend a broken heart . . .

Cloverdale is known for its winding roads, undulating hills and colourful cottages, and now for its Library of Shared Things: a place where locals can borrow anything they might need, from badminton sets to waffle makers. A place where the community can come together.

Jennifer has devoted all her energy into launching the Library. When her sister Isla moves home, and single dad Adam agrees to run a mending workshop at the Library, new friendships start to blossom. But what is Isla hiding, and can Adam ever mend his broken past?

Then Adam's daughter makes a startling discovery, and the people at the Library of Shared Things must pull together to help one family overcome its biggest challenge of all . . .

Step into the enchanting world of Lantern Square . . .

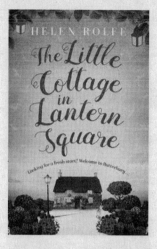

Looking for a fresh start? Welcome to Butterbury . . .

Hannah went from high-flyer in the city to small business owner and has never looked back. She's found a fresh start in the cosy Cotswold village of Butterbury, where she runs her care package company, Tied Up with String.

Her hand-picked gifts are the perfect way to show someone you care, and while her brown paper packages bring a smile to customers across the miles, Hannah also makes sure to deliver a special something to the people closer to home.

But when her ex-best friend Georgia arrives back in her life, can Hannah forgive and forget? With her new business in jeopardy, Hannah needs to let the community she cares for give a little help back . . .

Meanwhile, mystery acts of kindness keep springing up around Butterbury, including a care package on Hannah's own doorstep. Who is trying to win her heart – and will she ever give it away?